And They Went Up

A NOVEL FROM THE SAGA OF FALLEN LEAVES,
VOL. IV

J.L. FEUERSTACK

ILLUSTRATED BY ALANA TEDMON

Printed in the United States of America
Paperback ISBN: 978-1-961624-51-1
Ebook ISBN: 978-1-961624-52-8

Canoe Tree
Press

Canoe Tree Press is a division of DartFrog Books
301 S. McDowell St.
Suite 125-1625
Charlotte, NC 28204
www.DartFrogBooks.com

To My Fellow Reds, You'll Never Walk Alone

INTRODUCTION
LA TERREUR

The crowd was boisterous and joyful. All manner of people joined in the festivities: young and old, men and women, devout and disinterested, poor and those hiding their means. Vendors shouted above the noise and advertised delectable culinary delights. Other merchants peddled programs containing the names of the day or toys to entertain the children. The energy of the gathering added a shielding layer of warmth against the cold November day.

Vivienne Desruisseaux would have preferred to be at home reading. Her father had other ideas. He pulled her across the cobbles of the square known as Place de la Révolution. His grip on her wrist was a vice.

The Parisians fell silent for a moment. Vivienne looked toward the scaffold. A well-dressed woman, young, was led up the wooden stairs of the platform. She carried herself with an aloof demeanor. Some would call it confidence – others, arrogance. She stood before the slanted blade that would be her demise with neither fear nor bravery but only an unreadable blankness.

The pause of the crowd lasted only a moment. Men began to cat-call sexual obscenities and hurl denigrating remarks. Vivienne did not need one of the day's programs to know the name of the condemned was Olympe de Gouges, the advocate of female suffrage and equality.

"Do you see? For all her high-minded ideals, all of her writings, how do they address her? Like a whore," Vivienne's father said.

Her father was not a violent man. He was not a strict parent. If anything, he was lenient toward Vivienne and her brothers. He treated their mother with reverence. Yet, since he had found Vivienne reading pamphlets such as *Déclaration des droits de la Femme et de la Citoyenne*,[1] his demeanor had changed.

---

[1] Declaration of the Rights of Woman and of the Female Citizen

When news that the author of said pamphlet was to be sent to the guillotine, Vivienne's father had insisted they attend the execution. She did not like this version of her father. He was never prone to swearing and even if he was paraphrasing the mood of the crowd, it stung to hear him say the word "whore".

"This is where those pamphlets lead," her father said. His eyes were wide and wild.

Vivienne struggled to breathe. She felt as if she was in a very small room. She longed for the ordeal to be over. More than anything she wanted her father to discontinue his tirade, for it had given water to a thought that sprouted in her mind. *If they could send her here for writing it, could they not do the same to me for reading it? After all, children younger than fifteen have been sent to the blade.*

Once the terror and guilt took hold, they refused to relent. Vivienne stared down at the dirty cobblestones. Her father took her by the chin and forced her face toward the platform. Olympe de Gouges had been laid prone and her head secured in place.

Vivienne longed for some late reprieve for the woman of letters, though she knew there would be none. The blade fell with a swoosh and the head of the condemned toppled into a basket. Vivienne squeezed her eyes closed and felt tears forming in their creases.

Her father shook her face and commanded her to look. Vivienne opened her eyes to see the executioner holding the severed head aloft, much to the enjoyment of the crowd.

"Do you understand?" her father asked.

Vivienne nodded.

Shortly after the ordeal Vivienne left home. She never again touched a book or gave thought to ideas of suffrage, Liberté, Égalité, or Fraternité.

"You look lost in thought," Constance Silver said from within Aimé Rousseau, an officer of Marshal D'Erlon's I Corps of the Armée du Nord.

"Oh, my host has some pretty grisly memories of the reign of terror," Anna Gold said from within Vivienne Desruisseaux, also an officer of the Armée du Nord.

"They'll probably have some competition after tomorrow," Constance said.

"Indeed," Anna said.

The pair looked over the sea of tents – the French camp.

"Are you nervous?" Anna asked.

"More so for Zinc than for myself," Constance said.

"There's a lot afoot with Iron III seizing control of Napoleon," Anna said.

"A straightforward fight would be nice. This is all too complex. Protecting Zinc, keeping an eye out for duplicitous Angels. It all adds an extra element to the battle," Constance said.

"We'll do our part. Things will either go our way or they won't," Anna said.

"Either way, at least I'll have my sister by my side," Constance said. She placed her arm around Anna's host and gazed out across the rolling hills.

Anna smiled and recollected her host's thoughts. "Freedom, Equality, and *Sister*hood," she said.

Anorexia walked across the Great Hall of Hell. She encountered Scarlet Fever, Encephalitis, and Streptococcal standing before one of the sets of columns used to create departure portals. The Demons comprised Squad 2A of II Corps. They were to deploy to the area around La Haye-Sainte.

In addition to 2A, as the most senior Demon in II Corps, Anorexia was also responsible for the Squads 2B, 2C and 2D.

Anorexia longed to find adequate words for the occasion. As a member of the Triumvirate Council, Anorexia was accustomed to making decisions that affected the lives of her fellow Demons. Still, on the eve of what would likely be the most consequential battle in history, she felt the weight of her responsibility.

She steeled herself against terrifying thoughts of leading her fellows to death and ruin. With a thought back to her old squad mate Diphtheria, Anorexia said, "So, this is the sorry lot Titus gave me?"

Scarlet Fever smiled. The others seemed less amused.

"Well, I'll have to make the best of it. Just like all of you. This is going to be something big, we'll have to do our part," Anorexia said.

Anorexia opened a portal, then turned and took one last look back at the Great Hall.

Just in case I never see it again, she thought.

Chapter 1

How Stands the Glass Around

Day broke over the rolling green fields of the Kingdom of the Netherlands. The morning had degenerated into a disorganized farce. First, Streptococcal had returned from his position among the British artillery.

"What the fuck are you doing back here?" Anorexia shouted.

"I...I...I was told by...ah...um... a Wraith, that a Priest told her that I needed to be at the front lines," he said.

"You were told by a Wraith, who was told by a Priest? Streptococcal, *I* gave you an order. *I* sent you to the guns. Now get the fuck back there on the double. The battle is about to start. How can we hold the center without artillery support?" Anorexia asked. She knew her cheeks were flushed. She could feel the heat. She wanted to beat this idiot with a cudgel, but she needed him in the field – *now*.

Streptococcal scurried off. No sooner had he departed than a Wraith arrived with renderings of the Angelic Lords who were to be targeted by the gun crews.

"These are fantastically accurate," Anorexia said.

The Wraith nodded, flush with pride at the work of his contingent.

"Now if only the gunners were holding these parchments instead of me," Anorexia said. Her face reddened more.

The Wraith snatched the parchments back and fled.

While Anorexia attempted to calm her frustration, Streptococcal returned.

"The orders were from General Titus. Apparently, Satan felt too many Demons were assigned to the cannons. He ordered one per corps not one per squad," Streptococcal said. He cringed.

Her voice was calm...and unnerving. "Streptococcal, what is that you're holding in your hand?"

He looked down at his balled up fist. "Oh,…umm…renderings of Angelic Lords," he said. He paused. "A Wraith gave them to me… when I was…back by… the guns. I'm sorry."

Anorexia rubbed her forehead. She did not want to abandon her mortal host. She was the ranking officer in the area.

Her order cut through the clamor – a searing blade of anger and authority. "I need a runner!"

Several mortals arrived and saluted.

These buffoons are not what I need.

She gave mundane instructions. When she turned, she was relieved to see a Wraith awaiting instructions. The Wraith was fragile – almost immature looking.

"Get these to whomever is manning the guns."

"That would be Dysgraphia," the Wraith said.

Anorexia groaned. "They put a juvenile by himself? Where are Schitz and his Prussians?"

"Oh, they are wheeling around the flank."

"What?"

"Well, with the redeployment from the guns, Titus sent Schitz to the flank," the Wraith said.

"It might work. The French will send the Imperial Guard to meet them. All right, get these renderings to Dysgraphia on the double," she said.

The Wraith nodded and turned to leave. Anorexia grabbed her by the arm. "And thank you. You are an island of information in a sea of confusion," she said. The Wraith smiled and melted away.

Anorexia attempted to steady herself. The battle had commenced along the flanks. Smoke was billowing to her right from the buildings of Château d'Hougoumont. Likewise, signs of battle came from Papelotte Farm to her left.

"I'm sorry," Streptococcal said.

The French army came into view, an ocean of blue, spouting whitecaps of flashing bayonets. The French force was teeming with the auras of Angelic possession.

"Streptococcal, this is the battle we have long awaited. It will surely settle the score between Hell and Heaven. But you and I will not likely see the sun set on this day. Your apology is as unnecessary as it is insignificant. Please just give your all," Anorexia said.

"I will," he said.

"And spread out," she said.

This is it, Anorexia thought.

The French Infantry stormed the walled town of La Haye Sainte. From within the front line of the King's German Legion, Anorexia gave the order to fire. Muskets cracked and smoke filled the air. Still the foe approached. Anorexia rushed to reload her musket while the second line fired past her. The deafening explosions of their guns thundered in her ears. She returned the ramrod to its holder and raised her musket, along with the other soldiers of the first row. Anorexia picked her target and fired.

Before the shot had hit its mark, Anorexia leaped over the wall and rushed forward within the Celestial Realm. In her periphery she could see Scarlet Fever a few yards to her left, also within the Celestial. Encephalitis and Streptococcal had remained within their mortal hosts.

"We have to force them back into the mortals," Anorexia shouted to Scarlet Fever. The two Demons clashed with a veritable horde of Celestial Angels several paces ahead of the leading French troops.

Despite being outnumbered, Anorexia was the aggressor. She carried two sai and made great use of the short, tri-pronged weapons. The lead Angel swung a sword toward her neck while two others thrust toward her midsection. Anorexia narrowly sidestepped one blade while catching the other two in the grips of her daggers. She stepped between the foes and directed their swords into one another. The Angels shrieked as they impaled one another instead of the Demon. She launched forward and kicked another onrushing Angel in the midsection, wheeled, and stabbed another through the throat.

When the fatally stricken Angel began convulsing and choking on her own blood, Anorexia threw the enemy into a cluster of her opponents. The Angels fell over when struck by their dying compatriot. Anorexia set on them with vigor. She drove her sai through their throats one after the next. When she reached the last of the beleaguered Angels, a redheaded female, she put a sai through each of the Angel's eyes.

Anorexia rolled away from one crashing swipe and then another as more Angels attacked her. Having gained distance from the foe, she stole a glance toward Scarlet Fever. The academy instructor was holding her own against equally heady odds. Anorexia watched as Scarlet Fever decapitated two Angels simultaneously with her twin swords.

The front line of the French infantry reached the site of the Celestial slaughter.

"Fall back," an Angel commanded the remaining Heavenly soldiers.

I don't need a rendering to know an Angelic Lord when I see one, Anorexia thought. *Now is the moment.*

The Angels stepped back into mortal hosts and Scarlet Fever closed up next to Anorexia in the Celestial. She was covered in blood that matched her hair – she was untouched.

"That's the target," Anorexia said. She pointed across the expanse to the officer housing the lead Angel.

"Protect Lord Calcium," several Angels shouted.

Musket fire from the wall of La Haye Sainte cut down numerous French mortals, but the host of the Angelic Lord remained unharmed.

"We have to pull back. We're useless here in the Celestial without hosts," Scarlet Fever said.

"Give it one second," Anorexia said.

Come on Dysgraphia, she thought.

The ground in front of the possessed Frenchman erupted in a geyser of dirt and blood as the cannon shell obliterated both of his legs. The Angelic Lord within was tossed free of the host and landed in a seizing pile at the feet of the Demons.

Scarlet Fever and Anorexia rushed to dispatch him with maniacal glee. They severed the Lord's head and held it aloft. Musket fire from the King's German Legion sent the French infantry into retreat. Similarly, the Angels withdrew in the face of the fierce sight ahead of them.

Scarlet Fever wiped her brow with a bloody hand. "Whew, I thought they had us for a moment there."

"It's far from over. Look, the French are moving along both flanks of La Haye Sainte. You go shore up Rotavirus and his squad. I'll go look after Lymphoma and his cadre," Anorexia said.

She turned toward the walls of La Haye Sainte and motioned for Streptococcal and Encephalitis to hold. Then she took off. Anorexia's swift, Celestial steps carried her to the flank. The French were making better progress in this locale.

The squad containing Lymphoma, Ophthalmia Neonatorum, and Macular Degeneration was composed entirely of neophytes. The trio appeared to be too frightened to step into the Celestial. When Anorexia encountered them, the French had nearly routed the King's German Legion and Demons were firing frantically from within hosts.

I can turn this to my favor, Anorexia thought. The Angels were leaving several of their seizing comrades unguarded. *I'll make them pay for their carelessness.*

Anorexia mazed her way through the lines of French Infantry, setting upon seizing Angels as she went. She had just driven her sai through the palate of an Angel when she spied another Angelic Lord. As though connected by a telepathic link, a cannonball from Dysgraphia's position decapitated the Angel's host.

Several Angels attempted in vain to protect the fallen leader. Anorexia cut them down one after another until she reached the seizing Lord. He had recovered from his seizure and was sitting on his haunches. Anorexia hurled one of her sai. The main blade missed but the side spoke tore his throat open. A fountain of arterial spray showered the Angel's robes and he slumped to the ground.

The artillery battery began concentrating fire on the possessed French. They fled into the Celestial. Inspired by her arrival, Lymphoma, Ophthalmia Neonatorum, and Macular Degeneration charged into the Celestial and began slaughtering the disorganized Angels.

Soon the French and the Angelic contingent were in full retreat.

"Enfoirés, on peut faire ça toute la journée,"[2] Anorexia shouted to the retreating foes.

---

[2] Motherfuckers, we can do this all day.

She playfully punched Lymphoma in the arm and shook Macular Degeneration.

"You mustn't be afraid to leave your hosts," Anorexia said.

The trio nodded.

"It's far from over. Hold. The. Line," she said.

Anorexia broke into a sprint that carried her back to the central position at La Haye Sainte. A British regiment of Foot Guards, led by Lung Cancer and her squad, had arrived to reinforce the center of the line. Anorexia motioned for Encephalitis and Streptococcal to join her. They were soon met by a winded Scarlet Fever.

"How goes it?" Anorexia asked.

"The flank is secure. No casualties for our side. They're in good spirits," she said between gasps.

The ground began to tremble.

"Earthquake?" Streptococcal asked.

Anorexia stepped into a senior officer of the Foot Guards and shouted. "Squares! Make squares!"

"Cavalry charge," Scarlet Fever said. "Get into the front line of the box."

Streptococcal and Encephalitis followed the Academy Instructor's order.

Anorexia nodded in approval of Scarlet Fever's actions as she saw her move forward in the Celestial. She abandoned her host once the mortal orders were sorted and joined her confederate at the head of the formation.

"The mortals will hold them with the box formations. It's up to us to get the Angels they knock down," Anorexia said.

The charge was an act of desperation. The Angels could not keep up with the cavalry in the Celestial. Consequently, they could only ride into battle in possession of mortal troops. As the French troops thundered toward the Foot Guards, they began taking casualties from the defenders' musket fire.

Anorexia and Scarlet Fever set upon the Angels that had been shot out of the French Cuirassiers. The uninjured Angels were forced to abandon their hosts to assist their colleagues, which left the French mortals with no chance of breaking the British ranks.

Within the maelstrom, Anorexia cut her way through Angels with brutal efficiency. A pang of searing pain cut through her shoulder. She felt her left arm drop. An Angelic throwing knife was lodged in her shoulder blade. She yanked it free and continued to fight. A few strides later she was met by the same burning pain, this time in her quadricep. Anorexia buckled and fell to the ground. She rolled out of the way of several sword strikes and forced herself to her feet.

The leader of the Angelic contingent was some distance away. He was still within a mortal and was directing both mortal and Celestial units. *Come on Dysgraphia, three for three,* Anorexia thought.

Each step was painful as Anorexia's wounds howled in protest. For the first time all day, she dodged and avoided rather than cutting her way through the foe. The Angel was struck by a cannonball when Anorexia neared him. With a guttural war cry Anorexia raised her sai and drove both into the Lord's chest.

Unlike previous instances, the Lord's death did not send the Angels into retreat.

"Fall back," Anorexia called to Scarlet Fever.

The pair made their way back to the safety of the British lines. Each possessed a mortal. Moments later, another wave of the French horsemen collided with the bayonets of the Foot Guards' line. The combat was fierce. If the mortals were broken, the Angels would overrun the quartet of Demons.

Twelve times the French cavalry charged the lines and twelve times the 1st Regiment of Foot Guards held their lines. In the end, the French and Angels lost their will to advance.

"Here, let me help you with that," Scarlet Fever said. She began bandaging Anorexia's Celestial injuries.

"I'm fine, but thanks," Anorexia said.

"Do you think that's it?" Streptococcal asked.

Anorexia shook her head, "The Prussians have not arrived. The French will re-form and attack once more. Surely the Angels will be with them."

She scanned each face. Her squad seemed beyond haggard. Anorexia looked toward the hilltops to their rear and wondered if Dysgraphia was watching them through a field glass. She brought her hand to her mouth and gestured blowing a kiss.

"Our gunner has been striking down Angelic Lords like lightning bolts from Zeus. We have to do our part," Anorexia said. "Quick, Lung Cancer, Scarlet Fever, go get our flanking squads. We'll concentrate in the middle and deal them a savage blow."

Fatigue gripped at Anorexia. *There is no other day to save myself for*, she told herself. She summoned energy deep from within her. *All of II Corps are still living, we can win.*

The French and Angels bunched their cavalry and infantry for a combined assault. It was the fiercest fighting of the day. The forces under Marshal Ney struck at the British center with divine ferocity.

Once more Anorexia led her squad into the Celestial ahead of the British lines. Joined by Lung Cancer's squad and the rest of II Corps, they were even stronger than before. The Angels, though numerically superior, fell in droves.

Anorexia had just punched her sai into the throat of a dark-skinned Angel when she spotted a renowned foe. With flowing blonde hair and a sculpted build, he was surely Michael, Lord of the Zinc House. She charged toward him. As she approached, Zinc's host was struck though the midsection by a cannonball.

This is it. They'll never recover from such a loss, she thought.

Anorexia felt a longing akin to thirst as she neared the foe. She was joined by Streptococcal, Encephalitis, and Macular Degeneration.

A blur of blades intercepted their path. A female Angel with dark hair and fair skin put herself between the fallen Lord and the Demons. The foe blocked two swipes from each of Anorexia's sai. The blow from the handle of her opponent's sword dropped Anorexia to the ground. The Angel spun and threw a knife into Encephalitis's throat whose vacant eyes stared across at Anorexia as both lay on the ground.

Streptococcal bypassed the menace and lunged toward Zinc. He managed to stab him, but it was not a fatal wound. The female Angel ran Strep through with her sword a moment later. He howled and fell over.

We were so close, Anorexia thought.

She struggled to her feet as Macular Degeneration struck the female Angel over the head with a Celestial Morningstar. However, before he could deliver the coup de grâce, Zinc recovered and stabbed him through the heart.

With wobbling steps, Anorexia tried to reach Zinc. She was intercepted by a gaggle of Angels from the African Houses. She killed several and finally reached Lord Zinc. He had risen to his feet and ordered some Angels to carry away the limp female Angel. He appeared weak and ready for the taking.

Anorexia's path was interrupted by the arrival of a brunette Angel with olive complexion. The Angel was accompanied by another fair complected Angel. The pair engaged her with vicious precision. Their attacks forced Anorexia away from Zinc. As quickly as the pair had arrived they pulled back towards Zinc's path of retreat.

Anorexia assessed the scene. The tableau in front of her was dire. Asthma, Epilepsy, and Rheumatoid Arthritis lay dead. They had all been brutally dismembered. Rotavirus and Failure to Thrive were standing back to back and surrounded by a horde of Angels. An impulse shot through her mind to assist the pair, but they were struck down before she could react. Rotavirus was killed instantly. Failure to Thrive's weapons were knocked away from her. She was pinned to the ground and a sword was forced between her teeth. While others restrained her, an Angel stamped down on the blade and severed her head in two. The foe began to beat the corpse without restraint.

Anorexia cringed at the gory spectacle. Enraged by the brutality, she abandoned her sai and drew her sword. Anorexia set upon the cluster of Angels with a rage she'd never known before. At the conclusion of the slaughter, she pulled Failure to Thrive into her arms. The Demon was unrecognizable. There were no eyes in the misshapen top half of the skull.

Across the field Scarlet Fever and Lung Cancer rallied their forces and slew copious numbers of Angels with the survivors of II Corps.

"Fall back to the cannons," Anorexia called to her colleagues.

Disengagement brought further losses as ALS, Gonorrhea, and Ophthalmia Neonatorum were cut down while withdrawing. With each step of her flight Anorexia expected to feel the pain of an Angelic throwing star. Her lungs burned and her limbs ached as she propelled herself forward. Only when she reached the hilltop claimed by the Royal Horse Artillery did she feel safe.

Scarlet Fever finished wrapping a bandage around her wounded hand. "We must return to Hell."

Anorexia looked at the haggard survivors of the encounter: Scarlet Fever, Lung Cancer, and Lymphoma.

"I did the best I could," Dysgraphia said. "I picked off four of the Lords from those sketches the Wraith gave me. There were supposed to be three others."

Anorexia patted him on the shoulder. "You did great. They defended their Lords with surprising skill."

"We have felled many Angels," Lung Cancer said. She ran her hand across her face and wiped blood away from a superficial wound. "We should not retreat now. The French have not taken the field. Our entire strategy is based upon holding until Schitz and the Prussians shatter the French. We can kill scores more Angels when their hosts fall into disarray."

"They have taken La Haye-Sainte," Scarlet Fever said. "The British center is about to collapse. If it does, we will be the ones fleeing for a portal in terror. We must retreat."

Anorexia sighed. "There are still seventy to eighty Angels down there. The odds have gotten worse."

"Must be sixteen-to-one by now," Dysgraphia said.

Anorexia weighed their chances. "Fine," she said. "Fuck the orders. We were supposed to have four gunners; we will reduce the number to three. Scarlet Fever, Lymphoma, you stay with Dysgraphia and man these guns."

Anorexia punched Lung Cancer on the shoulder. "We will go forth to meet them."

This is it, the cataclysmic battle. How lucky I am to have made it this far, Anorexia thought.

Lung Cancer clasped Anorexia's arm and head-butted her.

The playful blow invigorated Anorexia like food to a starving woman.

"You two against seventy to eighty?" Scarlet Fever asked. "No matter what we do with the guns, you will die."

"It will not be a bad death," Anorexia said. "I just wish there were more Angels I could take with me."

Lung Cancer unleashed an unholy laugh. The two charged down the hill away from the gun crews and toward the British lines.

The capture of La Haye Sainte had posed a grave threat to the British center. Wellington and his allies maneuvered to secure the center of their lines. Anorexia and Lung Cancer reached the point of contact between the British and French Armies amid a hail of musket fire. Before them stood a multitude of the foe.

Anorexia led her confederate into the attack. She hurled her sai into two foes and slashed a third with her sword. The duo fell back toward the British lines. The Angels pursued and jumped into the French Infantry.

A cannonade of pinpoint fire obliterated the hosts of the Angels. Anorexia and Lung Cancer set upon the seizing Angels and dispatched those who arrived to protect them as well. An Angel knocked Anorexia to the ground and reared back to strike a killing blow. A sword pierced the Angel's midsection. Lung Cancer leaned down and hauled Anorexia to her feet.

"Look out," Anorexia shouted. She pulled Lung Cancer out of the path of a pair of throwing knives. One grazed her friend's scalp, but left only a superficial wound. Lung Cancer hurled a throwing star of her own. It caught an Angel in the eye and dropped him to the ground.

Another precise volley of cannon fire tore through the French lines. Again Anorexia threw herself toward the foe. The process repeated over and over. Yet, as her wounds accumulated, her progress slowed.

A dark-skinned male Angel stabbed Anorexia in the leg. The blade flayed her flesh. The pain was hot and pulled all of her focus to the weapon protruding from her leg. Anorexia howled and fell to the ground. The Angel withdrew the sword with intentional slowness. Blood spurted from the wound.

Lung Cancer rushed to her aid but was caught across the back by a fusillade of weapons and fell to the ground.

Cannon fire erupted again but was useless to them in the Celestial Realm. Anorexia longed for an out of any kind but all routes of escape were blocked. There were no mortals close enough to possess. There were no friends to summon.

I wonder how the broader battler went, she thought.

Lung Cancer dragged herself along the ground. She positioned herself atop Anorexia shielding her from the Angel that stood over them. Anorexia could feel the blood from Lung Cancer's wounded back running down her chest.

The Angel pointed his sword toward them and spoke. "It is noble that even now you try to defend her."

"She is my senior, my company leader," Lung Cancer said.

"Might I know you?" the Angel asked.

"I am Lung Cancer."

"Anorexia."

"Gabriel Hydrogen."

He stood for a moment. Anorexia could feel her life ebbing into the grassy field. She awaited the final strike.

An Angel shouted from across the field. "Father, we must withdraw! The French are collapsing."

The words might as well have been accompanied by a fanfare. *Our executioner is told to flee*, Anorexia thought. She could feel the effect of the words within Lung Cancer's frame.

"Though we are ended we are victorious," Lung Cancer said.

Gabriel held his sword in their direction a moment longer.

"What are you waiting for?" Lung Cancer asked.

"Your wounds are deep. You pale as we speak. I do not think you will leave this field. Your senior is already fading. There is no need for more brutality. Today has already seen enough," he replied.

Lung Cancer's breath was suddenly labored. Anorexia's mind screamed for air. The world around her grew dark. The last image she remembered was the Angel sheathing his sword and walking away. The last thing she heard was Lung Cancer's voice, "It is good to die beside a sister so fierce as you."

When she came to, Anorexia was met by the sensation of water – all around. A pair of strong hands pulled her from the water and she was face to face with Spanish Influenza.

"Good," he said and dropped her to the ground.

"They'll live. Thanks to you, Saturnalia," he said.

Anorexia looked along the bank of the Styx and saw the only useful Wraith she had encountered before the battle. The Wraith was sat beside Lung Cancer.

"You saved us?" Anorexia said.

"Nearly got blown to bits by your gunners, but yeah, pulled you two out," the little Wraith said.

"Thank you. Saturnalia is it?" Anorexia said.

The Wraith nodded.

"I won't forget this," Anorexia said.

"Well, if you ladies are all right, there's a protest I need to attend," Spanish Influenza said.

"Protest?"

"Yeah, well Satan is trying to put the blame for the casualties on Titus. The High Priest might be annoying at times, but he's the first individual in history to strategize us into such a winning position. Only for Satan to bungle it," Spanish Influenza said.

"Didn't we win?" Anorexia and Lung Cancer asked in unison.

"Well, sixty-two went out and twenty-three came back. Actually, they thought twenty-one came back. You two were classified as KIA, but yeah, not exactly great figures," Spanish Influenza said.

"But we killed so many Angels," Lung Cancer said.

"Hundreds actually, by the count of it," Spanish Influenza said. "But not enough."

Lung Cancer slumped.

"Wait, I'm coming with you," Anorexia said. She attempted to stand and fell over.

"You're lucky you didn't lose the leg," Spanish Influenza said.

"Help me then," Anorexia said.

By the time they reached the throne room, the protest was all but over. Anorexia managed to stick her head through the doorway before she was shouted away. A cluster of Demons stood outside the closed doors, deep in conversation.

"Did you give them the medals?" Spanish Influenza asked.

"Aye, all that we could collect," Schitz said.

Anorexia noticed that Schitz and his daughter Rabies each wore oddly unadorned robes. Equally so for Cancer, Autism, and other notable Demons. *How many others survived?* Anorexia thought. The cluster seemed so small. *He said twenty-five.*

"Would you mind helping me to my room," she said to her Demonic crutch.

Spanish shrugged and obliged. Halfway to her room, he scooped her up into his arms.

"It's easier this way," he said.

It felt utilitarian and romantic at the same time. Especially, the latter when he set her down in her bed.

"I feel like I could sleep for an age," she groaned.

"They must have fucked you up if you need to sleep. I think you might be the oldest Demon now," Spanish Influenza said. He helped himself to a chalice of brew from Anorexia's liquor cabinet.

"Schitz and Autism are older than me...oh, so Smallpox? Dad?" she asked.

Spanish Influenza shook his head. He filled a cup and brought it to her.

"I had a rough day too. My mother bought it and Trichomoniasis," he said.

"I'm sorry for your loss," Anorexia said.

"Ah, I had a complicated relationship with both of them...I have a complicated relationship with everyone I know, actually," he said.

Spanish Influenza seemed lost in thought for a moment then shrugged. He leaned over the bed and clinked his chalice against Anorexia's cup.

"Didn't we used to do this by the Styx?" he said, gesturing toward their cups.

"Yeah, but your late wife took issue with it," Anorexia said.

"Are you serious?" he said. Spanish Influenza shook his head. He seemed somewhere between irritated and amused. Then suddenly, he turned away and wiped his eyes.

"'Tis but in vain, for soldiers to complain," he said, quoting *How Stands the Glass Around*.

"Indeed," Anorexia said.

"Why would she object?" he asked. "It's not like we were fucking...were we?"

"Pardon?" Anorexia said.

"I do a lot of drugs. I don't always remember everything," he said.

"We were drinking partners," she said.

"In my experience that doesn't rule things out. If anything it increases the odds," Spanish Influenza said.

Anorexia felt herself blush. "We were just drinking friends."

"If you're ever in need of that again, consider my schedule open," he said.

His face was jovial, but behind his eyes Anorexia could see a deep well of agony.

"I would like that," Anorexia said.

"Well, until then adieu, enjoy your rest, neophyte," he said.

With a tinge of regret for opportunities long past, but no intent to act, Anorexia fell into a deep restful sleep.

"I think we could have done better," Constance said.

Anna sighed and looked about the room. Because one of them always recuperated on a cot in Zinc's room, the pair of bodyguards had acquired an extra bedroom. The room intended for Anna had been converted into a headquarters of sorts. Charts and diagrams festooned the walls. The bodyguards used the place to debrief and assess risks to Zinc. They also stored intelligence and summaries of various Heavenly personalities.

"I've told you before, it is better we arrive late," Anna said.

"He almost died," Constance said.

"We likely would have died if we'd entered the fighting earlier. Then we would have been useless to him," Anna said.

Anna looked down at a recreation of the battlefield. The miniature version was full of figurines representing the warring parties.

"What if I had joined Rachael?" Constance asked. She moved forward a tiny statue carved in her likeness.

Anna looked at the board. In her mind, all she could see was the Morningstar mace cracking Rachael's head open. She grimaced.

"Zinc would have probably asked you to carry off Rachael instead of getting one of her sons to do so. But her son's arrival brought the rest of the group that the Demon killed before we intervened," Anna said.

"Hmmm, true," Constance said.

"I heard she's going to be alright," Constance said.

"I was relieved to hear that," Anna said. Constance was like a sister to her. She knew of Anna's past relationship with Rachael. Which explained Anna's eccentric response to Rachael's injury.

"Are you okay?" Constance asked. She touched Anna's arm.

"I am...I guess I went a little overboard on the Demon that hit her." Anna said.

"Just a tad," Constance said.

Their unbridled, maniacal laughter echoed along the halls and chilled everyone who heard it.

"Whoa, that's a new one!" Salvatore said.

The corpse of Macular Degeneration lay on the prep table. He had died from a penetrative wound to the sternum. His heart was punctured. Such a wound was not unusual in battle but upon disrobing the corpse, Salvatore discovered Macular Degeneration had been emasculated – post mortem. Whoever had mutilated him stuffed the organs down the Demon's throat.

Salvatore chuckled in his solitude. "Certainly gives new meaning to telling someone to eat a dick with a side order of balls." He patted Macular Degeneration on the chest. "I'm sure you weren't alive for the experience, old boy."

The mortuary was small. Stacks of bodies awaited in the hallway.

"Most curious," he said. He patted the corpse on the shoulder. "Tell you what. I'll sew everything back in place. It's the least I can do."

Silver and Christa walked through the ruins of the temple of Aizanoi in what had been the kingdom of Phrygia. The temple was remarkably preserved with one wall and several pillars still standing. Much of the floor was undisturbed. Silver kicked a small stone. It ricocheted across the expanse sending echoes as it went.

"So no hidden chambers this time," Christa said.

"No, nothing, because Zinc ruined everything," Silver said. He clutched his head in frustration.

The pair had questioned Zinc at length when all of their research had pointed to the Gordian Knot. Much like the jade bowl, the knot was guarded by human sentinels rather than an elaborate tomb. In his campaign with Alexander the Great, Zinc had destroyed the knot.

"From what he said, he hacked the knot apart and it 'bled.' Then he left. The priests and priestesses of the temple were devastated. He wasn't clear whether they were all put to the sword," Silver said.

Christa shook her head, "The taboo around Titan artifacts was strong. I wonder what he meant by the reference to bleeding. Probably some sort of mechanism to prevent forced entry."

"Exactly, when he cut into it, he broke some sort of container the contents of which destroyed whatever was in the knot," Silver said. He kicked another rock.

"You think it was strong enough to destroy a piece of the sword?" Christa asked.

"It probably wasn't a piece of the sword. More likely an intermediary step. It might have been a scroll or something fragile, with additional instructions that was destroyed with the knot," Silver said.

"I can't believe the effects are still here," Christa said.

She pointed to a stone in the middle of the ruined complex, a rock bearing a black stain.

"That must be the blood," she said. Her voice was wistful.

Silver crouched.

"Look!"

Christa knelt beside him. Carved into the side of the bloody stone were words in a language unfamiliar to Silver. His limbs tingled.

"It's not in the language of the Titans," Silver said.

"No, it's Phrygian," Christa said.

"I never possessed a Phrygian mortal."

"It's been a dead tongue for about thirteen centuries now. Even when it wasn't, you could have gotten by in the region with Greek," Christa said. "I'm certain there is a book or two about it in the library."

"No, we can't risk any questions about our investigation." Silver glanced around. "There could be Wraiths nearby. You and I will have to decipher this on our own. Any ideas?"

It had been many centuries since Christa had encountered the language, yet like all Celestials, once she had possessed a mortal, her mind housed the acquired language for the rest of her life.

"Okay," she said. "Here goes. Oh…what – no why – yes, Oh why the vessel awarded the vipers," she said.

"It's talking about Zinc," Silver said. "He must not have butchered all of the temple attendants!"

"We know it's another anagram," she said.

He was surprised she could not hear his heart pounding. He was already processing the phrase into the Titan language.

"I do the language, love," Christa said. "The puzzles are up to you."

She stared at the letters.

"Anything?" Silver asked.

Christa glared at him.

"Alright, alright," Silver said. He held up his palms. "Well, while you're thinking, consider this. How did the vessel *award* the vipers? Right? I mean the vessel, the Gordian Knot, destroyed the clue. How is that an award?"

"I think it has to do with the prophecy that whoever unraveled the knot would be the undisputed king of all of Asia. It sounds like the survivor was lamenting that Alexander did go on to conquer the known world," Christa said.

"Then it might not be an anagram after all. It could just be an epitaph," Silver said. Disappointment painted his voice.

"Well, all I can come up with is: Heavy Tears show where depths lived," Christa said.

Silver's morose mood evaporated like a puddle in the hot Anatolian sun. He said, "That phrase matches the Titan translation as well. It is the same wording in both languages!"

"It does, you're right!" Christa said. She beamed.

"The knot didn't bleed. It cried when it was cut. But the vessel was meant to break regardless," Silver said.

"Yes, but Zinc smashed it willy-nilly. How can we recreate the effect that was supposed to take place?" Christa asked.

"Well the knot was secured to the walls. I've seen a painting of Zinc destroying it in his chambers."

Christa's words came in a torrent. "The painting is a dramatic recreation. I remember when Alexander's army reached Aizanoi. The ropes of the knot were suspended from iron rods driven into the ground."

They explored the floor of the ruined temple. Under the dust accrued from centuries of disuse they located the original positioning holes for the iron rods.

"Look – carvings in the floor. Figures," Silver said.

"Like the frescos in Aleppo," Christa said.

"So if someone had successfully untied the knot, they would have..." Silver trailed away.

"Ended up with one of the ropes in the rod corresponding to Demeter," Christa said. Her voice trembled. She depressed a stone upon which survived a carving of a woman surrounded by crops, other food, and what appeared to be pregnant mortals.

Christa broke into a jog, her eyes scanning the floor of the temple. She looked for other engravings.

"Eurybia... Primogenitorous. ...Theia...Hyperion... and Saturn," said. Her voice was triumphant as she depressed the last stone. Each stone had clicked when she pressed down on it.

Silver's voice echoed through the hall. "Where DEPTHS lived! The first initials of the Titans."

No sooner had he pieced together what his wife had already discerned than the ruins began to rumble. Bits and pieces of stone fell away from the columns and the sole remaining wall. The bloodied stone shattered and fell into a cavity below the floor of the temple.

Silver picked his way over to the new opening, wary of the potential of additional collapses.

"Yes, do be careful," Christa said. "We don't need a repeat of last time."

Silver reached into the hole in the floor and retrieved a small, stone box. The container bore elaborate carvings in the language of the Titans. Silver opened the box and felt his shoulders slump. Disappointment coursed through his frame.

"What is it?" Christa said.

"A key," Silver replied.

"Whatever was destroyed when Zinc hacked apart the knot was probably a clue to where to use the key," Silver said. "All this effort for a dead end."

"Not really," Christa said, "The cross guard was in the tomb of Primogenitorous. He was mentioned here as well. If the statue was right, and this is his sword, then the more we learn about him, the better we can discern where the clue was leading. In fact, I already have an idea."

Silver pressed his lips against Christa's mouth and clutched her tightly. "How wonderful it is having you by my side on this quest."

Dysgraphia made his way through the hallway with hurried steps. *Certainly, my absence will be noted. There are more dead than living attending the funeral,* he thought.

He rounded a corner and collided with a fellow Demon. He knocked her thin frame into the corridor wall, however she caught herself quickly. It was Anorexia.

"You look like you've seen a ghost," the elder Demon said.

"I thought I had for a moment," Dysgraphia said. He had been certain that Anorexia and Lung Cancer had perished during the final action of the day.

"But I am quite glad to see I was wrong," he said. "Glad you're still with us." He kicked himself mentally for his lack of linguistic agility.

"Glad to still be here – I guess," Anorexia said. "Funerals bring back lots of bad memories."

"I've been kind of delaying my arrival as well," Dysgraphia said. "It's unpleasant to say the least. I lost both my parents and all four of my grandparents."

Anorexia put her hand on his shoulder. For a moment Dysgraphia was compelled to remember a moment in the battle where Anorexia had turned and blown a kiss toward the artillery battery.

I'm sure that was just a spur of the moment type thing. She was probably grateful for the accurate fire, he thought. He was aware his pulse was racing. Dysgraphia did not have a mate. He wondered if the attractive widow was involved with anyone. He knew little about her.

The odds have to be in my favor, he thought.

"Are you alright?" Anorexia asked.

"Yes, just relieved you're well, and... wishing I could have done more," Dysgraphia said.

"You were amazing. You assisted in the killing of three Angelic Lords. Your accurate fire was instrumental in our ability to hold our position as long as we did. You'd have received a medal if such a dark cloud wasn't cast over the whole endeavor," Anorexia said.

"Really?" Dysgraphia said. He blushed at the praise and wished she had kept her hand on his shoulder.

"Oh yeah. It's scandalous really. Not to brag, but I should easily have been given a Knight's Pentagram, probably with crossed swords. I don't know if even Plague ever killed as many as I did in one outing," Anorexia said.

Dysgraphia had witnessed her ferocity firsthand but somehow seeing such bravado in such a petite package was still shocking.

"You were a menace indeed," he said. "It was an honor to fight alongside you."

"Thank you, Dysgraphia," she said. "You've just left the Academy, right?"

Dysgraphia loathed that he was so young.

"I have," he said.

"You'll do well. You've survived a horrid ordeal. From now on, we will depend on you and the other youngsters to carry the cause forward. Now, let's go. We faced the battle, surely we can face the wake."

They arrived in the Great Hall and slid into a line of Wraiths encircling the service. Anorexia walked through the formation of Demons to the front row. Dysgraphia remained in the back.

Titus was completing the eulogy. His words echoed across the quiet hall

"...for there is nothing more for me to say about the fallen and those of you who stand here today. You have said far more with your deeds than anybody ever could with words."

Dysgraphia looked through the formation of Demons to a large opening in the floor of the Great Hall. In the cavity the fallen lay in tight rows, much like the lines of the Armée du Nord or Wellington's Red Coats.

A quintet of Wraiths began playing a song Dysgraphia did not recognize. They played it on fifes. The shrill notes took Dysgraphia's mind back to the dreadful day of the Waterloo exchange. A detail of

Wraiths and Priests began covering the interred with black, marble floor slabs.

A choir of Wraiths sung along with the fifes.

How stands the glass around
For shame, ye take no care, me boys
How stands the glass around
Let mirth and wine abound
The trumpets sound
The colours, they are flying, boys
To fight, kill or wound
May we still be found
Content with our hard fare, me boys
On the cold ground
Why, soldiers, why
Should we be melancholy, boys

Why, soldiers, why
Whose business 'tis to die
What sighing fie
Damn fear, drink on, be jolly boys
'Tis he, you and I
Cold, hot, wet or dry
We're always bound to follow, boys
And scorn to fly

'Tis but in vain
I mean not to upbraid you, boys
'Tis but in vain
For soldiers to complain
Should next campaign
Send us to Him that made us, boys
We're free from pain
But should we remain
A bottle and kind landlady
Cures all again

When the song concluded and the interment was completed, the assembled Demons broke formation. Those who did not depart milled about in conversation. Dysgraphia looked down at the floor. The stones covering the grave bore one word: Waterloo. Below it were listed the subdivisions of the order of battle and their location: I Corps-Hougoumont, II Corps-La Haye Sainte, III Corps-Papelotte, IV Corps-Plancenoit.

Not just names on a map anymore, but places etched into the pages of history, Dysgraphia thought.

His thoughts were interrupted by the arrival of his sister, Dyslexia.

"How are you brother?" she asked.

"Fine I suppose. I heard you conducted yourself well during the battle," he said.

"I did the best I could as the sole gunner in my area," she said. "I heard the same of you."

"Odd song for the funeral. Fitting though," Dysgraphia said.

"Ah, it's a song of the mortals, and secular," she said. "Apparently Satan didn't want any of the traditional hymns sullied by association with such a disastrous operation. I heard Spanish Influenza picked the song."

"Everyone keeps saying how bad it was, but we killed boatloads of Angels and took the field. Spanish Influenza was with your detachment, right?" he asked.

"A pyrrhic victory at best," she said. "And yes, he saved us."

"Same for us with Anorexia," Dysgraphia said.

CHAPTER 2

OUR POOR POWER TO ADD OR DETRACT

Anna and Constance stood outside the wooden exterior doors of the sole building on the Isle of Neutrality. Anna scrutinized the elaborate merger of the cross and pentagram carved into the doors' surface. The symbols were offset by two pairs of wings – one feathery, the other belonging to a bat.

"Sometimes I wonder what would happen if we reached an agreement and Angels and Demons stopped fighting," Anna said.

"The Atrophy?" Constance asked.

"I mean we could still heal and infect the humans. We could just end the struggle where both sides imagine they are good and consider the other evil."

"God and the Devil would sure be upset," Constance said. "Might have to fight their own battles again."

Their conversation was interrupted when the doors opened and Zinc staggered out. He was arm in arm with a thin, male Demon. Zinc's compatriot had wild hair and five o'clock shadow. His chiseled face sat atop a muscular neck and a well-toned frame.

And he had only one horn.

His right horn was healthy – normal length. On the other side of his head was a nub.

"Ah, ladies," Zinc said. He steadied himself on the doorframe. "Would you go inside and recover Beatrice, please?"

The Demon leered. "So, that's her name. She was great!"

Beatrice knew Anna accompanied Zinc to the Isle of Neutrality. Anna went everywhere with the Angel she guarded.

"You've got to get permission for me to go," Beatrice had said.

"Zinc won't let you," Anna said. "You're from one of the disbanded Houses. You don't go into battle. Zinc sees the Island as a reward for warriors."

But Beatrice was insistent and Anna finally relented. When Zinc agreed to a "this is the only time" sort of invitation, Anna feared Beatrice might overdo things.

"She's your friend," Constance said.

"She's your mother!" Anna said.

The Demon looked at Constance and winced. "You might not want to go in there," he said. "No offense." He winked and made a lewd gesture with his tongue. It was overdone – and meant to be offensive.

"I'm well aware of my mother's lifestyle, thank you," Constance said.

"It's fine, it's fine, I'll go," Anna said. "Just point me in the right direction."

"You'll get lost, I'll take you," the Demon said.

The Demon pushed open the door with exaggerated deference. "After you," he said.

Anna stepped into a dimly lit hallway and was face to face with a young Wraith. She would have thought she was a Familiar, save for her pointy ears, catlike eyes, and sharp teeth. The Wraith was wearing a sheer dress that left nothing to the imagination.

"Welcome, dear, right this way," the Wraith said. Her smile was alluring.

"Oh no, Civateteo," the Demon said. "She's collecting a friend – not staying." He looked at Anna and raised an eyebrow. "Unless…"

Anna tasted bile at the back of her throat but knew better than to insult someone who appeared to be a friend of Lord Zinc.

"Oh, as much as I'd like it, I really have to get going," she said.

She turned. The Wraith was well inside her personal space. "Well, if you change your mind," the Wraith said, "showers and a change of clothes are there."

She pointed to a door. The sign above it was in Angelic, Demonic, and French: "Ladies."

Anna walked along the hall. The Demon trailed.

"And who might you be," Anna asked over her shoulder. "Oh, how rude of me, Spanish Influenza," he said. He raced ahead of her, bowed deeply, then took her hand and kissed it. She slipped away from his grasp.

"Anna Gold," she said.

"Charmed."

"You don't happen to know a Demon named Schizophrenia?" Anna asked. She hoped her eagerness was not apparent.

"Yeah, I know Schitz, why?" Spanish Influenza asked. His merriment vanished like fog under a blazing sun.

"Oh, I just had heard he was vicious. I wondered if he still lived," Anna said.

"Yes, he is among the living. Funny you would know his name."

Have I put Schitz in some sort of danger? Anna thought.

But Spanish's stimulant-infused mind could not focus on a single subject. "I wonder," he said, "am I known among your ranks?"

Anna breathed easier.

"Of course, I just had never put a face to the name," Anna said. "Interesting name at that."

The Demon re-assumed his jovial guise.

"Ah, I'm named after a global pandemic that's yet to happen. My father possessed a mortal strain carrier and foresaw a great illness and he knew I was destined for great things, so voilà!"

"Very impressive," Anna said. She was relieved to have moved the conversation away from Schitz.

Spanish Influenza reached out to grab the next door and said, "Miss Gold, I give you The Isle of Neutrality."

Anna's legs turned rubbery.

The room was large and dimly lit. Her eyes adjusted to reveal games of chess, groups of people engaged in conversation, and...utter debauchery. She saw a gaggle of Angels in lounges, mostly young males with a couple of females sprinkled in. The group members were either smoking pipes or drinking from chalices. The primary source of interest appeared to be a game of chess between two of the adolescents.

I suppose drinking and smoking are frowned upon for academy-aged Angels, Anna thought.

Her eyes drifted to another scene – heavier in its substance use. A cluster of older Angels and a pair of female Demons were seated around a table on which sat a large pile of red powder. At intervals, the participants used small, rounded knives to make lines of the powder, which they then snorted. They were also passing around a water pipe from which they inhaled thick clouds of smoke.

"This way," Spanish Influenza said. He gently touched her on the shoulder and led her through a maze of ornate chaise lounges. Upon one, a pair of male Angels embraced each other in the throes of passion.

Rachael and I could have come here, and been away from judgment, Anna thought. Of course there are others like me. The realization was driven home as she realized the corner of the room seemed to be exclusively occupied by same-sex couples. Anna's eyes lingered for a moment as she watched two female Angels ravish each other.

"Oh, this can be quite a nice corner – if one is so inclined," Spanish Influenza said.

"Are we taking a tour, or are you taking me to Beatrice?" Anna said.

"Alright, alright no need to get punchy," he said. He punctuated his sentence by smacking the posterior of one of the females that had caught Anna's attention. The Angel turned and snarled at him, but was pulled away from the disruption by her lover.

Spanish Influenza winked at Anna. "I'm a mayor of sorts around here, so I have to make my rounds," he said.

When they arrived in the far corner of the room, Spanish Influenza proclaimed, "Ah, at last we arrive at Le Cercle de Feu."

The participants in this corner represented an amalgamation of the other areas they had passed through. Arrayed around the perimeter was a group of fully clothed Angels and a handful of Demons. They were enthralled with the spectacle before them. Many had their hands under their robes, vigorously gyrating. In the center of the circle an orgy of Angels and Demons was in full bloom. Anna felt herself blush as she beheld a female Demon lying stark naked on the floor. An Angel continually covered her with the red powder Anna had seen earlier. All the while, several other male and female Angels and one Demon licked or snorted the powder off of her body.

At the back of this scene Anna noticed a large cauldron – a tub of sorts. Participants were swimming in the pool, having sex, or consuming the contents. Some were performing more than one of the activities at a time.

"I don't see Beatrice," Anna said over the racket.

"Ahh, well, she was here...I think she left quite an impression. Hold on," he said.

Spanish Influenza spoke to one of the watchers. She gestured to an area to the side of the spectacle. Anna followed the Angel's outstretched arm and saw Beatrice, face down behind a sofa. An empty goblet lay at her side.

"Your leg is so strong and hard... I wonder what the rest of you... feels like," Beatrice said. She was rubbing the leg of the sofa with intent.

"Oh, Beatrice, you've outdone yourself," Anna said.

Anna heaved her friend to her feet and slung her over her shoulder.

A rousing cheer erupted from the crowd in the Le Cercle de Feu. It started with a few instances of applause and the odd "huzzah," and culminated in a rousing chant of "Beatrice, Beatrice, Beatrice."

"Good Lord, what did you do?" Anna asked.

Beatrice giggled. "I'm...so high...and...so drunk...I'll tell you... later."

"I love you Beatrice," one of the watchers shouted over the crowd.

Anna looked over her shoulder. Spanish Influenza had taken a seat amongst the crowd. He noticed her gaze and tipped an imaginary hat in her direction.

What a crazy place, Anna thought.

"Oh, your friend was Beatrice," the Wraith at the door said. She popped around Anna to face her passenger. "Bye, Bee-Bee. Come back soon, alright?"

Anna pushed the door open. Zinc and Constance stopped mid-conversation. Zinc fell on the floor in a fit of laughter.

"Oh really, Mother?" Constance said, shaking her head.

"Alright, let's go," Anna said. "You think you can manage him?"

"I'll manage myself, thank you," Zinc said. He rose to his feet, but happily accepted assistance walking from Constance.

Anorexia and Lord Uranium II walked through the wreckage of a fort on the Chuenpi. The forces of the British Crown and the East India Company had pounded the fort into submission hours earlier. Around the Celestial pair, Royal Marines were still in the process of securing several hundred prisoners.

"There is no officially recognized conflict between my brother Lord Platinum and me. However, we do use conflicts such as this 'Opium War' to take shots at each other from time to time," Uranium II said.

"Oh, Xiang. To think I was worried about you surviving Waterloo and here you are seeking out your own dangers," Anorexia said.

"My world has and always will be very complicated," Uranium II said.

"It seems like I've always had an affinity to this part of the world and the Angels that oversee it, but I have to admit, I have some of the politics mixed up," Anorexia said.

He said, "Well, then allow me to enlighten you. The Mercury House is one of the original founding Houses. Hirokatsu Mercury I, Chikayoshi Mercury II, and Fusanosuke Mercury III all reached honorable retirement. They maintain a meditative vigil high in the Heavenly mountains, not far from the source of the Eunoe. Haruaki Mercury IV fell at the Teutoburg Forest. Before his demise he incorporated the Cobalt House.

"The name Cobalt had been in existence for many generations. Haruaki Mercury IV mistakenly thought his service at the Battle of Banquan would result in a dispensation – permission to form his own House. When he did not receive one, his son Lord Cobalt remained a Lord in name only. When Haruaki finally received the option to incorporate a House, he named his brother Yuxuan, Lord Cobalt I."

He paused to ensure Anorexia was keeping up. She nodded.

"Your dear friend, my mother Chu Hua, was Yuxuan's sister. Yuxuan Cobalt received my mother and my father, Jiao-Long, into his House to bolster Yuxuan's numbers – pretty typical for a new

House. However, shortly thereafter both of my parents died along with Lord Mercury IV at the Teutoburg. It is prohibited within the Asiatic Houses for an Angel who is not a Lord in his own right to be an orphan. Therefore, after Teutoburg Forest, Lord Yuxuan Cobalt became my father, in nomine solum, ah, in name only.

"Until this point, the Eastern Houses had existed in a state of balance. The descendants of the Mercury Lords knew nothing but loyalty and filial respect. I was accepted as one of Yuxuan's sons. I felt no different from his sons by birth to whom he granted Houses: Sadao Uranium I and Han-gyeol Platinum I."

"This is getting complicated," Anorexia said. "But it's fascinating. Please continue."

"Cobalt had conquered vast tracts of Asia via the Mongols. He divided them among himself, Sadao Uranium, and Han-gyeol Platinum. Thus, we existed in harmony. Despite my adopted status, I knew my pater in nomine would either name me Cobalt II or grant me a new House."

"What happened?"

"The peace was shattered. God named two Supreme Commanders of the Angels. The expressed intent was to avoid one sole leader from becoming too powerful. In point of fact, God's administrative decision ripped the Eastern Houses apart. One of the Angels he named as co-commander was Sadao Uranium."

"Lord Zinc II was the second," Anorexia said.

"Correct. Lord Yuxuan Cobalt could not accept such an affront and Han-gyeol Platinum agreed with him as well. They geared up for war against Sadao Uranium. I was thrust into the conflict when Lord Zinc assassinated Lords Yuxuan Cobalt and Sadao Uranium. Following the swift executions, he installed me as Xiang Uranium II. From then on, my brother Han-gyeol Platinum has waged unrelenting war against myself and my client Houses."

He took a breath. "And there is the history of the Angels of the Asian continent."

"I wonder why Zinc did not dispatch of Platinum when he started knocking off fellow Lords," Anorexia said.

Uranium II grinned. "You have a head for politics. Had he eliminated Cobalt and Platinum and left either Uranium I or me, the surviving Lord would have been powerful indeed – the solitary leader of the entire Asian bloc. All resistance would have fallen."

"Ah, so he elevated you and kneecapped you at the same time," Anorexia said.

"Indeed, but in spite of that, Zinc is a close friend of mine. I do not fault him for playing the game," Uranium II said.

"I do hope you'll be careful. I so value our friendship. I would hate to lose you, like I did your mother," Anorexia said.

Uranium II smiled and patted her on the shoulder, "I am as careful as I must be. If only you were born an Angel, then we could look out for each other."

The tranquility of the Heavenly countryside was shattered by the explosion of an 1853 Enfield Pattern rifle-musket. An old Elixir decanter disintegrated and fell from the branch of a far off tree.

"I love these new percussion lock muskets," Anna said.

"Well, consider it a retirement present, since I won't be going back to the Mortal Realm ever again," Lilly said.

"I think I'm supposed to get you the retirement present," Anna said.

Lilly chuckled. "Probably, however it is I who am forever indebted to you. Without your tutelage, I would have never lived to see old age."

"It's been a long time since it was Romans fighting Barbarians," Anna said.

"Yes, indeed. I've seen many empires of men rise and fall in my time. Lots of weapons, but I'm certainly glad I don't have to dodge the likes of those." Lilly gestured towards the musket.

"I'm glad you're safe," Anna said. She shouldered the musket. "Come on, let's get going."

They made their way across the countryside until they came upon the resting place of Gertrude Iron. The other Witch Hunters had already arrived to pay their respects, as they always did on the anniversary of The Confessoress's demise.

"It's good to see you Lars, Barnabas," Anna said.

The group exchanged pleasantries.

"We tried so hard to save her," Barnabas said. "Not a day goes by that I don't wonder if we could have done more."

"The past is the past, old friend. All we can do now is remember her," Lars said. He gave Gertrude's old flame a conciliatory pat on the back.

"How are things?" Barnabas asked Anna.

"Well enough. Zinc keeps me busy," Anna said.

"Indeed, you are the last of the Witch Hunters still actively employed. Congratulations Lilly, by the way," Lars said.

"What about you?" Anna and Lilly asked simultaneously.

"Oh, I passed things along as well," Lars said.

"Well, congrats to you also," Lilly said.

"So who heads up the secret police now?" Anna asked.

"Wouldn't you like to know," Lars said with a wicked grin.

"I could find out easily enough," Anna said. She matched his smirk.

"Oh, I'm sure you could," Lars said. "In many ways you are Gertrude's heir."

Silence hung over the assembly, then Lars shrugged his shoulders and said, "Pyotr took over for me."

"Oh, he's a sharp one," Lilly said.

"Implying I'm not?" Lars asked. He tried to act hurt.

"I'm not the one who retired you," Lilly said.

"The decision was my own, thank you," Lars said.

The Witch Hunters broke into laughter.

"It feels good to be back together," Barnabas said.

When the Witch Hunters bid each other adieu, Anna found herself followed by Barnabas.

"Ah, a word, Anna, if I may?"

"Of course, Barnabas. What is on your mind?" Anna asked.

"You know I keep mostly out of the affairs of running the Carbon

House. But recent events warrant my attention," Barnabas said.

"You mean Zinc executing Iron III and Palladium?"

Barnabas grimaced. "Yes, dreadful business that was. And yes, I know Zinc had his reasons. Iron III was ambitious and surely meant to take Zinc's position. It's just..."

"You worry Thomas, Carbon VI, and Zinc will do an equally lethal dance," Anna said.

"Straight to the point as always," Barnabas said. "Yes, Robert, Carbon V, loved Zinc. He died fighting for him in the duel with the Black Death coven."

"Aye, I recall. I also recall Thomas, Carbon IV, plotting to use Gold as a means to undo Zinc," Anna said.

"Your memory stretches far indeed," Barnabas said. "Yes, and poor Alonso paid the price. Unfortunately, it would seem both Thomases are unfortunately alike. I wish you could impress upon your master that Thomas VI is young. Your master need not be brutal with him. His ambition is born of youthful inexperience, not outright malice."

Anna shrugged, "Barnabas, you know you will always be one of my dearest friends. However, you also know Zinc makes up his own mind. I will relay your message, but in the end my master will chart his own course."

"I understand and I thank you," Barnabas said. "If only we schemed as much against the Demons as we did against our own kind."

"If that were the case, I'd be out of a job, for Zinc would hardly need a bodyguard," she said.

"To be clear, this is my mission," Spanish Influenza said for the umpteenth time. They walked through one of the trenches dug by the Union Army outside of Vicksburg.

Anorexia laughed. "Just because I'm your senior and a Triumvirate member, does not make this my mission. You're lead; I'm happy to lend my assistance. You've been fighting along the Mississippi for months. It wouldn't be fair for me to show up at the end and claim it as my own."

"I just don't want there to be any confusion once the bullets start flying," he said.

Anorexia knew control was important to Spanish Influenza. She kept her secret mission to herself. Anorexia had been tasked by Satan to observe Spanish Influenza in the field. He had performed remarkably at Waterloo and was being considered for a position of leadership. Satan was thinking of expanding the Triumvirate – creating a position for Spanish Influenza. Such an action would elevate him above several older, storied Demons.

"It's all yours. I'm only here as assistance from the Triumvirate. And in that spirit, I caution you: once the bullets start flying, please look after your soldiers. We are still severely thinned," Anorexia said.

Spanish Influenza waved his hand as though batting away one of the monstrous mosquitos of the region. The pair joined the rest of the contingent. Anorexia assessed those assigned to Spanish Influenza: Scarlet Fever, Lung Cancer, Typhoid, Liver Cancer, Brain Cancer, Gangrene, Cerebral Palsy, and Dyslexia. It was a sizable portion of Hell's fighting force. Anorexia hoped with all of her being that it would go well for Spanish Influenza. For a moment she was taken back to the Academy's lecture hall, watching Schitz answer a question and hoping his response would be correct.

"The tunnel is dug and the charges are set," Scarlet Fever said. The Academy Instructor was in possession of a woman of the 45th Illinois Regiment.

As valedictorian and an instructor she might well wonder why it is her brother leading this mission rather than her. Yet, Spanish Influenza commands respect from his subordinates, Anorexia thought.

"You all know your jobs. Follow me," Spanish Influenza said.

He has them well briefed and leads from the front. Recollections of Hastings and the impetuous young Spanish she had supervised flashed before her mind. He's come a long way, but he's never let go of that swashbuckling attitude.

The explosion of 2,200 pounds of gunpowder tore through the mine under the third Louisiana Redan. The seismic blast geysered dirt through the air – a shower of red mud. As debris settled upon the massive crater, a sea of blue uniforms filled the void.

Atop the peak, undeterred by the explosion, a column of gray took up firing positions along the ridgeline. Musket fire erupted from both sides.

Anorexia hated the feeling of being confined within the crater, however, Spanish Influenza had asked her to stay back with the mortals. Spanish Influenza, for his part, led Scarlet Fever and Lung Cancer forward in the Celestial.

The strategy was daring and simple. While the squad fired from within the Union soldiers and targeted any Angelic possessed mortals, the runners would advance in the Celestial and cut down any Angels the shooters picked off.

The Demons were assigned to predetermined waves. Spanish led the initial assault and soon reached the top of the ridge. From her position in the pit of the crater, Anorexia fired with unnatural accuracy at the Confederate position. Rounds whizzed past her like angry bees. Undeterred, she drove another cartridge down the barrel of her weapon, primed the percussion cap, cocked the hammer, and fired. Another headshot. She repeated the process over and over. All the while, Confederates possessed by Angels fired at her...and missed.

Typhoid and Liver Cancer were the next to charge up the hill within the Celestial. Anorexia instructed those who remained behind to continue their fire.

"Don't let up on them," she shouted.

The Union troops were in a dire position. The inaccurate assumption that the Confederates would be unable to form up in a coherent fashion following the explosion was a lethal miscalculation. The 45th Illinois was being shot to pieces.

Gangrene and Brain Cancer charged the hill next. Anorexia continued her fusillade. A round shattered the lower jaw of her host. While the mortal woman collapsed to the ground, Anorexia rolled into the Celestial and quickly selected another host. She resumed firing without delay.

Anorexia raised her musket, aimed, and blew the head off of another possessed mortal. She turned and signaled to Cerebral Palsy and Dyslexia. Together, the trio charged forward in the Celestial. The path up the crater was steep. Anorexia's legs burned and her breath came in ragged bursts.

At last, she crested the top of the hill and was met with a scene of devastation. Within the Celestial a multitude of Angels lay dead upon the ground. Still, the odds appeared insurmountable. All of the Demons who had preceded them were locked in ferocious combat.

How do the Angels take such abuse and still hold their ground? Anorexia thought. Then she beheld the answer to her query. Leading the Angels was the blonde haired menace she had encountered at Waterloo: Lord Zinc.

The Angelic Lord was continually organizing and compelling the Angels to keep up their efforts even as Spanish Influenza and his squad cut them down wholesale.

This fight can turn on a knife's edge. She knew neither Zinc nor Spanish Influenza was likely to yield. Similarly, the Confederates would not give up the ridge and the Unionists were stuck in the crater. It was a fight to the death.

"Follow me," Anorexia said to Cerebral Palsy and Dyslexia.

She followed a winding path through the brawl, bypassing numerous Celestial engagements. Zinc appeared unaware of her approach. Anorexia raised her sword and swung towards his back. The blade was intercepted by an outstretched sword and Anorexia was thrown to the floor.

The same damned bodyguard from Waterloo. The pale, brunette Angel seemed to have emerged from thin air.

Anorexia looked on helplessly as a bronzed, dark-haired Angel, also known to Anorexia from Waterloo, quickly dispatched Cerebral Palsy and Dyslexia. The former she decapitated with a Celestial axe; the latter she cut across the midsection.

Dyslexia, disemboweled and slowly dying, looked towards Anorexia. Her eyes begged for any sort of assistance.

Anorexia rose to her feet. Spanish Influenza passed her before she could re-engage Zinc and his retinue. The darker brunette sent Spanish sprawling back into Anorexia with a savage kick. His weight was almost unbearable, but the onset of fear was worse.

Any moment now they'll dispatch both of us, she thought. However, the foe had withdrawn by the time Spanish Influenza had extricated himself and hauled Anorexia to her feet.

"They're gone," Spanish Influenza said. His neck and cheeks glowed the deep scarlet of rage.

"It looks like you've taken the field," Anorexia said.

The Confederates were still firing down upon the Union troops. In the Celestial, a multitude of slain Angels lined the Confederate trench.

"Aye, but we should withdraw. We have sustained casualties," he said.

He fights like a madman, but he is more measured than in the past. He's learned a thing or two.

"You should have let me finish off those two elder Demons," Zinc shouted.

Anna and Constance followed him through the Great Hall.

"With all due respect, it was a volatile situation. It is our job to ensure your safety. Once we had a window, it made the most sense to pull back," Anna said.

Zinc was ready to continue the argument, but backed down and nodded.

"I suppose it was the most prudent path," he said.

An energetic crowd of Angels was making its way through the Great Hall. Zinc scrutinized the gaggle of Celestial soldiers.

"I wonder what is going on," he said. "Anna, go and find Silver. Inquire about the progress of his wonder weapon. I'd rather not have another day like today," Zinc said.

"Right away," Anna said.

"Come on, Constance," Zinc said. "Let's see what all the hullaba-loo is about."

Constance was happy to remain in her Lord's company. She fell back from him, as was typical when they were in Heaven, but kept him ever under her watchful eye. She walked with her hand resting within her robes, where she clutched a dagger.

Zinc doesn't want us too close to him in Heaven. He doesn't wish to appear weak and reliant on us for his security. But everyone knows why we are here.

Constance considered her former father-in-law. I've known him my whole life, the one true constant, even more so than my dear Adolphus, she thought. Her heart beat faster as Zinc snaked through the crowd. It was difficult to anticipate threats in such an environment.

The crowd moved to the banks of the Eunoe near a bridge that led to the island used to settle disputes. Across the flowing river, Lord Thomas Carbon VI, the Standard Bearer of the Carbon House stood holding a large spear and attacking a junior male of his House.

What the fuck? Constance alternated her gaze between the island and Zinc.

Constance noticed a line of members of the Carbon Household waiting to cross the footbridge that led to the island. She saw Anna in an animated discussion with the retired Standard Bearer, Lord Barnabas Carbon III. Constance felt herself tremble. She had never seen Anna in such a state of emotional upheaval. It shocked her to see the warrior crying in public.

Constance maneuvered through the crowd while keeping an ever watchful eye on Zinc. The crowd shouted and the next in line started over the bridge.

"I've lost too many friends and family. I'll fight him in your stead," Anna said. Her voice was painful…pleading.

I knew she was friendly with Barnabas, but not so much, Constance thought.

"I could not bear the shame of having such a dear comrade take my place in the tragedy brought about by my own lineage," Barnabas said. "Besides…I miss Gertrude. It is better I go than you."

"You won't be reunited with her," Anna said through streaming tears. "You'll just be gone."

"Just because our religion says that doesn't mean it is necessarily true. I have hope in a well-deserved paradise for us beyond this lifetime of suffering and war. Perhaps, the mystery is concealed from us, so that we don't long for it too much," he said.

Anna clutched to Barnabas. "Please, there has to be another way," she said.

The crowd shouted. Barnabas kissed Anna on the forehead.

"Do me one last favor," he said.

"Anything."

"Leave this place. I'd rather your memory of me be from our time spent searching for Gertrude," he said.

"Barnabas!" an authoritative voice sounded.

Constance looked up and saw God standing on a platform that provided a view of the island. She had not realized her sovereign was present. Of course, only he could sanction something like this, she thought.

Anna pushed her way through the crowd. Barnabas began crossing the bridge. Constance turned and saw Rachael Hydrogen walking toward Zinc. Rachael was considered to be one of the greatest threats of Zinc's safety.

Damn, I should have been paying closer attention, Constance thought. She clutched the handle of her dagger and made her way closer to Zinc.

Rachael rested one hand on Zinc's arm.

Where's her other hand? Constance thought. She looked for a weapon and kept pushing through the crowd. She was about to pull her weapon when Rachael raised her free hand and pointed toward the line of Carbons. After a few more words, Zinc began making his way toward the bridge.

Constance caught Rachael's gaze. Her eyes were unreadable, but contained a mixture of intense emotions. Constance looked away and followed after Zinc.

Constance arrived behind Zinc. He was speaking to a young Carbon maiden.

"Marry me!" Zinc said.

"To save my life?" Her question was blunt and without emotion.

Constance felt as though she would faint. Marry him? But...why, am I so sad? she thought. She had never truly explored her strong feelings toward Zinc. I thought I was just a loyal subject...but now, I don't know.

"And to make both our lives better," he said. He shrugged. "Of course, later on, you can change your mind, and I can just kill you."

"Your sense of romance needs a little work, my Lord," the maiden said.

Constance felt as though she was trapped within the confines of a horrible dream. She longed to awaken, to tell Zinc that she, like he, was so dreadfully lonesome.

God spoke next. "Do you, Lord Zinc, Standard Bearer of the Zinc household and Holder of the Golden Halo, take this Maiden to be your wife, to love her singularly, to father Angels by her, and to protect and defend her until death or into eternity?"

"I do," Zinc said.

God turned to the woman.

"And do you, Maiden Carbon, take this Angelic Lord to be your husband, to love him faithfully and devotedly, to bear Angels by him, and to protect and defend him until death or into eternity?"

"I do," she replied.

"I declare you husband and wife. I further declare the conclusion of the Trial by Ordeal of the House of Carbon."

"Excuse me, wife," Zinc said. "I don't even know your name."

"Eleanor," she said.

Constance followed the newlyweds back to his chamber. Zinc scooped up the young maiden. She giggled effervescently. Constance cringed. Zinc opened the door and dismissed Constance with a furtive glance over his shoulder and a nod of his head.

A disembodied walk carried Constance to the Manna bakery. She found Anna sobbing in a back corner. Constance slumped down beside her and put her arm around her. Soon she was weeping as well. The two held each other in a tearful embrace for a long while.

The sound of a bottle smashing against the wall echoed through the hallway. Angry words leaked through the door. Anorexia hesitated, then knocked Spanish Influenza answered. His face was a landscape of wrath.

"What do you want?" The growl of an agitated bear.

"You've been summoned to report to the Triumvirate," Anorexia said.

He brushed past her and stomped down the hallway.

Anorexia felt a rising sense of concern.

I hope he doesn't undo his good work by doing something rash.

She chased after him. "You need to calm down."

"I don't need, to do anything," he said.

Anorexia grabbed the youngster by the back of his robe and pinned him against the wall.

"You need to calm down."

Spanish Influenza's rage melted. A flirtatious gleam materialized in his eyes.

"Though she be but little she is fierce," he said.

"Not exactly the time for Shakespeare," Anorexia said.

"Oh, not a fan?" he said.

The nape of Anorexia's neck tingled with perspiration. Her pulse quickened and she felt an enjoyable, hungry sensation beneath her robes. I should kiss him, she thought. Anorexia pushed the thought away and stepped back.

"I was assigned to accompany you and to report on your capabilities in the field. Satan was planning on expanding the Triumvirate Council to open a seat for you," she said.

Spanish Influenza brought his hands to his head and clutched his drastically uneven horns. He groaned.

"I gave a stunning assessment and took full responsibility for the casualties," she said. "I was the one who led the inexperienced Demons into the Angelic Lord's scythe," she said.

Spanish Influenza's eyes were those of a pleading child longing for good news.

"The Devil was irate at the losses, which was why we're having this meeting in private. However, he is giving you a Knight's Pentagram, just not with the fanfare they showed to Scarlet Fever and Lung Cancer," Anorexia said.

"Fanfare is not the word for it," Spanish Influenza grumbled, "he had to double up, giving Lung Cancer a first class, and nearly all the survivors second classes so he could also give them first classes."

The rules were clear. Before you could earn a First Class, you had to have won a Second Class – and so forth. Consequently, he had bequeathed many of the Vicksburg combatants multiple awards.

"Those awards were more carryover from Waterloo if anything. Many Demons performed feats that were initially overlooked by Satan," Anorexia said.

"Yeah, I see they added a statue as well," Spanish Influenza said.

"Come on," Anorexia said. They began to walk.

"You know," she said, "no one has given me a Knight's Pentagram. And I've killed Angelic Lords. I led II Corps at La Haye Sainte, I—"

"But didn't the Angels capture La Haye Sainte?" Spanish Influenza asked. There was a glint in his eyes.

Anorexia smiled. She rolled her eyes and opened the door. The Triumvirate and Satan were already present in the room. Titus rose from the table and handed a medal to Satan. Anorexia walked over to the table and took her seat between Autism and Rabies.

Satan approached Spanish Influenza and said, "Every time your name is mentioned. I hear you are wild both on the battlefield and in your personal endeavors. Yet, no one can deny your accomplishments. However, I wish to caution you, as one of my Knights..." Satan paused to place the medal around his neck."...you must not be reckless with my army. God's army outnumbers us substantially."

"Yet, we persevere," Spanish Influenza said.

Anorexia heard several murmurs from those seated around her at the table. It was not exactly an interruption, however it was more brazen than most would have been.

He is wild, Anorexia thought.

"That we do. I wish I could tell you to take a seat at the table, but I'm certain that time will come soon," Satan said.

Spanish Influenza saluted and exited.

"Shame really," Satan said. "I have a Demon who went into the field and came back with all of his squad, but has no ambition to join my Triumvirate and another with unbounded ambition who gets his subordinates killed. And my current council as always is useless and complacent."

Having extinguished any positivity associated with the medal ceremony, Satan stalked off.

"Well, he certainly has a bee in his bonnet," the Priestess Erin said.

"After firing me, he's heaped a lot of his hopes on the Demons for leading his army," Titus said.

Anorexia thought back to the Idealists. "Our clans worked. He should never have disbanded them," she said.

"It's true," Autism said.

"Rather than rotating assignments from mission to mission, perhaps we could develop squads within the Triumvirate structure. If we don't change the assignments, it will be a de facto clan-like atmosphere," Titus said.

"Just like you did when you broke everybody up before Waterloo," Anorexia said.

"Precisely," Titus said.

"Satan might see through that. He was adamant about the stagnation he saw in the clans. The same stagnation he now apparently sees in us," Elise said.

"Humph, stagnation? He'd do better to assess what he's done for the cause lately," Mephistopheles replied.

Titus and the two Priestesses both giggled. Anorexia smiled. She could remember a time when blasphemy offended the High Priest. It seems leading the army cured him of that.

"Well, we can mull it over, but we should consider it before the next expansive campaign," Rabies said.

There was a murmur of agreement. Anorexia wondered what was next...for the Council... ...for Spanish Influenza....for her.

Chapter 3
Buried Secrets

Silver and Christa stood in the Celestial Realm under the shadows of the trilithons of Stonehenge. After years of researching Christa's hunch, the pair had settled on the ancient site as the most likely location marked on the map Zinc had destroyed when he hacked apart the Gordian Knot.

"Blasted tourists," Silver grumbled.

Unlike many of the other locations they had searched in their quest, Stonehenge was a center of everyday activity. Where Silver had been free to sneak into the meeting room of the Inner Circle hidden under the Teutonic Cemetery, and likewise had free access to the subterranean tomb in Aleppo and easily traipsed through the abandoned temple of Aizanoi, Stonehenge was littered with mortals.

"Well, it's part of their history too," Christa said.

Silver looked over at an amateur painter, a local of Wiltshire. He looked at the work and scrunched up his nose. "Hardly Michelangelo," he said.

Christa laughed, "Oh, be nice." She chuckled. "Besides, you can't draw a lick."

Farther from the painter, a family with more small children than either parent knew what to do with picnicked in the afternoon sun. The girls twirled small ribbons and pinwheels while the boys pelted each other with pebbles.

"Kind of reminds me of our brood," Christa said.

"Only if their aim was better," Silver said. He smiled and drank in the placid setting.

"We can wait until they clear out," Christa said. "I'll remember where the shadows fell."

"To be honest, we're grasping at straws anyways. We've been clandestinely excavating this site for what seems like forever. If it weren't for this Pax Britannica, I'm certain Wraiths would have sent a Demonic Army to seize the site," Silver said.

"But it was a Titan settlement," Christa said. "We've determined that the Titans named at Aizanoi lived here."

"We've searched every stone for lettering. We've dug. It might be time to start over at square one," he said, with a groan.

"You think?"

"Sometimes."

Christa rolled her eyes.

Silver kicked a pebble. It bounced along the ground, hopped, and struck one of the warring juveniles between the eyes. The victim, assuming the fault lay in one of his brothers, wrestled the nearest to the ground.

"Oh, Richard, do stop. So much of your father in you," the mother said. She cut daggers toward her napping husband.

Silver snickered. Christa punched him in the arm.

"Must you torment them so," Christa said.

"Hmm...fathers and sons," Silver said.

Christa's eyes lit up. "I know that look. What have you unraveled, brilliant husband?"

"These clues were left for a Titan. What are perilous challenges and riddles to us would be relatively straightforward to them. Perhaps this final step was meant to be self-evident once the Ancient arrived," Silver said.

"But how will we figure it out?" Christa asked.

"The anagrams," Silver said, "Man is a wolf to man. Treachery makes men wolves. The shepherd drives away the wolves."

"The shepherd doesn't live in the town," Christa said.

Silver pointed to one of the many rolling hills dotting the Salisbury Plain. "There," he said," "that's where he'd be – the highest hill over-looking the settlement. He'd be keeping watch for the wolves."

They walked to the top of the hill and began probing through the soil. Without human possession, the work was slow. Eventually, Silver unearthed a stone marked with the symbol of the Titans: symbols of the four elements surrounding a man.

"This is it," Christa said.

Silver could see her hands trembling. Silver lifted the stone. Beneath it was a box with a keyhole. Silver dug into his robes and retrieved the key from the Temple of the Gordian Knot.

The Grip and Pommel of the Titan's Sword

The box opened. Silver could hardly believe his eyes. The grip and pommel of a sword rested on a purple cloth.

"My quest began when Gold and I sacked the Temple of Rastuapati centuries ago," he said. "I never thought I would actually find these."

Tears welled in the corners of his eyes.

Christa pulled him to the grassy earth and pressed her mouth against his. He ran his hands over her lithe, muscular frame. After a moment, practicality returned.

"Let us away," he said. "As much as I hate to stop this, I won't feel safe until we've returned these items to Heaven and assembled the sword."

Christa scowled, but agreed.

"I think one of those megaliths will make for a perfect portal," Silver said.

Anorexia, Schizophrenia, and Rabies sat in the empty lecture hall of the Hellish Academy. The silence was awkward and palpable.

"I think these meetings between the faculty and the Triumvirate are very necessary," Rabies said. "Much of our firearms prowess has centered on quick reload times. The advent of breech-loading rifles will decrease our advantage immensely."

A Wraith arrived in the classroom – a frail, juvenile.

"Umm, Miss Rabies… umm… Dyslexia had a question for you," the Wraith said. She spoke as if remembering a script.

"Oh dear, Dyslexia is dead, you must mean Dyscalculia, she's one of my students," Rabies said. She rose. "I trust you two can carry on for a moment," Rabies said. She scrunched up her nose and winked.

Anorexia groaned mentally. When cornered by Rabies and pressed about her refusal to remarry and add children to the cause, Anorexia had confessed to her love for Schitz. In the time since, Rabies (ever the devoted daughter) had seemed singularly possessed with putting Anorexia and Schitz in the same room.

Why did I open my big mouth? Anorexia thought.

Despite the staccato presence of lusty thoughts for Spanish Influenza, Schitz was an ever present source of love, fantasy, and longing.

"I mean… even with breech-loaders…we'll still be way better shots than any of the Angels," Schitz said. "Hell's marksman are second to none."

Anorexia sighed. "Indeed."

"Are things alright…with us?" Schitz asked.

Oh, my word…first father…then Rabies…who knows who else has discussed my pining for him.

"Why do you ask?" she said. She forced solemnity into her voice.

"Oh, well. I don't know," Schitz said. "I spend a lot of time with Autism, but I never really see you anymore."

"Have you been expecting to find me under the robes of your horny students?" Anorexia muttered under her breath.

"I'm sorry?" Schitz said.

"Oh, I just said 'probably just busy instructing all of your students,'" she said.

Schitz smirked. "That's what I thought you said."

Anorexia's heart began to pound – a rolling drum at the beginning of a battle. "But…if you'd like to have a drink and reminisce some time, or see if I'm still a better shot than you, I'd be glad to oblige you."

Schitz smiled. He seemed relieved.

You fool! This is seduction? A drink, a play date at the firing range? What is wrong with you? Anorexia thought.

Anorexia longed for words to steer the conversation in a different direction.

Scarlet Fever walked through the room trailed by Rabies, and immediately playacted as though she was surprised to see the room occupied.

"Oh, Schitz, Anorexia, how pleasant to see you," Scarlet Fever said. "So much knowledge all in one room. Do you know, I was just telling Rabies that one of the most time saving procedures she taught me was never to let a meeting serve as the substitute for a memo. What are you all discussing?"

"The impact of new weaponry on weapons training here at the academy," Schitz said.

"Oh, tut-tut, Head Mistress, you're slipping. That would have easily been a report. I'm sure these two are quite busy," Scarlet Fever said.

Anorexia felt her shoulders slump in defeat.

Schitz used the intervention to excuse himself. Rabies gave her a "I did my best" shrug.

Anna sat cross-legged on the cot she shared with Constance when covering Lord Zinc's abode. Grown Angels did not need to sleep unless healing from injuries, but it was nice to be off her feet.

The door flew open and Michael Zinc entered carrying Eleanor Zinc. The two were locked in a passionate embrace. Before the door slammed shut, Anna saw Constance several lengths down the hallway. Anna rose and moved toward the door.

"Oh wait, Anna," Zinc said.

Anna continued to the door, opened it, and then pivoted.

Zinc turned to his wife. "Who was it, darling? Carter? Cartwright?"

"Clayton Cesium," Eleanor said.

"Yes, Clayton Cesium." He looked at Anna. "Please arrange for him to have a meeting with the late Lord Cesium," Zinc said.

Anna nodded and stepped out of the room. After a few strides, Constance joined her.

"You going to go back to HQ?" Constance asked. "I can wait here."

"Nope, we have a target for removal," Anna said.

"Another one? Let me guess, identified by Lady Eleanor Zinc?"

"None other," Anna said.

"I'd have thought the end of the Carbon House would have been the last of the hits," Constance said.

"Well, the hits keep on coming," Anna said.

"I mean, I have no problem with it," Constance said, "but what if something happens to him while we're away?"

"Missus Zinc will have to look out for him. She is actually quite fierce, despite being young," Anna said.

"Oh, yeah?"

"Yes," Anna said. "She came by the bakery a few times for the common remedy. During our conversations I gathered that she handles herself quite well in the field."

"You'd think she could settle her own grudges then," Constance said.

Anna sighed. Constance had confided in her, telling of her forlorn love for Lord Zinc and how loyalty to Adolphus had prevented her from acting on it. Now, another had laid claim to her prize. And she had to watch every day.

"We do what we're told, right?" Anna asked.

"Indeed we do. I'll go get a barrel; you get a Familiar," Constance said.

Outside the laundry, Anna beckoned to a Familiar. He was a young, sandy haired lad. The Familiar had a pin identifying him as one of Lilly's direct descendants. These Wraiths were generally spared the more dangerous tasks. Anna hesitated for a moment, but decided the errand was not overly precarious.

"Please inform Clayton Cesium that Lord Zinc would like to see him in his chamber," Anna said.

The Familiar nodded. His face was grave. He was old enough to know that not everyone sent to see Lord Zinc returned. A great many disappeared, as did those who looked for them.

Anna made her way back to Zinc's chamber. She stepped into a doorway of a room perpendicular to Zinc's room. From the outside of the door the sound of the bed frame rocking could be heard. *They sure are enamored with each other,* Anna thought. *I wonder what Schitz is up to. I wonder if he is alright.*

Footsteps approached. Anna glanced up into a small mirror she had placed in the top corner of Zinc's door jamb. The mirror, though usually unnoticed by passersby, allowed her to see down the hallway while remaining out of sight.

Clayton Cesium approached. His steps were tentative, but grew in confidence as he neared Anna. *He must figure he's really been called for if he makes it to the door,* she thought. For a moment she almost felt sorry for her prey. As always, she steeled her heart, reminding herself of the suffering she had endured at the hands of Angels.

Even poor Barnabas was killed by these bastards.

Anna stepped into the open. Clayton Cesium was a few strides away from her.

"Aww, fuck," he said. He glanced over his shoulder. Constance emerged from an adjoining hallway. Clayton's head dropped in resignation.

Anna stepped toward the target. She raised her hand to his face. The rag contained a mixture she had learned from The Confessoress's journal. Clayton fell to the floor limp as a ragdoll. Constance jogged forward and helped Anna scoop up the dead weight.

The pair dropped Clayton Cesium into the awaiting wheelbarrow they had stashed around the bend and covered him with laundry. It was convenient that Lord and Lady Zinc needed clean sheets almost as often as they required corpse disposal.

Anna and Constance made their way to the Eunoe and up through the countryside. The lump under the sheets began to groan and move.

"Ugh, it wore off quicker than expected," Anna said.

Clayton freed himself from the sheets and looked up from within the wheelbarrow.

"Why is this happening to me?" he asked.

"Your name was put on a list of traitors to Lord Zinc," Anna said.

"Tra-tra-traitor, it must be a mistake. I'm no traitor. I've only voiced some moderate criticism of Lord Carbon VI. I'm descended of the Carbons, it's within my right to critique my late grandfather, but I've never so much as thought a subversive thought of Lord Zinc. This is a mistake."

"What traitor would admit to his treachery when facing his doom?" Constance asked.

"But it's the truth. It must be a mistake, if only I could talk to Lord Zinc and… and… and explain. I am loyal. There is no need for this."

Constance huffed, but Anna held up her hand to quiet her.

"Perhaps a traitor to Lady Eleanor Zinc?" Anna said.

"I…but…what? She broke up with me. We never even did any-thing. Just kissed a little," he said.

Anna sucked her teeth. *I don't mind killing for Zinc, but this is a bit much,* she thought.

Anna looked over at Constance who looked like she was wavering as well.

"Look," Anna said. "I sympathize, I really do. But you understand, as much as we appear to be in Lord Zinc's favor, we are very different from you. We are slaves. The Gold and Silver Houses do not exist anymore."

"Neither does Cesium," Clayton said. "My father died in an altercation with Carbon VI after the ordeal. Zinc gave us to Platinum as vassals."

"So you realize you are obligated to carry out any of Platinum's instructions upon pain of death," Anna said.

"Aye, but this...this is murder," he said. "It could still be remedied."

"Unfortunately," Anna said – she drew a dagger from her waist, "...it cannot."

Clayton raised his hands in a futile defense.

"Hold still; it will hurt less," Anna said.

He did not listen. Because he dodged and deflected, the first stabs were nonlethal. Clayton Cesium howled in agony as Anna ran him through again and again. Constance stepped around Anna and plunged a dagger into his throat. The cries ceased. In silence the duo tied the body within the sheets. They added rocks from the riverbank and slid the shrouded corpse into the river.

"I did not enjoy that," Constance said.

"Neither did I, but like I told him, we are bound to follow orders. I'm not going to be on the wrong end of the sword, and I plan to stay above the water," Anna said.

"So...that's it." Zinc's voice boomed across the library. The Familiar librarians had long ago abandoned any noise enforcement when it came to things associated with certain Lords. In fact, most of the library's occupants, Angels and Familiars alike, were crowded around to see the unveiling of Silver's centuries long quest.

Silver felt his cheeks flush red. He had just unveiled the fully assembled sword of Primogenitorous. He felt as though he had exposed his manhood and been found to be comically short in stature.

Constance Silver

"Yes, this is called the Universal. In the language of the Titans it is pronounced 'Ur Lak.' It was left for Circades, the Ancient. It can injure creatures in any of the realms Mortal, Celestial, or Ethereal," Silver said.

He was aware that he sounded like a desperate salesman. He could feel Christa's arm on his shoulder, a signal to stop talking. His description of the sword did little to quell the snickering and gawking of the crowd.

Zinc appeared to have no intention of humiliating Silver. He looked around the room and extinguished all chatter and frivolity with an icy gaze.

"That is something," Zinc said. "My question is how we can implement such a find into our global strategy. I mean, even if it shot streams of fire, it would hardly be as impressive as modern artillery. So how is it a doomsday weapon?"

Silver had no answer. *This is a weapon of magnitude, but how do I make them see that,* he thought.

"My husband and I have completed the first half of a tremendous quest. Now we recommence our efforts in the literature to unlock the weapon's full potential," Christa said. "And it will be colossal."

There was a small round of applause.

"Oh, we all thought you were finished," Zinc said. "Alright, well done on finding the sword. We'll anxiously await the next portion."

"I feel like a buffoon," Silver said, once the crowd had departed.

"Don't be silly. None of them helped find it," Christa said. "But Zinc does have a point. We're missing something. The sword must have great potential – otherwise it would not have been hidden so well."

"You know what that means," Silver said. He turned to the rows of forbidden texts.

Christa sounded like a child who'd been told to eat more vegetables. "Woo hoo...more research."

The dimly lit room was filled with elaborate furniture and elegant chandeliers. The pungent smell of cigars floated through the air. Each puff of smoke intermingled with the aroma of aged bourbon. St. Petersburg could not have been farther from home for Zinc's Londoner host, however the man's mind was at ease among his fellow diplomats.

I suppose high society is the same all the world round, Zinc thought.

Zinc enjoyed the rare moment of reprieve. Since marrying Eleanor, Zinc had abandoned the Isle of Neutrality. Familiars kept him supplied with drugs, but the sensation of his host's mind being dampened, while his own remained sharp was also enjoyable.

The Anglo-Russian Convention of 1907 was the latest fruit of his efforts. Britain and Russia moved ever closer. The opponents who had dueled so viciously during the Crimean War decades earlier were now aligned. Zinc had orchestrated the same detente between Britain and France. As the centennial of Waterloo approached, the historic foes were resolute allies.

I've done well. To think how I struggled to cross the globe with only one empire aligned with Heaven. My efforts with Alexander and the Romans are dwarfed by the vast expanses I control with the powers of the Triple Entente, Zinc thought.

He looked over his shoulder and saw Anna within the Celestial. His beautiful bodyguard had seemed muted lately. He feared her conscience had finally caught up with her. *Constance also seems moody,* he thought. *But things will get better.*

Eleanor had apparently settled all her old scores – there was no one left to eliminate. *Hopefully, I can just use Anna and Constance for security now.*

When he'd ordered the killing of Mercury IV, Zinc had been convinced it would be "Just this one." But one assassination had led to another...and another...and still another. While there was blood aplenty on his hands, Zinc was about to reap the benefits.

Water & Air

Zinc stepped out of his host and made his way towards the lavatory. Anna preceded him into the room and opened a portal by tracing the symbols for water on the floor. She blew on them to provide air.

"Thank you," Zinc said.

Anna nodded.

They stepped through the portal and were met with the resonant strains of the Hymn of Return.

Anna made the sign of the cross and began to walk past

the Priests that were performing the Return Ritual. Zinc usually blew past everyone, but this time, he grabbed her arm. "Let's stay until the end of the hymn," he said.

Anna shrugged.

"Are you alright?" Zinc asked. A Priest looked at him – disapproving of the chatter – but knew better than to admonish someone so powerful.

"A bit weary, but committed," Anna said.

Her eyes were intense. Zinc was mildly disconcerted.

"I know you were close with Barnabas and I know you've been through a lot – since forever really. I can't thank you enough. When the Final Victory comes, I hope you will enjoy the peace more than anyone."

"Thank you," Anna said. She seemed sincere.

The hymn concluded and the pair began walking.

"I've called an assembly of sorts," he said.

Constance joined them as they made their way through the Great Hall. The atrium was sparsely filled with passing Priests and Familiars.

"Talk about a ghost town," Constance said.

"Well, the rest should be here soon," Zinc said.

They walked out of the Great Hall and into the perpetual sunshine. The Heavenly army stood in formation – House after House. Thunderous applause rose through the ranks when Zinc appeared.

His steps felt light – energized. He raised a hand to the crowd. The cheering swelled. Eleanor stood at the head of the formation with him and beamed. She embraced him in a socially appropriate way and pecked him on the cheek.

The crowd went wild.

Anna and Constance stood guard – just behind him – one on either side. He raised his hand for quiet.

"Thank you," he said. "Thank you all."

From her position behind Lord Zinc, Anna had a view of the Angelic Houses.

She was struck by the sheer size of the fighting force. After the decimation of Waterloo, the Angels had rapidly replenished their ranks. She looked down at Zinc's House and the unincorporated Houses that were his vassals. She saw Albert Silver and Christa. The former Lord had sired seven children. When they came of age, his offspring had continued the fertility. Silver and Christa (and their kin) had added nearly fifty Angels to Heaven's cause. Similar outcomes had occurred across all of the Houses.

After taking in the size of Heaven's army, Anna was amazed by the political homogeneity of the Angelic Houses. She had come of age during a time of backdoor alliances and intrigue. The part she had played in extinguishing that virulent spirit was evident to her. Zinc ruled over all. Hydrogen, his dear friend and Rachael's husband, commanded the African Houses and like Zinc, was universally feared and admired.

The only bickering was in Asia. Zinc's Co-Supreme Commander, Uranium II, was embroiled in an unending conflict with his brother Lord Platinum. Zinc had allowed the situation to simmer solely to handicap Uranium II. It also allowed him the ability to say, "I didn't kill everybody to create peace, look I left Platinum." Which was a feeble argument.

We've killed so many to create this unity, Anna thought. *And we have killed countless others for no reason. But what else could I have done? To leave Heaven like Gold would be folly and ruin. To ignore reality like Magnesium, wedded to principles, would be noble and foolhardy. I've hitched my wagon to Zinc's star. There is nothing left but to keep him safe and to hope for a happy conclusion.*

Anna's attention drifted back to her uncle, Silver and his wife. *They've found such happiness. I wonder if things would have been different for me if I had found a way to be with Schitz.*

Zinc droned on about his plans for victory, mortal empires, and glory. The crowd imbibed every word and grew increasingly drunk on every vainglorious syllable.

"This next great European conflict will spread across the globe and will be our vehicle for the utter annihilation of the Demons," Zinc said.

Anna cringed.

Circades walked around the Château Normandie, a countryside estate he had acquired in a game of chance with Napoleon III. Worldly wealth was of little interest to the Titan. He had watched humans fight and die over bits of metal and gemstones, land and pieces of paper. He would eventually leave the château for someone else. However, while it was his, Circades put the property to good use.

Hung from clothing lines that stretched from wall to wall were thousands of photographs. Where once social events had been held and where once guests had slept, even in what had once been the kitchen, there were only strings and photographs. The few staff he employed lived elsewhere and only maintained the property during the day. They had long since disregarded their employer's eccentricity, for he paid well.

Circades stopped and scrutinized a picture. The paper had been treated with the most up-to-date Autochrome Lumière process.

"Magnifique," he said to himself.

The photograph was taken in Vienna – a rendering of a crowd of everyday people passing through Minoritenplatz. Circades marveled at the details. He raised a magnifying glass to the paper, and assessed the women captured within – one after another.

Before the Titan's eyes he beheld each mortal in the various appearances her soul had manifested. The Austrian frauen became Russians, French, Celts, Egyptians, Aztecs, Hans, and all other possible backgrounds. One cluster of women showed a history of mostly European incarnations passing back through the Victorian Era, the Renaissance, the Medieval period, and Classical Antiquity. Some souls were newer, recent splits occurring from striking rocks in the Eunoe or the Styx. Others were older, stretching back millennia. Unfortunately, none were Pulwabi.

For so long, the world grew so big; more souls, more civiliza-
tions. Yet now, year by year, even as the population grows, the world
becomes smaller and smaller. Travel that once took years now takes
days or at most weeks. Information travels through the air and by way
of electricity. After all this time, Pulwabi is finally only one step away.

Circades had created a network under the guise of a textiles company. As fabrics and other materials passed from Indochina, or the
British Raj, or America back to Europe, so too did the photographs.
Once at Château Normandie, Circades meticulously arranged them
according to locale. He compared searches and established patterns. If the same thousand women walked through Hutatma Chowk
or Piccadilly Circus or Times Square, he could then deprioritize that
locale, once he was relatively certain Pulwabi was not among them.

For a moment he recalled the day he lost her. All their life they
had traveled. First along the Danube then along the coast of the
Black Sea. Pulwabi's youth had flowed away from her like the running waters of the Dnieper. With each step she grew older as they
crossed over land to the Don. Then after what felt like a day, he held
her in his arms, silver haired and wrinkled in the sun. Yet, he still
saw the young girl he had met so many years earlier. He laid her to
rest along the banks of the Volga.

The memory of the scene on the Volga receded and Circades
once more was within the master bedroom of the chateau. He began
to hum *The Song of the Volga Boatmen*, as he recalled her flowery
resting place beside the mighty river. "Ey, ukhnyem! Ey, ukhnyem!
Yeshcho razik, yeshcho da raz!"[3] Once more again, with renewed
vigor he began scrutinizing the photographs.

"Ah, plus ça change, plus c'est la même chose,[4] eh, Circades?" a
feminine voice said.

"Svaha," Circades said, addressing the Fire Elemental.

The Fire Elemental was a tall female. She had a dark complexion
and features similar to those of a Tamil woman. Within her dark skin
were signs of embers. Her flowing hair was a roaring flame. Svaha

---

[3] Yo, heave ho! Yo, heave ho! Once more, once again, still once more!
[4] The more things change, the more they stay the same

wore a sleeveless, white dress. The outfit consisted of two triangles – point to point at her waist – an hourglass of a dress to match her figure. The edges of her dress sparked while she walked. The singed cloth regenerated with every step. The repetition of the process gave the effect of waves on the shore.

Circades knelt and bowed his head. The Elemental strode toward him. He could feel his pulse racing and his frame trembling. He knew his sweat was not due solely to the sudden burst of warmth in the room.

Svaha rested her hand on Circades's shoulder.

"Mmm, you are right to kneel before me, but you may rise, Circades," she said.

Her voice was like honey poured from a jar, thick and sweet. Svaha brushed her hand and long black nails along Circades's cheek.

"What do you require of me?" Circades asked.

Svaha raised an eyebrow. She placed her hand to her chin as though thinking and walked among the rows of photographs.

"So dedicated to your search," she said. "I wonder what you would say if I demanded you service your goddess." Her eyes were dark, unreadable orbs.

"I am at your disposal…though I would fear replicating Primo-genitorous's mistake," Circades said.

"It was reckless for my sister and me to bear your grandfather's ill-conceived fruit. No, I had something more selfish in mind," she said.

In a motion like flames crawling up a jungle vine, Svaha ducked under a line of photographs and slithered across the long out-of-use bed. She reclined on her back and spread her legs.

His eyes had been glued to the floorboards. Circades glanced toward Svaha. Though her dress had fallen away from her bare legs, a sash from her waist covered her womanhood - barely. Circades looked down again.

Svaha's laughter was a thunder clap. She crossed her legs and edged off the bed. She unwound herself with a twirl and in a blur of motion traversed the distance between herself and Circades. This time, she did not duck under the lines of photographs. Instead, she immolated them as she went.

The acrid smell of chemical smoke filled the room as the photographs disintegrated. Svaha patted Circades on the cheek.

"Relax," she said, "I'm fucking with you." She placed her long fingers over his carotid artery.

"Your pulse, Circades!" she said. "Perhaps there is, indeed, some lust under that veneer of devotion."

Svaha held his jaw in her cupped hands. She stared into his eyes. Her proximity and physicality were daunting. Circades was taller than the average mortal male and yet felt very small since Svaha stood above him.

"You made my brother-in-law very powerful when you chose water as the element for mortal souls to pass though. I would have much preferred the Eunoe and Styx to be made of fire," she said.

"It was nothing personal. It was the easiest to teach," Circades said. "Besides, much of life is consumed by fire; you must not be doing too badly for yourself."

Svaha laughed again. The effect was more intimidating with her face mere inches from Circades.

"I am a jealous goddess, who will not tolerate your affection for any others," she said.

"Like I said, it was only a matter of practicality. It was not born of affection for Varuna," Circades said. "Besides, it has resulted in balance."

"Ah, that is why I am here, Circades," Svaha said. "All of us are concerned that your hunt for your woman is deflecting your focus. We need you to maintain the balance."

"I am, it is under control," Circades said. Still, the assassination of Archduke Franz Ferdinand of Austria had set off a string of events that made him very much doubt his pronouncement.

"Oh, Circades, you are an open book to me," she said. "You can save your lies. The situation has never been more precarious."

"What would you have me do?" Circades asked.

"We would like one side to win," Svaha said.

"History has proven that is easier said than done," Circades said.

"I'm sure it would be within your power, should you deprioritize your efforts toward finding the present incarnation of your wife," Svaha said. Her voice was a snarl.

"I pledged my neutrality," Circades said. "My immortality, all of my power, my essence is tied to my honesty. If I break my word, I am cut off from the Source. You know this."

Svaha groaned and released her grip on Circades's face. She ran her long fingers through her fiery hair in frustration. "Of course, that is true," she said.

"A humble suggestion, goddess; could you not decide a winner in the war between Heaven and Hell?" he asked.

"We have many powers. However, restraint is not one of them," she said.

Svaha gestured toward an untouched line of photographs. "Take this drawing of light for instance. I cannot remove part of it without irreparably damaging the whole." In proof of her point, Svaha touched the nearest photo. A pinpoint of flame expanded like a flash and spread until the photo was nothing but ash. Circades cringed.

"We are part of the loom as well. If we destroyed the Celestials, the Ethereal Realm would perish along with the Mortal one," Svaha said.

"I'll come up with something," Circades said.

Svaha pursed her lips. She smiled for a moment then said, "You had better not be putting me on, Circades, son of Plutus, son of Primogenitorous. Remember, I fuck with you, but you don't want to fuck with me."

"I will find a way for them to resolve the conflict without disrupting the balance or damaging the tapestry. I will do so without breaking my accord or severing myself from the Source. I will do these things and earn the right to look for Pulwabi," he said.

"Good, I know you will," Svaha said.

Circades breathed a sigh of relief.

Svaha sashayed across the room. She waved her hand and a fiery portal opened without the need for symbols or incantations. She stepped toward the gateway and turned as though gripped by an afterthought.

"Oh, and Circades, love, don't take this the wrong way, it is but... incentive," she said.

Svaha reached out and touched the nearest clothesline. In a flash, flames spread down the line and engulfed the photographs suspended from it. The inferno spiderwebbed across the other lines. In a moment, the room was consumed.

Circades ran through the smoke and out of the Chateau. He coughed violently as he emerged into the warm summer evening. After retreating a safe distance, he turned and beheld the blaze. The three floors of the estate were an inferno.

I have let time make me complacent. I need the means to defend myself against Ethereals and Celestials, he thought.

Circades often carried weapons to protect himself against mortals. However, weapons that could reach creatures of the other Realms were an entirely different matter. Svaha's mentioning of his father brought memories of the Titans' weapons to mind.

During the last days of the war between the Titans and Celestials, his father Plutus had hidden many items. He had dismantled and scattered Primogenitorous's sword (the key to the forge of Albion). Likewise he had concealed Demeter's earrings (amulets of elemental control). Circades knew that in the time since the last stand on Temple Mount, where God and Satan had slaughtered the last of his kin, the relics had been all but lost. Mortals sensed their power and sought them. Angels and Demons coveted them as well.

Gold had stumbled across one of the earrings and destroyed it to part the Red Sea – a trifling testament to the power within the amulet. King Midas had been buried with the other earring – his grave was lost to antiquity. The Angels had stolen the jade bowl containing the map to Primogenitorous's sword. While the weapons were useless to them, their theft prevented him from finding a valuable armament he knew how to use.

The earrings and the forge are beyond me, but the most powerful item of all is well attainable.

The city of Atlantis had been built at the height of partnership between the Titans and the Elementals. It was also the pinnacle of Titan arrogance.

Yeah, great idea, Hyperion – construction of a city with walls of water rather than stone. It was a stupendous notion until Primogenitorous banged both female Elementals, which simultaneously pissed off their husbands and created a race of power-hungry immortals.

Legend held that Hyperion perished with his aquatic city. He had ordered the doors to the throne room sealed tight enough to keep out the flood unleashed by the wrath of Varuna, the water Elemental.

All I have to do is locate Atlantis, access the throne room, and acquire the ring Hyperion wore. As long as I possess it, any weapon I wield will reach all three realms. The Elementals, God, and Satan will be as easy to kill as any mortal.

Circades heard a crash. He watched the Chateau shake, tilt, and collapse into a pile of smoldering rubble.

"This is just a bump in the road," he said. "It will not stop me, Pulwabi. I will find you."

Chapter 4

Schnall um deinen Säbel
und rüste dich zum Streit

The table of the Triumvirate was surrounded by a mob of Demons, Wraiths, and Priests. Spanish Influenza stood shoulder to shoulder with his kin and classmates.

Titus addressed the assembled, "It is the will of Lord Satan that this will be the last meeting of the Triumvirate Council."

Bedlam erupted.

"Order!" Titus shouted. "Our Lord recognizes the monumental struggle facing us in the days to come and has laid the foundation for an almighty victory by freeing you from the constraints of the Council."

Spanish Influenza shuffled his feet with glee. *I love being in the know,* he thought. During a recent drinking session, Anorexia had spilled the beans and informed him of the impending changes. She had even divulged that he was being given considerable authority. Anorexia had informed him that he would be under her (a phrase leading to crude innuendo on his part). She had also asked if he had any preferred subordinates.

How perfect I have just acquired Anthrax as a protégé with which to get rid of Schitz, and I get to have said protégé as my immediate subordinate, Spanish Influenza thought.

Spanish Influenza looked at Anorexia. She was in her seat at the table of the late Triumvirate. He felt an uncontainable lust for her.

Females are females, he thought. *You get the same thing from one as you do the next. But this female, this female has cleared the path for my ascent to the heights of unimaginable power. Her review got me a Knight's Pentagram. Her good word got me promoted and put Anthrax in place. I'd want to ravish her just for that, even without her looks.*

Titus cleared his throat. "Before I continue, I would like to thank my colleagues who have served on this Council: Erin, Desdemona,

Mephistopheles, Elise, Anubis, Anorexia, Autism, and those who came before you. You have given yourselves in the crafting of worthy strategies, and I cannot thank you enough. It has been my honor to serve with you."

The clapping started slowly, a few solitary palms slapping together. The sound rose in intensity until the chamber shook with thunderous applause. Titus felt the corners of his eyes burn, and the back of his throat tighten.

The old Wraith Mephistopheles rose to his feet and embraced the Priest.

"Thank you for that," he said into his ear. "I would rather have your recognition than a Knight's Pentagram."

Spanish Influenza cared little either way for the displays of emotion. However, he appreciated how his thoughts had been pulled from lusty fantasies involving Anorexia.

I know my cards, it's important I read the other players while they are dealt theirs.

Titus raised his hand to reestablish decorum. He glanced down at the scroll on the table.

"Satan has handed down an ambitious and remarkable plan," he said. Those who had survived Waterloo understood his sardonic tone. He continued. "The Mortal Realm will be divided into areas of responsibility. One will consist of Europe, Africa, and the Near East. The second will be North and South America. Asia and Oceania comprise the final area. Schizophrenia has been named the Commander of Europe-Africa-Levant. Autism the Commander of the Americas, and Anorexia the Commander of Asia."

Spanish Influenza assessed the players. Anorexia maintained her poker face. There were no visible signs that she was already aware of the announcement. To Spanish Influenza's surprise, Autism appeared to receive the announcement as new information. His eyes locked upon Titus and he appeared to be performing calculations within his head.

He's either a brilliant actor or very readable. He turned his attention to Schizophrenia. The elder Demon was visibly pleased and also seemed to be receiving the information for the first time.

Anorexia told me, but she didn't tell her brother or her old friend. I must be special to her. Perhaps she is interested in me.

Schizophrenia has always expressed disinterest in attaining power and authority. He had avoided joining the Triumvirate and oft expressed disinterest in controlling those around him. *He is loved and considered heroic because he acts laissez faire; 'follow me if you want'. But he had no problem marching Trichomoniasis to her death. He gave over so many to the slaughter all for the glory of his name. Yet, all they ever say about me is 'he's so wild, he's so crazy. What is to be done with Spanish Influenza?'"* Spanish Influenza thought.

Spanish Influenza was certain no one could read his thoughts. He knew how to control his emotions, even if he generally allowed them to run free.

It was soon announced that he was appointed Lieutenant Commander of the Far East. Spanish Influenza allowed a smile to spread across his face. Schitz took note. *Ah, you think I'm smiling because of my ambition. I'm smiling because I'm going to surpass and dispose of you. I will be the most senior Demon. I'll marry Anorexia and will ensure that I reach the zenith of power,* he thought.

The assembly broke up. Spanish Influenza wanted to talk to Anorexia, however, she left with her brother and Schizophrenia. Jealousy flared in his mind for a moment, but he decided there would be more than ample time later.

"You've done well for yourself," Scarlet Fever said.

"Aye, you as well, sister," Spanish Influenza said.

"Africa will be a challenge for sure. I'll be going up against Gabriel and his wife," she said.

"Ah, the Destroyer," he said using the nickname for Lord Hydrogen's storied wife. "I'm sure you're up to the task."

"Oh, I have something to tell Cancer. Good luck, brother," she said.

Spanish Influenza made his way back to his new room. Titus had concluded his briefing by reassigning rooms based on the new power structure.

A partner is overrated when I can find what I need at the Isle of Neutrality and then return here for blissful solitude. I wonder what type of wife Anorexia would be. Might she accept my proclivities, will she want to join me at the Isle, or would she try to change me?

His official appointment elevated him to a room formerly occupied by Schizophrenia.

"Soon," Spanish Influenza said aloud, "this will not be the only thing of his I possess."

Others reveled in their promotions and assignments. Spanish Influenza spent his time comparing his strengths to those of his rivals. He was level in authority with Cancer and Scarlet Fever, two valedictorians and respected Academy instructors, as well as fellow classmates, Hepatitis, Lung Cancer, and Typhoid. Spanish Influenza thought about his Academy cohort. Many of them were still alive. In fact, they represented the highest number and highest percentage of living graduates of any class save those sheltered from combat.

"They are strong warriors," he said to himself. "When the older ones have died off, they will be the heart of Hell's Army."

He stood only two steps removed from supreme authority. First, he would become a commander, then the not-yet-created-rank of Overall Ruler. He did not dream of challenging Satan for power over Hell even though the idea carried a certain appeal. He would be satisfied to lord over all the other Demons, and to report only to Satan.

Then I will never be helpless or powerless.

A knock on the door interrupted his scheming. When moving in, he had requested all the literature available regarding the Angels frequently seen in China, Japan, and Eastern Russia. An ancient Wraith stood at the door. She clutched a collection of leather-bound volumes in the grasp of her sole arm.

"They didn't have any full-bodied Wraiths available?" he asked.

"I volunteered to bring them," she said.

"Why?"

Spanish Influenza hated Wraiths with a burning intensity, due to the abuses he had experienced. Part of his mind knew it was unfair to loathe their entire species. It was also hypocritical, since he enjoyed the Wraiths that worked at the Isle. However, he held a special, deep hatred for Elise, Schitz's rearing Wraith.

She has to be the most arrogant bitch I have ever seen, he thought.

The withered old woman appeared to grow a few inches. Her smile was broad and devoid of anything other than malevolence.

"To tell you this," Elise said. "I know you delivered Rubella to the Angel that killed her."

The books clattered to the floor. Spanish Influenza considered killing the Wraith. He imagined snapping her neck, but he knew Wraiths were quick. Besides, there was no telling who else knew what she had just revealed.

"I might not have evidence," she said, "but I know what happened, and I will ensure that you pay the price for your treason."

He feigned indignation. "If you accuse me without proof, I have the right to challenge you to a duel. I don't think you want that, you deformed old hag."

She's not told anyone.

"Indeed," she replied, "that is why you are the first to know. Once I have evidence, you will be the last to find out."

She melted away into the shadow beyond the doorway of his room. He scooped up the books on the Asiatic Angels.

"I have to focus," he said aloud.

He tried—for an hour. But the stress of his new responsibility combined with the crone's accusation dulled his brain. He could concentrate on only one thought: the available indulgences on the Isle of Neutrality.

Well, I am going to be busy. It would do me good to relax a bit before I assume command.

Anna raised her field glasses and looked across the barren expanse of Verdun. The impact of an incalculable number of artillery shells had turned the landscape into a wasteland. Earlier in the day, the Germans had attacked the French position. Many of their dead and wounded lay around her in the barbed wire maze of no man's land.

As night descended, the artillery from both sides continued to rumble. Anna looked over her shoulder and nodded to Zinc and Constance. Both, like her, were in possession of French Officers. They had made their way through the shadows of dusk with their radio and were in command of mortal batteries.

"Are there enough to justify an attack," Zinc asked. He was crouched in the rear of the shell crater. Unlike Anna, he was less adept at concealing his aura. She had kept her cloak and methods of diminishing her aura a closely guarded secret.

"I see several Demons in the front line. They look like they're just a holding force after the failed attack by their mortals earlier," Anna said.

"Good," Zinc said. "Give the word."

Anna raised her hand and cadre of twenty Angels charged across the field in the Celestial.

Constance spoke into the radio, "Artillery Battery L1, L2, and L3, adjust fire to box F275."

The radio squawked with bursts of static, "L1 confirmé F275, L2 confirmé F275, L3 confirmé F275."

A moment later, shells began to fall in a tight cluster ahead of them, slightly off center from their position. Geysers of dirt flew into the sky.

Constance spoke again, "Artillery Battery L1, L2, and L3 adjust fire left 300, drop 100."

"Come on, come on, the sappers are almost at the trench," Zinc said.

"Relax," Constance said. Her voice was as level and calm as it was when she was communicating with the battery commanders.

The radio squealed over the static, "L1 confirmé left 300, drop 100, L2 confirmé left 300, drop 100, L3 confirmé left 300, drop 100.

Shells began to rain down on the German position directly in front of the Celestial runners.

"Artillery Battery L1, L2, and L3, feu pour effet, je répète feu pour effet!" Constance said. It was the first hint of emotion in her voice.

The battery commanders confirmed the order and unleashed their worst on the enemy position. Anna peered through her field glasses. Zinc rose to his feet and stood next to her. The German mortals had been forced back into their dugouts – no mortal shields for the Demons.

"I see at least two in departure seizures," Anna said.

"Perfect, now it is all up to Jeffery," Zinc said.

Anna grimaced at the mention of her cousin's name. Jeffery was the eldest son of Lord Silver and Christa. The setbacks of the conflict; bitter defeats at Tannenberg, Gallipoli, Tsingtao, East Africa, and more had forced Zinc to call upon his subordinate Houses, even the descendants of Gold and Silver.

While the shells continued to fall, combat erupted in the Celestial. A pair of Demons charged forward to cover their seizing comrades. A shiver passed through Anna's body. Memories of Waterloo and Vicksburg passed through her mind. The Demoness known as Anorexia was accompanied by Spanish Influenza.

Anna recalled meeting Spanish Influenza at the Isle of Neutrality when he assisted her in fetching Beatrice. She also recollected fighting him at Vicksburg. *Two vastly different experiences*, she thought.

"What in the blazes is he doing here?" Zinc said. "I thought he was in Asia."

"It seems like all of the Demons are focusing on France, just like us," Anna said.

Though outnumbered, the Demons held their own.

"Nobody got through to the seizing Demons," Anna said.

"And now they're back up on their feet," Zinc said.

Anna cringed as the Demons began eviscerating the Sapper squad. Then Jeffery managed to stab Anorexia. His sword punched through her abdomen and emerged out of her back. He lost hold of the blade as she fell to the ground.

"That's a notable kill," Anna said.

"Indeed, more than enough for the day," Zinc said. He gave the signal to fall back.

Constance fired a phosphorous flare into the night sky. As the red-tailed phoenix burst over the battlefield, she called into the radio, "Artillery Battery L1, L2, and L3, disperse your fire. We are pulling back."

The sappers, having seen the signal, fled back toward the French lines. The command trio joined them in retreat.

"No leave it in, leave it in," Spanish Influenza shouted.

Anthrax and Tay-Sachs were attending to Anorexia. Spanish Influenza stooped and scooped her up into his arms. He stared at her eyes, cloudy but not lifeless.

"Hold on, just hold on," he said. "Open a portal in the trench!"

Upon their arrival in Hell a Priest ceased performing the arrival ceremony and rushed to their aid with a vial of water from the Styx.

"Wait," Spanish Influenza said. He had seen enough injuries to know the best way to remove a foreign object. He snatched the vial and poured half into Anorexia's quivering, blood-stained mouth. As the effects of the healing water began to take hold, Spanish Influenza grabbed the handle of the sword and slid it out of her. He tried to be gentle. Despite his efforts, she convulsed violently and spit out a great deal of blood. Spanish Influenza poured the remainder of the vial into the cavity in her stomach.

"A second one," he said.

A Priestess handed him another vial. Spanish Influenza reclined Anorexia fully on the floor and poured the entirety of the second vial into her mouth.

"Something's wrong," he said.

"Hmmm, best to get Salvatore," the Priest said.

Spanish Influenza rose to his feet and struck the Priest across the face. The sound of bones crunching accompanied the blow.

"She needs help, not the mortician!"

The Priest clutched his face. "Salvatore is the foremost expert on anatomy, you brute."

"I'm...sorry...love," Anorexia said. Her voice was a faint wisp.

"Don't speak. Save your strength," Spanish Influenza said.

Memories of their time together flashed across his mind. Their first kiss – right after they had arrived in China. He might have laid her down then and there, except she had insisted on practical matters. They had found the briefest stolen moments during their time in Asia and after that in France.

There was something so innocent in our courtship: her naiveté, my uncharacteristic patience, cherishing the briefest of moments unaffected by the war. Now she lies dying before me, he thought. Helplessness clutched at his throat.

"Come, bring her to the morgue," Salvatore said.

Once more Spanish Influenza felt rage building within him, but understanding the Priest's meaning stayed any violence on his part. Anthrax assisted him in carrying Anorexia. The room dedicated to the preparation of the dead sent tendrils of dread through Spanish Influenza's frame.

*I've never thought about what would happen to me after I die. I mean for me it's game over, but to think this weirdo will have access to my body...*he thought. His stomach turned in revulsion.

Salvatore hummed a jolly tune as he assembled a collection of menacing knives, clamps, and other tools. He took up a small pair of sheers and cut Anorexia's robes. Next he picked up a small knife and sliced into her abdomen.

"What are you doing?" Spanish Influenza asked.

"Do you see how pale she is? Or the discoloration in her abdomen? The blade cut one of her main arteries. I assume you left it in or she would have never made it back. The Styx water healed the damage to the artery but also blocked it. With it blocked off it ruptured again," Salvatore said.

His voice sounded like a man discussing the weather. The Priest was soon proven correct. When he spread open the incision, blood began oozing out of the cavity. He clamped the artery and made several quick cuts with a smaller knife. Spanish Influenza did not ask any more questions.

"Boy, grab me that beaker and the dropper," Salvatore said.

Anthrax grabbed the requested implements and handed them to the Priest. Salvatore used the dropper to administer small amounts of Styx Water.

"She'll live," he said. His voice was bland as ever. He scrutinized her for a moment then added, "Ah, I remember her. She rebuffed my advances while I was preparing her husband for his funeral."

Spanish Influenza felt his blood boil, but he said nothing...did nothing. He scooped up Anorexia and took her to her room with Anthrax in tow. He gently laid her on the bed and stroked her face. She was unconscious but breathing.

He kissed her forehead and said, "Rest up, my love." One more chaste kiss. "Alright, come on Anthrax," he said.

The pair made their way to the Great Hall where they linked up with Tay-Sachs.

"I'm assuming command of the Asia/Oceania contingent in Anorexia's absence," Spanish said.

Anthrax and Tay-Sachs both stiffened as though the Devil himself had called them to attention.

"Tay-Sachs, find Lung Cancer and inform her that I am Acting Commander. Anthrax, find Hysteria and tell her to rendezvous with me at Avillers Aerodrome," Spanish said.

Both nodded and rushed about their tasks. Spanish Influenza opened a portal and made his way to the German airfield. A German march he'd learned while possessing a mortal hummed in his ears as he stalked across the airfield. "Schnall um deinen Säbel, und rüste dich zum Streit[5]," he said aloud as he made his way to the barracks.

"Herr Hauptmann, it's a bit early for heading out, no?" a lieutenant asked.

The woman's reservation evaporated when she was possessed by Hysteria.

"Actually, come to think of it, no time like the present," the woman said.

"It'll just be the two of us," Spanish Influenza said. "I think the Angels will still be occupying the artillery batteries they used to pulverize our position. Two planes shouldn't attract too much attention across the lines."

---

[5] Buckle on your saber and brace yourself for battle

"But what good is that without troops on the ground to finish them off?" Hysteria asked.

"I'm going to jump out of my host over the Angels," he said.

"Won't that kill you?" she asked.

"We'll see," he said.

"It wasn't pretty with Hepatitis," Hysteria said.

"Hey, I thought you were the one that liked flying," Spanish Influenza said.

They reached Spanish Influenza's plane. Crew chiefs were rushing to attend to the aircraft following the extra early muster.

"I just want you to know what you're getting yourself into, that's all," Hysteria said. "Once you're up there, that host is of no assistance. If you hit the ground you will die."

"Get to your plane," he said. He swatted away her concerns and clambered up the wing of the biplane.

"Phew, alright, here we go," he said aloud as he assessed the gauges and controls of the cockpit. He accessed the host's memories and knowledge of flight.

"Contact," the crew chief yelled.

Spanish Influenza flipped two magneto switches and yelled back, "Contact!"

The engine coughed and came to life when the crew chief spun the propeller. The bumpy, buzzing sensation of taxiing to the runway filled Spanish Influenza with a sense of anxiety. The fear was short lived. When he pushed the throttle forward and careened across the grass field, he felt a dizzying sense of exhilaration.

"Focus, old boy" he said. The cold morning air whipped through the open cockpit. Hysteria formed up beside him. She waved to him with enthusiasm. *I can see why she likes this*, he thought.

The two planes sliced through the early morning sky and over the trenches. Spanish Influenza kept them at a low altitude, hoping that the machine gunners and anti-air crews were not yet positioned for the day.

He looked down at a map strapped to his leg and adjusted his course. Soon they were approaching the most likely position for the French battery that had fired on their position. The shelling had continued through the night. Spanish Influenza was relieved to hear the booming of the big guns on the far side of a hill.

He rocked the wings of his Albatros D.II to signal to Hysteria. Spanish Influenza pushed the control column forward and descended even lower. When they passed the hilltop, he saw the French guns. Within the crews Spanish Influenza saw the light aura of Angelic possession.

He squeezed the trigger. The twin machine guns chattered and shook the plane's frame. Spanish Influenza raked the position with a stream of bullets. Mortals clutched their chests and fell. Hysteria followed suit. Spanish Influenza threw the plane into a loop. When he reached the nadir of the maneuver, he took a deep breath and released his possession of the host.

The sensation of falling was sickening and terminated abruptly. Spanish Influenza grabbed his ankle and howled. He pulled himself to his feet and tested his balance. *It's not broken – probably just a sprain.*

Hysteria made another pass over his head and opened fire again. Spanish Influenza saw six seizing Angels prostrated beside the guns. He hobbled over and unleashed cathartic fury on the foe before they could recover.

Once his work was concluded, Spanish Influenza limped to a dugout and opened a portal. He looked up toward the gray morning sky, however the two fighters had already departed. *This was a good strategy*, he thought.

The role of Acting Commander suited Spanish Influenza well. In many ways it was transformative. He stood straighter, spoke with greater authority, and exuded a confidence that outstripped his previous self-assuredness. He was like one of the Prussian officers he so routinely inhabited. His new found authority allowed him to pursue his new strategy to the fullest.

Spanish Influenza's sandals clacked on the marble floor of the Great Hall. While he walked he hummed Der Hohenfriedberger Marsch.

> *Auf, Ansbach-Dragoner!*
> *Auf, Ansbach-Bayreuth!*
> *Schnall um deinen Säbel*
> *und rüste dich zum Streit!*
> *Prinz Karl ist erschienen*
> *auf Friedbergs Höh'n,*
> *Sich das preußische Heer*
> *mal anzusehen.*[6]

Four Albatros D.IIs flew low over the Meuse River. The drone of propellers buzzed over the countryside as the warbirds cut south toward a position of French Artillery. Prior to takeoff, Wraiths had confirmed the presence of Angels within the artillery crews.

Machine gun and rifle fire tore through the air. Holes materialized in the canvas wings of Spanish Influenza's plane. Again, after one strafing pass and a breathtaking loop, Spanish Influenza released possession of his host and hopped over the side of the cockpit. He had grown accustomed to the fifteen foot fall and rolled when he hit the ground.

This time, however, Anthrax landed and joined in slaughtering the Angels. Hysteria and Lung Cancer remained in their aircraft.

> *Drum, Kinder, seid lustig*
> *und allesamt bereit:*
> *Auf, Ansbach-Dragoner!*
> *Auf, Ansbach-Bayreuth!*

The wheels of the German aircraft nearly touched the grassy field west of Fort de Vaux. Spanish Influenza, Anthrax, and Hysteria leapt to the ground after abandoning their hosts.

"Getting pretty good at this," Anthrax said.

"Indeed and without using a portal we've arrived completely

---

[6] Up, Ansbach-Dragoons! Up, Ansbach-Bayreuth! Buckle on your saber and brace yourself for battle! Prince Charles has appeared on Friedberg's heights himself to look at the Prussian Army.

undetected," Spanish Influenza said. The trio crept toward the fort unnoticed by the garrison.

Drum, Kinder, seid lustig
und allesamt bereit:
Auf, Ansbach-Dragoner!
Auf, Ansbach-Bayreuth![7]

Hab'n Sie keine Angst,
Herr Oberst von Schwerin,
Ein preuß'scher Dragoner
tut niemals nicht flieh'n!
Und stünd'n sie auch noch
so dicht auf Friedbergs Höh'n,
Wir reiten sie zusammen
wie Frühlingsschnee.[8]

Spanish Influenza looked at his wrist. The time piece, smuggled back into the Celestial, read 0800. When the dial on the trench watch moved to indicate one minute past, he led Anthrax and Hysteria up the stone steps to Fort de Vaux's exterior 75mm gun. Shells from the far off German battery began falling around the gun with supernatural precision. Anthrax and Hysteria dispatched the Angels that were sent into departure seizures. Spanish Influenza dealt with the handful that had managed to step into the Celestial Realm.

Ob Säbel, ob Kanon',
ob Kleingewehr uns dräut:
Auf, Ansbach-Dragoner!
Auf, Ansbach-Bayreuth!
Drum, Kinder, seid lustig

---

[7] So, boys, be jolly and all ready to go. Up, Ansbach Dragoons! Up, Ansbach-Bayreuth! So, boys, be jolly and all ready to go. Up, Ansbach Dragoons! Up, Ansbach-Bayreuth!

[8] Have no worries, Colonel von Schwerin, A Prussian Dragoon does not flee, never! And they also still stand so close together on Friedberg's height, We could ride them down like spring snow

> *und allesamt bereit:*
> *Auf, Ansbach-Dragoner!*
> *Auf, Ansbach-Bayreuth!*[9]

"Verdun was a disaster," Autism said.

Schizophrenia nodded in agreement.

Spanish Influenza shrugged and shook his head. Shells impacted over the roof of the dugout.

"I've had quite a lot of success dropping behind the lines," Spanish Influenza said. He smiled. *I'm the most successful of the three commanders.*

"We're going to need you more than ever at the Somme. The British are planning a major offensive there. If they break through, it could be the end of the Central Powers. Who knows what that would spell for our situation in the Mortal Realm," Autism said.

To Spanish Influenza's surprise, Schitz echoed the sentiment.

"Yes, we'll need you to interrupt their artillery as much as possible. We can't have them pinpointing the locations we send our Demons to," Schitz said.

They see me as their equal. They plead for my assistance, Spanish Influenza thought with glee.

"Say no more," Spanish Influenza said.

> *Halt, Ansbach-Dragoner!*
> *Halt, Ansbach-Bayreuth!*
> *Wisch ab deinen Säbel*
> *und laß vom Streit;*
> *Denn ringsumher*
> *auf Friedbergs Höh'n*
> *Ist weit und breit*
> *kein Feind mehr zu seh'n.*[10]

---

[9] Whether sabers, whether cannons, whether muskets, threaten us: Up, Ansbach Dragoons! Up, Ansbach-Bayreuth! So, boys, be jolly and all ready to go: Up, Ansbach Dragoons! Up, Ansbach-Bayreuth!

[10] Stop, Ansbach Dragoons! Stop, Ansbach-Bayreuth! Wipe your saber and leave the battle; For all around on Friedberg's heights Is far and wide seen no more of our Enemy.

A series of vicious holes appeared in the portion of the cowling covering Dysgraphia's engine. A moment later flames engulfed the Albatros. The plane fell into a death spiral.

"Fuck," Spanish Influenza said. *He's gone for sure.*

The Angels had gotten better at interdicting their insertion flights. With revenge in his heart ,Spanish Influenza slammed the throttle forward and climbed toward the foe. He shouted a battle cry when he opened up his machine guns. In a matter of moments three Sopwith Pups joined Dysgraphia's smoldering craft on the ground.

Spanish's squadron reformed around him. They had reclaimed the sky for the moment.

Alright, now we can head for the guns.

Und ruft unser König,
zur Stelle sind wir heut':
Auf, Ansbach-Dragoner!
Auf, Ansbach-Bayreuth!

Drum, Kinder, seid lustig
und allesamt bereit:
Auf, Ansbach-Dragoner!
Auf, Ansbach-Bayreuth![11]

Spanish Influenza hummed the marching tune as he walked through the Great Hall. *The war has been difficult, but I am excelling.* He made his way toward Anorexia's room. *I cannot wait to tell her the good news.*

---

[11] And calls our King, to the place we are today: Up, Ansbach Dragoons! Up, Ansbach-Bayreuth! So, boys, be jolly and all ready to go: To the Ansbach Dragoons! To Ansbach-Bayreuth!

The explosion that had been the Archduke's assassination had sent shockwaves across the globe. The conflagration expanded and spread and soon reached all manner of beings, Mortal and Celestial alike. The disturbance even touched Lord Silver's academic environ and he, too, was called to the slaughter.

"I should have seen it coming when Zinc drafted our children and grandchildren," Silver said. He was reclined in a trench possessing a British soldier of the 30th Division, III Corps.

"Speaking of our lovelies, Jeffery told me that he ran into Schizophrenia back at the start of all this," Christa said. She too was within a British soldier.

"How on earth did he survive?" Silver said. He reflexively touched his faux teeth.

"It was during the Christmas truce," Christa said.

"Don't suppose we'll have such luck today," Silver said. He peered over the edge of the trench across the dreary, shell marked, wire strewn expanse between their position and the German lines.

The objective of XIII Corps was to break through the German lines to enable the 30th Division to capture Montauban. Silver looked down at his host's wrist. The Roskopf trench watch read that it was 0721. The seconds ticked by. Precisely at 0722, explosions began sounding far behind them. Silver looked over his shoulder. The shells whistled overhead before exploding downrange at the German positions.

The barrage, termed a hurricane bombardment, was intense but short in duration. The shrill call of officers' whistles sounded along the trench.

"I don't know if I'm up for this," Silver said. "I've fought many times but I've never had so much to lose. And, these weapons are… terrifying."

"You'll be fine; we've got more than one ace up our sleeves," Christa said.

They climbed up two wooden ladders, side by side, and set out across the apocalyptic landscape of shattered trees, barbed wire, and craters. All around them a sea of drab green uniforms made its way toward the wall of artillery. Intelligence from the Familiars had indicated that the region was defended by the Demons Melioidosis, Cholera, and Anxiety. The overall area was under the oversight of the Demon Schizophrenia. Lilly had finally retired, however, she had ensured that Silver and Christa benefitted from the most accurate and detailed reports.

"Are you ready?" Christa asked.

"Now or never," Silver said.

The duo stepped out of their hosts and began focusing on their breathing. With each step Silver was more and more aware that his aura was diminishing. They had put the centuries since the Vatican debacle to good use. The couple had studied the ancient meditative practices needed to dim one's aura.

They moved through the soldiers like two shadows. The artillery barrage came to a halt when the British soldiers were approaching the position. When the contingent reached the first of the German lines, the enemy was only just emerging from their dugouts. They offered the bare hands of resistance-free surrender.

"Trickery?" Christa asked.

"No, they know they were outmaneuvered. If there are Demons nearby they planned to cede this territory," Silver said.

The mortal British troops pressed on toward their objective, the village of Montauban. Silver and Christa followed in the Celestial, their auras still concealed by their focused meditation.

Machine gun fire erupted from the top of a small berm. The rounds tore through the British troops. Silver crouched among the troops and looked up toward the machine gun position.

"Ah, there they are," Christa said.

Atop the berm, the dark auras of Demonic possession were visible among the gun crew. Silver drew the Ur Lak, the sword of the Titans, and ran toward the foe. Over his shoulder Christa possessed a mortal soldier. She ceased her meditation and immediately drew fire from the machine gun. Silver breathed a sigh of relief when he saw her dive behind a boulder. The machine gun rounds bounced off the large rock then resumed raking the British troops.

Silver was a few strides away from the gun crew when they noticed him. One of the possessed loaders recoiled in shock.

"It's a ruse, stay focused. This one can't touch us from the Celestial. Keep up fire on that one in the Mortal Realm," one of the Demons shouted.

It was not uncommon for long-range fire from artillery, aircraft, or snipers to be paired with a Celestial Assault. *They really think they're safe*, Silver thought. *They think that as long as their hosts are safe they're fine.*

Silver raised the Titan's sword and brought it crashing down on the neck of the possessed German. The mortal's head jumped from his shoulders. The Demon within was decapitated as well. Silver lopped off the machine gunner's head next. He stabbed the final mortal through the midsection. The Demon within rolled out of his host and lay on the ground, clutching a gaping abdominal wound.

"What are you?" the Demon asked.

"I'm the last soul you'll ever see," Silver said. He split the Demon's head in half like a ripe melon.

"The Somme is going to be a disaster," Zinc said from within the British command bunker.

Anna looked in his direction, but realized he was speaking more to himself than any of the HQ's occupants. *I wonder how this is all going to end*, she thought. Both sides of the mortal and Celestial conflict seemed content to maul each other to death.

A British colonel, possessed by her uncle Albert Silver, blustered into the bunker. Christa entered within the body of a Captain. They both looked weary.

Silver executed a brief kneel and handed Zinc a canvas bundle.

Zinc nodded acknowledgement and unfurled the bundle on a nearby table. Within the cloth was a bounty of Demonic weapons and personal effects.

"I killed three outside Maricourt," Silver said. "The route should be clear to Montauban."

"And just the two of you went out?" Zinc asked.

"Yes. I didn't want to risk more lives," Silver said.

Anna was impressed by Silver's demeanor. In the years since his marriage to Christa he had stayed true to his word. He was faithful and loyal to Zinc. Even when he had been pulled from his quest regarding the sword, he had remained submissive. *He truly is grateful for being allowed to marry Christa,* Anna thought.

"I wish the rest of my fighting force was like you," Zinc said. "We needed this to be a massive breakthrough, but it has been costly and slow."

"It's just day one," Christa said.

"Aye, but I can tell. We haven't caught them by surprise," Zinc said. "We're not moving quickly and they will organize a dogged defense." He looked at the married couple. "I wish they could give you each a decoration for this, but it would be impossible."

"Perhaps you would be gracious enough to allow us to continue the quest to unlock the full potential of the sword," Silver said.

Anna looked back and forth between Silver and Zinc. *I hope Zinc doesn't respond poorly.*

"It sounds like you have, killing three Demons easy as you like," Zinc said.

"We caught them by surprise and left no witnesses, but they will likely learn I am using the sword and develop tactics to counter it," Silver said.

Zinc scrunched his brow in thought. He looked at the wooden wall of the bunker and the maps nailed to it.

"Alright, you've done your part," he said. "I don't think two Angels and a magic sword will be missed too badly."

At least they get out of this mess, Anna thought.

"We are still serving you and the cause. The weapon will come through," Silver said.

"Yes, I believe it will. Please hurry. I fear this stalemate will never break," Zinc said.

"Aye, Lord Zinc," Silver said. He nodded to Anna and Constance and left the dugout with Christa.

Zinc looked down at the loot taken from the Demons. "Well, I'll take three to nil any day."

CHAPTER 5
NO MAN'S LAND

Anorexia had outgrown the need for sleep millennia prior to her injury at Verdun. Yet, the severity of her wound made slumber once more a necessity. Dreams were foreign, chaotic malice to her. They buffeted her mind with painful recollections; the death of

Chu Hua, Mono's funeral, and instances of combat long lost to her subconscious.

She bolted upright in bed and grabbed a dagger from atop the nightstand. *Did I hear something? Am I losing my mind, or am I still dreaming?*

"You are alive," a whisper sounded from the corner of her room.

A shadow loomed large and stepped into the light of the sole burning torch.

"Ah, Uncle," Anorexia said. She felt her body ease. She rested the dagger back on the nightstand.

"I had not heard from you for some time," Bubonic said. "I feared the worst, so I came to check on you."

"That's considerate, but aren't you at risk of being seen?" Anorexia asked.

"Hell seemed mostly empty," he replied.

"Things are rather busy in the Mortal Realm, from what I hear," Anorexia said. She grimaced as she adjusted in the bed.

"You are hurt though?" he asked.

"Nearly killed," she said.

"Good thing you have a comfy extra duvet," he said pointing to the pelt of the bear she had killed outside his cave.

A knock at the door interrupted the conversation.

"Hide!" Anorexia said.

Plague looked about in frustration.

"Where?" he asked in a whisper.

Anorexia pointed to her dresser. With quiet steps that seemed beyond his hulking frame Plague stepped over to the dresser. The armoire scraped along the floor when he moved it from the wall.

"Come in," Anorexia said.

She felt her heart leap when Spanish Influenza entered the room. He stooped over the bed and kissed her. Warmth spread through her frame. She also felt the painful awareness of Plague hiding in the corner.

"How are you feeling?" Spanish Influenza asked.

"The water of the Styx works wonders," she replied meekly, "but I fear you will have to carry on in your new capacity for a bit longer."

Spanish Influenza smirked.

I know him well enough to recognize that he revels in the power of his new position, she thought.

He leaned down and kissed her again, this time for longer.

"I thought I would never get the chance to do this again," he said.

"It would seem we were almost wrong when we said we would have time for this later, weren't we?" she said, though speaking was a struggle.

Spanish Influenza looked at her with a gaze that said, "No time like the present."

Oh no, he wants to do more now. Even if I wasn't in pain...

With the precision of a psychic, she said, "I want to, darling, I do, but I don't want my first time to be while I am rendered such an invalid."

"Of course," Spanish Influenza replied before he kissed her again, "and now adieu until the time is right."

She smiled in a girlish fashion and curled up within the sheets.

"I had my ears covered the whole time," Plague said. His rakish grin said otherwise.

Anorexia felt herself blush. She buried her face in the bear's fur and shook her head.

"I'm sorry, I picked a horrible time for a visit," Plague said.

"No, no, don't say that. It was sweet you thought to check on me," Anorexia said.

"I'm beside myself, waiting to get back into the action. Last I heard there was a war spread across the length and breadth of the globe," he said.

"Indeed, it has been all-consuming," Anorexia said.

"And yet Satan remains unwilling to introduce me to the fray," Plague said.

"Take it as a good sign, even more time to train. We'll pave the way for your arrival," Anorexia said.

Plague nodded. He patted her on the shoulder. She winced.

"Rest up," he said.

Anorexia yawned, the excitement had been enough to wear her out.

"Thank you for the visit. Let's do the next one at your place," she said.

Plague smiled and craned his head out of her doorway. He slunk out with silent steps.

I wonder if some part of him wanted to get caught so Satan would have to acknowledge his existence, she thought.

Anthrax stood beside the Albatros D.II and watched the flight crew complete the pre-flight procedures. Like most Demons, he thoroughly hated flying, but today he was on a mission. He could hear Spanish Influenza's voice and his diabolical instructions.

Once again, Anthrax cursed all humankind for the invention of powered flight.

"All ready, sir," the stocky crew chief said. "Happy hunting."

Easy for you to be cheery, Anthrax thought. *No one ordered you to ram your plane into one piloted by Hell's most illustrious Demon.*

The crew chief's voice rang out over the field. "Contact!"

The engine coughed and the wooden propeller began to spin.

A Wraith emerged alongside his aircraft. She raised her hands to her mouth and shouted to him. The engine roared in his ears. Anthrax motioned toward his ears and then toward the engine. The Wraith appeared to be at a loss.

I have to be going, but I need to hear what she has to say, he thought.

Anthrax motioned for the Wraith to come to the cockpit. The shadow moved up along the lower wing and hopped up into the cockpit. Anthrax adjusted himself awkwardly as she scrunched up in his lap. He began steering the plane to the runway.

"What is the plan?" he asked.

"Schitz said that he and Spanish Influenza are taking off from Ligny. Schitz wants you to ram his plane. Try to take him out when he has closed up behind another plane. He needs you to be a bridge so he can move from one plane to another unnoticed," she said.

Anthrax looked down at a map as the plane bounced down the runway.

"Shouldn't you be looking up?" the Wraith asked.

"Where I'm going is more pressing. I could fly this with my eyes closed," he said. As much as he hated flying, countless missions with Spanish Influenza had made it second nature to him. The plane lifted up into the air.

"You mean where *we're* going," she said.

"Oh, right, I can stay low so you can hop out," he said. He scanned the horizon for a field.

The Wraith clutched his arm. "I will do no such thing," she said.

Anthrax rolled his eyes and looked down at the map. He would have to head south from Grevilliers to meet Schitz and Spanish Influenza in the vicinity of High Wood. Conflicting thoughts buffeted Anthrax's mind, much like the wind rocked his Albatros. Schitz had been his mentor during his time in the Academy. Schitz had taught him, nurtured him, when he was a subpar student. Anthrax had no doubts as to his loyalty when Schitz asked him to spy on Spanish Influenza. The waters had become muddled when Anthrax served under Spanish Influenza. They had faced horrific fighting together and stood through it all side-by-side like brothers.

Why do I have to be in the middle of this? he thought.

"You're a good pilot, right?" the Wraith asked.

Anthrax had been so lost in thought he had forgotten about his passenger. "The best," he said.

The front was abuzz with aerial activity. Explosions of flak dotted the sky. In the distance black dots swirled around like a flight of angry hornets. Anthrax throttled forward and sped toward the heart of the battle. His vigilant eyes scanned the sky until he noticed auras of Demonic and Angelic possession. At long last, he spied Schitz and Spanish Influenza. The Demons were sandwiched between two RFC fighters.

Anthrax threw his plane into a loop, arcing away from his fellow Demons. He gave himself enough room to build up sufficient airspeed for his approach. Then he lined up on Schitz's Albatros. The shrieks of the Wraith rose in his ears over the drone of the engine.

He watched as Schitz abandoned his host and climbed onto the top wing of his bi-plane.

He is insane, Anthrax thought.

Schitz ran along the wing as Anthrax guided his plane toward the other. Celestial footsteps cut across the top of Anthrax's wing a moment before he slammed into Schitz's abandoned aircraft. The undercarriage struck the target's upper wing, tearing away his wheels along with the other plane's upper wing.

The Wraith shrieked and clambered over him.

"Hold still. This is hard enough as it is!" Anthrax said.

He looked down at the floor of the cockpit and was met with an image of the French countryside below. Not only had the undercarriage been pulled off, so too had a portion of the fuselage. The control column was also acting finicky. Anthrax looked over the side of the cockpit and groaned at the extensive damage his left wing had sustained.

"Alright, we're heading home," he said to the Wraith.

The trip back to Grevilliers was uneventful, the landing was anything but. To avoid fouling the landing strip, Anthrax intentionally overshot. The uneven field beyond the runway, coupled with the lack of landing gear resulted in the plane breaking apart upon impact. However, mortal host, Demon, and Wraith all walked away in one piece.

Anthrax abandoned his host and set out for the hangars to open a portal.

"Was Schitz alright?" the Wraith asked.

"From what I saw he made it into the other aircraft. After that, I was more concerned with keeping us in the air," Anthrax said.

"Thank you for that. I'm Josephine by the way," the Wraith said.

"Anthrax, but you already knew that," he replied.

"Listen, I know that no matter what happened, you'll be on the winning side. You either helped Schitz or Spanish Influenza," Josephine said.

"It helps that they both wanted me to crash into Schitz's plane," Anthrax said.

"Well, whoever wins, I want to be on their side as well," she said.

Anthrax opened a portal by pouring water over symbols he had traced in the dirt outside an open hangar.

"I won't worry too much. As far as I'm concerned I was up there alone and we've never met," he said. "Besides, hopefully this is all over now."

Earth & Water

Anorexia sat up in her bed. The knock upon the door was urgent. Her brother and Schitz walked into the room before she could say anything.

"What's the matter?" she asked.

The pair seemed to be in a huff. Autism went to the liquor cabinet without as much as a word. Schitz slid next to her on her bed and embraced her in a friendly hug. Anorexia felt her heart ricochet about in her chest. She held onto the embrace for a moment longer than was polite.

"I'm glad to hear you're making a full recovery," Schitz said.

I wonder how much I'm blushing, she thought. *I've committed myself to Spanish Influenza, yet Schitz sitting here in my bed sends me into hysterics.*

"Thank you. What has you both in such a tizzy?" she asked

"Spanish Influenza tried to kill me. He orchestrated an ambush and shot down the plane he thought I was in," Schitz said.

Schitz's words landed with the sensation of falling from a great height fixed with the feeling of being dunked in cold water. Anorexia was uncertain what to say in response. Her throat felt tight.

I don't want to believe it, but he is power hungry. He saw Schitz as an obstacle, but I never thought he'd go this far, now that we're an item...

Autism handed a cup of liquor to Anorexia and Schitz. As she looked down at the cup, Anorexia was ripped from her trance.

"Autism, that's not Brew..." she said.

She was too late. Her brother's face was as red as a radish. Tears were running down his eyes.

"...it's stronger," she said.

Spanish Influenza had gifted her the drink known as Ambrosia. Autism fanned his face and gulped.

"Are you certain?" Anorexia asked Schitz.

His face was unreadable. Anorexia wondered if she had hurt or angered him with the question.

"There can be no doubt, besides, it was witnessed by Anthrax," Schitz said.

My whole world has come crashing down. Even if I could bring myself to justify his actions out of my love for him. I cannot be with someone who could act so savagely. Schitz has done nothing to him. What am I going to do?

Footsteps sounded in the hallway.

"That must be him," Anorexia said. Her voice was a groan.

"Here, you two act like you're in mourning. Watch his reaction," Schitz said.

"It shouldn't be too hard to act upset," Autism said, still visibly influenced by the strong drink.

Schitz stepped back behind the dresser Plague had left pushed away from the wall.

The door opened.

"Is it not terrible news?" Spanish Influenza said. "A most tragic occurrence."

Schitz's voice sounded from the corner of the room, "News of colleagues falling in battle is always tragic."

"I..." Spanish Influenza stuttered.

Anorexia was glad that her brother had been pretending to console her. She leaned in to him. His embrace took on a genuine feel.

She felt steadied by his presence. She stared at the floor wishing for the drama to be over.

"I know," Schitz said. "You are overjoyed to see me and surprised, no doubt, since you watched my plane auger into the dirt."

"Precisely," Spanish said.

Anorexia felt her heart leap. *Could Schitz be wrong?* She continued staring at the floor. She feared her heart would break even more if she looked up at Spanish Influenza.

"Be man enough to admit what you've done, sorry, what you tried to do," Schitz said.

"How?" Spanish Influenza asked.

It felt like the sword that had impaled her. *If he only cares about "how" he is guilty.*

"Nothing with which you need to be concerned," Schitz said. "We are here to deal with your treachery. No one outside of this room other than your confederate knows what happened. Who was he, by the way?"

"Anthrax," Spanish Influenza said.

"Well, I'll have something in store for him," Schitz said, "but this is about you. You are hereby banned from combat operations anywhere on the globe. Busy yourself with a pandemic, or something else that serves our Lord and our people. I will deal with your treachery in my own time. Now, get the fuck out of my sight."

The door shut and Anorexia felt free to raise her gaze from the floor.

"Sorry, to involve you in all this," Schitz said. He drained his cup and looked toward Autism with disapproval. "We're going to need you back in your role as Commander. We cannot have him leading troops."

"Why not have it out with him now, or have him arrested?" Autism asked.

"The war effort hangs by a thread. Killing him or outing his treachery would be horrible for morale. There are many Demons who have fought alongside him and might feel sympathetic. He is also well connected. I doubt he would receive a death sentence if he went on trial," Schitz said.

"So what are you going to do?" Anorexia asked. She was unsure she wanted to hear the answer.

"A pandemic will aid our cause and send many mortal souls to the Styx. It won't make up for losing him as a fighter, but it should obviate any impact on morale. Once hostilities conclude I will decide how and when to remove him," Schitz said.

"Do you think there's no rehabilitating him?" Autism asked.

"I have no clue. Most of my enemies have held inexorable grudges against me, I don't see why he would be any different. I've done nothing to him, yet he tried to kill me," Schitz said.

"It's not because of who you are, but because of who he is. He is power hungry. While you are alive you will outrank him and he will always seek to correct that," Anorexia said. She knew the assessment was correct, painful as it was to give voice to it.

"I wonder why he went after you instead of one of us," Autism said.

Schitz shrugged, "Who knows, but do you think you can join us at the front again?"

Anorexia touched her abdomen. It was sore but not as painful as it had been. She stretched her legs over the side of the bed and rose to her feet. "If I'm needed, I suppose I don't have much of a choice," she said.

The salty air was frigid at the Austro-Hungarian naval base of Cattaro. Circades watched as his breath formed a thick white cloud with each exhalation from atop the conning tower of SM U-23. Its diesel engines propelled the craft away from port.

In the years since he had been tasked with ending the war between God and Satan, Circades had sought a way to gain access to Hyperion's lost city. The idea of freediving to Atlantis was not an appealing one. Thankfully, the mortals offered a solution in the form of their newly invented submarines.

It had taken Circades many years of bribery and influence peddling to put himself in the position of power within the Kaiserliche und königliche Kriegsmarine. From there he had taken part on several U-boat cruises to build practical knowledge of the vessels.

The port slipped farther into the distance. Circades had ordered several large steel drums, each containing bits of scrap metal, to be attached to the deck. From the conning tower he observed the ingredients for his ruse.

Over the course of several uneventful weeks, SM U-23 made its way to the Straits of Otranto. Circades did not interfere when the crew attempted to engage an Italian merchant. *This is pointless*, he thought as the captain offered him a look through the periscope.

"Linienschiffsleutnant, there is another contact maneuvering to our position!" the radar operator shouted.

The captain swiveled the periscope until she saw the source of alarm.

"Scheiße, a torpedo boat," she said.

"They're going to deploy a paravane," Circades said.

The captain looked skeptical. "They're moving to ram us," she said.

"At periscope depth, they won't have the draft," Circades said. He made his way to the corridor leading to the fore of the boat. He turned and said, "Hold position until I return."

Circades made his way down the corridor until he was directly under the deck barrels. He reached up to the ceiling and slid a specially installed lever. This released the barrels. Circades made his way back to the bridge. He hoped the torpedo boat's paravane, an explosive underwater sled, would strike the decoys rather than the ship.

"It just passed again," the captain said.

"Hard to port. All engines ahead full," Circades said.

The captain echoed the orders.

The U-boat began to turn.

The ship was buffeted about from the shockwaves of an underwater explosion. Lights flickered. Metal groaned. The crew scrambled for anything to hold. Then all was silent.

"Prepare to dive. One-third trim, niner zero feet, two degree up bubble," Circades said. "Now."

The crew executed the dive.

The captain had lost her cap in the turbulence and her hair had fallen down around her face. She wore a broad grin. While she readjusted herself, she asked, "The paravane?"

"Yes, it struck those barrels I had installed on the deck," Circades said.

The crew was elated. They knew they should have been killed by the torpedo boat. Circades felt glum. Though he had saved the crew for the moment, they would soon be discarded. He disliked killing mortals and tried to avoid it whenever possible. *This time there's no choice.*

Circades worked with the navigator until the U-boat was halfway between the Peloponnese Peninsula and Crete. There they ran aground on a shallow ledge.

The crew went into a panic once the ship settled.

"We should not have been traveling so deep, much is still unknown about these waters," the captain said.

"It is pointless now. We are stuck. You must make your peace with that," Circades said.

He made his way to the torpedo room. There the crew, though perplexed by the orders, removed a torpedo from its tube. Circades bid them well with a heavy heart and slid into the vacant tube.

All light vanished as the door creaked shut. A metallic clank echoed through the painfully narrow structure when the crew secured the hatch. Circades was laying on his stomach facing outward. After what felt like an eternity, the outer door opened and frigid Mediterranean water rushed into the tube.

When the turbulence of the tube flooding subsided, Circades pulled himself free of the submarine. His strong limbs propelled him along the underwater plateau. Circades was much stronger than a mortal. However, the feat he was attempting was at the borderline of his limitations.

Panic began to creep into his mind as he swam along the cobblestone streets of the vacant underwater city. The submarine had foundered on the edge of Atlantis, Hyperion's old domain. The royal palace was in the center of the old city. Circades's lungs burned and his limbs ached. He feared he was too far from his destination.

He willed himself on through the frigid water. At last he swam up the staircase that led to the exterior of the palace. Circades recalled visiting his relative millennia earlier. He knew the throne room was immediately after the main entrance behind a series of double doors.

Circades reached to his waist and retrieved an iron rod. He placed it between the two exterior doors and forced it open with herculean effort. The ocean filled the gap between the first set of doors and the interior doors. As with the torpedo tube on the U-boat, Circades enclosed himself within the vestibule before attempting to open the interior doors.

The aperture of his vision had begun to contract to a pinpoint when he used his last ounce of strength to push the stone doors open. He collapsed into the dry throne room. Circades chest rose and fell as he gasped ragged breaths. He writhed in agony for a moment and then began to breathe normally once more.

He staggered to his feet and made his way through the ancient abode of one of the original Titans. A creeping sadness entered Circades's mind. Primogenitorous had acted rashly when he bedded Svaha and Vasundhara. The violence their husbands unleashed could have been expected. Yet, it was a tragedy that Hyperion, his wife Theia, and their progeny were killed by the Elementals, and not just Primogenitorous.

They did not need to destroy Atlantis, Circades thought.

What had once been a festive, happy court was now a tomb. Circades walked across the stone floor of the throne room. The air was beyond stale. While swimming, Circades had been able to see thanks to sunlight penetrating the water. The throne room was pitch black. Yet, in his memory, Circades could see the columns that lined the approach to the throne, the stairs leading to the royal chair, and the rest of what had once been.

Circades's hands recoiled when they came into contact with the rough texture of naturally mummified flesh. The conditions in the room had impeded decay. Nausea rose in Circades's stomach as he felt down to the hand of the corpse.

"There it is," he said, when his fingers touched a solitary ring.

He gently slid the cool copper off of its former owner and placed it on his left ring finger. An intense sensation passed through his body.

"Thank you, Hyperion," Circades said.

He retraced his steps back to the entrance. This time Circades left the interior door open when he opened the exterior. He allowed the sea water to flood the throne room. Once the room was engulfed, Circades swam out into the city and began his slow ascent to the surface.

He was halfway when he noticed that the flood had collapsed the palace. The sinking effect continued across the rest of the submerged city and then the plateau as a whole. The entire shelf began to crumble and to slip farther into the depths.

Circades cringed as he imagined the plight of the trapped U-boat crew. *What a terrifying way to go,* he thought. Circades noticed that his efforts toward reaching the surface were having less of an effect. He strained further and harder, as he was pulled down with the sinking shelf. The frightening realization that he was being dragged down with Atlantis dawned upon him.

With the strength born of deathly terror, Circades fought the water's pull. He was barely conscious by the time he broke into the sunlight.

It's good the city fully sank. The mortals are always expanding their borders. It would have been bad if they found it.

Circades floated in place. The waves lapped around him. There was no land for miles in any direction. He knew he could float for a while, but something would have to help him gain land or he would eventually drown. His plan had not included an escape route.

Hours passed. Circades contemplated the end of his journey. *Oh, Pulwabi, it was reckless of me to seek the ring. I just longed for a way to protect myself from those who could instruct me to abandon my search for you,* he thought. *I am the last of my kind, it is such a pity. I wonder which element my soul will pass through. I wonder, to which Elemental will I be bound?*

His thoughts were interrupted by the arrival of a Greek fishing vessel. Circades felt his limp body wrangled and lifted from the water.

"Some catch today," the boat's captain said. He was a burly man who patted Circades with a heavy hand.

"I can't thank you enough," Circades said. He spoke in Cretan Greek.

"Your uniform is Austrian, but you sound like us," the fisherman said. His astounded voice drew attention from the rest of the crew.

"My father was from Heraklion, my mother from Vienna," he said.

The crew seemed to accept the explanation. They covered him with a blanket and led him below deck. Circades was offered a warm meal and a change of clothes.

"We will throw your old clothes overboard so you don't have to explain yourself to the authorities. Tomorrow we make port in Kalamáta. You can make your way home from there," the captain said.

"What was your father's name?" the fisherman asked.

"Stelios," Circades said. He had spent enough time in Greece that it was no challenge to produce a believable name

"In my youth I knew a Stelios from Heraklion. He worked at the tavern my father would take us to when we made port there. Tall fella, friendly. Maybe your father?" the Captain said. His eyes were alight with memories of bygone days.

"Very well may be. I will ask him when I get back to Vienna," Circades said.

"Tell him Konstantinos from Rethymno said hello," the fisherman said.

"I will," Circades said.

"Well, get some rest. It is not long to Kalamáta," Konstantinos said.

Circades nodded. When the fisherman departed he thought of Plutus, his actual father. They had never reconciled. Plutus had expected him to fight against the spirit walkers; God, Satan and the other abominable offspring of Primogenitorous and the female Elementals. Circades could have returned to the Titans after Pulwabi's death.

The search for her felt far purer than any conflict between the Realms. But still, I left him and my family to face ruination and death. He looked down at Hyperion's ring. Perhaps I don't deserve the aid of my ancestors. But I will not sink into despair. I am alive, and while I live there is still a chance I will find my beloved, my Pulwabi.

Zinc sat upon the roof of the lumbering iron giant that was the Mark II tank. He leaned down into the aperture of the top hatch and shouted down to Hydrogen.

"Remember, they're going to light you up with armor piercing rounds, so stay in the Celestial!"

"Yes, for the hundredth time my brother, none of us are possessing hosts," Hydrogen shouted from within the hulking beast.

"Alright, well just making sure. Everything is riding on you and your squad," Zinc said.

"We won't let you down," Hydrogen said.

Zinc slid down the back of the tank and landed ahead of a platoon of the 2nd Canadian Division. The Canadians were using the tank for cover as they advanced on the German positions at Vimy Ridge. An assortment of thirty Angels from the House of Zinc proper and his subordinate Houses were arrayed among the mortals.

"Fan out, we're almost at the trench," Zinc commanded.

Ten Angels maneuvered to the left, another ten to the right, ten remained with Zinc. In addition to Zinc's contingent of troops, Anna and Constance maintained a watchful eye.

"They're going to make a stand here; they can't fall back," Zinc said to his bodyguards.

Bullets began to ricochet off the sides of the tank. Artillery from both sides exploded around them. Zinc felt alive in the fiery furnace of battle.

The war has been costly, but at last we are forcing them into no-win situations, Zinc thought. The Demons could not afford to let the Entente sweep over the globe. The unified world would be one of peace, prosperity, medical advances, and all else that sent mortal souls to the Eunoe. Yet, they were reaching a point where they could not fight either.

The three Demons manning the machine gun position before him were outnumbered more than ten-to-one. Yet, if they fled, they would sacrifice the strategic position of Vimy Ridge and further hasten the demise of their mortal enclave.

It is perfect, he thought.

Scarlet Fever sat behind a Maschinengewehr 08 heavy machine gun. The gun was silent and for a moment, fire from the advancing Canadians was directed elsewhere. Then, like a burst of artillery, squads of enemy infantry brimming with Angelic possession rushed from behind the tank they were using for cover.

Scarlet Fever pushed the trigger in with both thumbs and the gun chattered to life. She swept the gun from side to side raking the enemy with 8mm rounds.

"If only I had more troops!"

Her accurate fire had cut down several mortals, sending their possessing Angels into departure seizures. Yet, with only Bornholm and Streptococcal Pharyngitis by her side, she lacked the numbers to charge forward and dispatch the seizing foes.

Sweat beaded the nape of her host's neck. Scarlet Fever could feel the mortal woman's anxiety as the large tank lumbered toward her. Bornholm rushed along the trench within a German soldier. She slid along the dirt when she reached the sandbag encircled platform housing the machine gun.

"The armor piercers," Bornholm said through breath shortened by her exertions.

"You might want to hold on. I can't tell if the Angels are in the Celestial or the tank crew," Streptococcal Pharyngitis said. He was the youngest of the trio. Scarlet Fever could see his hands shaking within his host as he looked through a pair of field glasses.

Scarlet Fever's Demonic vision allowed her to see the Angelic auras through the hull of the tank. However, like her subordinate, she could not tell if they were in possession of hosts.

"We need to stop that tank; this whole position is reliant on this machine gun staying up," Scarlet Fever said.

Bornholm loaded the chain of armor piercing ammunition into the gun. Scarlet Fever pushed the cocking handle two times. The Maschinengewehr 08 burst to life when Scarlet Fever depressed the trigger. With her position revealed by her fire, rounds from the tank and small arms fire from the infantry began striking around her position.

Scarlet Fever flinched as rounds tore past her, but continued to pepper the tank. After a few moments, the behemoth ground to a halt. It appeared that the Angels within were in the grips of departure seizures within its hull.

"I can dispatch them," Bornholm said.

"It's not worth it. Move to the flanks, we have to hold this position," Scarlet Fever said.

Bornholm ran along the trench to her right and Streptococcal Pharyngitis departed to her left. Scarlet Fever emptied the remainder of the chain into the tank for good measure and motioned for a non-possessed mortal to reload the gun.

A woman of the 261st Infantry Reserve regiment fed another belt of ammunition into the gun. She tapped Scarlet Fever on her helmet twice. Scarlet Fever worked the cocking handle and opened fire on the advancing infantry.

She stole a glance to her right. The Canadians had reached the edge of the trench and were engaged in vicious close quarters combat. Bornholm was still in her host and had two seizing Angels at her feet.

If only we had more Demons, she thought in frustration. *Of course I never received an explanation for Spanish Influenza's reassignment.*

Scarlet Fever reached to her waist and drew her host's Luger P08 pistol. The combat involving Bornholm was well outside the 50 meters effective range of the weapon.

Fuck it.

Scarlet Fever emptied the eight-round magazine, dropping a possessed mortal with each shot. Bornholm stepped out of her host and began dispatching the seizing Angels in the Celestial. Scarlet Fever ejected the magazine from her pistol.

To her left, Streptococcal Pharyngitis was fending off a cluster of Angels in the Celestial. The Canadians appeared to be pinned back on that side. Scarlet Fever motioned to Bornholm to assist Streptococcal and returned to firing the machine gun.

We might just hold them off, she thought.

Zinc had watched the initial phases of the battle unfold from behind the immobilized Mark II. He had kept possession of a mortal host. Once the battle commenced on both sides of the German machine gun, he scampered up the back of the tank. He dropped through the hatch and manned one of the Hotchkiss M1909 machine guns.

As he had anticipated, the Demon firing at them was occupied with the infantry assault. She had temporarily ignored the tank. Zinc unleashed a burst of fire. He grinned. The possessed gunner's head came apart when it was stuck by multiple rounds.

On cue, Hydrogen and Rachael rose from their feigned departure seizures and clambered out of the tank in the Celestial. Zinc remained in his position and continued to fire on the trench. A few brave mortals attempted to take up the vacant machine gun. He gunned them down without mercy.

Zinc watched as Hydrogen and Rachael dispatched the Demon that had been operating the machine gun. He abandoned his position and exited the tank. Zinc led his contingent of possessed infantry to the front line of the German trench. With the machine gun position captured, the Canadians made rapid gains.

Eleanor stepped out of her host and kissed Zinc with enthusiasm.

"The day is ours," she said.

Zinc looked across the trench. The mortals were mopping up and advancing into the German defenses. In the Celestial, his Angels had placed the three deceased Demons side by side at the base of the German machine gun.

"I don't know any of them," Zinc said to his significantly thinned contingent.

"Get one of the Familiars," Zinc instructed to an Angel of the Silver House.

The Angel saluted and scurried off. Zinc assessed the survivors. Of the twenty who had attacked the flanks, five were yet remaining.

"Why does everybody look so glum? We just killed three Demons," Zinc said.

"Jeffery Silver fell in the assault," one of the Angels from the Zinc House said.

Zinc felt a shiver run down his spine. Albert's son was well-regarded and renowned not only in his house but also among all the Angels fighting in France. *Silver will be furious with me*, he thought.

A Familiar arrived with a handful of scrolls. She looked through them with a franticness that indicated her desire to spend as little time as possible at the front.

"Ah, alright, it seems we have Scarlet Fever, Bornholm, and not sure of the last one, my Lord," the Familiar said.

"The females are quite storied," the Familiar said.

Zinc reached down and removed a pentagram shaped medal from one's neck and a similar medal pinned to the other's robe. *It won't be much, but maybe Silver will accept these as a gesture of my gratitude and remorse,* he thought.

Spanish Influenza and Anthrax walked through the U.S. Army Camp Hospital No. 45 in Aix-les-Bains, France. There were rows of soldiers near death. Yet, they were not casualties of battle.

"And after centuries of explaining my name, the world now has The Spanish Flu," Spanish Influenza said.

"That must have been a powerful strain carrier your father possessed, to see so far into the future," Anthrax said.

"Indeed. Plague once said his coven would prevent the need for this pandemic. He sure was wrong," Spanish Influenza said.

Anthrax nodded and the pair walked on in silence. Spanish Influenza assessed the mortals and admired his handy work. Although he had spent his entire life infecting mortals, he had only recently focused on perfecting his illness.

The Celestial pair passed a cluster of nurses. The mortals wore cotton face masks covering their mouths and noses. Spanish Influenza snarled.

"It's frustrating that something so simple can negate all of my hard work," Spanish Influenza said.

He unhooked the band of a nurse's mask so that it slipped from her face. The Demon breathed in the mortal's face before she could raise the mask.

"Mortals are pretty stupid. Outside of the hospital I don't think many will want to wear masks," Anthrax.

"Good point," Spanish Influenza said.

The duo exited the hospital.

"I'm sorry about your sister. She was a fierce warrior and a talented instructor," Anthrax said.

"Thanks, but I've got too much on my mind to worry about Scarlet Fever," Spanish Influenza said.

"Schitz?" Anthrax asked.

"Yes, and whatever he has planned for us," Spanish said. "I don't like it. He should have fought me right then and there or reported me. But this, reassignment to pandemic duty and waiting to see what he does, it's maddening."

"What are you thinking?" Anthrax asked.

"I might have to expand this clique of ours. Don't worry, I won't tell whoever I recruit about you. It would only needlessly endanger you for more Demons to know your involvement with me. I just appreciate you're still with me," Spanish Influenza said.

"To the bitter end," Anthrax said.

Silver and Christa sat in silence at a table in the Heavenly library. The Ur Lak and the jade bowl lay on the table amid a mountain of books. Silver looked down at the pair of Demonic medals Zinc had given him.

"We knew this could happen when we started a family," Christa said.

She reached across the table and held his hand.

"I know, I just blame myself," Silver said. "If I could have found the use for this damn sword maybe Zinc wouldn't have called on our family to fill the ranks."

Christa chuckled, a wistful half-laugh.

"He looked so nervous when he came over here. It was as if you were the Lord and he the vassal," she said.

"I guess it was because I was fond of Jeffery. I mean everybody was fond of him. He was upright, and brave. Nobody would have thought he was the descendant of an unincorporated House," Silver said. His voice cracked.

"We have to keep going forward. Jeffery was one of fifteen that fell in that engagement alone. There are countless mothers and fathers in the Mortal and Celestial Realm asking why their sons and daughters died," Christa said.

"I agree. It will be a fitting testament if we can end such suffering for generations to come," Silver said. He flicked at the medals. "You know me, I'm not much for stripping the dead. I've never taken tokens from the battlefield, it's kind of gauche."

"Ah, there's the air of superiority that made me fall in love with you," Christa said.

"Still," he said, "I will keep them for him. From what I've been told, he gave a good accounting of himself in the war. He deserves some decoration."

"That's nice," Christa said.

"You know, sorry to change the subject, but I think I'm onto something," Christa said. "This diary was kept by Stephan the Wise. He says there are several inscriptions of Titan lore referring to something called The Forge of Albion," she said.

Silver looked around the library until he saw the tapestry of a Priest holding his own head in his hands.

"Ah, yes, the Second High Priest of the Heavenly Church. Lost his title with his head back when Priests led the Angels into battle," Silver said.

"That's the one," Christa said. "But here's what is interesting. He speaks of the key to the forge being a weapon of great power in and of itself."

"Ah, so you think the Ur Lak is a weapon and a key?" Silver said.

"It would make sense." She stroked his hand. "And I would assume a forge would be way more valuable to us than a single weapon. Imagine if every Angel could strike at Demons in either Realm all at once."

"That would definitely be a game changer," Silver said. "Where do you think the forge is located?"

"Well, the diary ends shortly thereafter," Christa said.

"And his successor Carolus was significantly less interested in the Titans," Silver said. "After all, he was the first High Priest after the alteration of the dogma stating that God came before the Titans and created the world and all things, et cetera."

"Well, he might have some knowledge on the subject," Christa said. "Don't you think?"

"Indeed, I do," Silver said. My love, I believe we need to have a word with the High Priest."

Chapter 6

Betting on the Wrong Horse

Lilly sat in a public house a few blocks from Trafalgar Square. She wore a large hat and gloves to conceal her Familiar appearance. Likewise, the members of her company were heavily dressed as well. Mephistopheles wore a workman's cap. His fellow Wraith, Elise, wrapped her head in a shawl. The group could easily be mistaken for an elderly trio of mortals.

The pub was festively decorated with Union Flags and like coloured bunting. The passage of a few months had done little to dampen the euphoric patriotic swell brought on by the Armistice. Lilly felt certain there was nowhere on earth farther from conflict. Yet, she still felt anxiety in the pit of her stomach.

"I could have never imagined when I let you go at Teutoburg Forest that'd we all be sitting here," Mephistopheles said with a chuckle.

"Or that you would become such a legendary commander of the Familiars," Elise said.

"Oh, I'm retired," Lilly said.

"Good for you, I wish we had a similar option," Mephistopheles said.

"I won't lie, it is quite nice. I spend most of my time teaching a sketch class to the younger Familiars," Lilly said.

"Ah, one of our tricks," Elise said.

"I don't know who pioneered it first. Both of our organizations seem equally talented," Lilly said.

Mephistopheles raised his pint. "Here's to that. Distant relatives finding a common ground."

They clinked glasses. Lilly felt at ease.

Mephistopheles is quite friendly and Elise seems mostly overprotective of her husband, but not hostile, she thought.

"So, my saviors, why have you sought this reunion?" Lilly asked.

Mephistopheles sipped from his beer, clearly more than happy for Elise to proceed.

Elise said, "I have a favor to ask of you. It may seem odd, but it is extremely important to me, and since..."

"I owe you a life debt, I'm obliged to agree," Lilly said.

"Well, when you put it like that," Elise said.

"Come, I'm not young and naïve as I was when we first met. Tell me what you require," Lilly said.

"I need you to provide intelligence to a nondescript Angelic House. Two Demons will be leading a squad of Whites to Ipatiev House on February 2. I will give you the details pertaining to their arrival. The ambush should be rudimentary," Elise said.

"The place where Tsar Nicolas and his family were murdered?" Lilly asked.

"Yes, your target will be informed that the assassinations were a ruse and that the Tsar is still captive," Elise said.

Lilly felt intrigued. *It smacks of Zinc's style of housekeeping*, she thought.

"I imagine you would prefer Angels lacking in notoriety," Lily said. "They will be less likely to question how I came upon the information and happy to accept the assignment."

Elise touched her nose and smirked.

"Consider it done. You two are like parents to me in a way," Lilly said. "I owe my life to you. It is a small favor really."

She was intrigued why they wanted to kill two of their own. *Their reasons are theirs, I suppose.*

"I still believe we have more in common than not," Mephistopheles said. "Both our sides treat us shoddily."

"I'll drink to that," Lilly said and raised her cup.

Anthrax lay on the snow covered hill overlooking the Ipatiev House.

"I don't think this is a good idea," Anthrax said.

"We really don't have much of a choice," Spanish Influenza said. His voice was a snarl.

Anthrax had been with Spanish Influenza while he spread the eponymous pandemic through America when they had been contacted by Anubis. The Wraith carried orders, purportedly from Satan. They were instructed to investigate rumors that the Tsar had not been executed and, if proven true, to possess him. Logic said a restored Monarchy in the possession of Hell could counter the post-war progress Heaven was making toward solidifying the League of Nations.

Anthrax felt anxiety within his White Army host. Yekaterinburg was no longer close to the front line as it had been when the Tsar and his family were reported murdered. In the time since, the Bolsheviks had expanded their influence.

The detachment of ten men had maneuvered far behind enemy lines. It did not take much intuition to see it was a suicide mission.

"I've sent Encopresis and Ganser Syndrome to scout Schitz's location as well as Anorexia's and Autism's. All of them are tied up in Ireland. If it is an ambush, we'll more than have an advantage over whatever Demons they sent," Spanish Influenza said.

Anthrax thought of Encopresis and Ganser Syndrome, neophytes Spanish Influenza had seduced into his clique. *They don't know what they're getting themselves into,* Anthrax thought.

"Alright, so we infiltrate the house. Most likely confirm it is empty. Otherwise we rescue the Tsar and ferry him and his family back to friendly territory, no sweat," Anthrax said.

"Right, let's get this over with," Spanish Influenza said.

Anthrax clutched his host's M1891 bolt-action rifle. The snow crunched under his boots.

This whole mission is fucked. First, we have to schlep here with a squad of Whites because the minds of Red hosts might be too committed to preventing the Tsar's escape. Then we have to break into a place where at least Anubis and probably others know we're coming. Worse, none of this may have originated from Satan.

The quiet of the night erupted into a storming hail of gunfire. It was more a firing squad than a firefight. In a moment, the Whites were eviscerated. The wily Demons within, both veteran campaigners, managed to abandon their hosts before they died.

"I knew it," Anthrax groaned.

"Come on," Spanish Influenza said. "They're not possessed. We can continue into the house."

No sooner had he spoke than the entire Red contingent assumed Angelic auras.

Spanish swore. "Bastards held back so we wouldn't spot the mortal soldiers lying in wait."

The pair of Demons drew their swords and stood back to back as a horde of Angels descended on them.

"Any bright ideas?" Anthrax asked. He could feel his pulse in his throat.

"We'll break the encirclement and I'll make a run for it," Spanish Influenza said.

"You'll?" Anthrax said.

He felt a massive shove in his back as he was thrown into the advancing Angels. Anthrax battled to recover his breath after careening into the foe. He'd dropped his sword. Anthrax was vaguely aware of Spanish Influenza racing past him at a dead run. But he did not make it far.

A moment later Spanish Influenza was struck in the back by a throwing knife and set upon by a vicious cluster of Angels. He howled as they stabbed at him over and over.

Anthrax felt a sea of hands raise him to his feet before shoving him back to his knees.

There's nowhere to run, no mortals to possess, no way to fight, he thought.

"I surrender," Anthrax said.

An Angel stood over him. He looked perplexed and unsure of himself.

"Can we take him prisoner?" an Angel asked.

"Surely not," another said.

"The orders were to kill both of them," another said.

"A prisoner could be useful."

"I'm content to be your prisoner," Anthrax said. "As you can see, my senior did not treat me particularly well. I'll happily divulge any information you might require."

An Angel looked at him with suspicion. "It'll all just be lies and deceits."

The debate continued to swirl around him. *Perhaps they will take me prisoner,* Anthrax thought. He considered imprisonment. *It would be better than death, perhaps one day I'd see my boy Ebola again.*

The Angel who stood before him nodded to one of the Angels standing behind him.

Oh, no.

The first strike was painful. He howled and was dimly aware of his face hitting the snowy ground. The next blow was oddly blunted. All sensation had already begun to leave. Though his eyes were open, his vision darkened until he was no more.

Lord Dysprosium scowled at his younger brother and said, "You didn't have to do it so savagely."

Timothy Dysprosium shrugged. "Their side is not known for civility."

The younger brother had struck the Demon over the back of the head with the broad side of his sword. It had taken several barbaric whacks to ensure all life had left the foe's body.

"Regardless, we hold ourselves to a higher standard," Lord Dysprosium said.

Timothy Dysprosium rolled his eyes.

"I hope our places are never reversed with this poor wretch," Dysprosium said.

"I for one never plan on surrendering," the younger Angel said.

Elise hummed as she walked through the Great Hall.

"You seem particularly happy, especially considering the current state of affairs," Mephistopheles said.

"Well Josephine just informed me that she had successfully retrieved the bodies of Spanish Influenza and Anthrax," Elise said. "Everything went according to plan."

"Well done, but didn't Schizophrenia tell you not to meddle in his affairs?" Mephistopheles asked.

"Oh please, he doesn't know what's best for him, never has," Elise said. She waved away the objection with her sole arm.

"If you say so," Mephistopheles said.

"Besides," Elise said, "there's no way Schitz will even find out how his rival met his end."

From their perch on the rocky, barren expanse of the Ethereal Realm, the Elementals, the entities that fashioned the Earth and (albeit inadvertently) the Celestial Realm, looked down on their creation.

"I am so fucking bored," Vayu, the Air Elemental, said. He tossed down a set of playing cards with disgust.

"Maybe you'd be less bored if you were winning." Varuna, the Water Elemental, chuckled, picked up the cards, and shuffled.

While the two males played cards, their wives, Svaha and Vasundhara reclined next to their respective spouses.

When the next hand was dealt, Svaha sat up and looked at Vayu's cards. She covered her mouth and whispered in his ears.

"I know how to play the game," Vayu replied. But he reorganized his hand in accordance to his wife's advice.

Svaha snickered and returned to her reclined position.

Varuna played his first card, face down. Vayu hesitated and then placed his card also face down.

The game was simple. A round consisted of five duels. The players each selected a card from their hand. The highest card won each duel. At the end of the round, the player who had won the most duels collected all of the cards. The game continued until one player possessed the general, the highest ranking card in all five suits.

At this point in the game Varuna held three generals and Vayu held two.

They flipped their cards. Varuna had played a general and Vayu had played a private.

"First duel to me," Varuna said with a grin. "Will you risk your generals in this round? You won't have many foot soldiers left at this rate."

"Just play your next card," Vayu said.

Varuna played a lieutenant. Vayu played a captain.

"Ah, all tied up," Varuna said.

Vayu glanced back at his wife before he played the card.

"It's not really fair that you have such talented help," Varuna said. His gaze toward Svaha contained thinly veiled lust.

Vasundhara yawned and looked toward the game. "I'm sorry I'm not more help. The game is just so violent. I don't see why you can't play something without winners and losers."

The others ignored Vasundhara. The next duel was a tie. Both Elementals played a general.

"Oh, it is getting feisty now," Varuna said. "Will you risk your last general? Do you think I will play another general, or try to beat you with an officer?"

Vayu sighed and played his cards. Once more both tied, each playing his last general.

Varuna was no longer playful. His play was aggressive and reckless. And the game was still up in the air.

They placed down their cards. For the first time, Vayu smiled.

"Care to go first?" Vayu said.

Varuna flipped his card with disdain.

"Ah, a major," Vayu said. He rocked his knees in a fidgety motion and giggled.

"Look, don't draw it out, just play your card, if it's better..." Varuna said.

"A colonel," Vayu said triumphantly.

"Like to see you do it without Svaha," Varuna grumbled under his breath.

Vayu was too happy to notice his colleague's remark.

Varuna rose to his feet. "You're right, this is boring," he said.

"Maybe you'd be less bored if you were winning," Vayu said.

Varuna glared at Vayu. Then his scowl turned into a grin. "Well played," he said.

"Another?" Vayu asked.

"No, I think I will go to the Mortal Realm," Varuna said.

"Oh, no. Please think of the poor mortals," Vasundhara said. "Every time you go, you cause a tsunami or a flood or a drought."

"You're such a bleeding heart. Come on, let's go. I don't trust you alone with Vayu," Varuna said.

Svaha laughed.

"It's even worse when I go," Vasundhara moaned. "Earthquakes and volcanic eruptions and landslides."

"It will be alright, we'll tread carefully," Varuna said.

Reluctantly, Vasundhara followed her husband.

Anorexia stood in a lonely alcove of the Great Hall. She looked up at a life-sized statue of Spanish Influenza. The Wraiths had done a remarkable job. The representation was accurate down to his broken horn, the hash mark tattoos on the tops of his hands and forearms (tallying the slew of Angels he had slain), and the medals he had cherished so much.

"I'm sorry I didn't come to your funeral. It's taken me a while to be able to come here," Anorexia said. She fidgeted and felt awkward. *I wonder if I should speak to the statue or the floor he's buried beneath.*

She settled on the floor. The face of the statue was carved in a fierce, sneering guise and she preferred to remember him in more carefree moments.

"You know, Trichomoniasis once told me I knew nothing about you. I think she was right. We drank and smoked together. We spoke. We kissed. But did I know you? Would I have known you if we had time to develop our relationship? Or would you have forever been a mystery? For certain, now you always will be. But I did love, even having not really known you," Anorexia said. She wiped her eyes.

"I think I could have forgave you for killing Schitz. I mean if you ever explained your reasons. I just didn't have the heart to side with you over him while you were both alive. I'm sure you thought it a betrayal. I'm sorry for that. I'm sorry for a lot of things."

Anorexia gave up on wiping her face and let the tears run down her face.

"You should be sorry too. You know, you left me here. You took away my loneliness and then gave it back to me in spades. You gave me optimism for the future and took it with you. You were a junkie, and a philanderer, and a sadist, and so much more than those things. Just because you're gone doesn't mean I have to stop loving you. I can love you, so I will," she said.

The statue stood on a small platform, but Anorexia was able to reach up and caress the cold, stone face. She ran her hand over it for a moment and then turned away. Anorexia exited the alcove to the main atrium of the Great Hall. The mood among the occupants of Hell was one of gloomy vigor. There was a population boom, massive training and drilling, all the preparations for the next great war.

Despite the activity, there was a deep sense of foreboding as well. The forces of Heaven had created a global empire in the form of the League of Nations. The organization was far from universal, but by AD 1934, it comprised much of the world's major countries.

The Angels used the League to deescalate crises in the Åland Islands, Upper Silesia, Albania, Memel, Mosul, conflicts between Poland, Lithuania, and the Russian SFSR, border disputes between Colombia and Peru, the referendum for the Saar to unify with Germany, and more. Each one of them could have ignited broader regional conflicts.

It's quite the strategic stranglehold they've carried over from the Great War, Anorexia thought. *With one hand they re-arm the Allied nations for the next conflict. With the other they promote peace and modern advances that choke the Styx. We're already on the back foot and the next conflict hasn't even started.*

Schitz interrupted her musings. Anorexia felt her pulse quicken. He scrutinized her appearance before he spoke. *Oh, I must look a mess. I wonder if it is obvious I've been crying*, she thought.

"Are you alright?" Schitz asked. He placed his hand on her shoulder. "You seem upset."

His hand felt enticing. *How is it that I was just mourning Spanish Influenza, and now one touch from this guy has me weak in the knees?*

"Oh, I'm just depressed about the state of things. Our current disposition looks weak compared to the Angels," she said.

"Oh, ye of little faith," Schitz said.

Schitz had recently been dubbed the Supreme Commander of the Demons – a rank Spanish Influenza would have adored.

"I have faith in you," Anorexia said. "But the political landscape looks bleak."

"It's not as bad as it looks. The peace achieved by the League of Nations is an illusion. Autocratic rulers will always wage wars of conquest. Germany, Italy, and Japan are in the early stages of building empires destined to smash the League of Nations and competing countries to smithereens. Our forces are preparing rigorously for when that conflict comes. We will perform better than in the last war."

Something about Schitz's demeanor filled her with an odd confidence.

"Well, when you say it like that, I feel better," Anorexia said.

"I'm on my way back to the Mortal Realm right now," Schitz said. "There's a lot to learn and master in terms of new weaponry," Schitz said.

"Don't forget, you still owe me that drink and trip down memory lane," she said. Anorexia ran her hand through her hair. *I hope I sound friendly and flirtatious, not desperate.*

Schitz smiled, "Yes, definitely before the next conflict starts."

Schitz half-embraced her and headed off. Anorexia made her way to the departure portals and thought, *Why not? It's been a while.*

She made the symbols for a tea house in Shanghai. China was embroiled in a civil war, however the port city was far enough from any engagements. The conflict would not interfere with her jaunt.

The attire of the mortal women and the furniture in the room had modernized. But the tone of the gossip seemed locked in time.

A shadowy figure sat beside her and addressed her in a low voice. "Finally you have come. He's had me waiting for you forever."

Before Anorexia could reply, the Familiar departed. A few moments later Lord Uranium II arrived.

"Ah, Xiang, good to see you," Anorexia said.

Her old friend appeared rattled. He hugged her more out of courtesy than affection, and sat. Uranium II rubbed his temples like a man with a migraine.

"What's wrong?" Anorexia asked.

"Platinum," he said, "and other things. I've been anxious to see you."

"I would say so," Anorexia said. "Your spy nearly jumped into my lap the moment I appeared."

"Sorry about that," he said. "Didn't mean to scare you. I just...uh...well...this is delicate."

"Spit it out."

"I need to have a way to warn you – if and when the situation warrants," he said.

Anorexia felt the hair on the back of her neck stand at attention. "Xiang, your mother and I were very clear. Our friendship always avoided even the appearance of impropriety. What you're talking about sounds like treason."

Uranium II rubbed his teeth with his index finger as if cleaning them for what he was about to say. "It may well be...but...but only in the most benign of ways. All I need is a way to tell you...should circumstances require...for you to...ah...make yourself scarce on a given day."

"You mean from Hell," she said.

"Ah...yes...ah...precisely."

My friend wants to spare me from something. And if I know something is pending, could I save myself without warning others?

"I have a feeling I'm going to be pretty busy in the Mortal Realm soon enough," she said, "but I suppose you could use a newspaper. My Wraiths bring me *The Telegraph* every day. You can possess an editor and put in a combination of advertisements. Let's say 'Cigars' on the top left and 'Gin' on the top right. Only use that combination when you need me to be out of residence," she said.

"Yes, our intelligence service uses those too. I'm partial to *The Asahi Shimbun*," Uranium II said.

"You're not going to tell me what all this is about, are you?" Anorexia asked.

"I cannot," Uranium II said, "but when you see the warning, please avoid Hell."

Anorexia shook her head. "Sounds like doomsday."

"Don't pry," he said with a chuckle. "Let's change the subject. How's your love life?"

Christa looked up from a mortal newspaper.

"Look at this," she said. She tossed the newsprint across the table.

"American archaeologist, O'Neill Hencken, completes first modern survey of Cornwall's ancient standing stones: Mên-an-Tol," Silver said. "They always put the nationality first when they're not British, like somehow the work is suspect. Oh, well it is good work, for an *American*."

"Ugh, read the part about the locals," Christa said with an eye roll.

"Hmm, local Cornish farmers are reported to crawl through the hole in the stone to cure arm and back pain. Women climb through the hole in the stone to improve fertility. Children with rickets are passed through the stone and are said to experience curative effects," Silver said.

He drummed his fingers on the table. "Cornwall's about 200 miles from Stonehenge. You know, it makes sense. I can see it. Stonehenge was some sort of bastion and this Mên-an-Tol is right on the water. The Titans didn't have the option of traveling via portals, so it makes sense for the forge to be near a port. From there they could disseminate weapons across Europe over rivers and land or through the Mediterranean to the Levant," he said.

"I think the forge will be there," Christa said. She leapt from her seat, overcome with excitement.

Silver picked up the Ur Lak and said, "This is just the key. The Forge of Albion will be the advantage that will win us the war."

Elise, Mephistopheles, and Anubis sat around the table that had once been the meeting place of the Triumvirate Council. The mood was sullen as were the countenances of the assembled Wraiths.

"I see no way around it," Anubis said.

Mephistopheles picked up a copy of the Divine Dictum and said, "The last part of Operating Clause 2, Section C states, 'Members of the monitoring organization may act in concert, in assistance of, or collaboration with other associated forces of God or Satan, so long as such actions are undertaken for brief instances.'"

"I'm sure our involvement will be quite brief. Most of us will be dead within minutes of entering into combat with the Angels," Anubis said.

"What about Operating Clause 4, Section A?" Elise asked.

"Hmm," Mephistopheles said. '...all species created by, utilized, or indentured to God or Satan for any period of time, or any purpose, are entitled to due process regarding any form of lasting or severe punishment.'"

"I don't see how that applies," Anubis said.

"Well, like you said, we won't last long in combat. Our very genetics put us at a huge disadvantage," Elise said. "I believe mobilizing the Wraiths for combat against the Angels is tantamount to a form of punishment inflicted without due process."

Mephistopheles and Anubis sat in silence. They were both visibly working out the merits of the argument.

"Here's the problem," Anubis said, "and I'm not saying it's a very strong argument, but do you remember Schitz's trial? Satan is the sole arbitrator. Anybody could see the case against Schitz was farcical, at best. Yet, he was still banished. If we invoke our right to due process, Satan, the originator of the idea to use us in combat, will lambast us."

"I see another problem with it as well," Mephistopheles said. He looked saddened. "Failing at trial would likely be a devastating blow to our fellow Wraiths. We might have to consider the reality of our situation and accept it."

Elise threw her sole hand in the air. Her face was red, "So that's it, we cultivated intelligence gathering skills over millennia, and now we're mere cannon fodder?"

"I think we can take a two-pronged approach," Anubis said. "First, we can quadruple our efforts to ensure the initial phase of combat is highly successful. Remember, we're being activated as a reserve, not as the first wave. If we can provide stellar intelligence, perhaps the Demons can carry the day without our having to enter the fray."

"We already provide stellar intelligence," Mephistopheles said with a grumble.

"What's the second part?" Elise asked.

Anubis glared at Mephistopheles and continued. "Second, we should work on identifying Wraiths who have exceptional, but unacknowledged skills. We can protect them so that they can carry on our good work after this folly. Schitz has already taken steps to ensure Josephine is not part of the Wraith combat battalion."

"Ex...ex...excuse me?" Elise said.

Mephistopheles put his hand on her shoulder.

"After all I've done for him. After all we've done for him. I mean he said, he would keep me out of combat, but that was before he started looking into the Spanish Influenza business..." she said.

"Ugh, I wish we'd never gotten involved in that. For all we know, Schitz suggested the entire thing to Satan as retribution," Anubis said.

"For killing his mortal adversary?" Elise said.

"For getting involved in his business," Anubis said.

"Enough, enough, what's done is done," Mephistopheles said.

Elise recalled meeting with Schitz in Paris. He had an underlying hostility. *Was he baiting a trap? Or giving me one last chance to come clean?*

"So, we redouble our efforts and identify the next generation?" Anubis asked.

"I thought it was quadruple," Mephistopheles said, testiness in his voice.

"Yes, it is a good plan Anubis. A trial would have been...messy," Elise said.

The morning sun was rising over the grassy fields of Southwest England. Silver and Christa crouched on their haunches. They were in possession of a local mortal husband and wife. They peered anxiously through the opening in the middle of the Mên-an-Tol stone.

The sun's rays crept toward another tall stone where they had hung the Ur Lak.

"It has to work. All of the research points to the sword being a key and the Mên-an-Tol being the lock," Silver said.

The sunlight reached the sword and a reflected beam terminated upon a barren patch of earth.

"That's it," Christa said. Her voice was giddy. She rubbed her hands together like a child on Christmas morning.

They began to dig. They broke through the topsoil and after a few feet, encountered a stone slab. The pair dug around the stone until they could lift it. Under the stone was a large bowl fashioned from a rock.

"What's that?" Silver asked.

"It looks like a witch's cauldron," Christa said.

"Let's pull it up," Silver said. He reached down and grabbed the stone by its handles. It did not move.

"It's heavy as fuck," Silver said.

"Come on," Christa said. She reached down and grabbed one of the handles. Silver pulled at the other side. With a groaning effort they pulled the stone cauldron out of the ground.

"It's not very big, why is it so heavy?" Christa asked. Her breaths came in wheezing gasps.

"I think it's these," Silver said. He reached into the pot and retrieved an odd, black rock. Although the object fit in his palm, his hand shook as he tried to hold it. After a moment Silver dropped the rock to fall back into its holder.

"It's a kiln," Christa said. "Look."

In the ground were an anvil and a set of bellows.

Silver and Christa lugged the other artifacts out of the hole.

"Whew," Silver said, rubbing his arms. "Well that must be it: the Forge of Albion."

"It seems we've moved away from codes and cyphers, as this is quite literally a forge," Christa said.

"Yes, and thankfully no traps either," Silver said

"Let's use the Mên-an-Tol to get out of here," Christa said.

"Good call, I'm not trying to lug this stuff farther than I have to," Silver said.

"So then where are we setting up the forge?"

Earth & Water

"Let's do it by the river," Silver said. "I think access to water is useful when smithing and we need to be away from prying eyes."

"Say no more," Christa said.

She began tracing symbols in the dirt below the Mên-an-Tol. Next she poured water from a canteen on top of the symbols. The portal opened. With enormous effort they pushed the kiln, anvil, and bellows through the portal.

"Ladies first," Silver said, gesturing toward the portal.

When she stepped toward the stone Silver grabbed her on the shoulder.

"God in Heaven..." he said.

"What is it?" Christa asked. She looked around in a panic and clutched at a pistol her mortal host carried at her waist.

"We left the bloody sword up on the rock," Silver said.

Christa fell over laughing as her husband jogged over and retrieved the Ur Lak.

"Could you imagine if we left it there after all those centuries looking for it?" Christa said.

The amused Angels abandoned their hosts and leapt through the portal.

Anna stood in the Celestial Realm in the elevated gallery of the main room of the Palais Wilson. She yawned and looked down to the chamber floor where Zinc and his wife Eleanor moved about to possess various world leaders and diplomats. They did so to exert the most influence they could over the League of Nations.

It's like watching a medic work on a soldier who has lost his arms and legs; a frantic ultimately pointless endeavor, she thought. Anna felt a deep sense of pity for her overlord. His unending fixation was to create a worldwide empire. He tried with Alexander the Great, Rome, Napoleon's France, the Entente, and most recently the League of Nations.

For all of the earlier success following the Great War, the League had begun to falter. Italy invaded Abyssinia; Spain fell into a civil war; Japan invaded China; the Soviet Union had invaded Finland – all without effective action from the League of Nations.

The meeting Zinc was so frantically trying to influence had been called in response to the German and Soviet invasion of Poland. Anna watched as Zinc was rebuffed from possessing any mortals of the Soviet delegation. Their minds were steeled by the knowledge of what would happen to them should they deviate from the party line.

Sadness had burdened Anna of late. She could not pinpoint a cause, but she was lonely...empty. She had lost good friends to death (the Confessoress and Barnabas) and romantic partners to circumstance (Schitz and Rachael). She still had comrades in Lilly, Beatrice, and Constance but felt cut off from them.

Lilly basked in her retirement and seemed to have an emotional wall against current events. Beatrice was occupied with her revolving door of romantic liaisons. Constance remained a jealous wreck and was in a perpetual foul mood because of Zinc's marital bliss.

I miss the fellowship of the Witch Hunters. I miss the intimacy of romance. Damn, I even miss the thrill of offing targets for Zinc, Anna thought.

Zinc motioned to her. Anna vaulted over the edge of the gallery and landed with the grace of a ballet dancer next to Zinc and Eleanor.

"This meeting was pointless," Zinc said. "This global empire has no teeth. From now on our efforts will be directed towards other ventures."

Anna nodded and said, "So another world war it will be."

Zinc shrugged. "Perhaps, but come, we have to collect Constance. There is something major going on."

They made their way to a backroom where Zinc opened a portal to the Great Hall. To Anna's great surprise there was a vast contingent of Angels and Familiars from most of the Houses assembled in front of the departure portals. Alongside the formation stood a brooding Constance Silver. Anna made her way over to her confederate.

"Any idea what's going on?" Anna asked.

"I can only assume we're going to Poland or Finland, or both," Constance said. "One or more of the places where there's fighting."

A group of Familiars were opening portals between several columns. They were taking great care to be exact with the symbols.

I wonder what we're up to, Anna thought.

Zinc addressed the assembled. "On this truly historic day, we depart on the grandest of endeavors. It will be a terrifying and monumental struggle, but in the end we will be victorious. Lord Uranium II will brief you on some details."

Zinc was joined at the head of the formation by his fellow Co-Supreme Commander. Uranium II looked like a caged lion at the

Colosseum. He appeared thirsty for battle, ready to be unleashed. He began his speech with a shout, "Banzai!"

The contingent of Asian Angels echoed the call. Other Houses cheered and applauded the animated commander.

"We are going to a place of great darkness. Therefore, you will blindfold yourselves now so your eyes may adjust quicker," Uranium II said.

A horde of Familiars handed out lengths of cloth.

"I don't like the idea of neither of us having eyes on Zinc. You leave yours on. I'll keep mine off," Anna said. "Just be prepared to protect him once we get to the other side."

Constance nodded.

"Hands on the Angel in front of you," Uranium II commanded.

The assembled stepped into the portals. Anna moved forward. She held Constance by the wrist. They passed through the portal a moment behind Zinc and Eleanor.

He was not lying, Anna thought as she emerged at the destination. Her eyes hurt as her pupils expanded.

Constance lifted her blindfold. "Are we in…"

"Hell," Anna said.

"Now you can appreciate the secrecy surrounding this venture," Zinc said.

They had arrived in a forest of twisted, black trees. Uranium II put several Angels to the task of hacking some down.

"Hang tight for now," Zinc said. "This is his venture, but if it is successful it will mean the end of the war."

"Why are they felling the trees?" Constance asked.

Zinc gestured toward the edge of the wood. Anna squinted in the moonlight. Beyond the trees she saw luminescent, blue water. *That must be the Styx*, she thought.

"We need a bridge," Zinc said. "We will cross the river and storm their Great Hall. Once there, we will kill Satan."

Anorexia sat in her room and reviewed reports of the growing conflict in Europe. A scraping noise announced the arrival of the post.

Let's see what the mortals are saying about the war, she thought.

Anorexia stooped and collected the evening edition of *The Telegraph* for Wednesday, October 25, 1939. When she saw the advertisements, fear constricted her throat.

Havana Cigars on the left.

Gin on the right.

"It's the signal," she said.

Anorexia snatched a cup of Brew off her desk and dipped a finger in the chalice. She traced a set of symbols on the floor in front of her door. *New York City is far away from any fighting*, she thought as she completed her work.

The fear of the unknown was a foreign emotion to Anorexia. She had seen battle for countless centuries. Combat offered dread and worry, but it was not virgin territory to her. The current unknown menace from which she fled was all the more terrible due to its mystery.

Anorexia breathed over the symbols for water and air and pushed her door open. She stepped through the portal. *I wonder what I'm fleeing and what will be here when I return.*

Anna drew back on a celestial bow. The weight was no different from a mortal weapon. However, the novelty of firing a ranged weapon in the Celestial was exciting. The bridge had been placed across the Styx successfully, however, no sooner had the final anchor been set than it was attacked by a solitary fighter.

From the far bank Anna had struck the enemy twice and he had fallen into the river. For a moment, it seemed that victory was at hand. Then the foe emerged from the waters. Anna fired another arrow, but the enemy ducked behind some rocks.

"The waters must be curative like the Eunoe," Constance said.

"They're injurious to our troops," Zinc said. "To make matters worse, he damaged the bridge. It no longer reaches the far bank."

"Why didn't we just land on the far side?" Constance asked. She loosed an arrow even though there were no viable targets.

"We needed to conceal our arrival. The woods were the best location for that," Zinc said. "Who would have thought we'd arrive at such an inopportune time?"

Anna's pulse raced. She could not think of a single option to turn the tide in their favor.

"Keep up your fire on that Priest. Send more lumber to the front of the bridge," Uranium II shouted.

A Demon arrived on the far side of the river bank. He scurried behind the rocks as the arrows continued to fall. More Demons arrived. The reinforcements began hurling throwing stars at the Angels on the bridge. The landing party was forced back. Several were struck and fell into the Styx. Their howling screams echoed across the eerie countryside.

"This venture is blown," Zinc said. He gestured toward Eleanor and his bodyguards. "Let's get out of here."

CHAPTER 7

ROT SCHEINT DIE SONNE

The early morning beams of the coming day shone through the window of the New York skyscraper. Circades stretched his arms and looked out the window across the midtown landscape and as far as Queens.

I hate New York, he thought. He much preferred the unadulterated countryside like the region along the idyllic Danube. However, the boardroom fit for the impending meeting and New York's population always warranted a thorough search for Pulwabi.

At last I will be able to look for her without pesky interference, he thought.

Water & Air

Circades's plan was simple. He would convene the meeting. When God was presenting his case, Circades would shoot him. His finger moved instinctively to Hyperion's ring.

After all that time worrying about how I would execute Svaha's decree, the answer fell into my lap. God and his Angels massively violated the Divine Dictum we set forth when they expanded their conflict into the Celestial Realm by invading Hell.

The Celestials were unaware, but should they wipe each other out entirely, their Realm would collapse. The limitations on their conflict in the Divine Dictum were designed to engineer a way for them to fight without annihilating one another. If the Celestial Realm were to fall, the Ethereal and Mortal Realm might also be destroyed. While the mortal souls fueled the construct through constant death and rebirth, passing through the Styx and the Eunoe, the Celestial beings held together their portion of the construct simply by their existence. God and Satan, the ignorant offspring of Vasundhara and Svaha respectively, threatened to tear apart the fabric of being with their sibling rivalry.

"Primogenitorous had no idea what he was doing getting into bed with those Elementals," Circades said to himself.

"Indeed it was a grave error with grave consequences," a booming voice said.

Circades turned to see Varuna standing behind him. His wife Vasundhara stood behind him. Circades felt the hairs on the back of his neck stand on end. He had a pair of colt 1911s holstered under his vest. However, the Ethereals were quicker than either Celestials or Titans. He knelt before the Elementals.

"You have no reason to be afraid," Varuna said as though he had a window into Circades's mind.

Circades rose and assessed the water Elemental. He was much stockier than any of his contemporaries. His blue skin stretched and bulged to accommodate his heavy musculature.

I gave him this frame when I selected water as the element for God and Satan to shepherd mortal souls through, Circades thought. The glut of psychic energy from the Eunoe and the Styx had rendered Varuna massive though he bore it with forcefulness rather than lethargy.

"God and Satan are expected here any moment," Circades said. He directed the Elementals to an adjoining room.

"That is why we are here. I've heard of Svaha's plot to entice you into ending the war between the Celestials," Varuna said.

"Svaha said she spoke for all of you," Circades said.

"Hardly. Some gamesmanship is surely afoot though I know not how she intended to use the end of the war to bring things to her advantage," Varuna said.

"Are you lot at war?" Circades asked.

Varuna's laugh shook the room. His jowls gyrated with his chuckle and his frame pitched like a swelling ocean. "If we went to war, all of existence would be destroyed. Our kind merely squabbles. Look at the ancestor you spoke of earlier, Primogenitorous. We cut him to pieces, but we did not take out our rage on our wayward wives," Varuna said.

Circades glanced at Vasundhara. He felt pity for her. Legend held that her good nature had been exploited by Primogenitorous. She loved all living things, and he had used this empathy to seduce her. Conversely, the lusty Svaha was said to have demanded Primogenitorous's attention after hearing about the affair between the Titan and Vasundhara.

"So, what does your squabbling have to do with me?" Circades asked.

"Well, obviously you are not going to end the conflict between God and Satan," Varuna said.

"I'm not?" Circades asked.

"No," Varuna said. He folded his tree trunk arms across his barrel chest.

"And Svaha?" Circades asked.

"She won't bother you anymore," Varuna said with a laugh.

"That sounds sinister," Circades said.

"Hardly, we wagered on a game of chance. She lost. She'll get over it and return to her scheming," Varuna said.

"And if she had won your little game?" Circades asked.

"Then I would have let you end the conflict. I presume that is the purpose of today's meeting," Varuna said.

"It was. Now I'll have to devise a different outcome," Circades said.

Varuna shrugged. "I'm sure you'll think of something."

Without further ado, Varuna turned away from Circades. He snapped his finger and a portal opened in the doorway. Vasundhara folded her hands in front of her chest and bowed to Circades politely.

Circades exhaled. He heard muffled voices coming from the board room.

The first was God's "Well, Brother, you are looking healthy."

"To your disappointment, I'm sure," the Devil replied.

Circades pushed the door open and entered the room. *They know my kind is fierce. They still remember the war with my kin. They will listen to what I have to say, as they always have,* Circades thought.

"This meeting will be brief," Circades said. "You will each present your information. My determination will be swift and final."

God looks like a schoolboy about to get the ruler. If only he knew what my original plan entailed. He felt the weight of his pistols in their holsters.

Each of the deities had brought a representative.

The Devil's Priest spoke first. "We are here today because the forces of Heaven, under the command of the one who refers to himself as God, have breached the central tenant of the Divine Dictum – that all conflict be contained to the Mortal Realm." He tossed a handful of Celestial arrows up the conference table. "Additionally, they have produced weapons banned by the Divine Dictum."

God's representative spoke next.

"What constitutes conflict?" she asked. "A conversation? The movement of troops? I would contend the only acceptable definition of conflict in our context is an action resulting in violent death or severe, irreparable injury. Did any Angels or Demons or other living beings die in the events mentioned? The answer is a resounding 'no.' No one died. Were any maimed? No. We are willing to accept censure for the creation of the banned weapons. We made them… we will accept the consequences."

She looks just like Pulwabi, Circades thought. *The resemblance is remarkable, but there are more pressing matters at hand.*

Circades leaned on the table. "I accept that the presence of Angels in Hell is a novel experience. However, I can hardly see why I should be bothered with this matter. Surely, conflict arises any time you are in proximity to each other. Let's say this. You will only be in proximity to each other in the Mortal Realm. In the Celestial, you will maintain distance and you will stay out of each other's abodes. As to punishment, I will not hand victory to Hell over such a minor thing as this."

God sighed audibly in relief.

Circades continued. "Still, I would like to see this resolved. Heaven, you will turn over to Hell fifty percent of the Angels that participated in the incursion, and they will be dealt with as Hell sees fit. Punishment for Hell, you will cede the area occupied by the Angels while in Hell to Heaven."

Satan erupted. "Why should we be punished?"

Circades's eyes grew dark. "For wasting my time."

The delegations departed. Circades looked out the window, taking in the bright morning. The building would soon be filled with mortal businessmen. They would be entirely unaware that their boardroom had just served as the stage for one of the most consequential debates in history.

Circades donned a fedora and made his way down to the street. The hustle and bustle of the day was ramping up into full swing. He took a right at the corner.

Where to next?

The Ju 52 transport aircraft lumbered across the Sea of Crete. The red rays of the early morning bathed the camouflage green exterior of the three engine aircraft. The Fallschirmjäger[12] within were in high spirits. They had trained tirelessly and the day was at hand.

Anorexia looked at the seventeen mortal paratroopers, three of whom were possessed by Cancer, Hysteria, and Brain Cancer. Schitz had assigned the all-female quartet with the daunting task of ensuring the success of the airborne invasion of Crete.

The invasion, codenamed Unternehmen Merkur,[13] was intended to expand Axis control over the Eastern Mediterranean. Schitz had sent Anorexia and her cadre to ensure the battle did not result in an Axis defeat, and to draw Angels away from the upcoming invasion of the Soviet Union.

Anorexia looked out of the window of the transport and thought about Uranium II. He had warned her to be away from Hell on the day the Angels invaded. His alert was unnecessary in the end since the Angels had been unable to launch a full scale assault on Hell. It

---

[12] Paratroopers

[13] Operation Mercury

was incredibly considerate of him to warn me. I wonder what would have happened if they were successful? she thought.

It's bad enough I'm nearly the oldest surviving Demon. If Xiang had succeeded maybe I would have been the last Demon left. The consideration sent a chill down Anorexia's spine.

She turned away from the window and looked at the rest of her companions. They seemed comfortable within the mortal women. None were novices. Cancer was growing into a celebrity of sorts. She had acquired a following; they worshiped her like a deity. Hysteria was an artillery expert and had fought well at Waterloo and in the American Civil War. Brain Cancer was an academy valedictorian and the sole survivor from her cohort.

An explosion rocked the aircraft. It was followed by another and then another. She looked out the window and saw small black clouds; *Flak.* The clear sky soon sported an outbreak of countless black dots – like malignant measles. The menacing plink of shrapnel striking the fuselage of the aircraft sounded through the cabin.

Anorexia's watch read 7:58 am. She held up her thumb and index finger to the paratroopers. Her frame tensed with the explosion of anti-aircraft fire. At this height, the Demons were just as vulnerable as their hosts.

This is it, Anorexia thought. She rose to her feet, hooked up to the static line, and hauled the door open. The cabin filled with cold, violent air. Kreta lay outstretched below, a patchwork of dusty brown and dark green. Anorexia had experience flying during the interwar period, however, she was entirely reliant on her host's training for parachuting. The woman's thoughts were primarily focused on the mission to capture the airfield at Maleme. She was also thinking of home and a love for the Vaterland. Deep in the host's subconscious lay the confidence in training that gave Anorexia the courage to throw herself from the plane.

Anorexia grasped either side of the doorframe with her hands. The metal was cold even through her gloves. She could almost reach out and touch the clouds of flak. Anorexia bent her knees and pushed off from the edge of the door.

The sensation of falling was exhilarating and sickening. Anorexia was forty meters from the plane by the time her parachute opened.

The jarring deceleration yanked Anorexia upright underneath the canopy.

At least it opened.

Machine gun fire from the enemy below quickly reminded Anorexia that the fall from the plane was not the primary danger. While in the parachute, she could control very little in terms of her descent. It was a relief when her boots struck the dusty, rocky ground.

Anorexia unbuckled from her parachute and detached her MP 40 submachine gun from her gear. She had landed in a small defile that provided a great deal of cover. On the other hand, she was quite far from the airfield she was meant to secure.

The rest of the squad including the three other possessed mortals arrived at her position.

"We missed our target quite substantially," Anorexia said.

"But we jumped on time," Cancer said.

"The pilot must have steered off course to avoid the worst of the flak or the wind was stronger than predicted," Anorexia said.

She looked at the sky as more Ju 52s passed overhead. Most of the III Regiment was scattered away from the airfield. Anorexia removed a map from inside her tunic and assessed the situation.

"If we can move to this hill here, 107, we can take a commanding position overlooking the airfield," she said.

Cancer nodded. "Perfect spot to call in the Stukas."

The squad of Fallschirmjäger set out across the barren, rocky expanse. Soon they were in contact with soldiers of the 2nd New Zealand Division. The German troops were outgunned. The New Zealanders were armed with machine guns and rifles while the paratroopers only had submachine guns or carbines and a few grenades.

"Do you see them?" Cancer shouted over to Anorexia. They were pinned down behind a ridgeline halfway up the hill. Bullets whizzed overhead like angry bees.

"Yeah, there's a large group of Angels on the hilltop," Anorexia said. "They're probably going to charge our position."

As soon as Anorexia had spoken, more German troops arrived at their position. They were Luftlande-Sturm, glider troops. An Unterfeldwebel saluted Anorexia.

"It looks like you're in charge here, Frau Hauptmann. We're at your disposal," the Unterfeldwebel said.

"Where did you land?" Anorexia asked.

"The dry riverbed over there; the steep banks offered good cover. From what we could see from the air, the units that landed to the south and east were wiped out," the Unterfeldwebel said.

Most of the glider troops were as lightly armed as the paratroopers, however, Anorexia noticed one holding a full variant of the Kar98k equipped with optics.

Anorexia addressed Cancer. "Feldwebel, please relieve the Unteroffizier of his rifle.

The glider troops looked hesitant.

"Don't worry," Cancer said. "I'm the best shot in the regiment."

"Dig in here and prepare for their attack," Anorexia said to the Unterfeldwebel. "We're going to harass them a little."

The four Demons backtracked the dry riverbed. They passed the wrecked gliders. Discarded gear littered the dusty ground.

Anorexia looked at her map and then across the countryside.

"Look," Anorexia said. She pointed to a hilltop in the distance. "There's a monastery between Hill 107 and Xamoudochori. You can take up a position there. You'll be able to see all across the top of 107."

"I'll have to avoid the town and locals between here and there," Cancer said, pointing to the map and the town of Vlakheronitissa.

"Nothing else can be done, that's the only vantage point," Anorexia said. "We'll approach the hilltop from the south so you can track us."

Cancer shielded her eyes from the merciless sun and scanned the expanse. "It has to be fifteen hundred meters from the monastery to the top of the hill. Are you sure you don't want to take the rifle?"

"Everyone here is an expert," Anorexia said. She nodded to Hysteria and Brain Cancer. "All well vetted at Waterloo and in the Great War. We're counting on you, Head Instructor."

"Ah, you pull the Head Mistress card when you need something, right?" Cancer grinned. "Just don't hold it against me if my aim is wild."

Anorexia patted Cancer on the shoulder.

"Alright, let's get to climbing," Anorexia said.

Crete was hot and dusty. Cancer's host clawed her way up the rocky terrain. The New Zealanders were concentrated to her north and east, however she still proceeded with caution. She knew the locals would be as hostile as the enemy.

After an exhausting climb, she entered an ancient monastery. Cancer had already drained her canteen. She buried her face in a holy water font. It was tepid, but better than nothing. Without pausing, Cancer reached to her waist and drew her Walther PP pistol. She pulled back the hammer and pointed the sidearm in the direction of a cluster of clergy. Only when she had drained the font did she turn to face the monks.

She wiped her mouth and in Cretan Greek said, "The bell tower."

One of the monks pointed to a doorway at the rear of the chapel. Cancer ascended the stone steps and emerged into the cramped belfry. She rested her rifle against the wall. She raised her binoculars.

"Come on girls, where are you?" she asked.

The view from the top of the monastery was breathtaking. The bright blue sea stretched out in the distance. In the foreground lay the patchwork of green and brown hillsides. The Maleme airfield was obscured from view behind Hill 107. However, pillars of black smoke gave away its location. The sky was filled with flak and German dive bombers. The Ju 87s were pounding the airfield and its defenses.

"There you are," Cancer said. She had spotted her comrades. They were just under the crest of the hill. Cancer let her binoculars hang around her neck. She pulled off her host's lightweight scarf and wrapped it around the rifle's ZF41 telescopic scope to cut down on any reflection that might give away her position. She rested the rifle on the ledge of the belfry's low wall.

"Alright ladies, ready when you are," Cancer said. She moved the crosshairs a few feet to the right of Anorexia.

"Do you think she's made it to her position yet?" Hysteria asked.

No sooner had she asked than a bullet stuck against the hillside beside Anorexia's foot.

"I'd say that answered the question," Anorexia," said.

The drone of attack aircraft and the constant boom of anti-aircraft fire rendered the shot silent.

"Horrido!" Anorexia shouted.

The squad climbed the last few steps to the top of the hill and began firing on the enemy infantry. A withering barrage of return fire sent the paratroopers ducking behind the crest. Anorexia abandoned her host and ran across the hilltop.

There were several Angels within the Celestial. Anorexia closed the distance and engaged them in fierce combat. She wielded two sai and worked with ruthless efficiency. Anorexia caught the foes' swords in her tri-pronged weapons or sidestepped their attacks. She stabbed one Angel through the throat, then another. A third she tripped to the ground before stamping down on her throat.

The Angels stepped back under the fury of her onslaught and possessed mortal New Zealanders. One after another, each one collapsed to the ground. Blood and brain matter jettisoned into the sky with each headshot.

While Anorexia dealt with newly arriving Angels in the Celestial, Hysteria and Brain Cancer dispatched the Angels that had been sent into departure seizures. The Angelic defenders of Hill 107 fell into disarray. Those who attempted to possess mortals were immediately cut down by a sharpshooter from an unknown location. Angels remaining in the Celestial were disorganized and easily hewn down by Anorexia and her colleagues.

Anorexia spotted two Angels crouched by the entrance to the mortals' HQ. They were frantically trying to open a portal.

If they get away they might call for reinforcements.

Anorexia threw her twin sai across the hilltop. Both Angels slumped to the ground. When she walked over to retrieve her weapons, she realized one of the Angels had survived the strike. One had exsanguinated when the blade severed her carotid, but the other was only paralyzed.

Anorexia saw a light of recognition and terror in the foe's eyes. He was young with blonde hair and freckles. She pulled the sai from his neck and drove it through the base of his throat. After retrieving her second weapon, Anorexia assessed the scene across the hilltop.

The Angels had been routed. They lay dead across the hilltop within the Celestial Realm. In the Mortal Realm, the New Zealanders were concentrating machine gun fire on the far-off monastery. The hosts Anorexia and her squad had arrived within had scampered off down the south side of the hill.

The Demons repossessed the German paratroopers, made possible by switching hosts since neither Demon nor Angel could possess the same mortal twice. They returned to the rally point where they were met by a jaunty Cancer.

"Good shooting Frau Feldwebel," Anorexia said.

"Yeah, I thought so myself," Cancer said. She spun her pistol around her index finger, a western gunslinger. "I executed a bunch of monks on the way back too – just for fun."

"All in a day's work," Anorexia said.

The airfield of Maleme was considerably quieter by the time Schitz arrived to assess the situation on the first of June 1941. Anorexia felt the need to temper her excitement in the presence of her subordinates. Yet, when he emerged from a portal between one of the hangar doors, she could not help but broadly smile.

"It looks like you led quite a successful campaign here," Schitz said.

They walked in the Celestial among the graveyard of destroyed and damaged transport aircraft. Ju 52s littered the runoff area around the airstrip.

"I would say so," Anorexia said. "It was iffy at the start for us and the Germans, but after we cleared the Angels from Hill 107, it got a lot easier. The New Zealanders abandoned it and we used the position to call in air strikes against the airfield's defenders. More Angels showed up, but they were too late to turn the tide of the battle and we dealt with them easily enough."

"That's good, very good and just in time for the big offensive that's about to kick off in three weeks."

"Unternehmen Barbarossa?"

"Yes, it is going to be a big expansion of the war," Schitz said. "The Angels were obsessed with building a mortal empire, but our Axis forces continue to overrun them left and right."

Anorexia felt her heart race. It was exhilarating to have time with Schitz, even if Cancer and company walked behind them.

"I wonder if my actions in Crete were enough to merit a Knight's Pentagram," Anorexia said.

"I can recommend it. You've earned one many times over," Schitz said. "Although, I'm sure your after-action report will speak for itself."

"I guess, I just want to be recognized for my worth," Anorexia said. *Either by Satan or you.*

Schitz touched her arm. "Satan can be very picky when it comes to decorations. Once he decides someone is unworthy, it's hard to change his mind. Waterloo cast a shadow over all of us old timers."

Anorexia hardly heard the words but her small frame tingled under his fingers. Her legs felt squishy and she heard the quiet giggling behind her.

Schitz turned to the rest of the squad and allowed his hand to fall away. "I was just telling your leader that you all have fought remarkably," he said. "I hope you will all be ready for the war's next chapter."

The three Demons nodded. Anorexia noticed something disconcerting when he turned and assessed the others. *They are all enamored with him,* she thought. It was incredibly annoying that Schitz held the carnal interest of virtually every female Demon.

With Crete deemed secure, the Demons departed for Hell. After the Return Ceremony Schitz left.

Anorexia felt a hand on her shoulder while making her way to her room.

"You know it's none of my business, but you and Schitz..." It was Cancer.

The heat rose in Anorexia's cheeks. Her fists clenched. "You're right, it's not your business," she said.

"Hear me out nevertheless," Cancer said. "It's not a secret you desire him despite his...enthusiasm for intimate liaisons. So, if that's the case, life is short. If he won't come to you, take matters into your own hands."

Anorexia recalled the awkward time she'd thrown herself at Conjunctivitis in drunken stupor. "My dignity in this subject area is hanging by shreds," she said. "I don't know if I could survive an outright rejection."

"Then succeed, or find someone else," Cancer said. "But don't waste your precious time casting him longing glances. You deserve to be happy."

"Thank you, I appreciate that," Anorexia said.

They reached her room.

"You're always welcome at one of our gatherings," Cancer said. "It's mostly just the Demons with carcinogenic nomenclature, but anyone is welcome."

"I've heard of your gatherings," Anorexia said.

"And?"

"Oh, I guess, I mean, no offense, but I thought that area of life was already covered by the Isle of Neutrality," Anorexia said.

"It's so much more than that," Cancer said. "My adherents share a deep connection with one another. Their communion is not just physical, but emotional and spiritual."

Anorexia looked at the Academy instructor. She was gripped by the alluring pull of her amber, piercing eyes and smooth, feminine features. *I wonder what would happen if I let this spell continue to manifest*, Anorexia thought.

"Well, that is definitely something to consider," Anorexia said. She exhaled and only then realized she had been holding her breath.

Cancer giggled. "I like you. There's an honesty to you, it's refreshing," she said. "Keep in mind what I said. Don't wait. You deserve more than longing looks and pats on the back."

They embraced. Cancer departed and Anorexia stepped into her room. A pile of reports had been left for her on her bed.

"Oh, right, aside from all this, there's a war on," she said to herself.

The sun was setting over the Oxfordshire hills to the west of RAF Brize Norton. The mortals had already departed the flight training school for the day. Within the cockpit of a Supermarine Spitfire MK1, Constance Silver sat in the Celestial. Anna stood on the wing of the single-seater fighter and looked into the open cockpit.

Anna pointed to a series of gauges on the right hand side of the cockpit. "There's your radiator temperature gauge, your oil temperature gauge, and your fuel pressure warning lamp. All of that is important if you take damage or if you're overworking the engine," she said.

"This is a lot," Constance said.

"Yes, they've definitely taken things up a notch since the last war," Anna said. "But remember as soon as you possess a mortal you'll gain all of their aviation knowledge. We just do this in case you end up possessing a mortal with less than exemplary skill. I don't want you at a deficit."

"I wonder if Zinc is even going to keep having us go out with him anyways" Constance said. There was dejection in her voice.

There were very few surviving vestiges of the old rivalries. There were no challengers remaining to Zinc's supreme authority.

"I don't see any Angels taking a shot at Zinc, but he's paranoid. He'll likely always keep us watching his back," Anna said.

Constance moved the control column as though she were flying the aircraft. She squinted through the gun sight.

"Rat tat tat tat tat!"

"Bandits?"

"Or Eleanor – either one," Constance said.

Anna laughed. "Well, as long as you feel comfortable should our Lord need us to protect him in the skies."

"I won't know until I'm up there, but yes, I think I'll be alright," Constance said.

Lord Uranium II stood at the periscope of the Japanese Imperial Navy Submarine I-168. The Angels were fighting mostly within the Allied armies. On the continent, Uranium II often fought within the Chinese Nationalists or Communists. However, in the Pacific he could not bring himself to support the Americans.

They are a people devoid of cultural achievement or refinement, he thought as he looked across the expanse between the I-168 and the aircraft carrier USS *Yorktown*. An explosion jettisoned fire and a geyser of water into the afternoon sky.

"Kuso!" Uranium II said.

The first torpedo had struck a destroyer alongside the *Yorktown*. His disappointment was short-lived as the next two torpedoes struck the aircraft carrier.

"Got you," Uranium II said.

The bridge crew cheered. However, they all knew there was a fight yet to be had. Uranium II ordered a dive to 200 meters. The first, eerie explosion sounded overhead. The muffled boom lightly rattled the ship. The next was closer and jostled the crew about.

Here we go.

The depth charges exploded closer and closer until the I-168 was caught in a violent subaquatic storm. A massive explosion along the bow was followed by darkness. A moment later the unnerving, red hue of the emergency lighting filled the craft.

Uranium II knew he could abandon the submarine and her crew to their fate, however, he wanted the challenge of saving them.

We can get away yet.

Alarms blared. The crew reported catastrophic flooding in the torpedo room and the maneuvering room.

"Masks, masks, masks," an Officer shouted.

Water flooding the batteries could release deadly chlorine gas. Uranium II directed the crew to move bags of rice to the rear of the submarine to counterbalance the weight of the flooding bow.

"Hayakushite!"[14]

The I-168 steered away from the depth charges. But Uranium II knew that they could not stay submerged much longer. The batteries were nearly depleted.

We'll surface and fight it out however best we can. It had never been in his nature to relent. He thought of his longstanding feud with his adopted brother, Platinum. *I am a stubborn son of a bitch. Well, let's see what's waiting for us on the surface.*

---

14 Hurry!

Commingled dismay was met with relief when Uranium II assessed the situation. The Americans had blundered and were hunting over 10,000 meters from the submarine's position. The crew set about repairing the motors and clearing the air below decks.

The American destroyers fired a few rounds from their deck guns. The shells all landed a significant distance away. Uranium II knew they had done more than their fair share of damage to the American fleet. With the cover of night approaching, the I-168 submerged and easily evaded the enemy as she fled west.

They arrived at Yokosuka twelve days later where they took on fuel and one passenger.

"It's good to see you, Anorexia," Uranium II said.

The two sat in the Captain's cramped quarters.

"I wanted to thank you in person for your warning," Anorexia said, "even if it wasn't fully necessary in the end."

Uranium II shook his head. "It was a good plan to end the war, but unfortunately, it came undone."

"Thank you for looking out for me nevertheless," Anorexia said.

Uranium II batted away her thanks. "You're an old friend. Mother might not have warned you, but she was more by the book than I am. If I can, I will always look after you."

"I wish there was a way for us to be on the same side," Anorexia said.

"Well, Demons and Angels are distant cousins," Uranium II said. "Perhaps someday this war will end and we can get along."

Anorexia closed her eyes and rocked peacefully with the motion of the ship. "That would be nice," she said.

The Saharan sun beat down on Constance and Anna with merciless delight.

"Bring back memories?" Constance asked.

Anna glanced over, then returned her attention to the looped sight of her host's Lee-Enfield rifle.

"Egypt? Not too many pleasant ones," Anna said.

"I wish I was alive back then," Constance said. "It would have been something to see the Gold and Silver Houses fighting against all of Heaven."

"You would have had to fight against Lord Zinc," Anna said.

The pair glanced at Lord and Lady Zinc. They were commanding the Angelic effort as part of the British 8th Army outside of El Alamein.

"What was he like back then?" Constance asked.

"Eh, I didn't know him too well," Anna said. "Back then he was under the shadow of his father, Zinc I. He was bright though. I ran into him at the Academy a couple of times."

"Do you think they'll attack today?" Constance asked. She checked her Bren Mk.1 light machine gun.

Before Anna could answer, a shadow flitted across the dunes a few hundred yards in front of them. From her time training and time with Lilly, Anna had developed an understanding of Familiars and Wraiths. Both were descendants of Titans and mortals, with some Celestial genealogy as well. When they moved, Wraiths and Familiars were mere shadows. When they were stationary they were visible both to Mortals and Celestials.

Anna was certain the shadows moving across the dunes were Wraiths. She tracked one and fired her rifle.

"Oh shit," Constance shouted.

The Bren opened up with a rapid chatter. The trench was teeming with possessed mortals who also began opening fire across the seemingly empty expanse. Anna worked the bolt of her rifle and fired another round. The recoil slammed into her shoulder. She pulled the trigger with her middle finger, so her index finger was free to work the bolt faster, a technique developed for firing the Lee-Enfield. The Brits called it "the mad minute technique."

Despite the fusillade, many Wraiths made it into the forward position. The shifty foe posed the most danger to the Mortal troops, for just as the Wraiths were vulnerable to mortal weapons, so too could they inflict damage upon the Mortals.

Anna stepped out of her host and drew her sword. Constance had been sent into a departure seizure by one of the foe. With a broad sweep of her weapon, Anna decapitated two Wraiths who charged Constance.

In the Celestial we have a huge advantage over them, Anna thought. She defended Constance while the seizure ran its course. The other Angels abandoned their hosts in similar fashion. Anna looked across the British defensive position and assessed the scene. Zinc and Eleanor seemed safe. They had moved forward in the Celestial and were slewing scores of Wraiths. It seemed the Wraiths were in the process of being wiped out.

Anna hauled Constance to her feet.

"Tricky buggers," Constance said. She caught her breath. "They nearly got me there."

"Yeah, they're quick," Anna said, "but we dealt with them easily enough."

When she checked on her master again, she saw him lying on the ground. Eleanor crouched over him. Fear clutched at Anna's throat. *My attention was pulled away for one moment. How could I let this happen?*

To Anna's relief, Zinc sat up. He held his head, injured, but very much alive. Eleanor gestured toward their left flank. A pair of Demons had plowed into the Celestial ranks. Anna looked to the right flank. Her fears were confirmed; a second pair of Demons was attacking there as well.

The Demonic assault was accompanied by the chatter of incoming machine gun and rifle fire. The mortal Afrika Korps was attacking the British position in conjunction with the Demons' arrival.

Fuck, we're all out of sorts.

The Wraiths had sent the Angels into the Celestial, which meant that the Demonic ambush was causing a high rate of casualties. Similarly, without Angels possessing them, the British troops were equally vulnerable.

The Defensive position was quickly becoming untenable.

"Get Zinc and Eleanor out of here," Anna said. "We can't hold the line here."

Constance nodded and fell back.

Anna charged along the sandbag covered parapet toward the foe – two females. Their fighting style was in complete synchronicity. The Demons were slaughtering the entire contingent covering the right side of the position. Anna made eye contact with the lead Demon – cold gray eyes and blonde hair dyed with streaks that matched her eyes.

The Demon ducked. The second foe hurled a throwing knife in Anna's direction. Anna leapt to the side to dodge the blade and swung her sword toward the foe. They hacked away at each other. All the while, Anna remained wary of the second Demon, who stayed back at the edge of the confrontation.

The foe was of equal skill to Anna. She snarled at Anna when their blades came together. Then Anna saw the slightest glance of her enemy's eyes beyond her shoulder.

A voice screamed in Anna's head – *Duck!*

The second Demon had thrown another knife. As Anna dropped to her knees, she felt a burning, painful sensation rip through her scalp. She winced and clutched the handle of her sword and prepared to defend herself, but her opponent crumpled to the ground and lay motionless. Her eyes glazed over in a wild, vacant expression. Blood flowed from the corners of her mouth. A Demonic throwing knife protruded from her throat.

Anna charged the remaining Demon. She had a pale complexion offset by long, emerald-green hair. The foe hurled another throwing knife at Anna before drawing her sword. It sailed wide. They came to blows in a vicious round of combat.

Anna recalled her bout with Silver when he had predicted her series of movements. The Demon, though skilled, was following a pattern where she loosened her grip to gain speed. Anna anticipated and knocked the sword from her foe's hand.

Once disarmed the Demon dove at Anna. Anna swiftly side-stepped and tripped the Demon. With the foe face down on the ground, Anna drove her sword through the Demon's back.

Anna pulled the blade free. She rolled over and looked up at her.

She's quite striking, Anna thought. It's such a shame that we have to fight each other.

The light faded from Demon's eyes. Anna looked across the battlefield. The left flank was also crumbling. Anna could not identify the Demons, but could see that copious amounts of Angels were falling under the onslaught.

The German troops had nearly captured the forward trench. Anna possessed a mortal woman and picked up a discarded Bren. She opened up on the enemy troops with withering effect. The Germans began to retreat across the dunes.

Anna assessed her surroundings. Zinc, Constance, and Eleanor had withdrawn from the fight. The British had withstood the onslaught at a critical position in their lines. Anna saw little need to charge into the fray once more.

I've done my part for the day.

She vacated her host and trotted away from the fighting. Once a safe distance away she opened a portal and returned to Heaven. She rushed through the Arrival Ceremony and ran into Zinc. He was busy arguing with Eleanor and Constance.

"Didn't lose too much brain matter I hope," Anna said.

Zinc turned toward her red faced, but her joke seemed to break the tension.

"It was only a graze," Zinc said.

"The knife caved in your skull," Eleanor said. "It was the best decision to pull back."

Eleanor patted Constance on the shoulder. Anna cringed inwardly, but Constance, to her credit, accepted the compliment.

"Yes, Lady Zinc, we did not know how many there were and their attack was unorthodox and well-coordinated," Constance said.

"How were things when you left?" Zinc asked.

"We took a battering, but I took down two of theirs and the mortals held the line. I don't think the German will break the lines there," Anna said.

"Good, good. Well done," Zinc said. "We have to regroup and get back there. The Germans cannot be allowed to take the Suez."

A Familiar arrived and handed Zinc a parchment. He read it, crumpled it, and tossed it across the marble floor.

"Another meeting." Zinc groaned. "It's almost as if my fellow Angels would rather sit around and talk about the war than fight it." He dragged himself to his feet. "Okay, let's go see what everyone has to say."

Chapter 8
Drawn Swords and Crossed Swords

The clang of a hammer striking against an anvil resounded across the Heavenly countryside. Silver grunted as he pounded the heated metal over and over until he was satisfied with the shape of the blade. Once the metal had cooled he filed the sides down to a keen edge.

"Ready?" Christa asked.

"I hope so let's go find Lilly," Silver said.

The couple met with their old friend and traveled to occupied Reykjavík.

"I swore I'd never come back to the Mortal Realm," Lilly said.

"This is pretty far away from any active fighting," Christa said.

"Besides, you can never say no to me," Silver said.

Lilly rolled her eyes.

The Celestial trio made their way to a house of ill repute. The brothel was teeming with British soldiers eager to spend their pay. In an upstairs room Silver and Christa possessed a pair of mortals who had recently completed their liaison.

From within the red-headed Mancunian, Silver looked about the humble room. *Kind of quaint, actually,* he thought, taking in the Nordic decorative touches.

Lilly handed him his recently forged blade. Celestial weapons dropped by Angels did not cross over into the Mortal Realm. Lilly, a Familiar, existed in a place between the Mortal and Celestial Realm. Therefore, she could transfer objects, such as the sword Silver had fabricated with the Forge of Albion, between the realms.

Christa held out the hand of her host. Silver opened a deep laceration in the mortal woman's palm. He cringed at the thought of cutting Christa. However, as had been the case on their multitude of prior attempts, the Angel within shook her head.

"Nothing?" Silver asked.

"Nothing beyond the usual sensation of a host's injury, but my hand is fine," Christa said.

"Damn it all!" Silver said.

He handed the sword back to Lilly.

The Angels departed their hosts. Freed of possession, the mortal prostitute unleashed an unearthly howl that contradicted her petite frame. She fired off a profuse tirade in Icelandic. The mortal man was at loss and frantically tried to calm the girl.

A moment later, two burly locals burst into the room. In the Celestial, Silver fell to the floor in a heap of laughter. The new arrivals, brawny imitations of the isle's Viking heritage, manhandled the perplexed Brit and pulled him from the room.

"Oh, poor lad," Silver said between giggles.

"Are we done here?" Lilly asked. She suppressed a grin.

The Celestials made their way back to Heaven.

"I know I can trust you to keep our lack of success to yourself," Silver said.

"Of course," Lilly said. "I would imagine Zinc would be quite frustrated with you." "Indeed, although he seems quite occupied at the moment," Silver said.

"Yes, I've heard from my descendants that his work with The Order of St. Patrick is quite involved," Lilly said.

"It's bought us some time to try to sort this out," Christa said.

"What exactly is the issue?" Lilly asked.

"We've tried all sorts of metals, copper, iron, gold, silver, lead, and all types of alloys, but none have replicated the Ur Lak," Christa said.

"It's bloody frustrating," Silver said. "We didn't go through all that just to find a single weapon. The forge is the real prize."

"Could there be something else we need to discover?" Lilly asked.

"I don't think so. Mên-an-Tol definitely felt like an 'X marks the spot' type of deal," Silver said.

"Well, I wish you luck, let me know next time you need to test out something in the Mortal Realm," Lilly said.

The Familiar departed.

"So what now?" Christa asked.

Silver shook his head in frustration, "I don't know. And although I appreciate that Zinc is distracted with his knightly society, our progeny and the rest of Heaven who are not part of St. Patty's Order are being slain at an alarming rate. We need to tilt the scale in our favor, now."

"I don't know, what was that mixture we just tried? Iron and..." Christa said.

"Zinc alloy, of all things," Silver chuckled. "Our overlord's metal does not seem to be the key."

"Maybe back to the library?" Christa asked.

"Wonderful," Silver groaned.

Anorexia walked through the Great Hall of Hell. She stopped for a moment beside Bubonic Plague's statue. It commemorated his victory at the fall of Babylon.

I wonder how my uncle is doing, surely he is itching to get back into the fight, Anorexia thought.

Schitz had called for a meeting of the senior Demons. When Anorexia arrived by the columns used for departure portals, the meeting was about to begin. Anorexia kept to the back of the crowd. She felt her pulse quicken as she watched Schitz address the gathering.

"Gentlemen and Ladies," he said, "I have called you away from your various ventures because our very existence is in far greater peril than ever before. The sinister forces of Heaven are waging a relentless campaign against the most esteemed of our ranks. While we have slaughtered innumerable foes, we are hemorrhaging on all sides. We must turn this pattern on its head and bleed their best and brightest."

Anorexia clapped her hands together as the assembled Demons applauded Schitz's enthusiasm. For her part, Anorexia felt far from hopeful. She had recently encountered Cancer and found out that the Demon's following had been experiencing catastrophic losses.

I wish we could just find an end to all this suffering. She looked at Schitz as he provided instructions to a Wraith.

"Travel to the Eastern Front. There is a rapidly approaching German offensive. Make sure that you are followed."

"Sir?"

"You heard correctly. Make no effort at stealth. Certainly, a Familiar will begin to tail you," Schitz said. "Let the Familiar overhear that I will be meeting Autism to plan an assault here." He pointed to a map of Kursk. "This is where the Soviet defenses will be at their highest, the perfect opportunity for the Angels to launch an ambush. Autism, you will already be there. You must both make the communication appear genuine, something exposed out of haste and not as intended deception."

Autism and the Wraith nodded in unison, saluted, and began making the requite symbols to open a portal to the Mortal Realm.

Anorexia thought about Cancer's advice vis-à-vis Schitz. *I should just put it on the table, I have wanted him for centuries.*

Schitz resumed his instructions. "The rest of you will arrive only at the time of the ambush. I am certain the Angels will attack. Until then, remain out of sight."

Schitz handed out maps.

Anorexia looked at the rendering of a portion of the front line within the Kursk Oblast region. *This is going to be brutal.*

"You will arrive exactly at 0945 hours. You cannot be seen until the moment you enter the fray," Schitz said.

Anorexia instinctively looked down at her wrist. She had taken a trench watch as a souvenir during the Great War. It was set to GMT. She would have to change to the local time for Kursk Oblast.

Several Demons began to mutter around her. They were voicing her sentiments.

"You will be leaving yourself exposed," she said. "If the plan deviates even slightly, the Angels will have you."

"I know," Schitz said. "I am the required bait for this plan to succeed but I firmly believe we will triumph if everyone does things right."

Schitz met her gaze when answering her question. Anorexia's knees turned rubbery. *He's always been dashing and brave – even when he was an awkward youth.*

Schitz walked from one veteran to the next, clasping each one upon the shoulder or by the hand. "Today, we will reverse the tide of the war. Today we will take back our own destiny," he said

Schitz made his way through the cheering formation. When he reached Anorexia, he put both of his hands on her shoulders. Her heart fluttered. For a moment she imagined he might kiss her. Then the spell broke and Schitz moved on and the acclaimed warrior stepped through the portal provided by Autism and Malchus.

The assembled Demons set off on their individual tasks.

"Looks like we're working together again," Cancer said.

"At least this time we don't have to jump out of a plane," Anorexia said.

"I hope Schitz is right. This squadron of Angels appears to be targeting my people in particular. I lost Liver Cancer and Fallopian Tube Cancer in Russia recently. I was almost killed as well," Cancer said.

Anorexia embraced the Academy Headmistress. "Well, now we're going to turn things around. They want to take on our best. We'll show them what we're made of."

Cancer nodded, "I hope so. It looks like we're crewing the same tank, the Tiger I. Are you familiar with it?"

"Yeah, I've commanded a few, you?" Anorexia asked.

"Yes, I'm quite comfortable with them," Cancer said.

"Good, I'll be counting on your accuracy on the gun," Anorexia said.

"I can't wait , I'm ready to get some payback," Cancer said.

The air was thick and humid among the lush countryside of West Hubei. Overcast clouds released a drizzle across the rural expanse outside of the town of Changjiao. AIDS had been tasked by Schizophrenia with raising hell in the Far East. The Empire of Japan had provided the perfect army for the task.

AIDS looked across the formation of Japanese soldiers. They were a sea of khaki and brown marching through the Chinese countryside. The mortals under his command had just massacred thirty thousand civilians over a three day period.

Uranium II hates that stuff, AIDS thought. He had read copious reports about the Angels he could expect to encounter in the Far East. The leader of the Asiatic contingent, Uranium II, was notorious for his skill in battle. However, his temperament was prone to frustration. AIDS knew from Wraith reports that his adversary was likely in Europe. *News of the slaughter will get back to him and he will be itching for a fight,*

He checked his pistol and holstered it. AIDS fidgeted and adjusted his host's katana scabbard. He knew the Nationalists and Angels would be reorganizing and setting up an ambush along the road to Taishi Bridge.

Memories of the Eastern Front filled AIDS's mind. He remembered being trapped in a mortal surrounded by Angels while Soviet tanks and infantry assaulted his position. *I learned a lot that day. I won't let myself get pinned down again.*

The lessons from the battle in the Soviet Union at Lushno had influenced AIDS's leadership style. He had taken recent Academy graduates Marburg Hemorrhagic Fever, Coronavirus, Huntington's Disease, Vampirosis, and Alzheimer's Disease under his command.

In a break from the typical team approach, AIDS had devised his own improvised course of instruction and then scattered his team across the map. They took up positions in China, Indochina, and the Solomon Islands.

We have to be able to stand alone. Our numbers are too few. With this global war it is better we learn to be comfortable fighting alone.

His squad was nimble and used Wraiths to communicate. The messengers allowed them to stay in the field and stay up to date on everyone's movements. If they encountered a large contingent of Angels, they could reinforce each other. Otherwise, they could assist the Japanese Empire and pick off the Angels left in Asia.

I wonder how the war in Europe is going. He thought of Schitz. A warm sensation of overwhelming admiration ran through him.

Schizophrenia had saved his life and taken the time to coach him. *I can never repay him. He also entrusted me with this important mission of seizing Asia for ourselves, I won't let him down. I can't let him down.*

AIDS's thoughts were interrupted by the staccato chatter of machine gun fire. Rounds cut through the Japanese soldiers and kicked up plumes of muddy water from the dirt road. AIDS dropped to the roadside and looked in the direction of the enemy fire.

The Chinese troops had concealed a trench with tree branches and foliage. The location of the machine gun gave them maximum advantage. However, the defenders were vastly outnumbered by the imperial troops. AIDS observed a trio of Angels manning and supporting the machine gun.

Perfect. His contingent's loose formation meant the Angels had spread out looking for him. It was difficult to locate a single Demon in an entire region. AIDS often encountered these small sentry clusters – they were easy to overcome.

AIDS rolled out of his host and possessed another mortal. Machine gun fire tore through his former host's body a moment after he had abandoned the possession.

Too slow. He raised the sight of his new host's bolt action rifle and fired just above the flashes coming from the machine gun. The mortal gunner and the Angel within collapsed to the ground. The remaining two Angels made the expected move into the Celestial to protect their seizing companion. By the time the foes had abandoned their mortals, AIDS had already hurled two throwing knives across the expanse. One knife struck the seizing Angel in the throat. The second knife struck its target in the chest.

The Japanese troops unleashed a withering barrage of fire in the direction of the silenced machine gun. The hailstorm of lead lasted for a moment, the stillness covered the countryside.

""Ni, Lai-Lai," a Japanese officer shouted, instructing the Chinese soldiers to come out in their native language.

A dozen Nationalist soldiers emerged from their position with hands raised. The cessation of the mortal battle spelled the end of the Celestial confrontation. AIDS looked in the direction of the surviving

Angels. A dark haired female was dragging an injured male Angel along the road. The throwing knife was still in his chest. He looked grim. AIDS raised two fingers to his forehead in a sarcastic salute.

The Chinese prisoners were standing in a line facing their captors. AIDS took the opportunity to possess a surviving Rikugun-Shōi. Once he was within the lieutenant, AIDS drew the officer's sword and in a swift motion decapitated the first prisoner. The severed head rolled along the muddy ground. AIDS looked toward the surviving Angel with a maniacal grin. She had given up on lugging her mortally injured comrade.

AIDS brought the sword crashing down on the neck of yet another helpless prisoner. Then another and another. The muddy road was awash in ever widening pools of crimson. When there were only three prisoners remaining, AIDS wiped the blade and nonchalantly returned it to it's scabbard.

"If you had surrendered right away, I would have spared all of you," he said to the prisoners. AIDS used the tactic to sow fear. The three survivors would relay their tale as well as the message to countless others. Now they would be hesitant in battle and quick to surrender.

AIDS's current possession was the highest ranking officer to survive the ambush. He roused the men to their purpose. Once more the column of troops advanced through the Chinese countryside. The imperial troops were in high spirits despite sustaining casualties.

Their grievance with the foe was quickly avenged, AIDS thought. *There's nothing soldiers enjoy more than seeing the fighting spirit stamped out of their enemies.* He could hear the men hum the strains of the Battōtai, the gunka song of the *Drawn-Sword Regiment.*

AIDS had a spring in his step as he looked through the light, summer rain across the green of the lush countryside. *These troops are fierce as tigers, they are good for my purpose.* He hummed along while marching.

Ware wa kangun waga teki wa
Tenchi irezaru chouteki zo
Teki no taishou taru mono wa
Kokon musou no eiyuu de[15]

Coronavirus stalked through the dense jungle foliage of New Georgia. The Japanese soldiers were more accustomed to the rugged conditions than their American counterparts. From within an imperial officer, the Demon surveyed the U.S. command post near Zanana Beach. The mortal troops had been harassed for several days. Coronavirus could tell the Americans' nerves were frayed. Their shooting was undisciplined and haphazard. The Demon stayed back allowing the first wave to disrupt the foes' position. In the night, he could see the Angelic silhouettes clearly. He remained low to the ground. Most of the Angels moved into the Celestial, choosing to avoid the carnage the Japanese were unleashing on the Americans.

---

[15] We are the Imperial Force and whoever disobeys us are the foes forsaken by the Heaven and the Earth. The head of the enemy, a legendary hero compared to none throughout history.

Coronavirus rose to his feet. He shouted to the next wave of infantry and led them into the fray. When he reached the end of the enemy's command post, he stepped into the Celestial. With a swipe he disemboweled an unsuspecting Angel. He moved on while her screams pierced the muggy night air. He decapitated the next foe and kicked the severed head toward his next target. When he raised his hands to cover his face, Coronavirus plunged his sword through the Angel's heart. He left the sword impaled in the victim. He reached to his back and drew his weapon of choice: a heavy ball and chain flail.

The surviving Angels encircled Coronavirus. He spun the flail over his head. He crushed one skull, tripped another Angel, and brought the weapon crashing down on her face. The surviving Angels retreated in disarray.

All around Coronavirus the Japanese troops shouted in victory as they captured the American position and routed what was left of the enemy.

Kore ni shitagou tsuwamono wa
Tomo ni hyoukan kesshi no shi
Kijin ni hajinu yuuaru mo
Ten no yurusanu hangyaku wo[16]

Huntington's Disease looked through a pair of worn field glasses. His gaze tracked the steep ridge on which the Japanese defensive position was constructed down to Tambu Bay below. He had spent the better part of a month possessing various officers and troops. Each host had detailed and accurate instructions embedded in his mind. The beach below was well and truly pre-sighted. When the Australians and Americans arrived, they would be caught in an ornate killing pattern.

Huntington's Disease slipped into the Celestial and sauntered through the jungle down to the beach. The Demon reclined against

---

[16] All the soldiers who follow him are the fearless warriors prepared to die. Although their courage rivals the fiercest god whoever rebel against the Imperials.

the trunk of a Papuan wattle tree and waited for the foe. When they arrived, he would be ready.

Okoseshi mono wa mukashi yori
Sakaeshi tameshi arazaru zo
Teki no horoburu sore made wa
Susume ya susume moro tomo ni[17]

Vampirosis shoved a five-round clip into her Type 30 bolt-action rifle. Incoming rounds sliced through the air around her. Branches snapped and cracked as the fusillade from the Chindits sailed past.

The Chindits were a special operations branch of the British military that conducted long range penetration missions behind Japanese lines in Burma. Angels frequently used these patrols to strike at Japanese positions.

Vampirosis spotted a burst of muzzle fire. She moved her sight over the target and fired. She ejected the spent cartridge and pushed the bolt back into place. Vampirosis spied a light aura through the Burmese undergrowth. She ducked behind a large Banyan tree. A storm of lead struck the trunk as the Angels targeted her host.

Vampirosis tossed her helmet to one side of the tree and broke cover on the other. She raised her rifle and fired at the possessed mortal. The Angelic aura dropped into the Celestial a moment before Vampirosis's shot cut down the Chindit.

Ah, a veteran, she thought. Vampirosis glanced to her flanks as she ducked back into cover. She saw a shadow moving among the trees. *And they're using Familiars.* The Demon pulled a Type 97 fragmentation grenade. She pulled the cord attached to the safety pin and tossed the frag in the direction of the shadow.

Gunfire erupted from behind the Japanese position. *They have us surrounded.* She saw a pair of Angelic auras amongst the new column of mortals. Vampirosis led her host through the brush as the chaotic fighting whirled around her. She put her back against a

____

[17] Those the heavens do not tolerate, none of them have prospered through all ages. Until our enemies fall, go forth, go forth, all together.

broad tree and embedded a thought into her host's mind: turn and fire on the British. Vampirosis stepped into the Celestial and drove a dagger into the trunk of the tree. She crouched behind her host so her aura would still be near the mortal. Vampirosis snapped her fingers next to the host and the mortal leaned out from cover. She fired a shot but was cut down a moment later.

Vampirosis stepped back behind the tree and grasped the handle of the dagger. She pulled herself up into the lowest level of branches. The Angels arrived in the Celestial in a tactical formation. They approached the tree from three separate directions. *Experienced fighters for sure.*

The Angels sensed a ruse and looked up into the tree. The Demon hurled a throwing star from each hand and dropped from her perch. The stars caught their targets in the throat. Vampirosis pinned the third Angel to the ground and punched her in the face. She struggled to wrestle free but went limp under the onslaught of blows. She throttled the foe until her eyes rolled back in her head and her frame spasmed.

Vampirosis retrieved her throwing stars from the vacant-eyed Angels. She drew her sword and began humming as she made her way through the Burmese jungle in the Celestial toward the next engagement.

Tamachiru tsurugi nuki tsurete
Shisuru kakugo de susumu beshi
Mikuni no fuuto mono no fu wa
Sonomi wo mamoru tamashii no[18]

Alzheimer's Disease sat in the cockpit of a A6M3 Zero Japanese fighter. The nimble craft zipped through the early morning sky over the Solomon Sea. Her host, Rikugun-Tai-I Fumiko Hasegawa, was an extremely accomplished aviatrix. However, the prospect of combat aviation was daunting for any Celestial.

The Demon's supernatural vision allowed her to spot a flight of American P-38s. Dustups between the Japanese flying out of Rabaul and Americans out of Bougainville had become fairly common. Even at the extreme distance, Alzheimer's could see the light aura that indicated Angelic possession within two of the cockpits of the enemy single-seater fighters.

We got the jump on them, Alzheimer's thought. She ordered half of her flight to attack directly while she climbed to a higher altitude. Alzheimer's considered her situation. Two against one was not ideal. On the ground such odds were trivial, but in the air it was a different story altogether. No matter how good she was, she could only engage one Angel at a time.

AIDS is radical in his stand alone strategy. Yet, I suppose, starting out at the worst possible odds means things can only get better during the battle. And the Angels are always looking out for my imaginary backup.

She pushed the Zero into a dive and lined up on the lead Angel. Her fighter shuddered as 7.7mm machine gun rounds flew from her plane. Alzheimer's smiled with glee when she saw the rounds tearing into the port engine of the P-38. She pressed the right rudder pedal and the Zero swayed to the right. Alzheimer's pulled the lever for the 20mm cannon.

Tracer trains arched across the cerulean sky and exploded over the cockpit of the twin-engine fighter. The large caliber shells shredded

---

[18] Unsheathing your swords glistening like a gem, go forth, resolved to die! The spirits who have defended the custom of the Imperial Land and the Samurais' bodies.

the mortal and sent the Angel into a departure seizure. The P-38 entered a death spiral towards the sea below. Alzheimer's pushed the throttle forward. There was no time to celebrate, the second Angel had broken into a turn and was maneuvering behind her.

Alzheimer's threw the Zero into a loop. The Angel followed, either in bloodlust or ignorance. The P-38 could not match the Zero in the maneuver. Alzheimer's came out behind the green fighter. Her prey banked and swerved, but the end was inevitable. The starboard engine caught fire and exploded, tearing the wing from the fuselage. Mortal and Angel within cartwheeled into the sea.

"Tennōheika Banzai!" Alzheimer's Disease shouted.

Ishiin kono kata sutaretaru
Nippontou no ima sara ni
Mata yo ni izuru mi no homare
Teki mo mikata mo moro tomo ni[19]

Marburg Hemorrhagic Fever rubbed her hands together. *Fuck, does it ever get warm here*, she thought. The Aleutian island of Attu was a barren rocky expanse. Even in the summer months, the Arctic air was cold.

Her detachment of troops was in a hopeless position. The American fleet controlled the waters around Attu and the combined American and Canadian Infantry divisions outnumbered the Imperial troops five-to-one.

"For the Emperor!" Marburg Hemorrhagic Fever shouted to her troops.

Blood-curdling cries of "Banzai!" echoed across the landscape. The imperial soldiers charged the American position. Marburg Hemorrhagic Fever cut her way through the mortals before her until she encountered a cluster of three Angels. The Demon made short work of the foe, cutting them to ribbons. The soldiers of the

---

[19] After the Restoration, all of them remain abolished, but we are still able to brandish our Katanas. We are honored to come back to life, all of our friends and foes.

301st Independent Infantry Battalion made their last stand. They fell in fierce hand-to-hand combat.

> *Yaiba no mono ni shisu beki ni*
> *Yamato-damashii aru mono no*
> *Shinubeki toki wa ima naruzo*
> *Hito ni okurete haji kakuna*[20]

Uranium II sat back in a chair in a Soviet Command bunker along the Kursk region. Arrayed across his host's desk were a myriad of intelligence reports pertaining to the upcoming German offensive. Yet, the Celestial report a Familiar had just brought him was all he could think about.

They are tearing through the heart of Asia and I am helpless to stop it, he thought. He seethed at his current predicament. He was required to be with Zinc and the Order of St. Patrick in Europe while his preferred region was being overrun by the Demons. He thought back to the assistance he had given the Imperial Japanese Navy at the Battle of Midway. *It would seem that they have more than enough help lately.* Wars in Asia were nothing new. However, the idea that the Demons could take hold of a mortal kingdom, let alone one so powerful as the Empire of Japan, was jarring.

I have to get back. His pulse raced and he glanced half-heartedly at the dispositions for the upcoming mortal battle. *This is not the way. As much as I love a good fight, this is not how we will beat them for good. We need to give the mortals a truly awe-inspiring weapon – one that will end the war and make future conflicts irrelevant, or give our side such cataclysmic power that we would obliterate any foe the Demons raise against us.*

There were books in the Heavenly library that detailed all sorts of concepts barely grasped by the mortals.

---

[20] They must fall beneath our blades, for those who possess the true spirit of Japan. Now is the time to die, do not bring yourself shame with delay.

Teki no horoburu sore made wa
Susume ya susume moro tomo ni
Tamachiru tsurugi nuki tsurete
Shisuru kakugo de susumu beshi[21]

AIDS looked across the dimly-lit briefing room of the Imperial Japanese Army Air Service base. The place looked vacant to the airfield's mortals – and the charts and maps appeared unattended – but the six Demons AIDS had summoned were hard at work.

He addressed the assembled, "This is the second part of our strategic design. You have all reported encounters with small, reconnaissance sized cadres of Angels. This is likely due to our dispersed approach – most of the Angels are in Europe. The remaining ones are stretched thin in the Pacific from the Aleutians to the Solomon Islands. It is time to concentrate our efforts in a coordinated hammer blow of a strike. All six of us will be involved."

AIDS pointed to a map of the operational area.

"We will strike the American airbase at Guilin. Wraiths report that the Angels have prioritized halting the Japanese Army here in China. Their efforts in the Pacific have been grinding and slow. We can expect a concentration of Angels working within the CACW.[22] Huntington's, you'll lead the bomber formation. Alzheimer's and Vampirosis will escort the bombers. From the air you will target the American airbase. Coronavirus and I will infiltrate on the ground to take out any Angels you send into departure seizures. Any that manage to takeoff you can kill in the air."

He looked across his assembled squad with glee. *They have been forged into veteran warriors.* He was particularly proud of his daughter, Vampirosis. She looked like her late mother, red hair and petite features. She was developing a reputation as a skilled aviatrix. *This mission will go well. I wonder how our comrades are faring in Europe.*

---

[21] Until our enemies fall, Go forth, go forth, all together! Unsheathing your swords glistening like a gem, Go forth, resolved to die!

[22] Chinese-American Composite Wing (Provisional)

The engine of Anorexia's Tiger I tank clanged and banged across the barren terrain of the Russian steppe. Throughout the morning she had checked her watch with obsessive regularity. Everything depended on a timely arrival.

Anorexia heaved open the cover of the turret and peered through her binoculars.

"Amazing," she said.

Schitz and Autism each manned an artillery piece. Various Phobias followed orders and fired. A squadron of five Soviet tanks leveled a barrage on an artillery position. Three tanks burned at the crest of the hill. The ground ahead of Anorexia overflowed with Angels. She did not hesitate.

She shouted her orders to Cancer. "One hundred and fifty meters, dead ahead, zero elevation, fire on the lead!"

The shell clanged into place. Anorexia could see a contingent of Angels within the Soviet T-34. *Come on Cancer*, she thought.

A moment later the steel colossus shuddered with an ear-rending explosion as the 8.8cm round was fired. Anorexia's vision jostled.

Downrange the lead tank exploded into flames. The round had struck between the turret and the chassis.

"That's a kill," Anorexia said into her headset. She smacked the roof of the turret and pumped her fist. The other tanks in the formation opened up on the remaining Soviet tanks with devastating effect. Schitz's plan had come off perfectly.

The battle between the Demons and Angels progressed into close quarters combat. Anorexia was still a hundred meters away. She cursed the slow progress of the tank. Schitz and Autism were still greatly outnumbered.

Anorexia dropped into the turret. She tapped Cancer on the shoulder and said, "Stay with the tank. If any other vehicles arrive, blast them."

Cancer nodded. "Good luck."

Anorexia left her host and pulled herself through the open hatch of the tank. She sprinted across the dusty, barren landscape. Ahead of her Schitz was perched atop a disabled tank. He tossed a handful of throwing knives and cut down five Angels. It was a miraculous feat. Anorexia could hardly believe what she had witnessed. She flushed with joy. The decisive engagement was going their way.

All happiness evaporated when Schitz stepped into a mortal host, an officer who immediately took a bullet to the head. While Schitz seized on the ground an Angel approached him with a raised sword.

Anorexia sprinted across the distance. *I could run the Angel through, but he still might bring his sword down on Schitz,* she thought. Anorexia dove forward and blocked Schitz's throat with her sword. The Angel's blade sparked against hers. Anorexia carried her forward momentum into the Angel and bowled him over.

The combatants tumbled away from Schitz. Anorexia was first to her feet. The Angel's sword was ten feet away. Anorexia raised her blade to dispatch him – until...

"Xiang!"

Lord Uranium II met her gaze, but said nothing.

Thoughts of Chu Hua crossed Anorexia's mind. *I will not repeat that folly, simply for loyalty to my side.*

"Your side is losing. Go while you can," Anorexia said.

Uranium II looked across the battlefield. Anorexia followed his gaze. The Tiger Is had closed the distance and were mowing down the remaining Russian infantry. Most of the Celestial combat consisted of the Demons finishing off the few surviving Angels.

Uranium II nodded in agreement. "Thank you, Anorexia," he said.

Anorexia felt relief. She took a deep breath and watched as Lord Uranium II scampered into a trench and hurried away. With her friend safe, she turned her attention back to Schitz. He was still lying on the ground.

Anorexia stretched out her hand and hauled Schitz to his feet. She looked into his cold, intense eyes. *They're filled with pain. Perhaps gratitude? If I had been a moment later, I would have never seen him again. How many close calls have there been over the centuries?*

She pressed her lips against his. He opened his mouth and brushed his tongue against hers. She wished it could have lasted longer.

"Glad you're still here," she said.

"Glad to be here," he said.

Something's wrong. He should already be back at a hundred percent. The seizure is long over, but he looks so ill.

"Please find me a portal," he said. "I can't be out here like this."

Autism arrived by their side and assisted in bracing up Schitz.

"Come on," Autism said. "We can use the hatch on that Tiger tank to get him home. Then we can attend to the others."

"The others?" Schitz asked.

"The field is ours," Autism replied, "but there are many wounded. I've never seen anything like it in all my life."

"That was a battle for the ages," Anorexia said.

Earth & Water

They staggered to the nearest Tiger tank. Anorexia made the requisite symbols in the dirt around the hatch of the tank and Autism began the ancient incantations while she lit a match. She looked about for an ignitable material. "Here," Cancer shouted from inside the tank. She tossed up her canteen and scampered through the hatch.

"Thanks," Anorexia said. She adjusted the symbols for earth and water and poured the contents of the canteen over the dirt.

As they lowered him into the tank, Schitz said, "See to the others."

Anorexia climbed down from the tank. Cancer followed her.

"You know from where I was seated, it looked like you and Schitz..." Cancer said.

"Oh, mind your own business," Anorexia said.

"Well, good to see you taking my advice. Maybe the two of you will attend one of my gatherings after all," Cancer replied.

"Hey, look at this one, rather famous he is," Autism said.

Anorexia walked over to where Autism was assessing an Angelic casualty. She was met by a familiar face, the Black Angel she had encountered at Waterloo. He had been cut down by Schitz's wondrous throw. A Demonic throwing knife still protruded from his heaving chest.

Autism raised his sword.

"Wait," Anorexia said. "His wounds are deep. He turns pale as we speak. I do not think he will leave this field. There is no need for more brutality. Today has already seen enough." She had quoted what Hydrogen said to her and Lung Cancer when he met them outside La Haye Sainte.

The Angel looked in her direction and cracked a weak smile.

"I remember you," Hydrogen said. His voice was weak and he choked on the blood in his mouth.

"Waterloo," Anorexia said.

"Aye," Hydrogen said.

"We can afford you the dignity of doing it yourself," Anorexia said.

Hydrogen nodded. "If you would help me up," he said.

Anorexia and Cancer helped Hydrogen onto his knees and handed him his sword.

"It is finished," Hydrogen said and fell on his sword.

Though impaled, the Angel shuddered and clung to life. Anorexia drew one of her throwing knives and drove it into his throat, ending his suffering.

Autism shrugged and resumed his search across the battlefield. Cancer assisted a handful of wounded Demons back through a departure portal.

"We got another one," Autism called to them. "Oh fuck."

All Demons knew the Archangel Michael Zinc II. He had grown in notoriety over the centuries much like the Angel they had just dispatched.

Anorexia was preparing her exit when her brother spotted the injured Angel. The foe was within an incapacitated host. The duo of

Demons possessed nearby mortals so that they could deal with the straggler.

Anorexia was immediately aware that her mortal host was full of respect for the mortal the Angel was possessing. *If it's the same for the other vacant mortals this could be tricky*, she thought.

The Angel was within an injured German and the surrounding mortals would be hesitant to kill the host.

"So, you shot the Rottenführer," Autism said.

He was addressing the mortal possessed by Zinc. The surviving panzergrenadiers had assembled around their injured comrade and listened intently. Zinc's host was an SS-Untersturmführer, the highest-ranking among them. It was clear the mortals sided with Zinc's host.

"Yes," Zinc replied. "Apparently, he lost his mind; he shot Hans, Gunther, and Fredrick. He shot them all dead."

"It's true, sturmscharführer," one of the non-possessed grenadiers said.

"Jawhol, sturmscharführer, I saw it as well," another soldier said.

Autism and Anorexia were the only Demons still in the field. Autism cursed under his breath. The mortal's injury hid the Angel's aura, so he had not been finished off during the fighting. If more Demons had been present during the mop-up, they could have possessed all the surrounding humans, deemed Zinc a traitor for killing the other Germans, and executed him. Alas, this was not to be.

"I had no choice, sturmscharführer," Zinc said.

Anorexia felt her pulse race. They were so close to killing two of Heaven's most storied Angels. Yet, without mortal violence they could not kill the Angels host or the Angel. Her frame shook with frustration when she saw the Angel smirk within his host.

He knows that there's nothing we can do to get him, Anorexia thought.

"Take him to the field hospital at once," Autism said.

He sighed as he stepped into the Celestial.

"There's nothing we could do about that one," Anorexia said. "He's just lucky. Maybe he will bleed out before he gets back to Heaven."

Autism shrugged. "One can only hope."

"Only two of them got away—that one and the one I got off Schitz," Anorexia said. "All in all, we brought down nineteen Angels. We only lost three: Claustrophobia, Autophagy, and Seasonal Affective Disorder – all juniors."

Autism stepped up to the Tiger's turret.

"Ready for a hero's welcome?" he asked.

"That's the spirit," Anorexia said.

She dropped through the hatch and passed through the portal in the process.

"Having a good sleep?"

Anna opened her eyes and was met with the vision of her glaring overlord. He lifted her from the cot by her throat. Anna coughed. Zinc dropped her.

Anna rolled on her side – and saw Constance.

The cobwebs began to clear. They had been in a Soviet tank keeping an eye on Zinc. When a shell hit the T-34, both Anna and Constance went into departure seizures. She remembered nothing else. She had not experienced a departure seizure for a long time. Anna knew experiencing one after a long time could lead to a violent sickness.

That's why I was unconscious, she thought. *I could have died. I wonder if I was even attended to.*

"Our tank was hit," Anna said.

"So were all the others," Zinc said.

He collapsed onto the floor beside the cot and rested his head in his hands. After a moment, he looked up – apology in his eyes.

"Sorry, about that," he said. "It wasn't your fault."

Anna rubbed her throat and tried to hide her rising resentment.

"Don't worry about it," she said.

"We lost Hydrogen and his sons," Zinc said. "Uranium lost many of his kin. The Order of St. Patrick has been decimated." His voice caught – almost a sob. "It's Teutoburg Forest all over again."

A heavy silence fell over the room.

"It's not really though," Anna said.

"How?"

"Well, the old politics are gone," Anna said. "No enemies will rise up to challenge your position. You and Uranium II are codified as unassailable leaders. You are secure in victory or defeat."

Zinc leaned forward and embraced her. It was as jolting as when he had choked her.

"You're right," he said. "We will dust ourselves off and go again."

Anna nodded.

"Get some rest. I'll be counting on you two."

Anorexia touched the Knight's Pentagram around her neck. It made her think of the way Spanish Influenza had lusted after awards and recognition. She wasn't immune to such emotions herself. She had waited a long time to enter the pantheon of Hell's knights.

I can't wait to show Bubonic Plague, she thought.

The Great Hall was full of Demons. All were in a festive mood. The engagement at Kursk had been a long awaited, decisive victory.

Titus approached her with a broad grin plastered across his face.

"I heard it was you who brought back the lion sword of Gabriel Hydrogen," Titus said.

"Have a look yourself," Anorexia said. She reached to her waist and drew the curved sword she had taken off of Hydrogen. The handle was composed of ornate gold and the pommel was shaped like a lion's head.

"Truly impressive," Titus said.

"Keep it," Anorexia said. "Add it to the Church's haul of trophies and relics."

"Most generous of you," Titus said.

"I already have a Standard Bearer's sword," she said. "And this." She pointed to the Knight's Pentagram.

"Yes, congratulations. That was much overdue," Titus said. The High Priest reached into the pocket of his robe and retrieved a medal. "Perhaps you could give this to Schitz for me?"

Anorexia took the medal. Her eyes widened.

"Knight's Pentagram with Crossed Swords. I haven't seen one of these in a long time."

"Yes, Satan was rather enraged that Schitz carried out the mission against his orders. However, he was equally impressed with the result. So, yet another unceremonious pinning ceremony for Schitz. Hence why he didn't want me to give him the award directly," Titus said.

"He favors that method," Anorexia said. She recalled the time Spanish Influenza was knighted without fanfare after Vicksburg. Schitz had told her that he received his Second Class in a muted ceremony.

"But why was Satan angry?"

"He told Schitz to scrub the mission," Titus said. "Satan didn't want you, Schitz, Autism, Cancer, et al in the same place at the same time. Thought it too risky."

"I didn't know we were going rogue," Anorexia said. "Now it all makes sense. No wonder our Lord looked so furious during the ceremony."

Titus chuckled. "It all worked out. And it would seem the Devil is happy enough. He called the Crossed Swords a 'peace offering' or 'peace overture' something like that. Point is, he would like to get along with Schitz."

Josephine cut in on the conversation.

"Excuse me, Titus," she said. "The artisan Wraiths have some questions regarding the Kursk statue."

Anorexia assessed the Wraith. The elevation of mortal consciousness that had accompanied the advent of gunpowder and the rise of the modern age had affected the passage of time. Wraiths reached their perpetually elderly state much quicker than in days of yore. Josephine, though young, appeared as a late middle-aged woman. The decimation of the Wraiths in battle had elevated her to the most senior position. She was known for her effectiveness and charisma.

Well, her skills and her romantic relationship with Schitz seem to have aided her career, Anorexia thought.

"Ah, pardon me, dear," Titus said.

"I'll make sure to give your regards to Schitz," Anorexia said.

A smug look passed across Josephine's face at the mention of Schizophrenia. Anorexia hated the Wraith for the glint in her eyes, and the meaning behind her smile. She turned away before her frustration became obvious.

Is there anyone he hasn't slept with? No, I will not dwell on such thoughts; today is a happy day.

Anorexia's pulse was racing when she knocked on the door of Schitz's room.

"Come," he said.

Anorexia pushed open the door,

"They finally gave it to me!" she said.

She fairly pranced around the room, gesturing toward her neck.

"The Knight's Pentagram," he said. "I'm proud of you."

Schitz sat up, slowly. Anorexia dialed back her celebration.

He's still looking ill, she thought.

"Are you feeling better now?"

"Yes, I am, thanks," Schitz said. "And I mean it; I am so happy for you. You've earned the award three times over now."

"And you deserve this," Anorexia said. She tossed a medal into Schitz's lap. She hoped she appeared care-free and playful.

Schitz stared at a Knight's Pentagram with Crossed Swords.

He's happy, even if he's less outwardly exuberant than me.

He smiled. It was a little weak, but the grin still aroused her.

"Titus said to give it to you," Anorexia said. "He called a peace overture from Satan."

She grinned from ear to ear and stepped closer to Schitz. An uneasy silence enveloped the room.

Ugh, say something.

"I... I never thanked you sufficiently for saving my life," he said.

Anorexia leaned forward. "What constitutes sufficient thanks?" she asked.

Anorexia could hear Cancer's advice ringing in her head. "Take what you want,"

She flicked her tongue across his lips. She felt warmth rising within her.

"I cannot give you what you want," he said.

Embarrassment, frustration, rejection and all sorts of emotions swirled in her mind. Tears formed in the corners of her eyes.

"Just once," she said. She placed her hand on his chest. "Just once, let me be the one who pleases you."

She closed her eyes and rubbed his chest. Her other hand slid down his torso.

"Just once," she said, her mouth by his ear. "It's all I've wanted for as long as I can remember."

This time, he did not move away. *Maybe he's giving in.*

"I wish I could," he said.

"I don't understand," Anorexia said. She was beginning to pout. "You have slept with more than your fair share of maids after Rubella."

Indignation sprawled across Schitz's face. He raised his palms.

"Let me explain," he said. "Sit down for a second."

He patted the bed. She sat beside him with her arms folded across her chest like a disappointed child.

"It is true," he said, "I have had my dalliances, but I have never replaced Rubella with any of those women. I have not given any part of myself to them. Each time I considered it, that woman has died." His voice cracked a little. "The way you love me... the way you love me, I don't deserve it. It's amazing. If I were to be with you, I would give all of myself to you, and if anything were to happen to you..."

This is so awkward. Why are we both crying?

She wiped his cheek.

"I have to keep you at a distance," he said. "I cannot lose you—"

"That's unfair. Don't I have a say in this?"

Schitz chuckled. "Actually, you do not. I am the elder... I am in charge."

She huffed in disgust.

"Let's do this," he said. "Lie here with me."

The two reclined onto his bed in a lovers' embrace. Satisfaction spread across Anorexia's face.

This is nice, even if it's not what I came for.

After a long while, Schitz spoke. "So, how awkward was my absence?"

Anorexia convulsed in laughter. "It was grossly obvious. Everybody kept on insisting they should go and get you. They applauded your bravery, and your miracle throw is now the stuff of legend. Last I heard someone tell the tale, you brought down a dozen Angels with only four knives! Ha!"

She laughed so hard she started gasping for air. "Satan was furious, but there's nothing he could do. You sort of left out the part about his not approving your mission."

She slapped at him with both hands, beating on his shoulder while she cackled. Then... the mood grew serious.

Anorexia felt her moment slipping through her fingers. *I have to do something.*

"I understand we can't be together, but I have waited for you my whole life," she said.

"You mean, you've never?" he asked.

"Never," she replied.

I wonder if that's alluring, or pathetic, in the eyes of such a playboy.

"What about while possessing a human?"

"Never."

"What about Mono?"

"Never."

She waited... he waited... the silence grew oppressive.

"I deserve to feel like a woman," she said.

"I really don't deserve you," Schitz said. "But consider this a one-time, never to be repeated, post-award celebration."

I didn't even know it was possible to be so committed to being non-committal. At any other time, the mood would have been shattered. But this was her moment.

He kissed her mouth, then her neck... her chest... her stomach. He opened the folds of her robe, baring her smooth sex. Instinctively she raised her knees on either side of his head.

Anorexia's grip upon the lion's skin blanket turned her knuckles white. Her body went rigid. Then she surrendered to a sea of ecstasy.

They held one another for hours. Finally, Schitz broke the silence.

"I'm sorry, that we cannot be more to each other."

Little does he know, this is just the start.

"You fool," she replied. "This is the most wonderful day of my life. I'll always love you, Schitz, and I'll always have this moment with you."

Schitz appeared to accept her sentiment.

If it takes him thinking there are no strings, so be it. Today, I won't be denied.

Schitz offered no resistance when Anorexia climbed on top of him.

Chapter 9
The Destroyer of Worlds

Uranium II made his way through the Heavenly library. He felt ill at ease amongst the quiet of the academic center. He felt more at home on the training ground. *Scholarship has its uses, but I prefer the knowledge passed on from senpai to kōhai over that which resides in dusty manuals,* he thought.

He had gone through the irritating, bureaucratic process of acquiring permission to enter the restricted portion of the library. He collided with the defrocked Lord Silver when he rounded a bookcase.

"Ah, pardon me, Albert," Uranium II said. He pronounced the name with a French accent.

"Oh, thank you, most mispronounce it," Silver said.

Uranium II shrugged, "You and your brother's story was always fascinating to me. More interesting than most of what you'd find in these books anyway."

Silver smiled, "You must be a rebel then as well. And yet, you have your permission slip there atop your books."

"How did you get back here?" Uranium II asked.

"A while ago, I punched one of the librarian Familiars in the face. After that, they kind of let you do whatever you want," Silver replied.

Uranium II chuckled. "That would have saved me some time. The Priests are horribly slow when it comes to paperwork."

"Most Priests are horrible when it comes to anything useful," Silver said. "What are you looking up?"

Uranium II felt uncomfortable sharing the details of his work. He did not know Silver – he'd only heard the gossip.

"Don't worry, say no more," Silver said, reading his trepidation.

"It's just..."

"No, no it's fine, I should have figured it was something secretive," Silver said. "Mortal sciences and all. I'm sure it's fascinating."

I suppose I wasn't very clandestine, only grabbing books about fission and fusion.

"Well, thank you for understanding. It was nice to make your acquaintance," Uranium II said.

"Likewise, Supreme Commander," Silver said.

"Call me Xiang. After all you are my elder," Uranium II said.

Silver's false teeth flashed in a bright smile. He began walking towards the exit.

"I thought we couldn't leave with the sensitive volumes?" Uranium II said.

"Just punch them in the face," Silver said. Several Familiars looked up; none said anything.

Uranium laughed. *I like him. He definitely lives up to his reputation.*

Mortals often confused the Devil as a fallen Angel, whereas the actual fallen ones were the brothers Gold and Silver. The pair were indeed charismatic and full of personality. It was no surprise that mortals lusted after their associated metals long after the curative effects of the elements had dissipated.

Uranium II left the library and made his way to Los Alamos. The New Mexican desert was picturesque and beautiful in their rocky, barren expansiveness. The distant Sangre de Cristo Mountains rose with grandeur toward the sapphire sky.

Such a wondrous locale for such a devastating laboratory, Uranium thought.

He deeply regretted his part in giving such a weapon to Americans. Uranium II shook his head as he made his way through the laboratory in the Celestial.

I would have preferred to have gifted atomic weaponry to an Asian country. These Demons have stolen so much from me. After Kursk he had been free to return to Asia, however, the Demons had embedded themselves deeply within the Empire of Japan.

How frustrating that I have to give this knowledge to such a horrible people. Well, no point in dwelling on it. The sooner the war ends, the sooner we can consolidate our gains and unify the world against the forces of Hell.

The concepts Uranium II had gleaned from the ancient materials had existed for time immemorial. However, humans had been far too simple to unearth the designs during previous eras. The most recent elevation in mortal consciousness (that had brought about firearms) had given rise to countless advancements.

Uranium II gazed from scientist to scientist. *I have to be strategic, for I can only possess each mortal once. Yet, they are smart and know some of the mystery already. Let us unleash the power of the atom.*

The Manna bakery operated at a frenetic pace during the later years of the Second World War. Anna often had to decide between overworking the addict Familiars and running out of life-saving bread. A fine balance, one complicated by the copious time she spent looking after Zinc.

"You seem busy," a recognizable, feminine voice said.

Anna turned to see Rachael leaning against the doorway to the storage room.

"Rach!" Anna said. She embraced her platonically and kissed her on the cheek.

Rachael returned the hug.

"It's good to see you," Anna said. "I'm sorry about Hydrogen."

"Thank you. He was a good and decent Angel. I'll miss him dearly. It's an added pain that he was killed by Schizophr— the Demon that murdered Benjamin," Rachael said.

Anna tensed. Suddenly the storage room felt very small. She realized Rachael stood between her and the only exit. *It's like so many of the ambushes we instigated for Zinc,* Anna thought.

Memories of Rachael attempting to gouge her eyes out flooded Anna's mind.

"Oh, no, no I'm so sorry! I didn't mean it like that," Rachael said. "It...it has nothing to do with you. I see now how horrible it was of me to take that out on you."

She stepped forward and touched Anna on the cheek. Anna hated the feeling of being vulnerable as much as she hated being helpless. Yet, she was relieved by Rachael's words.

"You've already apologized for that a long time ago," Anna said.

"I still feel bad. I think I always will. But the truth is, this whole conversation has gotten horribly sidetracked," Rachael said. She moved her hand from Anna's cheek down to her shoulder. Her gaze was both unnerving and alluring.

Rachael continued, "The truth is. Although, I am devastated by Gabriel's demise. I have been presented with an unprecedented opportunity. I've been offered the lordship of the Hydrogen House. Apparently, God would be happy to see me as its Standard Bearer, rather than see it unincorporated."

"A female Standard Bearer?" Anna asked.

"I'd be the first," Rachael said.

"And well deserving. Your record is beyond compare. I don't know of an Angel living or dead who has killed more Demons," Anna said.

Rachael smiled. Her grin was almost self-effacing, which was uncharacteristic for her.

"Well, I didn't come to brag, to my teacher," Rachael said, "but thank you. You are very kind. I know you spurned a full reconciliation before. I thought maybe...now with things being different, perhaps you would consider being...the Lady of a House."

"You mean, your wife? Would that even be allowed?" Anna asked.

"You've never cared much about what was allowed," Rachael said.

Anna felt warm with excitement and arousal. Yet, her mind protested with all the reasons she was scared to be vulnerable to Rachael. Her thoughts were silenced when Rachael pressed her lips against hers. Anna ran her hands over Rachael and pulled her closer.

Rachael grabbed Anna's hair close to her scalp and jerked her head back. Anna gasped. The brief moment of pain was followed by Rachael delicately nibbling on her neck. Anna groaned. The sensation of pleasure was almost too much to bear. Rachael moved down, kissing her chest. She parted Anna's robe and continued down.

Anna's legs were wobbly. She tried to steady herself and knocked several containers of Manna to the floor. Rachael turned her head in the direction of the fallen containers.

"Don't stop," Anna said and pushed Rachael's face back between her thighs.

Anna almost succeeded in stifling her screams as she climaxed. Fighting to catch her breath she pushed Rachael onto her back and reciprocated.

Beatrice's voice echoed through the rear of the bakery. "Oh, you know she might be in the storage room," She was speaking much louder than would have been necessary.

"Shit!" Anna said.

Rachael scampered to her feet and crouched in the corner beside the door. A moment later the door swung open. Zinc stood in the doorframe.

My robes are a mess, Anna thought. *I hope it isn't incredibly obvious.*

Zinc looked at her, glanced down at the scattered Manna, back at her. A look of fascination crossed his face, then vanished.

"Meet me in the Great Hall in a few minutes," he said. "I fancy an air mission."

Since his second wife, Eleanor, had passed away, Zinc had been perpetually gruff in his interactions. He stalked away without waiting for her to reply.

"Want me to help you pick those up?" Beatrice asked.

"Oh, that's alright. I've got things well in hand," Anna said.

"Oh, I'm sure you do," Beatrice said with a wicked grin.

The award ceremony for AIDS was a quiet affair. Demonic casualties were high following the Allied invasion at Normandy. The legendary Academy Headmistress, Cancer, had fallen. Her death had left many sullen Demons. Even Huntington's Disease, originally assigned to AIDS's Pacific contingent had been killed after his redeployment to Europe.

However, despite the pall among Hell's fighters, there was joy in AIDS's accomplishments. After he had been awarded the Knight's Pentagram, many fighters milled about the Great Hall, anxious to hear tales of his exploits.

Anorexia looked across the assembled. She felt a twinge of jealousy. Schitz was engaged in conversation with AIDS and Josephine the Wraith. From what Anorexia could hear, Josephine was telling a story about the Great War. The trio laughed and Josephine clutched Schitz's forearm with familiar affection. Anorexia's blood boiled.

"How goes it, Sis," Autism asked.

Her brother handed her a chalice of Brew. Anorexia swirled the cup and took a large gulp.

"Do you remember celebrating after the fall of Babylon?" she asked.

"Feels like forever ago," Autism said.

Anorexia gazed through the large open archway past which the Styx flowed. She remembered Mono and Mumps battling for her attention while Measles boasted about the Angels he had killed. Schitz and Rubella had been farther along by the river's edge. In her memory, the old timers were there too: Diphtheria, Bubonic, Smallpox, Syphilis, and others.

"So many are ghosts now," Anorexia said.

"I'm sorry?"

"Oh, nothing, just so many that celebrated on that day are gone," Anorexia said.

"Well, we have to enjoy life while we can. I miss Reye's Disease a lot. It would have been pointless to wait until the final victory to look for happiness. I'm glad we had our time together, even if this unending war cut it short," Autism said.

Anorexia thought of Schitz. She longed to seize happiness with him. He had been insistent that there were no strings attached to their liaison, but she was certain she could win him over.

"I agree. Our world is bleak, where and when we can find some joy it is important to take it," Anorexia said.

"I have to admit, I'm a bit jealous of AIDS though. I had to wait forever for my Knight's Pentagram, you too."

"It just means that much more to us who waited for it," Anorexia said. Her gaze involuntarily strayed over to Schitz.

"Oh dear," Autism said following her stare.

"No, it's fine, things are quite good with us recently," Anorexia said.

"Alright, he's my friend, but I don't want to see you get hurt. I think he'll always be a bit of a man-whore…" Autism trailed off as Schitz approached them.

"Friends!" Schitz said. He pulled both siblings into an embrace with either arm. "I'm so glad to see you well." Schitz kissed Anorexia on the cheek and tousled Autism's hair.

"Likewise, and congrats on your friend AIDS there. I was shocked to hear you tasked a youngster with tackling all of Asia and even more shocked he came out on top," Autism said.

"Yeah, I got the chance to fight alongside him during Barbarossa. He's very talented," Schitz said.

"Do you think we'll be switching over to his area of operation? Things seem almost wrapped up in Europe. I doubt the Allies are going to bother invading Norway or Denmark," Autism said.

"I don't think so," Schitz said. "I'd rather prepare for the next war. Even if we could save the Empire of Japan, I don't want to give the Angels any chance at a large-scale, pitched battle. We saved our cause with the casualties we heaped on them at Kursk, but we are still vulnerable to a crippling defeat."

"Fair enough, I wonder what the next war will be like," Autism said.

"Well, I'm sure it will be here soon enough. Until then, do either of you fancy spending some time with a fighter squadron?"

"I hate flying," Autism said.

"All the more reason to hone your skills," Schitz said.

"I'll go for a ride," Anorexia said.

A mischievous look passed across Schitz's face. "Lovely, let's get to it."

Anna walked alongside Zinc and Constance. They passed by a row of Yak-9, single-seater fighters of the Soviet Union's 278th Fighter Aviation Division.

"I don't like it," Constance said.

There was only one active female pilot in the squadron, which meant only one of Zinc's bodyguards could accompany him.

"It'll be fine. Anything that can end this war sooner," Zinc said. "If I can help these Russians on their way to Berlin, we can consolidate our gains sooner and get ready for the next war."

"We'll be back in no time," Anna said from within her mortal host.

Anna climbed up the wing of the sturdy Soviet aircraft and stepped into the cockpit. *I hate flying,* she thought. She did not dwell on the vulnerabilities of air combat. Anna ran through her host's skillset and taxied to the runway.

Angels and Demons had canny eyesight and could see the auras of friends and foes from great distances and even through objects. Anna was appreciative of the Celestial cloak that hid her aura, especially when flying. She could blend in with the rest of the mortal squadron.

Once they were aloft, Anna alternated between watching Zinc and scanning the sky for enemy aircraft. As the fighter cut through the air, Anna found her thoughts drifting.

I never actually gave Rachael an answer, we just fell into intimacy. I guess she's assuming that was a way of saying yes, but still, I should confirm. Should I? I'm never going to find Schitz again. I should be happy. I am. Aren't I?

"Hitlerovtsy, ahead and below," Zinc said over the radio.

Anna's focus returned to the task at hand. They were in an advantageous position – higher than the foe with the sun to their back. Anna could see a Demonic aura within one of the 109s. She throttled forward and followed Zinc into a dive.

Although the German fighter was outnumbered and at a disadvantage, he did not retreat. Anna gritted her teeth as she watched

Zinc's phosphorous tracers sail wide of the mark. Worse than failing to shoot down the enemy, Zinc sailed past the German craft and ended up directly ahead of the foe.

Anna maneuvered her plane and aligned her gunsight over the enemy fighter.

I got your back, Lord Zinc.

A vicious series of explosions rocked the cockpit. It sounded like hail striking a window pane. Machine rounds punched through the cowling of the Yak-9's engine. The barrage only lasted for a split-second before the enemy zipped past.

"Fuck!" Anna shouted.

Any hope of assisting Zinc died with the fatal blow to the Yak-9's engine. Thick plumes of smoke belched from holes in the plane's skin. Anna moved the control column, but it had little effect. The propellers were still spinning but without effect. Flames licked across the canopy.

Anna considered bailing out, but a glance at her altimeter told her she was too low.

"Come on, keep it together for me," she said to the plane.

Anna did her best to guide the stricken craft to the ground.

"Fast enough not to stall, slow enough not to crash," she said to herself. She watched the German countryside grow larger with every second.

Anna screamed at the shock of the impact when the Yak-9 hit the ground. The fighter burrowed its way across the grassy field and came to a groaning stop. The engine's flames filled the cockpit with unbearable heat.

Anna opened the canopy and threw herself from the aircraft. She took a few steps with her host and then stepped into the Celestial. It was an odd sensation to be back on the ground so quickly. She looked toward the sky. There were other oil trails cutting across the blue expanse. From the ground it was difficult to tell the outcome of the battle. However, Anna had the sense that the Soviet squadron had been shot to pieces.

There's not much I can do for Zinc. I hope he fared better than me.

Anna began looking for anything she could use to construct a portal.

AIDS and Vampirosis sat on the wing of a RAF Gloster Meteor from the 616 Squadron in Melsbroek, Belgium. They had stayed behind in the Celestial after the pilot and ground crew departed. Father and daughter conversed as the warm summer evening settled in around them.

"I prefer the Me-262 to the Meteor," Vampirosis said.

"Any particular reason, other than it being what we used during the war?" AIDS asked.

"It handles better and feels more solid in a dive," Vampirosis said.

The war in Europe had ended with the death of Hitler and demise of the Third Reich. For the Demons committed to the European struggle, the end of hostilities offered the opportunity to learn about the other side's machinery.

"Fair enough. I try to avoid flying when I can," AIDS said, "Dangerous stuff."

"It's only dangerous if you're unskilled," Vampirosis said. Her extra sharp, abnormally long teeth glistened when she smiled.

"I didn't say I was unskilled," AIDS said, "just that I don't prefer it. I've logged my hours. I simply prefer my feet on the ground."

Vampirosis kicked her legs back and forth in the empty air under the wing of the jet fighter. "I love the freedom of flying. It is intoxicating. Sometimes I wish I could stay up there forever."

"You're a good pilot, and a good fighter," her father said. "I'm proud of the work you did back East."

Vampirosis grinned. "Do you think we'll be going back?"

"No, Schitz seems to be done with this war. He's already focused on preparing for the next one," AIDS said.

"You get along with him well?" Vampirosis asked.

"He saved my life during Barbarossa," AIDS said. "I was stuck and surrounded, fighting for my life. I got myself into a horrible position; couldn't leave my host – enemies everywhere. He showed up, killed all the Angels one, two, three, and I got to go home. I owe him a lot for that."

"Is that why he tasked you with the Asia mission?"

"In part. He said I did well despite ending up in such a precarious position. I also happened to be present at the moment he needed someone to lead."

A Wraith emerged from around the nose of the jet. "There you two are," she said. "You have to get back to Hell at once. Something big has happened."

AIDS and Vampirosis looked at one another. They shrugged and followed the Wraith back to a hangar where she opened a portal. Upon arriving back in Hell, AIDS was shocked to see the Priest station vacant. No one was performing the Arrival Ritual.

"Never seen that before," AIDS said.

"There he is," a voice shouted from a crowd of Demons assembled in the Great Hall. AIDS never really felt shy, but the convergence of attention in his direction made him take a step back. The crowd engulfed AIDS and propelled him into the hall. He looked back toward Vampirosis. She smiled and shrugged.

"Ah, there you are," Schizophrenia said from the head of the assembled. Schitz was standing at the foot of the statue commemorating his victory at the Plains of Abraham.

"What on Earth is going on?" AIDS asked the senior Demon.

"Well, it would seem the Angels were not too happy with the control you established over the Empire of Japan," Schitz said. "Even after we pulled you back to Europe, the units and commanders you influenced have been leading a war that would make any Demon proud. To combat that, the Angel Uranium II has gone rogue and given the mortals technology far beyond their current understanding. They've dropped a bomb with the power of the sun on a Japanese city."

The news stunned AIDS.

Why are they all so happy though? He thought.

Schitz continued. "The Angels were already on thin ice after their invasion of Hell. Surely, this violates the Divine Dictum. The Titan must hand us victory in the conflict."

AIDS smiled. He had enjoyed running riot across the continent of Asia, but he could have never imagined that it would trigger such a response.

"Well, that's some good news," AIDS said.

The crowd of Demons erupted into more raucous cheers.

Circades paced the length and breadth of the empty boardroom. *They can find me too easily*, he thought. He recalled the Familiar informing him that God wished an audience with him. *It was just like Svaha and Varuna, they can always find me with ease.*

As though summoned by his thoughts, Varuna the Water Elemental entered the room through a portal formed in the doorway. Circades slid his left hand, along with Hyperion's ring, into his pocket. He knelt and bowed his head.

"No need for all that formality, appreciated as it is," Varuna said.

"What do you require of me?" Circades asked. He noticed that Varuna was not accompanied by his wife. *I wonder if that's of any significance*, Circades thought.

"I heard that you're meeting with God. I can only assume it is about the two bombs?" Varuna asked.

"You are certainly well informed," Circades said.

"Indeed. Those bombs represent a threat to...everybody, even us Ethereals," Varuna said.

Interesting, they have vulnerabilities beyond Titans and Celestials now.

"Do you still want me to keep the war between God and Satan going?" Circades asked.

"Yes, it keeps both sides weak and ensures a steady flow of souls through the waters of the Styx and Eunoe," Varuna said.

"Alright, I'll come up with something," Circades said.

"Good, you just keep things the way they are. Keep me strong and maybe one day I will tell you the location of your elusive love," Varuna said.

Circades remained silent, stupefied.

Varuna laughed, a deep rumbling bellow. "Her soul passes

through water whenever the mortal life of her host ends. It flows through either the Styx or the Eunoe. I'm aware of her and all mortal souls at all times."

Circades's hands trembled and his facial muscles twitched. *All this time, all this effort, and he could have just told me! I could have spent every lifetime with her,* Circades thought.

"You seem upset," Varuna said. "Well, hard work is its own reward, or something like that." His laugh was harsh and hollow.

"I will continue to maintain a balance here on Earth. However, I am neutral in their conflict, if one side should gain the upper hand, there is little I could do," Circades said.

"They're both very resourceful at avoiding destruction," Varuna said. "Just do your part."

The Elemental turned from Circades and snapped his fingers. A portal opened in the doorway of the boardroom. For a moment Circades considered shooting him in the back. Hyperion's ring rendered the bullets in his sidearm lethal to Elementals and Celestials.

I could do it. I could end him. But what would that mean for the world, for me, for Pulwabi. I risked everything to get the ring, but do I have the balls to use it now?

Varuna vanished through the portal just as the door swung open. God and his attaché, the Priestess Gertrude, entered the room. Circades's mind swirled with conflicting and unpleasant emotions. His very public search for Pulwabi made him an easy target – in the past Gold, and more recently Varuna played him at will.

"Good morning," God said. The deity wore an intrigued expression.

The Titan masked his inner turmoil with indignation.

"This is the second time in very quick succession that you have called me to a meeting," he said. "I am intrigued that your brother is not here."

God coughed awkwardly. He looked at his legal counsel, then back at The Ancient.

"This is an internal matter of clarification, but I thought it warranted your attention via a sidebar," God said. "A subordinate of mine—"

Gertrude jumped in. "Without our knowledge or authorization—"

She reminds me of Pulwabi, but someone else also – something in the posture – her bearing. Who is it?

"Yes," God said, "without our knowledge or authorization imparted a great deal of information about us to the mortals. He went crazy. I thought it was a clear violation of the Dictum. However, I do wish to spare his life."

In the manner of many attorneys, Gertrude struggled with remaining quiet. "And to report it properly to avoid any sanction," she said.

Ah, of course they go by the same name. She is much like Gertrude Iron. He had known the Angel called, The Confessoress very well. He recalled their close friendship. *If there was ever one who could have tempted me to abandon my search...*

Circades cracked a rare smile and said, "Gertrude, you remind me of someone I knew once."

"I hope it was someone you held in high regard," she replied.

"The highest." He sounded almost flirtatious.

Gertrude blushed and looked away. The Ancient reacquired his serious demeanor and looked at God.

"By the letter of the law, you must sentence him to death," Circades said. "But you do not need to kill him instantly. Use these symbols and the corresponding incantations to accelerate the Atrophy. He will die unless he completes great exertions to reverse it. This will fulfill your obligation and allow you to spare him."

Circades sketched several ancient symbols and a series of phrases on a sheet of paper.

God shrugged as he glanced at the sheet of paper. "Is this a loophole?"

"I assume you are familiar with the language of the Titans?" Circades asked.

"I am," God replied, "thank you."

"Thank you for not evading your obligations," Circades said.

God and his representative seemed relieved.

"You know who it is? You remind me of another Gertrude, Gertrude Iron," Circades said.

"Oh, The Confessoress. She was very close with my parents. In fact, I'm named after her. It's an honor that you would be reminded of her through me," the Priestess said.

"Give her my regards," Circades said.

Gertrude's joyful demeanor evaporated. "I'm sorry to say, but she passed away some time ago," she said.

A pang of regret struck Circades. "I'm sorry to hear that. Such a pity. Well, I bid you good day."

He turned and walked toward the door. He could hear the conversation at his back.

"Seems fair," Gertrude said. "Uranium II works back his debt, or he dies. Radiation has brought much suffering to the world. Now maybe some good will come from it."

If only they knew the dangers Uranium II has unleashed. They would not be so calm.

Anorexia and Uranium II walked through the grounds of the Summer Palace. The former imperial gardens had become a public park, still splendid despite wars and the passage of time. The pair strode in the Celestial past many ancient buildings that dated back to the early part of the Qing Dynasty.

"It is with great irony that we come to this place known as Longevity Hill, while I waste away before your very eyes," Uranium II said.

"I heard you were behind the atomic bombs," Anorexia said.

"That Demon, AIDS, he took such a strong hold of the Empire of Japan. I wanted to wipe it from the face of the Earth. I wanted to start with a clean slate and to leave no foothold for Demons on the Asian continent," Uranium II said.

"I think you went a little overboard, Xiang," Anorexia said.

"So does most of Heaven. I've earned a nickname: Metatron, 'the youth'. Ironically, of course," he said.

Anorexia cringed. Her friend looked like a withered, elderly man – a shadow of his former robust self.

"But you can reverse it?" Anorexia asked.

"Yes, but it takes a lot. I have to heal many, many mortals of disease. It is not easy," he replied.

"I don't know how your God could condone this," Anorexia said. "You are one of his archangels." She clenched her small fists in indignation.

Uranium II chuckled before he was nearly strangled by a coughing fit. He recovered, turned, and spit something nasty onto the floor.

He said, "You know there's a lot of debate about that. Of course human mythology has always been caught up in our lore. Iron would fight a battle in Mesopotamia and all of a sudden he was An. Gold and Silver spent time in Egypt and might have been seen as Ra and Set. You get the picture. I've often made my way into mortal dogma as Uriel. My proper name, Xiáng Guāng, means 'Auspicious Light,' much like Uriel is 'God is my Light.' So by some accounts I am an Archangel; by others, the only two are Michael Zinc and Gabriel Hydrogen. Some accounts hold that Rachael is an Archangel. However, her name is often masculinized as Raphael."

"You ramble like an old man," Anorexia said.

Uranium II grumbled and quit talking.

"Oh, I was just joking," Anorexia said. She grabbed his arm with affection. "What's going on with The Destroyer, anyways? I heard that she inherited her late husband's House."

"Yes, Rachael is the first female Standard Bearer. You are incredibly well-informed," Uranium II said.

"I have to be. It is essential to survival," Anorexia said.

"Indeed, I find it is the case that both Angels and Demons are obsessed with understanding their opposite numbers."

"I've always felt close to Angels," Anorexia said, "even though they were my enemy. I've often wished I was born on your side of the conflict."

"I've wished the same since I learned of your friendship with my mother," Uranium II said.

Anorexia giggled. "Yes, I recall you saying that flirtatiously over the years."

"You used to say you were too old for me," Uranium II said. "Now I think I am too old for you." He grinned for a moment.

"Please stay well, old friend. Heal some mortals, as many as it takes. You never know, there could yet be hope," Anorexia said.

Uranium II nodded, though he looked bereft of hope.

Anna hummed as she sorted the ingredients for an experimental batch of Manna. She had spent time in the Heavenly library and cross-referenced some ancient volumes with The Confessoress's journal. The result was a Manna designed to rid the bakery's Familiars from their chemical dependence.

Patrice approached her. He was followed by a handful of sober Familiars, all of which had eaten her concoction.

"They say that they feel better," Patrice said. The Familiar's eyes beamed as he showed off his redeemed brethren.

"Aye, but what... um...am I supposed to do with all me free time now?" a Familiar asked. She scratched at her arm while waiting for a response.

Anna shrugged. "Anything you want. You're lucky that you don't have to risk life and limb in the Mortal Realm. I understand work in the bakery can be monotonous, but read a book, play a game, or go back to the drugs, whatever you prefer. What I've given you is something you never had before; a choice. Use it wisely and well."

The Familiar nodded and grinned with a gap-tooth smile, "That's right, I used to like games when was little, alright. Come on, let's give that a go."

The Familiar led the cluster of her newly recovering peers out of the bakery.

"Oh but their shift isn't done yet," Patrice said.

"It's alright, I'm sure they'll be several magnitudes more productive now that they're clean," Anna said.

"That's true, and demand is down with the world war having

come to an end. I can't thank you enough for all you've done for us," Patrice said. "Nobody thinks of the Familiars. We're seen as less than garbage, but you, you trained Lilly, you freed us from the vice of Manna. We all owe you a debt of gratitude we could never repay."

"You owe me nothing, I'm just happy to help when I can," Anna said.

Constance stomped through the bakery tossing pots and kicking equipment.

"Oh no," Anna said.

Patrice took one look, nodded at Anna, and fled.

"What is going on?" Anna asked.

Constance's face was beet red. "I just, I can't with this guy. I thought, I'd have my chance once Eleanor was gone, but he's in his quarters railing some bitch right now," she said.

"I'm sorry, love," Anna said.

"He's the guy," Constance said. "He's supposed to come on to me. I've been dropping hints since Eleanor croaked. But nothing. Then I went to check on him and well, suffice to say it was 'do not disturb' time."

"I don't know what to say, but maybe it's just a passing fling," Anna said. "You know, he's never gone back to the Isle of Neutrality, even after Eleanor's death. You'll win him over yet."

"The worst part is that I have to stand guard by the door. He's not feeling secure in his title since the debacle with Uranium II and the atom bombs. He thinks someone might want to depose them both. So, I have the joy of listened to his grunts and groans without enjoying them."

"I'll watch the door. Just take some time to cool off, alright?" Anna said.

Constance embraced her with sisterly affection. "Thank you, Anna," she said.

"And no more kicking things around the bakery," Anna chided her with a grin.

Constance broke into a smile and wiped her eyes. "Fine," she said.

Anna made her way to the corridor of Zinc's room. *I don't think that anybody has the nerve to go against Zinc or Uranium II, Anna* thought. Despite the reduced Angelic ranks after World War II, Zinc still held a firm grasp on his authority.

The door to his abode creaked open and Rachael stepped out into the hallway. Anna felt a sinking feeling in her stomach. She steadied herself and tried to suppress any emotions from rising to the surface.

Rachael froze in place. A shameful look was etched across her face.

"I..." Rachael said.

Anna tried to stomach her tears.

"I didn't mean for things to go like this. After the other day with us, Zinc and I..."

"You don't have to explain anything," Anna said.

She stepped back and then remembered that she was meant to be guarding Zinc's doorway.

"I am required to stay here for his safekeeping," Anna said, gesturing toward the door.

"Anna, I didn't plan for any of this," Rachael said.

"Did you mean any of it in the bakery?" Anna asked.

"Of course, I did," Rachael said.

Rachael stepped forward and caressed Anna's cheek. Anna flinched at the contact and withdrew.

"Just, don't," Anna said.

Rachael pulled her hand back.

"When I came to see you, you were all that was on my mind. I had no intentions toward Zinc. But when he pursued me, I—" Rachael said.

"I can fill in the blanks," Anna said. "What's not fair, is that you came to me, after all of our history, and you proposed to me. Then you just run back to him?"

"It's not that simple. I have history with him too, Anna," Rachael said.

"So, I guess I should just be happy for you two then," Anna said. Her sadness was transitioning into rage.

Rachael sighed and said, "I think we were always like this. We have chemistry, but look at us. You're ready to bash my head in.

Maybe rightfully so, but still. Anna, it was wrong of me to dredge up the past. I felt something incomplete with us, a love that still flickers, but, like you said once before, one that can never be."

Anna looked down at her clenched fists. She felt hypocritical, but still wounded. She took a deep breath. *Who knows if I'll ever get the opportunity to be honest with her.*

"Rach, I feel embarrassed. I was ready to commit to this whole pioneering, socially unaccepted, intoxicating plan. A plan that you brought to me. Now I find out that you are also involved with him. Maybe it was naïve of me to assume your offer implied exclusivity. But I've always been a bit naïve with you. I just feel foolish for letting you in again," Anna said.

"Don't feel foolish," Rachael said. "I'm the fool and I'm sorry, Anna. I really am. I, I shouldn't have come to you until I was fully committed. I guess things with us will always be complicated."

Anna wiped her eyes. Rachael stepped forward with her arms out but stopped short of hugging her. She looked to Anna for permission. The two embraced and Anna felt some sense of closure.

"Look after yourself," Rachael said. She walked away down the hallway.

Anna leaned against the wall and looked at the door behind which was Lord Zinc's abode. *It's not his fault,* she thought. *Besides, he is dangerous. There is a veritable graveyard on the bottom of the Eunoe thanks to him. As far as I know, Rachael may have saved my life by not putting me between her and him.*

"But what of Schitz?" a voice in her head asked.

Anna slid to the floor of the hallway and ran her hands through her hair. Word of her Demonic beau frequently made its way to Heaven. *But my love for him is like a statue carved out of smoke. I dare not breathe near it, least it be gone. He is the most hunted being in existence. Any day there might be word of his demise. And even if not to death, I surely have lost him to another lover.*

As she often did, Anna pushed thoughts of Schitz from her mind. She knew confirmation that he was forever beyond reach would be far more devastating than what she had just experienced with Rachael.

She stared at the wall and mumbled without any care about who might hear.

"We should have run away together all those years ago."

CHAPTER 10

DUPLICITY

The air around the Chosin Reservoir stung with every burning breath. The cold knifed through the clothing of Anna's host. The young woman was a native of Guǎngzhōu and unfamiliar with the bitter winter of the Korean Peninsula.

Anna glanced toward Zinc. He was within the body of an officer of the 9th People's Volunteer Army. Both the host and the Angel within seemed miserable.

He's been distant for so long now, Anna thought. *First, it was marital bliss with Eleanor, then grief-stricken isolation after her death. Now it's his current tryst with Rachael. There had been a time when Constance and I were his closest companions.*

Anna shrugged. She was not overly concerned if Zinc was her friend or not. *Keeping him alive is my responsibility, and the safer he is, the safer I am as well.*

Zinc continually shifted between glancing down at a map and back up at a ridge defended by American Marines. He seemed unnaturally obsessed with the map. He looked in her direction.

"You remember the plan?" he asked.

"Oddly specific, but yes," Anna replied.

Zinc raised a tin whistle to his lips. Anna crouched and prepared for the assault. *I wonder why he' so certain there will be Demons here.*

Zinc blew his whistle and a human wave under his command surged towards the enemy lines. Anna looked ahead of her. The UN forces opened up on the Chinese troops. A wall of lead tore through the formation. Zinc kept pace with the Chinese soldiers who hurled themselves at the UN force's machine guns.

Anna dropped to a prone position and rested her DP-27 light machine gun on its bipod. She raised her sights toward the top of the hillcrest.

He was right! That's uncanny. Zinc had been incessant that the Demons would be arrayed across the top of the hill. She could make out the dark auras within the entrenched positions. Ahead of her, Zinc was reaching the crest of the snow-covered hill.

Zinc's lungs screamed for relief from the cold. It still felt odd using Schitz's intelligence. At every turn he expected a trap. Yet, each time, the Demons were laid out helplessly before him, ripe for the plucking. He glanced down at a crudely drawn map indicating the Demons' locations. Incoming fire struck the snow around his boots. He pressed forward.

The Chinese troops were being mowed down wholesale. Zinc stepped into the Celestial as he neared the UN troops' position.

Anna depressed the trigger of her light machine gun. It jumped on its mount as a series of pops sounded in her ears. Anna swung her sights over the next machine gun nest and fired once more. She moved her sights to the third and final emplacement and fired.

On the hilltop, Zinc sprinted across the front line and dispatched the seizing Demons with ease. He waved to her from the hilltop; the signal to depart. Anna shivered within her host. *Not a moment too soon.*

Anna abandoned her host and fell back to the Chinese entrenchment where she could open a portal. *That all felt too easy.* She and Zinc arrived back at the Great Hall at the same time. He opted to remain while the Priests conducted the Arrival Ceremony. Anna made the sign of the cross and continued into the Great Hall.

"Were you two alright?" Constance asked her.

"It was easy as pie, or however the mortal saying goes," Anna said.

"I worry after that time you two were shot down. I like to go out with you both," Constance said.

"It really was straightforward through. Almost, unnaturally easy," Anna said.

"How so?" Constance asked.

"I've never seen such accurate intelligence. Zinc knew right where the Demons would be and when they would be there. It was a turkey shoot, well, it was a Celestial bloodbath is what it was," Anna said.

"You say that like it's a bad thing," Constance said.

"No, just unexpected," Anna said. "What's up, why do you look so funny?"

"Well, I just hate when I don't get to go out with him. Seems like he's either with you or with *her*. I feel out of the loop," Constance said.

"I'm sure it's nothing," Anna said. "He relies on you. He might just be keeping his distance considering all the hints you were dropping right before he got with Rachael. She can be jealous; he probably wants to avoid any shenanigans."

"Yeah, I guess," Constance said with a dejected voice.

"Come on, let's go see how the recovery program is going for the bakery Familiars," Anna said.

Silver walked absentmindedly through the library and out into one of the adjoining hallways. His thoughts meandered from concern for his children and grandchildren, to frustration over reproducing the Ur Lak, to lusty desires for Christa.

"Shit!" Silver said to himself. He saw Zinc walking along the hallway in his direction. Silver looked down at the floor and tried to pass by unnoticed. He was stopped when a strong arm abruptly halted his progress.

"Ah, Lord Zinc," he said looking up and feigning surprise.

"Silver, how are you?" Zinc asked.

"Well, is all is well thank you. No complaints," Silver said.

"Silver," Zinc said.

"Yes?"

"You know what I'm going to ask you don't you?" Zinc asked.

Silver dropped his false smile. "The sword?"

"Yes, the sword," Zinc said. "Any progress?"

"We're still working on it, exploring different types of metals in the forge," Silver said.

"I've been very patient. You promised a war winning weapon."

"I know…The forge has just been an unanticipated…complication," Silver said.

Zinc sighed and rubbed his temple. "Well, see what you can do before the next world war, alright?"

Silver nodded and continued on his way. *Ugh, he makes me feel like a fucking child,* Silver thought.

"What's the matter?" Christa asked, when he had arrived at the forge.

Silver kissed her on the forehead and said, "Oh, nothing. I ran into Zinc. He seems impatient with our progress. It's annoying, but that's neither here nor there. What has me really upset is my doubt that we will ever reproduce the Ur Lak. So far, all I have is this stupid sword I spent centuries looking for."

Struck by a sudden impulse, Silver snatched up the Ur Lak and dropped it into the fire of the forge.

"What are you doing?" Christa asked. She shouted over the roar of the flames.

She tried to push past him to remove the sword from the coals, but he held her off.

"Look, one sword is useless. I can melt the blade down and fashion it into two smaller weapons. At least that way we can each have one," Silver said.

"Fine, but it is rash of you," she said. "If you destroy the Ur Lak, we could be taking a step back, especially after all that work."

Silver's frustration had reached a frustration point as hot as the forge. When the blade of the Titan's sword glowed orange, he grabbed a pair of tongs and placed the blade on the Anvil. Silver began hammering at the molten metal. The handle and pommel separated and fell to the floor. Silver grunted and continued his work. He struck the sword until it separated into two pieces. He worked with the expertise honed from decades of practice.

After folding and pounding, folding and pounding, two dagger-sized blades took shape. Silver felt a frantic, small hand tapping at his shoulder.

"What is it?" he asked.

He was met with silence and more tapping. Silver let the hammer fall and turned to Christa.

His wife had one hand over her mouth and the other on his shoulder. Having acquired his attention, she pointed to the ground where the handle of the Ur Lak had fallen. The grass was scorched around it. Attached to the handle was a new blade, identical to the one Silver had melted.

"It grew back?" Silver asked.

"Uh huh," Christa said.

"It grew back!" Silver said.

"I know!"

Silver swept Christa up in his arms and spun her around. He kissed her with all the emotion unleashed by his prior disappointment turned to joy.

"We can make as many swords as want," Christa said.

"Swords?" Silver asked.

"Yeah, you just made two, but we can continue making enough for every Angel," Christa said. "Surely, that's how the Titans armed their people."

Silver scooped up the self-repaired Ur Lak and held the tip in the fire of the forge until it glowed bright orange. He hammered away at the anvil until the molten segment broke away. He dropped the rest of the sword and went to work on the small bit of moldable metal. He scrutinized and hammered some more. Silver repeated the process and then scooped up the tiny bit of metal with the tongs and dipped it in the Eunoe. He held in submerged for a while and then brought it back up. Taking his creation in his hands he tossed it from palm to palm.

"Eh, eh, still a little hot," he said. Then with a broad grin he held the cone-shaped hunk of metal between his thumb and his index finger. "Now what does that look like to you?" he asked.

"It looks like the projectile for a 7.62×51mm rifle cartridge," Christa said.

"It sure does. Now think of it. Nine millimeter, 50 caliber. Shit, we can make tank shells, artillery rounds, aerial munitions, rockets, mortars. The only limit is the imagination of mortals," Silver said.

"It'll take an army of Familiars working around the clock to churn out that arsenal and to smuggle it back into the mortal world," Christa said. "We'll need a way of tracking it once it's sent back. We don't want to end up facing our own munitions." Her mental wheels were spinning at full tilt.

"No, no, no, we will only use Lilly," Silver said. "She can bring back the bits that don't need the special metal – stuff like cartridges, gunpowder, shell-casings. We can manufacture the rest ourselves. And nobody else will know – not even Zinc."

"Isn't that a bit much? Everybody knows what we're working on," Christa said.

"No, it's not," Silver said. "I was so focused on using the forge to create more swords. It never dawned on me until just now that with an infinite supply of malleable metal, we can make anything in vast quantities. Why not modern munitions?"

"But why not tell Zinc," Christa asked.

"Loose lips sink ships," Silver said. "And although I'm certain Michael is not a traitor or a fool, we now have the materials in place to end the war. We should keep the secret to ourselves, least the Demons find out and develop a counter strategy."

"We should move the forge into the hinterlands," Christa said.

"Good idea," Silver said. We will construct the grandest arsenal the world has ever seen, but we'll have to be quiet about it."

Anorexia and Vampirosis sat inside the cramped fire control cabin of an S-75 Desna surface-to-air missile site. The metal box was hot and packed with displays and instruments. From within her Soviet host, Anorexia scanned two cathode ray tubes that displayed the azimuth-distance and azimuth-elevation of the target they were tracking. She read the parameter, speed, and altitude of the target from a set of analogue indicators. Anorexia called the information aloud.

In the corner of the cabin, Vampirosis transcribed the information by hand onto the fire control plot table. She drew the path of the target based on the information relayed by Anorexia. The crew adjusted the control wheels to the specified elevation, azimuth angles, and distance.

Anorexia glanced at the PPI scope, a round gauge that displayed the target based on the feedback from the site's radar. The moment had arrived. She gave the order to fire.

Outside of the fire control cabin, two massive explosions sounded in quick succession. A pair of S-75s screamed skyward. At the edge of the atmosphere the first missile struck the target: an American U2 spy plane.

Anorexia had recollections of standing at the helm of a U-boat, looking down at her pocket watch while the torpedoes ran toward their target. *There are always these heart-in-mouth moments of waiting,* she thought.

The blip disappeared from the radar screen. The crew within the fire control cabin cheered. Anorexia opened the door to the cabin and stepped into the noontime sun. She looked up into the sky high above. Her Demonic vision allowed for her to see the smoke trails of the missiles that had destroyed the American plane.

"If there was an Angel in there, he's as dead as a coffin nail," Vampirosis said.

"I don't see a chute," Anorexia said. "Come on let's go check on the R-12s"

"Portal?" Vampirosis asked.

Anorexia looked over to the edge of the SAM site. There was a pair of senior, female officers in discussion with the site commander.

"Might as well take a drive," Anorexia said.

The pair exited their current hosts and possessed the officers. They boarded a Soviet GAZ-67 jeep and set out across the Cuban countryside. The road was a winding dirt expanse that led across grassy fields and at times skirted the coastline.

"Do you think they'll retaliate," Vampirosis shouted over the jeep's sputtering engine.

Anorexia shrugged. "I mean, if they didn't want to get shot, they'd stay out of other people's backyards right? But I don't know, they might. It could kick off a big exchange."

"Is that why we're going to San Cristobal?" Vampirosis asked.

"If the Americans do attack, we have to be prepared. If the MRBMs are launched, it will start a global war of annihilation. Might as well be the first to know," Anorexia said.

"Things have been getting very crisscrossed since the Second World War," Vampirosis said. "There are Demons in the NATO forces and the Warsaw Pact nations and same for the Angels."

"The Angels have been trying to establish a presence in the Mortal Realm for as long as I can remember. Now they use the United Nations to improve the lives of mortals through medicine and education, spreading liberal democracy, decolonization, and all that nonsense," Anorexia said. She was interrupted by a violent jolt as the jeep bounced along the rustic road.

"However, with such an expansive organization, member states will be at war with one another. In this modern world it is easy for us to slip into Communist forces in one conflict and Western troops in the next," Anorexia said.

"I wonder what Schitz and my father have planned if there is a nuclear exchange," Vampirosis said.

"They sure have been spending a lot of time together lately," Anorexia said. She was shocked by how audibly bitter her voice sounded.

"Yes, they've grown quite close. I hope my father will benefit from Schitz's tutelage. Maybe he can even fill me in on some secrets to survival," Vampirosis said.

"If anyone's going to, it's Schitz. He sure is good at…surviving," Anorexia said.

"Well, you too. You're as old as Schitz right?" Vampirosis asked.

"Schitz is a little older than me, but yes, we were in the same Academy class." Anorexia said.

Vampirosis leaned back in her seat. "I can't imagine all you've seen."

A deep sense of nostalgia swept over Anorexia. She felt her throat grow tight. *There has been so much loss and grief. Too much to consider.*

"Yes, I've seen mortals go from chariots to supersonic jets. I've seen the map redrawn too many times to count. And I've seen the same opera of greed and selflessness, love and hate, cowardice and valor, play out in their world and the Celestial over and over again," Anorexia said.

"I'd like to see how it all ends," Vampirosis said.

"You just might today," Anorexia said with a chuckle.

"If that's the case, I'd like to see it from a cockpit. High above it all, while everything below fries and turns to ash," Vampirosis said. Her eyes held a wicked mischief. They were deep pools of incalculable malice intermingled with delight. Her abnormally long incisors gave her a menacing smile.

"How did you get your name anyway?" Anorexia asked.

The youngster giggled. "I picked it myself. My given name is Hematolagnia. I infect mortals with the desire to consume blood, and the communicable diseases therein. However, due to my teeth and my dislike for the moniker 'Hema,' I decided on Vampirosis," she said.

"Fair enough, suits you," Anorexia said. "I can see you didn't fall far from your father in terms of your disease craft."

"Yes, actually my illness can help spread his," Vampirosis said.

The jeep followed the road through a tract of dense foliage into a clearing. Rising before them was the nuclear-tipped behemoth: an R-12 Dvina 8K63 Medium Range Ballistic Missile. Anorexia parked the jeep and the pair hopped out.

"A long way from catapults, I guess," Vampirosis said.

"The mortals' capacity for destruction knows no bounds," Anorexia said.

The scream of jet engines sounded in the distance. Anorexia's keen ears identified two rapidly approaching aircraft. "They're coming," she said.

"Fuck, they're retaliating for the U2," Vampirosis said.

"They well, may be," Anorexia said.

The mortals around the missile site began running. Vampirosis relieved a security officer of his Kalashnikov rifle. She ejected the banana clip, inspected it, returned it to the rifle, and chambered a round.

"Now what good is that going to do?" Anorexia asked.

"Something's better than nothing," Vampirosis replied.

A pair of single-seater jets, RF-8A Crusaders, zipped toward them at treetop height. The anti-aircraft guns surrounding the MRBMs opened up with a deafening fusillade. Vampirosis fired her rifle. Several of the scrambling infantry saw her and followed suit with their small arms.

The jets screeched past and disappeared beyond the trees.

"Nice shooting, I think you hit the lead one in the wing," Anorexia said.

"Yeah, didn't do anything though," Vampirosis said. She tossed the rifle back to its owner.

"Well fortunately and unfortunately they were only carrying cameras.

"Why, unfortunately?" Vampirosis asked.

"We're on that film. When it goes back with those jets, any Angels monitoring the situation will know we're here," Anorexia said.

"Their Familiars are probably all over the island anyway," Vampirosis said.

"True, but they could fall prey to our Wraiths and are limited to the ground they can cover," Anorexia said. "That photo is indisputable and will get back quicker. We should bounce. If they're taking pictures, they're still a long way from dropping bombs or invading."

The Demons left their hosts and set about making a portal.

The clang of a hammer against metal reverberated in the small, hot, subterranean room.

Silver bellowed. "Chi del gitano i giorni abbella? La zingarella!"

"God, your singing voice is as awful as ever," Christa said. She stepped into the cramped room that housed the Forge of Albion.

Silver looked up and smiled. He wiped his brow. "It's the false teeth; they interfere with my naturally melodic voice."

"Hmm, likely story," Christa said. "Well, loving husband, what are we working on?"

"This is a 155mm shell for a howitzer," Silver said. He set down the shell and allowed it to cool.

"Lilly sure is good at getting components from the mortal world," Christa said. She gestured toward the half-assembled shells awaiting the addition of Silver's anti-Celestial piece.

"From what she's told me, her descendants bring the mortal weapons to the Academy. They always claim they are needed for training. Then all she has to do is cook the books and bring them here."

"This is going really well," Christa said. She touched one of the completed Howitzer shells.

"Oh, do be careful though, we're vulnerable to them," Silver said.

"Yes, dear," Christa said. She motioned as though she was going to push over one of the shells.

Silver rolled his eyes.

"I mean, don't the mortals store and transport these things without them going off?" she asked.

"Yes, of course," Silver said, "but I hate spending all this time near such dangerous explosives. God forbid something sets this all off."

Christa looked through the doorway of their bunker to the storage room. Silver had used some of the few remaining, drug-addled Familiars from the bakery to dig an expansive cavern for the forge and storage of its products. The poor wretches would have no memory of the location or even digging and constructing the bunker.

"Quite the arsenal you've built," Christa said.

"It still pales in comparison to what we need," Silver said. "In a modern conflict, an army will burn through millions of rounds of ammunition and thousands of pounds of ordinance in no time. We also need to build NATO and Soviet variants, since we won't know which side we'll be fighting on," Silver said.

"I know, but we're making good progress," Christa said.

"Exactly, so do you fancy some time with the hammer?" Silver asked.

"Oh, tired?" Christa said. Her voice held a hint of mockery.

Silver smirked. "Let's see how many shells you can complete."

"You're on," Christa said.

The ring of the hammer once again sounded throughout the bunker.

Circades glanced down at the morning paper. The headline read: Khrushchev Orders Removal of Missiles. *Well, look at that, the world won't end,* he thought.

"St. James's Square is that way," a gruff voice said.

"I'm sorry?" Circades said. He looked up to see the elderly operator of the newsstand.

"The library is at St. James's Square. Otherwise, that's tuppence-ha'penny," the man said.

For a moment, Circades considered his holstered pistols. *I should teach him some manners.* In the end, he fished into his pocket and dropped a thruppence into the man's hand.

"Keep the change," Circades said.

"Yeah," the man said. He appeared satisfied with the exchange.

Circades walked along the London street. It had been seven months since he'd found and lost Pulwabi all in one evening. His emotion had oscillated between depression and motivation. He looked at the pictures of women in the newspaper. Involuntarily, he scanned through their past incarnations.

Old habits die hard, he thought. Her soul was in a fetus, yet to be born. *No reason to be looking for her in the paper.* He dropped the circular into a bin and continued his stroll in no particular direction.

He recollected the exchange with the newspaper man. *I need to build up wealth and influence.* Circades thought of the chateau Svaha had burned. He'd always been good at accruing and scattering mortal fortunes. *I need the power to influence nations. That will take some time.*

His walk carried him through Covent Garden and into Islington. Circades found himself walking past Priory Green, one of the city's many council estates. It was still early in the morning and few people were out.

A cluster of youths were hanging about the estate's derelict playground. One noticed Circades and motioned to the others. In a flash they closed the distance between them. The posture and stride of the young people was full of menace and bravado. The mop-topped, adolescents stood in front of Circades in silence. Then one spoke, "You appear to be lost. There's nothing for you this way, Guv."

"All the same, I'll be going where I please," Circades replied.

His response was met by raucous laughter from the locals.

"Oh, is that right?" the spokesman said.

He pulled a knife from his pocket and stepped closer to Circades. The would-be gangster was tall and lanky. Circades had to crane his neck to meet his gaze.

Circades calmly unbuttoned his suit jacket. The youth broke eye contact to glance down at the holstered weapons.

"Oh, shit," one of the other gang members said.

"It's a bit early for all the fuss, eh?" Circades said.

The ringleader raised his palms and stepped aside. The rest parted like the Red Sea, moving to either side of the pavement.

"We was just having a gas," one of the youths said.

Circades continued on his way.

"Think he's with the Firm?" Circades heard one of the youths ask his fellows. The entire exchange had lasted but a few moments. Yet, the impact on Circades was monumental. *That's it. I could start a business and amass a fortune, but then what? I would become a Prime Minister, or a Chancellor, or a President? Comrade Circades? That's stupid. Yet, notorious criminals have power and influence as much as any politician.*

Circades knew of the West End gangsters the youth had mentioned - nightclub owners who ran all sorts of illicit ventures. *This is how I will rise. I will become somebody with reaching influence and power in the underworld.* The only drawback he could see was that, despite his resourcefulness, delving into illegal activities could land him in prison. *Notoriety is both an asset and a weakness. I will build myself up, but I will remain a shadow.*

Anna and Constance walked through the Great Hall. Neither had been in high spirits as of late. Anna looked about the various Angels, Familiars, and Priests coming and going.

"It's easy to feel lost in this living sea," she said, more to herself than Constance.

"I've been trying to be more positive, but yes, it is," Constance replied.

"I think pinning your hopes for happiness to others is a recipe for disaster, but solitude can be pretty bitter also," Anna said, ignoring the part about attempted positivity.

"Look," Constance said. She gestured toward the departure portal arches.

Rachael stood surrounded by a large contingent of African Angels. The cadre was immersed in some sort of briefing.

"She's the Standard Bearer of her House now," Anna said.

"Which is all well and good, but where is Zinc?" Constance asked.

"Ah, we left him with her," Anna said. She felt her pulse quicken and her face flush. Part of her reviled Zinc, yet years of doting over his safety had embedded an almost maternal instinct.

"This has been happening too frequently!" Constance said.

"Well, let's start with Rachael, she was with him last," Anna said.

"Good idea," Constance said.

The pair made their way to the fringe of the meeting.

"...Also, things are also getting very dicey in Rhodesia and Portuguese East Africa. The Demons seem more interested in Angola and the Congo, specifically Katanga, but be mindful of the east as well," Rachael said.

The assembled Angels nodded in agreement and departed. Some opened portals; others walked off through the Great Hall.

Anna felt a slimy awkwardness crawl across her skin. She had seen Rachael in passing a few times since Rachael's abrupt withdrawal of her proposal.

"This is so uncomfortable ," Anna said.

Constance glanced at her and stepped forward to Rachael.

"Excuse us, but we're trying to find Zinc," Constance said. Her voice thinly veiled her hostility.

"Oh, hi Anna," Rachael said, looking past Constance. "What do you need from Zinc?"

"We are meant to provide his security at all times," Constance said, refusing to be overlooked.

Rachael turned her attention to Constance, much in the way a cat might scrutinize an aggressive mouse.

"And who gave you that task?" Rachael asked.

I wonder which one of my students would prevail in an altercation, Anna thought. She sized up her two former pupils. Both had fiery personalities and could be quite vicious. It was fitting they were both deeply in love with Zinc.

How sad that they both ended up this way. Constance had been a talented student, a loving wife to Adolphus, and continued to be a brave and talented Angel. Rachael had been innocent and idealistic when Anna met her. Anna recalled Rachael telling her of her revulsion at the Passover massacre and her fear in battle.

As much as I care for them, they're both violent, vindictive bitches.

"Lord Zinc," Constance said.

"Then I'm certain if he needed you, you would not have to be looking for him," Rachael said.

The tension was palpable, but Anna gleaned something else.

"Alright, thanks Rach," Anna said. She pulled Constance away from the exchange.

"But she didn't tell us where Zinc is," Constance said.

"She did tell us that she doesn't know where he is either. Although she'd never admit," Anna said.

"Ah, you do know her pretty well," Constance said. "So what are we going to do now?"

"We'll have to hope he's capable of looking after himself. It's altogether possible he's just relapsed and gone back to the Isle of Neutrality," Anna said. "Speaking of relapses, let's go check on Familiars at the bakery, shall we?"

Across the Great Hall, Uranium II watched Anna and Constance move away from the departure portals. He did not have to hear their conversation with Lady Hydrogen to surmise that they had been looking for Zinc.

Uranium II recalled a conversation he had with his fellow Supreme Commander in which Zinc had stated that he was never without his security. *Very interesting.* Uranium thought. *Right now, he is with neither his lover nor his bodyguards. He must be up to something underhanded.*

He coughed violently and spat blood onto the marble floor. Uranium II grimaced. *Time to heal some sick mortals*, he thought.

Craig Walters of The Central Intelligence Agency walked through a dense swath of Colombian jungle. He swatted ineffectually at clouds of voracious mosquitos, pausing only to wipe his brow. The primitive trail, if it could be called such, gave way to a grassy clearing.

"Whoa, that is a lot of dead Communists!"

In the middle of the clearing was a mountain of stacked corpses. The pile of entwined limbs, vacant eyes, and gaping mouths made Walters's hands twitch with excitement.

Several men in fatigues were dousing the pillar of humanity with gasoline from red plastic containers. They might as well have been watering a crop.

"Communists, peasants, students, traffickers, even two anthropologists studying the Carabayo," a man in a light-gray suit said.

"Eh, this country has more letters than a spelling bee: FARC, ELN, PRT, MOEC,EPL. All I see are Communists. And the best kind at that, dead ones," Walters said.

The man shrugged. They shook hands

"You must be the man of the hour," Walters said. "What was your name again?"

"You didn't have it before, so it is not possible for you to have it again," the man said, "but you can call me La Sombra."

Walters chuckled. Most types he dealt with sought anonymity, but it did not take Langley long to figure out who they were. The man standing before him was unique; he had remained a mystery.

"That's apt," Walters said. "You've been casting a pretty big shadow over these parts as of late."

"Then call me La Larga Sombra and leave it at that," Circades said.

"You're about your business, I can respect that," Walters said. He unshouldered the pack he was carrying and handed it to La Larga Sombra.

To Walters's surprise, his contact took the pack, walked over to the man commanding the soldiers, and handed it to him.

"Not going to count it?" Walters asked.

He shook his head.

"Not going to keep any of it?" Walters asked

He shook his head, again.

"You certainly are an odd case," Walters said. He retrieved a cigarette from behind his ear and lit it. "But I like your results."

"I'm glad to hear it. I would like to maintain a mutually beneficial relationship," Circades said.

The soldiers ignited the pile of corpses.

"I can see no reason that would deter me," Walters said.

In truth, Circades was nauseated by the man as well as the

wanton violence. *This is the path I chose, I have to see it to its end. To Ragnarok*, he thought.

"I'll be in touch," Circades said.

Svaha walked through the forest along the Bitterroot River. Around her pine needles and fallen branches burst into flames. A herd of deer sought sanctuary from the blaze by standing in the water's flowing depths.

The fire Elemental snarled. *Always defeated by Varuna*, she thought. The sound of scampering hooves caught her attention. A fawn had fallen behind. Svaha raised her hands and a wall of flames rose before the panicked animal. She giggled when the fawn turned only to find an inferno behind it as well.

The tiny, quivering heap soon succumbed to the heat and smoke. A blur of tears and wailing passed through the flames and scooped up the tiny animal.

"Why must you be so cruel?" Vasundhara asked.

Svaha fell into uncontrollable laughter. "I'm sorry," she said through her mirth. "It's just something about you holding the little dangling legs."

Vasundhara stared silently at her sister and rested the fawn back on the ground.

"Come, come you know you can't hold it against me," Svaha said. She held her arms open.

"You push my good nature to its limits," Vasundhara said. She stepped forward and begrudgingly embraced her sister.

"Well, you know Varuna gets jealous. What was so important that you needed to tell me away from the men?" Vasundhara asked.

"The Titan Circades has been industrious," Svaha said. "I've been paying close attention to him."

"There's nothing new about that. I think you're obsessed with him," Vasundhara said.

"Hmmm, be that as it may, he's become quite involved in the affairs of mortals," Svaha said. "It's been rather interesting actually. Watching him grow in power and prestige. But I wonder about his motive. Varuna outmaneuvered me when I attempted to goad him into ending the Celestial civil war."

"Yes, why did you try to meddle in that?" Vasundhara asked.

"I am tired of all the mortal souls passing through water," Svaha said. Her eyes smoldered with an intensity that dwarfed the forest fire around them.

"I get that. But why wish destabilizing everything? Why risk enraging our husbands?" Vasundhara asked.

"You mean, why risk enraging your husband. Vayu goes along with everything I say," Svaha said.

"I'm pretty certain he doesn't seek conflict with Varuna regardless," Vasundhara said.

Svaha giggled. "I called you away from them to see what you thought about getting rid of both husbands."

"Have you gone mad?" Vasundhara asked.

"Hardly, you know things would be better without them," Svaha said.

"We all serve our purpose: the Elementals, the Celestials, and the Mortals," Vasundhara said.

Svaha sneered, "You're the mad one. The Celestials? You mean those abominations we birthed from Primogenitorous? Don't tell me you even feel something for them as well?"

"I have love for all living things, especially God," Vasundhara said. "Do you not ever think of your son Satan?"

"I could care less," Svaha said. "This got off track. I recognize the current balance requires one Celestial and the one Titan to keep them in line, I guess. But I fail to see what Varuna and Vayu offer to the equation. We could rule over the Cosmos. You can create and I can destroy without petty jealousy. And we can both be free to love as we choose."

"Oh, is that it?" Vasundhara asked. "Is there someone you want to be with? If it's the Titan, you're wasting your time. He'll only ever belong to that mortal of his – what's her name. Ah...Pulwabi."

Svaha flushed and the flames that were her hair glowed brighter. She said, "If the river of incarnation was made of fire instead of water, I could devour her soul and take what I wish. But that is not your concern. You should worry about your freedom, dear sister. I know you hate being shackled to Varuna. I know you wish you could be free, like before – amongst the vivacity of life – back when you could have knowledge of mortal men and women as you pleased. Don't you wish to be known as Ianna, and Venus, and Xochitlicue, without fear of jealous Varuna?"

"How would you do it?" Vasundhara asked.

"With my darling Titan of course," Svaha said. "I just need to know I can count on you when the time is right."

"And there would be peace throughout the Cosmos. In the Ethereal, Celestial, and Mortal Realms?" Vasundhara asked.

"Yes, silly. You and I will rule the Ethereal with the balance of creation and destruction. God can rule over the Celestial provided he agrees that the Eunoe be comprised of Fire. Lastly, my bride-groom-to-be Circades will oversee the Mortal Realm," Svaha said.

Vasundhara stood in silence for a moment. She knew her sister was relentless when she set her mind to something. It had been the same when Primogenitorous caught her attention. *Now it's the same thing with Circades,* she thought. *But it is better to go along with her than to argue.*

"You can count on me," Vasundhara said.

"Good. I knew I could, sister," Svaha said.

The fire Elemental continued to burn her way through the forest. She climbed a mountain that rose above the Bitterroot. From the summit she looked down at the scarlet blanket she had draped over the landscape.

Bubonic Plague and Anorexia sat in Plague's cavernous abode. They each held a chalice of Brew.

"I get the sense that something odd is going on," Anorexia said.

"Explain," her uncle said.

"After every war, we refit and get ready to go again. We took a beating in the Great War, but we came back again just a few decades later. We took a walloping in the Second World War, but we've rebuilt again and yet, no full-scale global conflict," Anorexia said.

"But there is fighting?" Plague asked.

"Of course," she said. "It looked like there was going to be a nuclear war between NATO and the USSR. And there are conventional wars. We fought one in Korea, there are a million in Africa, and a nasty one in Indochina, but I am talking about something different."

"Is it not just the changing nature of the Mortal Realm?" Bubonic asked. "Satan said that nuclear weapons are a game changer – something about an Angel giving the mortals knowledge they hadn't fully grasped on their own yet."

Anorexia saw her friend Uranium II in her mind. *I really wish Xiang hadn't done that*, she thought.

"It could be. I think it's more the parity," she said. "At Teutoburg, Waterloo, the Western Front, and other great battles, we fought the Angels to a stalemate, but it was always on a knife's edge. We could have tipped the scale toward the final victory or we could have been annihilated. Now, there are casualties, but there is also, stability."

"Stability?" Plague asked.

Anorexia took a sip of her Brew. "Yes, it's almost like trading horses. Like, 'here you take this one and I'll take that one' type of deal."

"That's odd. Are you sure it's not just a coincidence?" Plague asked.

Anorexia shrugged and said, "It might be. It might also be the side effect of having one singular leader. No clans, no council, no regional commanders, just Schitz. Maybe his leadership is yielding uniform results."

Bubonic nodded. Anorexia was surprised. Typically, mentioning Schitz sent Bubonic into a blind rage.

"I hear he's been quite the leader," Plague said. He looked like he had swallowed bitter medicine.

"Uncle! What has happened to you?" Anorexia asked.

"Well, recently Satan has insisted that I get past my previous misgivings for Schizophrenia. He is my half-brother, and we may well need to work together to defeat the forces of Heaven," Plague said.

Anorexia burst out laughing.

"Hey, I'm trying. I've always been a servant of Hell. If Satan says to do it, I'll do my best," Plague said.

Anorexia continued to laugh.

Plague grumbled something about 'a weasel' under his breath.

"All joking aside, that's actually really nice to hear. It also sounds like the Devil might finally be close to calling you out of the shadows," Anorexia said.

"I think so, I really do. I've spent enough time here in the dark and skulking quietly around the Mortal Realm. I'm ready. Even if it means working with...him," Plague said.

Anorexia reclined in her seat and drained her chalice. "Ah, that makes me feel better. I was probably just overanalyzing things anyway."

Chapter 11
Cauld in the Clay

Rachael reclined in Zinc's bed. *He has earned himself a rather opulent bedchamber,* she thought. *Hmmm, we've earned ourselves.*

She did not spend much time in the room that had been hers and Hydrogen's. She took a drag from a hand rolled spliff. The acrid smoke warmed her throat and chest. She held the pungent smoke for as long as she could then exhaled a thick cloud through her nose and her mouth.

The dried herb had a strong effect. It left her tingly and light headed. She stretched and closed her eyes. The room spun around her. *Ah, this is nice.* Part of her wondered where Zinc was, another part was happy for the time alone.

Everything is within my reach. Uranium II is decrepit. I will utilize the deal that would have elevated Hydrogen to get myself appointed Co-Supreme Commander. I will use my authority to seek out and kill Schizophrenia. Then I will know rest. My vengeance and my ambition will be fulfilled.

She took another deep drag from the spliff and unleashed a maniacal laugh. *It was cruel to toy with Anna.* She had dangled the lure of a legitimate relationship with love and passion solely to seduce her. Anna had so readily took the bait. *It bothered me, the time she spurned me. Now I am the victor; she holds nothing over me.*

It was an added bonus that she got to have her way with the Angel who was so in love with her nemesis. *That's right, Schizophrenia. I bedded your long, lost love and I discarded her.*

A niggling thought undermined her cold, calculating thoughts. *But as tough as I act, part of me has always loved Anna.* Rachael thrashed around atop the covers. It was as though the physical motion might drive the thought from her head.

She inhaled the last bit the joint had to offer and tossed the rest across the room. Rachael exhaled with her eye lids pressed tight together. *Oh, Benjamin, my life has not gone the way I imagined it would.* For a moment she could see her late twin's face. *I miss you. I miss Gabriel too. You both were, stabilizing.*

The room, much like Rachael's thoughts, continued to swirl. The drug did enough to bring her as close as she could go toward sleep without grievous injury. She remained in the listless, in-between state for some time. When the effects of the smoke subsided, Rachael rose to her feet and staggered over to the liquor cabinet. Her mouth was dry. She remedied it with a swig of Elixir.

"Where the fuck is Zinc anyway?" she asked the empty room. *He had better not be out sleeping around.* She decided to take a walk to clear her head and shake off the cobwebs from the Devil's Grass. Rachael looked down at the decanter of Elixir and shrugged. *Who can judge me?* She took it with her on her stroll.

The Great Hall was busy as always. *Perhaps it will be even after I'm gone.*

She took a swig from the decanter. Throughout her walk she was greeted by many Angels from her House and others. Rachael had mothered many children and they all had been prolific. Her kin treated her with reverence whenever their paths crossed. Likewise, many Familiars and Priestesses were very cordial to her.

I suppose they see progress when they see me, she thought. *The first female Standard Bearer, the Destroyer, the Archangel.* Rachael considered the mix of love and antipathy she held for Anna. It much mirrored the feelings she had for herself. *I am fond of myself and I hate myself. I accept who I am...who I love, and I reject it.*

Rachael drowned her philosophizing with more Elixir and made her way back to Zinc's room, her room, their room, she was not quite sure how to think of it. *I suppose it doesn't matter, as long as he isn't sharing it with anybody else.*

Rachael came through the doorway to what had become their chamber. Zinc had returned. *I wonder where he was,* she thought. *Perhaps we should wed, so that my claim on him is official. I've mourned Gabriel long enough.*

"We found him," Zinc said.

"Who, love?" she asked. She embraced Zinc and kissed him on the mouth.

I wanted him so badly in my youth yet circumstance contrived to keep us apart. I need to quiet my thoughts and be happy with him now.

"The one you have sought for so long," he said. "He's usually meticulous in the field, but I think the mortals' technology has caught up with him. A Familiar who knows his voice heard him speaking through a mortal over a field radio in Indochina."

It can't be. He's found Schizophrenia? Here I am awash in self-hate and doubting Zinc. All while he was out securing this boon for me. The future is bright.

Rachael tossed the empty container of Elixir on the bed and shook herself, assessing her level of inebriation. *I'm good,* she thought.

Her face reddened with excitement. "He's in Vietnam?" she asked. "Let's assemble a team."

Zinc remained silent. He wore an awkward expression. He stepped closer and kissed Rachael hard. He ran his hands over her body, searching for the special spots he knew would unleash her riotous passion. Instead of responding, she laughed.

"Not now, lover," she said. "Once we get back, I will wear you out. But now we have work to do."

Rachael felt her arousal growing, both for Zinc and for the impending hunt. She thirsted for both – always, but she controlled her lust and led the way to the Great Hall.

Rachael roused several members of the Hydrogen and Krypton Houses. Her preparation was precise; her focus unwavering.

Zinc departed for a moment and returned with two Familiars Rachael had never seen. They provided their rendition of what they had learned while monitoring radio communications. Rachael could feel the hairs on the back of her neck stand on end. She longed to be underway.

Zinc's infuriating, love-struck bodyguard Constance Silver arrived with a message. Uranium II and God had summoned Zinc to an urgent meeting. Zinc looked at Rachael.

"Go on. Don't let him slip away," Zinc said. "If it's quick, I'll join you."

He motioned her away from the assembled group. His voice broke a little. "Be careful."

He acts like he'll never see me again. With the advantage we're carrying into this, we're sure to be successful, Rachael thought.

Zinc kissed her one final time. "I love you," he said.

"I love you, too," Rachael said.

Rachael felt a giddy sensation. It felt rewarding to be affectionate with Zinc in public. They had been sloppy in their younger years, displaying their desires, even when he wed. *Now, we are finally free to do so with legitimacy.*

The Familiars assisted with the crafting of portals designed to take them to the best possible location from which to interdict the Demons. Rachael savored the moment, looked across the Great Hall, and departed.

Anorexia sat within a mortal host at the Cần Thơ base camp of the U.S. Army's 9th Infantry Division. Her host, Sgt. Carreau, was as bored as she was. It was oppressively hot. The air seemed as much an enemy as anything waiting for them in the jungle. She half-reclined on a cot. Anorexia looked up from the pages of a magazine and watched as her brother, Autism, played cards with an assortment of mortal enlisted men and women. He was murdering them.

It probably helps that he can see what cards they're holding, Anorexia thought. She rolled her eyes as the Demonically possessed Sgt. Winston let out a celebratory hoot and dropped down yet another winning hand.

"Your brother's funny" AIDS said from within the body of a corporal. He sat down at the foot of Anorexia's cot. She moved her boots to give him more room.

"I don't see the point in playing a rigged game," Anorexia said.

"That's what makes him funny," AIDS said.

Anorexia shrugged and glanced back at her magazine.

"You know what else is funny?" AIDS asked.

"I'm guessing you're going to tell, regardless of what I say," Anorexia said.

AIDS gave her an amused look and fulfilled her prophecy, "Schitz has all of us sitting here at this base for a while now. How can his intel still be fresh? I understand going into combat right after scouting, or going to a big battle and playing the odds that Angels will be there. But we've been here, what two, three days? Waiting. How could anything that merited all these senior Demons being present still be in place?"

"Those sound like questions for your buddy Schitz," Anorexia said.

"But you don't think it's odd?" he asked.

"It's too hot to get worked up over it one way or another," she said. She yanked at her collar and groaned.

Schitz's voice thundered from outside the tent. "First Platoon, mount up."

Anorexia grabbed the M16 resting against her cot and donned her helmet.

AIDS was making his way to the entrance.

"Corporal, you carry the claymores," Anorexia said. She slapped AIDS on the back and stepped out into the blinding sunlight. Anorexia nodded toward Schitz. He looked rather dashing within his host.

They made their way to a row of helicopters.

Of course AIDS is correct. If the intel was hot, we would have moved right away. If Schitz knew the Angels would be arriving later, why have us sitting around? None of it really adds up.

The roar of the rotors and the task ahead pushed any misgivings to the background. *Whatever's going on, it must be heavy if he wants all of us in on it.*

As the UH-1, "Huey," lifted off the ground, Anorexia reflexively tapped her gear. Everything was in place.

The helicopters conducted numerous false landings along the way to conceal the true LZ. When the time came to exit, Anorexia hopped out of the helicopter and gained her footing. She peered across the clearing to the tree line. There were no signs of movement.

The squad disembarked and began maneuvering across the jungle terrain. Anorexia felt her heart racing. Autism and AIDS led a separate squad through a large clearing. They were meant to serve as bait for an ambush. She stepped over roots and around tree trunks, and hoped her squad would arrive in time to provide assistance.

The distant sound of gunfire disrupted the humming sound of the insects. The clatter of small arms and machine gun fire masked their approach toward the Vietnamese position. Arrayed before them was a squad of Communist guerrillas, several emitting Angelic auras.

Schitz signaled the squad to fan out. Anorexia raised the iron sights of her M16. Schitz's rifle cracked. The round tore through the machine gunner's beige helmet, smashing through his skull, and splattering brain matter on the surrounding foliage. With Schitz's shot as a signal, the Americans unleashed hell on the Viet Cong position.

Anorexia fired, killing her target. She swept her sight to the next possessed Viet Cong. She was too late; the enemy had turned and was sighting her up. Anorexia made the decision to roll into the Celestial. A moment later, a round tore through her former host's face. The sergeant collapsed to the muddy ground.

Anorexia looked about for another female host. To her right a private was taking cover behind a large tree. The Demon sprinted to her and possessed Private Caroline Bass. When she accessed the host's memory, she encountered little self-preservation instinct. *Good thing, this host is a little wild,* she thought.

Anorexia bounded from cover and became the central focus of the enemy. She fired toward the foe while on the dead run. Anorexia reached a dead VC and scooped up his discarded RPG-7. She raised the grenade launcher. Bullets tore past her, snapping branches and tearing bark from the trees.

The RPG-7 was loaded. Anorexia pulled the trigger. Her frame shook when the launcher discharged its ordnance with a loud bang. An explosion erupted around the surviving Viet Cong and sent the surviving Angels into departure seizures.

Schitz stepped into the Celestial and dispatched a pair of seizing Angels with his knives. He jumped into another American and made his way along the tree line. He waved to Anorexia and gestured to the clearing beyond the tree line. Anorexia left her host and ran into the sundrenched clearing in the Celestial. Ahead of her, LAWs and RPGs pounded their opponents.

The VC that had entered the clearing were sandwiched between Autism and AIDS's squad and Schitz's troops. It was a turkey shoot. Anorexia ran toward her comrades, both in the Celestial. Autism waved toward her and shouted, "We need a mortal."

Anorexia groaned. *I just left a good host,* she thought. The engagement between the guerrillas and the Americans was progressing away from them as the surviving VC retreated. Anorexia jumped into one of the female troopers and jogged back to Autism and AIDS.

"We got one pinned down in the defile," AIDS said. "But if she stayed in her host…"

"I get it, I get it," Anorexia said. Of course they needed Demons in the Celestial and Mortal Realm to cover all options.

Schitz jogged up to them in the Celestial. He sported a wide grin. The scene was surreal with gunfire sounding across the countryside and the quartet of Demons standing around their cornered prey.

A pair of pale, Angelic hands reached up to the edge of the defile and the infamous Angel known as the Destroyer, Rachael Hydrogen, pulled herself from the trench. Anorexia looked into the natural depression cut by a small stream. Huddled on the muddy ground was an injured Viet Cong. Rachael's former host appeared to be out of ammunition and had been injured in the shoulder.

Anorexia raised her M16 and shot the woman three times in the chest. She slumped over in a heap of black pajamas and an oozing puddle of blood. The Angel seemed irritated by the gratuitous slaughter. It filled Anorexia with joy, to have gotten a rise out of her.

The Angel glared at the Demons. Schitz addressed her. "They will kill you," he said, "and they will take your corpse with them to Hell and hang it along the Styx for your brethren in Limbo to see. It will happen, but in the spirit of warriors, I offer myself to you, one-on-one, as it should be."

Why aren't we just killing her? Anorexia thought. This smacks of Plague's idiotic duel.

"I agree," Rachael said.

The Angel launched a throwing star. Schitz ducked and hurled a knife at her. Before it sailed wide, he'd already drawn his short sword. It had barely cleared its scabbard when Rachael swiped at him with her own blade. The battle was joined.

Anorexia felt a sense of helplessness. She longed to help Schitz. Yet, she dared not involve herself. He was clear about the terms of the duel.

While Rachael backpedaled to avoid Schitz's sword, AIDS tripped her.

Anorexia's eyes grew wide. *The duplicity.* Anorexia wondered if Schitz would be sporting and allow his foe to recover.

He did not.

The Angel rolled across the ground, a lithe and gymnastic move. But she could not avoid Schitz's boot. He smiled when his toe connected with the side of her chest. Still in possession of her sword, Rachael lunged – a final, desperate swipe. Schitz knocked it away as easily as he would have dismissed an annoying fly, then he sliced through her midsection.

Schitz grabbed the Angel by the throat and lifted her from the ground.

He looks like a fisherman, lifting his prized catch. I shouldn't have expected him to be upset with AIDS. Of course he would delight in defeating his nemesis under any circumstances.

Rachael smirked. "Your wife called out for you while I was skinning her alive, and you weren't there; always remember that," she said.

Anorexia recalled Rubella. The Angel Schitz was battling was famed for wearing Rubella's preserved skin. Anorexia had never been overly fond of Rubella, but her fate seemed hardly just. Anorexia shivered. *To be flayed alive. I could hardly think of a worse fate. I hope Schitz drags this out.*

Schitz flung the Angel down into the ditch beside her deceased host. Her body crumbled like a discarded doll. He followed her into the ditch and loomed over her. Her eyes were beginning to dim. He growled into her face.

Anorexia could not discern the nature of the conversation, however, she was certain he was enjoying every moment of it.

He couldn't be. No, he is. Anorexia thought. Schitz handed the Angel his dagger. *She is going to end her life, just like her husband did at Kursk.* Anorexia recalled the African Angel, Lord Hydrogen. He had taken his life with a chilling dignity of purpose.

The Angel plunged his dagger deep into her abdomen. She howled as she dragged the knife up through her innards. Schitz brought his sword down on her neck and severed her head from her body in a clean swipe. Her decapitated crown rolled along the bottom of the trench and her body slumped to the side.

Schitz withdrew his dagger from her body.

With sacramental reverence, he removed the skin cloak from her headless shoulders and cradled the grisly garment in his arms.

A heavy silence descended over the clearing. The firefight had petered out. The Celestial business was concluded. There should have been shouts of celebration, yet the solemnity of the moment dispelled all joy of victory. Anorexia's brother broke the spell.

"We're not taking the corpse?" Autism asked.

"It only matters that she's dead," Schitz said.

They headed toward the tree line to construct a portal.

"That was some really good intelligence. It allowed us to catch a big fish," AIDS said. His voice was jovial.

Anorexia searched Schitz's face. He appeared annoyed. *This was an oddly perfect boon,* she thought. She recalled AIDS's discussion with her at the base camp. An inkling of a blasphemous thought crossed her mind. *Schitz is hiding something and he's hiding it in the place least likely to be scrutinized – in success. His triumphs contain some dark secret.*

"Indeed, but do me a favor, next time trip her sooner. She almost got me with that knife," Schitz said. He playfully shoved AIDS, who bumped into Autism. Autism then shoved AIDS back into Schitz.

As Anorexia walked behind the others, it felt like she had been transported back to the Totem pitch, or some other part of her childhood. Once more she was outside of the clique, a common locale for her.

Perhaps that is why I have never been able to recreate our post-Kursk liaison. In many ways Schitz still acts like a juvenile. Will

I be forever waiting for him to give me the attention he so easily heaps onto others?

Anna glanced about the Great Hall. The usual assortment of Angels, Familiars, and Priests went about their business. Anna looked back to Lord Zinc. Her job of ensuring his safety had taken her around the world from battlefields to meeting rooms. She had executed some seedy orders for him. *Things could be worse, I suppose. I'm alive, a lot of Angels would give anything to be in my position,* she thought.

Guarding Zinc had become a mundane affair after the removal of his foes and their accompanying threats to his life. Providing for his security on the battlefield remained treacherous, however he had recently taken to conducting unaccompanied excursions.

He can be so moody. He's a good fit for Rachael, Anna thought.

Anna assessed Zinc's fellow Supreme Commander, Lord Uranium II. The Asian Standard Bearer was affected by a divine affliction that caused him to rapidly age. By many accounts Uranium II was required to offer substantial healing to the mortals to prolong his own survival.

The Order of St. Patrick didn't eliminate all the Cancers, but they did a good job. Now radiation cures the mortals of any types of that terrible disease.

Constance arrived by her side.

"How's it going?" she asked.

"Eh, nothing remarkable, you?" Anna replied.

"Just trying to figure out what he's up to," Constance said. She gestured toward Zinc. "He had me interrupt a briefing with Rachael with instructions to announce that he and Uranium II were called to a pressing meeting with God."

"But he is talking with Uranium II," Anna said.

"Yeah, but there was no meeting with God," Constance said.

"Fishy," Anna said.

"He's always scheming," Constance said.

A Familiar strode across the hall toward the two Supreme Commanders. A tingling sense gave Anna the inclination that the Familiar was a part of whatever was happening.

"Come on, let's be overprotective," Anna said.

The pair of bodyguards intercepted the Familiar's path. He was a young lad. He wore a pin identifying him as one of Lilly's descendants, a privileged bunch. There was terror in his eyes when confronted by Zinc's security.

"I..I..I have a message for Lord Zinc," the Familiar said.

He removed a scroll from his robes, making sure to appear non-threatening. Constance took the report and motioned for the Familiar to depart. He did so with haste. She handed the scroll to Zinc.

Anna noted Zinc's reaction as he read the communique. He acted as though stricken by grief. Yet, to anyone who knew him as well as Anna, his response was obviously contrived. The news was not a shock to him but to Anna, the report was a painful, unexpected blow. Lady Hydrogen had been killed in action.

Time passed in a blur. Zinc's demeanor became erratic. Despite the news not coming as a surprise, he did appear genuinely devastated. Then there was the sudden unexpected return of Zinc I, Lord Zinc's long-lost and presumed dead, father. The elder Zinc reported an unbelievable tale of escaping from captivity in Hell.

Anna sensed that 'something was rotten in the state of Denmark,' but also recognized it had little to do with her. She attended Rachael's funeral as Zinc's bodyguard and also as a private mourner.

The sound of bagpipes filled the Great Hall. Anna knew Rachael had loved the instrument and assumed their inclusion in the service was intentional. The slain Angel lay atop a stone slab. A thick, white scarf was wrapped around her neck to conceal the presence of injuries. Anna had heard talk that Rachael had been decapitated – a violent end to a tumultuous life.

Anna felt a lump in her throat as she watched as six pallbearers, Zinc among them, lay Rachael next to Lord Hydrogen.

Her death brings a close to a chapter of my life. Though their romance had been brief, it had bound them to one another. Anna would have accepted Rachael's flippant proposal. Her withdrawal of the marriage offer had been painful. *I'll never know what possessed her to offer herself to me again only to run to Zinc a second time. But I do know that she never fully accepted that she could feel romantic love for a female, and her lack of acceptance always expressed itself in antipathy for me.* One who loved her so deeply also hated her beyond expression.

Such was the legacy of Anna and Rachael.

Rachael's son, Lord Krypton, made his way from one griever to the next. He was an attractive youth with the features of his mother and complexion between hers and his late father's.

"I don't think Lord Zinc is in any danger today," he said when his path brought him near to Anna.

"I'm sorry?" Anna said.

"He did not need to bring his bodyguard to the funeral," Krypton said.

"I'm also here as a friend," Anna said. Her voice was testy. Her response brought a change to the young Lord's demeanor.

"Oh, I apologize," he said. He rested his hand on her shoulder, a brief reconciliatory gesture.

"I did not realize. How did you two know each other?" he asked.

"We met during my House's rebellion. We fought against one another. Later when my House was subjugated, she asked me to train her in combat. She was a good student and a ... good friend," Anna said.

"You were her instructor!" Krypton said.

"Yes, is that so hard to believe?" Anna said.

"No. She spoke of you often, but always refused to name you. She said she didn't want anybody else apprenticing with her master," Krypton said. "She said she owed you everything for forging her into an adept warrior."

"That's very kind of you to tell me," Anna said. "She was a very talented student."

"Would you be willing to take me on?" he asked.

"As an homage to your mother, sure, why not?" Anna said.

"Thank you, I'll be in touch," Krypton said. He nodded and moved on to other mourners.

The Familiars playing the bagpipes continued the sad refrain. Anna knew the tune well, *The Flowers of the Forest*. In her head she could hear the lyrics.

I've heard them lilting at our ewe-milking,
Lasses a-lilting before the dawn of day;
But now they are moaning on ilka green loaning–
The Flowers of the Forest are a' wede away.

Schitz stood alone over the opening in the floor of the Great Hall. The Wraiths had removed the stone covering Rubella's final resting place. He cringed when he looked down into the burial cavity. Rubella was wrapped in a black cloth. Schitz had not considered how they would respectfully inter somebody who had been skinned.

"I'm sorry I wasn't there," he said. "I'm sorry for a lot of things. I caused you much pain in our time together. I wish I could have been better; better to you, better in general. But we loved each other. I hope that was enough."

The only reply was silence. He placed the cloak Rachael Hydrogen had fashioned from Rubella's skin into the burial pit.

At bughts, in the morning, nae blythe lads are scorning,
The lasses are lonely, and dowie, and wae;
Nae daffin', nae gabbin', but sighing and sabbing,
Ilk ane lifts her leglin and hies her away.

Private Bass inhaled from her cigarette and flicked the butt toward the perimeter fence. The sun was setting over the Mekong Delta.

"Heard you got the Bronze Star," Lieutenant Eisenhower said.

"Something like that, sir," she replied.

She placed two cigarettes in her mouth, lit both, and passed one to the Lieutenant. He nodded in acknowledgement.

"It's getting dark. Might not want to be flicking that lighter out here in the open," Eisenhower said.

"Snipers?" Bass said.

Eisenhower nodded. He looked uneasily toward the tree line.

"I think there's a lot less gooks out there after today," Bass said.

"That there are, but if I'm honest, seems the more we kill the more come right back," Eisenhower said.

"I guess we just gotta keep doing what we've been doing, till there's none left," Bass said.

Eisenhower chuckled. "Well, that's one way of putting it," he said.

"Be honest LT, can you tell the difference between the zipperheads we're supposed to be wasting and the ones we're supposed to be saving? None of 'em want us here," Bass said.

"I suppose you are right, private," Eisenhower said. He flicked the cigarette and patted her on the shoulder. "I suppose you are right."

In har'st, at the shearing, nae youths now are jeering,
Bandsters are lyart, and runkled, and gray;
At fair or at preaching, nae wooing nae fleeching–
The Flowers of the Forest are a' wede away.

"Địt Mẹ Mày!"[23] The doctor swore and punched the chest of the unresponsive patient. "Why did you have to go and die on me?" he asked. Surgery in the dimly lit, subterranean room was far from ideal. Nevertheless, the Viet Cong physician hated losing a patient. He kicked the makeshift operating table. The corpse's arm jostled from the impact.

"Đồng chí,[24] there was nothing you could do," the doctor's assist said. She placed her hand on his shoulder. "You did your best."

The doctor placed his blood soaked hands in his hair, gripping his scalp in frustration. "He was so young...his whole life was ahead of him," the doctor said.

---

[23] Motherfucker
[24] Comrade

At e'en, in the gloaming, nae younkers are roaming
'Bout stacks wi' the lasses at bogle to play;
But ilk ane sits drearie, lamenting her dearie–
The Flowers of the Forest are weded away.

Zinc vomited the burning mixture of Elixir and stomach acid back into the carafe from whence the liquor had originated. His nose and throat were a searing agony.

"How could I have done this," he said to himself.

He looked about his empty room. It should have been a happy time, a happy place, not a lonely reminder that she would never again share his bed. Zinc tried in vain to recall Rachael when she was living. But all he could see in his mind's eye was her still cold body at her funeral.

"How could I choose? How could he make me decide?" he said.

Dool and wae for the order sent our lads to the Border!
The English, for ance, by guile wan the day;
The Flowers of the Forest, that fought aye the foremost,
The prime of our land, are cauld in the clay.

Amanda Neon and Khadija Krypton sat under a tree in the Heavenly countryside. The young lovers had neared graduation from the Academy. Yet, a pall hung over what should have been blissful youth.

"What are we going to do now? I had hoped your great-grandmother would open the door for the rest of us. But she died almost as soon as she became the first female Standard Bearer. What hope do we have?" Amanda said.

"Rachael opened the door to all sorts of possibilities. It is up to us to make sure our opportunities didn't die with her," Khadija said.

"She survived all those years only to die now. She could have really made a difference," the Neon maiden said.

We'll hear nae mair lilting at our ewe-milking;
Women and bairns are heartless and wae;

Sighing and moaning on ilka green loaning–
The Flowers of the Forest are a' wede away.

Anorexia and Uranium II sat in a tea house in the city of Nagasaki, Japan. The setting was more modern than their traditional spots for meeting. The women sported collared blouses and short skirts of the 1960s aesthetic. They were a long way from the ornamental robes of yore.

"Interesting choice of locale, all things considered," Anorexia said.

The pair was seated in the Celestial Realm at a vacant table.

"I enjoy seeing this city recover and regenerate. It gives me hope that I too can revive," Uranium II said.

"You are looking well," Anorexia said.

"I've spent countless hours healing cancer patients at the Red Cross Society hospital not far from here," Uranium II said.

"Oh Xiang, I wish you had never given the mortals that cursed bomb," Anorexia said.

"Indeed, I regret it as well. I found fission and fusion in the books of mortal sciences. Perhaps if they had been allowed to develop the sciences at a later time, their first inclination wouldn't have been to build world-annihilating bombs," Uranium II said.

Anorexia giggled and said, "But it was *your* idea to give them a weapon."

"Yeah, ugh I guess, but look at where they've taken it. I gave them a twenty-one kiloton bomb. Now they have missiles with one-point-two megaton yields," he said. "That's all on them. I intended to deliver a weapon so terrifying it would turn the mortals away from war."

"They're never going to turn away from fighting. It's part of their biology," Anorexia said.

Uranium II shrugged. "Nothing can be done now."

"You seem tense, Xiang," Anorexia said.

"Just a lot going on back home. Everyone's mood is kind of sour after our recent loss," Uranium II said.

"Rachael Hydrogen?" Anorexia said.

Uranium II nodded and said, "I mean, don't get me wrong. I was not close with her, but her loss seems to have upset my colleague Zinc quite a lot. They were...involved."

"I was there for the battle," Anorexia said. "I saw everything."

"Oh, were you now? There are a lot of folks in Heaven who would like to talk to you," Uranium II said.

"Is that so?" Anorexia said.

"One of our most storied warriors was killed and those accompanying her were wiped out to the man. So yes, her death is a haunting mystery. Come on, do tell how your lot managed to pull off such a brutal victory," he said.

Anorexia shifted in her seat. It felt odd, to debrief with an Angel, even one as close as Xiang.

"It was just a regular engagement, "Anorexia said. "We surrounded her squad by splitting up and picked them off until it was just her."

Silence hung over the conversation. A palpable degree of awkwardness arose. Both went to speak at the same time.

"It's just..."

"Well, I mean..."

"Oh, sorry," Anorexia said.

"No, no you go ahead," Uranium II said.

"Well, I was going to say. It's just as simple as that. I'm not leaving anything out. It was a straightforward counter-ambush. The Angels maneuvered to ambush one of our contingents. We slipped in behind them and took them out instead. Textbook, really. But...considering who our foe was, and considering how easy it was, something was definitely amiss," Anorexia said.

"It felt odd to me too," Uranium II said. "Lord Zinc is well-known for being a bit brutal in terms of killing off Angels and Familiars. He doesn't exactly conceal the fact that he disappears people. I mean, I participated with him in an impromptu double execution right after Waterloo. That was quite public. But he also kills off opposition secretly as well. And, he was acting odd right before Rachael's death."

"That's interesting," Anorexia said.

Sounds just like Schitz! she thought. *He was acting odd before the battle too.*

"What is it?" Uranium II asked

"Oh, it's just that our lead Demon, Schitz, was also acting weird before the battle," Anorexia said.

"Weird how?"

Anorexia recalled all of AIDS's concerns when they were waiting at the Cần Thơ base camp.

"It seemed like we were oddly prepared for the battle," Anorexia said. "Like we knew where to be in advance. It wasn't like we were responding to an intel report or anticipating enemy movements. It was uncanny. We were right where we needed to be."

"I see," Uranium II said.

He stroked his chin and ruminated for a moment.

"This might sound preposterous, but what if they were working together?" Uranium II asked.

Queasy nausea accompanied hearing Uranium II give voice to her fears.

"But why? Or how? Do they even know each other?"

"Perhaps they met at the Isle of Neutrality or La Rue de la Croix Nivert," Uranium II said.

"No, Schitz is notorious for avoiding those places," Anorexia said.

"Then perhaps in the field," Uranium II said.

"I don't feel comfortable accusing him of treachery if we cannot even prove they were at the same place at the same time, let alone know each other," Anorexia said.

"An Inquisition summons," they both said in unison.

"Can you arrange it?" Anorexia asked.

"Yes, and I can do it with discretion," Uranium II said.

"I have a terrible relationship with the head of the Purists," Anorexia said thinking of the creepy Salvatore. "But, I have a good rapport with the High Priest. Their organizations are separate but perhaps he can do me a favor."

"Wonderful, we will acquire the results and compare the two. If there is a pattern, our suspicions will be confirmed," Uranium II said.

Anorexia sighed and felt a lump growing in her throat.

"I know you have feelings for him. Is he still distant, since... well you know," Uranium II said.

Anorexia blushed. "I really wish I had a female to complain about my love life with," she said.

Uranium II chuckled. "I'm all you've got, old friend. Now don't hold back, what's been going on?"

"He has been distant," she said. "Sadly, when I first considered the collusion I thought, 'Oh, that could be an excuse for his aloofness,' but sadly I have to accept that he will never feel about me the way I do about him."

"There'll be someone better for you," Uranium II said. He gave her a mischievous look.

"You're married Xiang!" Anorexia said. She playfully waved her hand toward him.

"Ah, I didn't say me," he said with a laugh.

"Right," Anorexia said. She nudged Uranium II with her elbow.

They absorbed the light-hearted banter for a moment. They both needed the moment of emotional reprieve. They settled into a platonic embrace and quietly watched the mortals go about their business.

Titus busied himself cleaning the main temple. There was an army of Wraiths at his disposal, but he found it therapeutic to attend to the details himself. Dust was as persistent an enemy of his chapel as the Angels were for the Demons. He hummed while he set about tidying the altar and surrounding displays.

A quiet set of footprints approached. He turned to see the thin, elder Demon, Anorexia. Titus felt a swell of paternal affection. Anorexia had been one of the Demons who assisted in training him when he was assigned to lead Hell's army. In the time since her childhood, she had grown into one of the pillars of Hell's army. He had very much enjoyed serving with her on the Triumvirate Council.

"It's good to see you Anorexia," Titus said.

"And you as well Titus. How have you been?" Anorexia asked.

"Well, I have been well thank you," Titus replied. "Trying to stay busy since there is no longer a council on which to serve. I find that my office as the High Priest and my scholarly research more than fill the void though. At the same time, it's hard not to feel out of the loop."

Anorexia was silent for a moment. Then the two chuckled. Titus was known for long-winded answers to simple questions.

"Mephistopheles would have said, 'That was the longest possible way to say, 'I'm good,'" Titus said. "Ah, I do miss them, poor souls."

He glanced toward a corner of the temple dedicated to the memory of the lost Wraiths. The servant class of Hell was mostly buried in mass graves without fanfare or dedication. However, despite Satan's protest, Titus had established a section of wall bearing the names of many heroic Wraiths. It was a simple tribute, consisting of three perpetually burning candles that rested in boxes carved out of the wall under the inscription. "May They Know the Peace They Knew Not in Life."

"They were good comrades," Anorexia said.

"Yes, yes they were. How can I be of assistance? I doubt you came to reminisce," Titus said.

"Oh, I brought you this," Anorexia said. She had taken a small, ornamental sword from Rachael's waist. It bore the same lion's head as Hydrogen's famous sword.

"You're becoming quite generous. Are you sure you don't want it for your personal collection?" Titus asked.

"No, you have it. It will go well with its mate," Anorexia said.

"Ah, so this came from the legendary Destroyer, the Demon Killer, Rachael Zinc Hydrogen?" he asked.

"Yes, indeed," Anorexia said.

Titus took the blade, briefly admired it, and set it in a display panel beside a matching larger blade.

"I can't thank you enough," he said." "To think the swords of the House of Hydrogen are here, trophies in Hell. We must be close to winning the war."

"Well, that's another reason I'm here," Anorexia said.

Titus felt his skin tingle with intrigue. He remained uncharacteristically quiet.

"Titus, we worked together for centuries on the Triumvirate and we've known each other even longer," she said. "I trust you with my life. However, I know you are very close with Schitz as well. What I ask of you now, must stay with you. It must."

Titus felt a hint of a threat from Anorexia's tone and posture. *Whatever this is, it must be serious*, he thought.

"You can tell me, my child – anything," he said.

Anorexia's posture relaxed. Titus breathed a small sigh of relief.

"I believe Schitz is in league with an Angel," Anorexia said.

Titus could not fight the urge to laugh. "My dear, he is the most storied warrior living today. He might be the most illustrious warrior Hell has ever produced. His victories are the stuff of legend. How could it be that the slayer of so many Angels is a traitor? It belies reason. I don't mean to laugh as I see you are serious. It's just that I am confounded by the notion."

"I know it sounds preposterous, but hear me out. If Schitz is innocent he will be able to account for his actions during an Inquisition. Correct?"

"Well, yes, but..."

"And can it not be applied randomly, to ensure all soldiers are conducting their affairs correctly at all times?" she asked.

"Yes, it's not the same thing as a trial. It's more quality assurance, but it hasn't been done in some time. It's just a practice that remains on the books, so to speak," Titus said.

"Well, who better to start with for its revival, than our illustrious leader?" Anorexia asked.

"You know, I'll have to convince Salvatore?" Titus asked.

Anorexia nodded.

"You know he and I don't get on?" Titus asked.

Anorexia nodded again.

Titus groaned.

"I hope I'm wrong," she said.

"I do too," Titus said. "If you're right you will have uncovered the greatest deception in our history. If you're wrong—"

"I will be punished," Anorexia said.

"No," Titus said. "If you are wrong, you still had the courage to do the right thing for our cause. And I will defend you to the death."

Salvatore swung the driver in a smooth arching motion. He struck the ball with a rewarding ping. He watched as it took flight and sailed out over the Styx. He squinted to track the ball. Priests had the worst low-light vision of Hell's races.

"Hmm, wind's a little strong today," he said.

"It takes some effort to find you," Titus said.

Salvatore groaned at the invasion of his private time.

"That is entirely by design," Salvatore said.

"Yes, your attendants were less than specific," Titus said.

"Still, I'll have to fire them nevertheless," Salvatore said. "How can I help you Titus?"

"I'd like you to take up the Inquisition," Titus said.

That's an odd request, Salvatore thought.

He teed another ball, squared his stance, and smashed another ball.

"Not bad," Salvatore said.

Titus squinted and followed the flight of the ball. It kerplunked into the Styx.

"But I thought you liked the Demons. Why do you want me digging into their business?" Salvatore asked.

"Well, I feel out of the loop; no more Triumvirate to assure the quality of their work and only one Demon at the top."

"Ah, so you feel put out to pasture," Salvatore said. "I can relate. There have not been many deaths and the current bloodlines are easily verifiable. Not so much work for the Purists. But it's not all bad, gives me time to work on my swing."

"Yes, what are you doing?" Titus asked.

"It's a sport of the Mortals," Salvatore said. "Quite infuriating actually, but at the same time can be therapeutic, if you are a masochist."

"And what, you just hit the ball?" Titus asked.

"In the mortal game you have to put the ball in a hole," Salvatore said.

"It sounds tough, how big is the hole?" Titus asked.

"It's not much bigger than the ball, but you don't have to get it in in one go. That almost never happens," Salvatore said.

He placed another ball down and focused with extra attention. He raised the club. The swing was exactly what he was looking for.

"But if you get it just right..." Salvatore said.

Both Priests craned their necks and followed the flight of the ball. It arched high over the Styx. Buffeted by the breeze it sailed toward the ramparts of the Limbo fortress.

"No way," Titus said.

The ball struck one of the Angels manning the battlements. The aura tumbled from view.

"Ahh, hole in one," Salvatore shouted. Titus laughed alongside him. Excitement ran through Salvatore's veins.

"You're good luck Titus. You should take a swing," Salvatore said.

"Oh, I don't think I could manage that," Titus said.

"I hear you're an adept fencer, it shouldn't be hard for you," Salvatore said. He handed Titus the driver.

"Don't try to smash. Just focus on completing a smooth, sweeping motion like your arm was the blade of a windmill," Salvatore said.

They worked on Titus's swing until he was able to hit the walls of the bastion at Limbo.

"So you want me to look into Schitz then?" Salvatore said.

"What makes you say that?" Titus asked.

"Don't be coy, you said there's only one leader. You think he's doing a bad job?" Salvatore said.

"No, but I know that absolute power corrupts," Titus said. "Best to give him a reality check. The Priesthood is at the top of the pyramid, even if Schitz lords over the army, he is still subordinate to us."

"That's a good point. I've no problem reviving the Inquisition," Salvatore said.

"Thank you," Titus said. "I knew you would see the logic. Well, I'll leave you to your game. Give them Hell."

An odd feeling pricked at Salvatore, the desire from camaraderie. He fished into his bag and retrieved another club.

"Why don't you stay until we empty the bucket?" Salvatore said.

"Sure!" Titus said. The ambitious High Priest took a ball and eyed it with the hunger of a starving tiger.

The shot sailed over the ramparts of the Angelic fortress. "Almost got one," Titus said.

Salvatore laughed. "You're a quick learner, well done."

Titus smiled.

"Now tell me, I know you and Erin are an item, but what of Desdemona?" Salvatore asked.

Titus shrugged. "I suppose I could put in a good word for you," he said.

Salvatore smirked and teed up another ball.

"Who invented this game?' Titus asked.

Salvatore grinned. "The Scots take credit for it, but I am sure our Lord Satan conceived the idea."

"Really?" Titus said. "Not God?"

"Oh no," Salvatore said. He topped a shot and swore viciously. "No figure described as 'loving and gracious' would even design something so damnably diabolical."

Chapter 12
Waiting Below the Surface

Vampirosis made her way through a narrow corridor of Hell. Her hands trembled as she reached a heavy wooden door. She pressed it open. The Triumvirate had been dissolved before her birth, therefore she had never had the opportunity to attend one of its open meetings. She felt like a trespasser.

Seated at the table were her father, AIDS, and the ancient Demons Anorexia and Autism.

"You called for me?" Vampirosis asked.

"Tell us about the shoot down back in '67," her father said.

Goosebumps speckled her arms. The room was suddenly cold. Her father's voice was stern.

"That was ten years ago," she said. She was certain she had failed to sound as nonchalant as she intended.

"A long weekend from our perspective," Autism said with a roll of his eyes.

AIDS glared over at the elder Demon and said, "Yes, and I think the events would stick in your memory, harrowing as they were."

"I bailed out from a fighter jet, I mean—"

Anorexia cut her off. "Nobody is saying you did anything wrong. You're a skilled aviatrix. Yet, you were shot down while working with our side's most successful fighter pilot. On top of that, the Angels believe you died from a mid-air collision with Schitz. Hardly seems like the expert flying we might expect from the two of you."

Vampirosis's neck warmed. Irritation replaced her previous nervousness. "Is he the most successful?" she asked.

"He shot down over one hundred across both world wars," Anorexia said.

"I shot one-hundred and fifteen with the Japanese Imperial Navy and Army Air Force, thirty in Korea, and twenty-two in Vietnam," Vampirosis said.

"Well, I guess you two can have a pissing contest sometime," Autism said. His voice was moody.

"Look we're not here because of you per se, but something you told your father," Anorexia said.

"It was stupid, just something dumb after almost dying," Vampirosis said.

"You said that you thought Schitz shot you down," Anorexia said.

Vampirosis looked about the room half expecting the ancient Demon to be lurking in a dark corner. Her gaze settled on her father. He looked uncomfortable when their eyes met.

"Like I said, it was stupid. I must have made a mistake," Vampirosis said.

"Why did you think it back then and why is it stupid now?" Anorexia asked.

Vampirosis sucked her teeth and rolled her eyes. *I'm not some Academy whelp; they might be older than me, but they have no right to ambush me like this*, she thought.

"When I got hit, my plane was blown to bits, but the Angel's MiG was firing his guns. That means I was struck by a missile. So where did it come from? Schitz was the only one left in the engagement. Therefore, the logical conclusion is that he hit me with an air-to-air missile. Was he aiming for the MiG? Maybe. Was it a SAM I didn't notice? Possibly. It's just weird, because Schitz bailed out after I went down, but the MiG was already crippled, so how did he get shot down? I didn't see any smoke trails from ground fire. It was all suspicious," Vampirosis said.

"How did you survive anyway? That shit sounds wild. I hate flying," Autism said. He appeared genuinely interested.

"The front half of my jet stayed together," Vampirosis said. "I bailed out low. It didn't do anything to save the pilot, but I jumped into the Celestial right before hitting the ground. Only broke my ankle."

There was a moment of silence after her description of her harrowing ordeal.

"My daughter is an expert," AIDS said. "If she thinks she was shot down by Schitz, that's what happened. But I've worked with Schitz and he is a fiercely committed warrior. Perhaps he was aiming at the

MiG. I've had my suspicions about his behavior as of late, but to think he would engage in such duplicity, I don't know if I can believe it."

"Yet, you so readily confirmed my sister's suspicions," Autism said. He banged his hand on the table.

"Well, what do you want from me?" Vampirosis asked. "It's not like it's so easy to say. 'Oh, by the way, storied killer of Angels, by any chance were you trying to kill me or are you just incompetent?' That's not a formula for success either."

Vampirosis hands shook with rage.

"Alright, alright, that's understandable," Anorexia said.

"I thought we were supposed to get the Inquisition to deal with this," Autism said.

"The Inquisition?" Vampirosis asked.

"It hasn't been active as much in your time, but the Inquisition is a form of...quality control. It's supposed to be a randomly assembled panel that reviews the work of an arbitrarily selected Demon. Not really a trial, just a mechanism for keeping everyone on their toes," Anorexia explained.

"Oh, that doesn't sound so bad," Vampirosis said.

"Well, you can be put to death if you're found wanting," Autism said.

"Hence, why it fell out of practice," Anorexia said. "The negative impact on morale was seen to outweigh the benefit."

"So..." Autism said with his hands in the air.

"Titus said that Salvatore requested permission from Satan to reinvigorate the procedure, but he is still waiting to hear back," Anorexia said.

Titus, Salvatore, and Satan, this goes all the way to the top, Vampirosis thought.

"In the interim we must continue to keep an eye on Schitz. AIDS, as his protégé that falls heavily on you," Anorexia said.

"I always keep a close eye on him," AIDS said. "I'm meant to be learning from him. I want to believe this is all folly or a misunderstanding."

"So do we!" Autism said. "He was my buddy in the Academy. I've known him for millennia. Anorexia...is extremely close with him also. Don't you think we want our friend, our leader, to be beyond reproach? But think about it. If he meant to kill Vampirosis, then why? To save the beleaguered Angel? To get the kill himself? Both are insane theories. We need to know the truth."

Vampirosis felt sympathy for her father. AIDS looked like he was being squeezed in a vise. *I don't need to stick around for more of this. They might be my seniors, but I am as decorated as they are.* Her exploits had earned her the Knight's Pentagram and the lesser gradients. She found little need to stand before them as though she had committed some offense.

"If you need me, you know how to find me," Vampirosis said. She turned and left the meeting.

The outskirts of Lisbon were quiet in the afternoon hours of the early June day. The air was warm and the breeze peaceful. The Turkish diplomat's black sedan creeped up to the front of his residence. The breaks squeaked as the old Fiat came to a stop.

Parked within a nondescript Citroën, Zinc's father, the Elder Zinc I, watched the diplomat arrive. He was in possession of a mortal Armenian.

"I might be an old-timer, but I fail to understand the point of this," Lord Zinc I said.

"He likes to maintain certain global conflicts so there is fighting everywhere. International terrorism provides a convenient loophole to the Divine Dictum. The JCAG are avenging a genocide from decades ago. Wherever they take violent action there is cover for us to do battle, it keeps all regions open to us; we just have to keep the embers burning from time to time," Anna said.

She too was in possession of a mortal Armenian.

"Seems excessive, just to kill a mortal," the Elder Zinc said.

"Your son actually started a global conflict doing something like this once but today shouldn't have that effect," she said. She recalled Zinc's assassination of Archduke Ferdinand.

Zinc I shrugged and shifted in his seat like someone waiting for a film to start.

Within the diplomat's vehicle the administrative attaché of the Turkish consulate stretched and yawned.

"We should have just had lunch in the city," Erkut said.

"There aren't any good restaurants in this city," his wife Nadide said.

"Ah, well, nothing like lunch at home," he said.

"Hassiktir!"[25] the driver shouted.

Erkut looked away from his wife to the front of the sedan where his driver and bodyguard were sat. Beyond them, through the windscreen, he could see a woman holding an assault rifle. She was dressed in a track suit and wearing a ski mask over her face.

The metallic sound of the door handle of the Fiat sounded through the interior of the car. Erkut looked to his left and saw a similarly dressed, masked man trying to open the locked door.

"Kapıyı aç!"[26] the woman shouted. She held her Kalashnikov sideways so the driver had full view of her weapon and then re-sighted the barrel in his direction.

Before Erkut could tell the driver not to comply, a heavy clunk indicated the lock had been disengaged. He felt sick in the depths of his stomach. *I hope they are here to abduct me*, he thought.

Zinc, in the possession of a mortal, opened the rear door of the diplomat's sedan. He raised a silenced Makarov pistol and placed the sights over the terrified, middle-aged man's balding head. The small caliber pistol coughed. A cloud of red mist filled the interior of the Fiat. Zinc lined up the woman seated beside the deceased diplomat and shot her in the face. She slumped in the seat.

"Çek git!"[27] Constance shouted to the driver and bodyguard.

They emerged with their hands raised above their heads.

---

[25] Shit!
[26] Open the door!
[27] Get Out!

"Alright, piss off," Constance said. She gestured with the Kalashnikov, in a shooing motion. The men needed no second invitation and scurried away down the block.

Zinc could sense his host's subconscious screaming to abandon the murder weapon. *This Armenian is strong-willed to interfere with my possession*, Zinc thought.

"Fine," he said. He tossed the Makarov under the vehicle, then jogged toward the getaway car. Constance and he had barely piled into the backseat before Anna stomped on the accelerator.

"Some security they were," Constance said. She punctuated her sentence with a maniacal laugh.

"Good help is hard to come by," Zinc said. There was a lightheartedness in his voice.

Anna glanced into the rearview mirror for the briefest moment. Zinc was kissing the neck of Constance's host.

Oh, it finally happened. Hopefully, now she won't be so morose all the time, Anna thought. *Although Zinc is a whirlwind; he is oft times damaging to those around him.*

Anna's attention was pulled away from the backseat when she realized Zinc's father had rested his hand on her host's thigh. She looked down and might as well have seen a cockroach on her leg. She stifled the nauseating feeling growing in her stomach.

"Here's good enough. The mortals can take it from here," Anna said. "I'm sure they won't be caught by the authorities," Anna said.

"Good, it's always useful to keep a cell operational," Zinc said.

Anna parked the car and the four Angels exited their hosts. They made their way along a quiet street. Anna felt relieved to be out of the car.

"You three can head back to Heaven. I just have something to check on real quick," Zinc said.

"But..." Constance said.

"I'll be fine, it's just an errand God asked me to take care of alone. I'll be safe," Zinc said.

Anna opened a portal in a quiet doorway arch and the trio returned to Heaven. *Whatever old man Zinc does, I'll do the opposite*, Anna thought. Zinc I opted to remain for the arrival ceremony. Anna continued on her way after making the sign of the cross. Constance followed her.

"You and Zinc seem to be getting along well," Anna said.

Constance replied by doing something Anna had not seen her do in a while, she broke into a broad grin. It was infectious and Anna found herself smiling as well.

"Good fortune has finally rid him of Eleanor and Rachael, ah, sorry... but yes, I am quite happy. He has finally accepted my affections," Constance said.

"I'm happy for you," Anna said. She placed her arm around her friend's shoulder.

The pair made their way to the Manna bakery.

"I think Zinc's father has a thing for you," Constance said.

Beatrice seemed to emerge out of thin air. Her salacious guise left little doubt that she had overheard Constance.

"Oh, hello girls," Beatrice said.

Constance embraced her mother and kissed her on the cheek. The three stood in silence for a moment.

"Well, go on," Beatrice said. "Old man Zinc has his eye on Anna?"

"You're the worst," Anna and Constance said together.

Beatrice chuckled. "So I have been told. Nevertheless, dish."

Anna sighed. "Zinc mentioned his father's interest. And for his part, the elder Zinc hasn't been very subtle."

"Is he that repulsive to you?" Constance asked.

"Even if he wasn't awkward as Hell, always leering at me. He's spent almost my entire lifetime locked in a box. He knows very little of modern etiquette, even less of the mortal world. He might have the Angelic appearance of eternal youth, but after a few minutes of conversation, he very much seems ancient," Anna said.

"Yeah, he was a bit rusty in the bedroom," Beatrice said.

"You're unbelievable," Anna said.

"What? Somebody had to welcome him home," Beatrice said.

"Well, if I needed any other reason to be repulsed by him," Anna said.

"Oh, don't be so harsh, his intentions were admirable, just lacking refinement," Beatrice said. She giggled. "In all seriousness though, you might have to be prepared if he takes a more direct approach. We are all subject to Zinc's whims. What if he orders you to wed his father?"

"I don't know if he'll push the issue. I know where all the bodies are buried, and I assure you, not all of them deserved to be there," Anna said.

Constance's smile evaporated, but she remained silent.

I'll have to be careful moving forward. Constance only has one allegiance, and it's not me, Anna thought.

Zinc cracked his host's knuckles while sitting in a chair in the communications room of the Al Hurriya Air Base of the Iraqi Air Force. The skies were relatively quiet in the dead of night, but soon that would change. With the arrival of morning, all manner of deadly birds would take to the air over the battlefield.

Lord Plutonium entered the communications room within an Iraqi host. Zinc assessed the Asian Angel. He was the eldest son of Lord Uranium II. Plutonium carried himself with poise and self-assuredness. *I suppose centuries of supporting his father in the rivalry with Platinum forged him into a commanding persona,* Zinc thought.

"Supreme Commander," Plutonium said. He saluted.

Zinc returned the gesture.

"Quiet night," Plutonium said.

"For now. Are your forces ready for their mission?" Zinc asked.

"Just waiting for the word," Plutonium said.

"Timing is going to be everything for this one," Zinc said.

"The MiG-23 is a powerful ground-attack aircraft. We will do our part. The rest is on Gallium," Plutonium said.

Zinc nodded. "Very well. But don't loiter. There are reports of F-14s in the area. Their range of fire and speed are not to be underestimated."

"It is not in my nature to avoid a fight," Plutonium said.

"Ah, I see so much of your father in you," Zinc said.

The younger Angel broke his stoic demeanor and smiled. "That is quite the compliment," he said.

"But temper your exuberance," Zinc said. "You don't want to expose yourself or your House to unnecessary risks. Up there, it's not a matter of courage. The most skilled pilot is helpless if his plane is inferior."

"We'll deliver success," Plutonium said.

"I have no doubt you will," Zinc said.

Plutonium started to leave then turned back and said, "Oh, do you want me to station one of my House here to watch your back?" He looked around the room. "Usually, you have your feminine protective detail."

"I'll be fine, thank you for your consideration. I think you'll need all your pilots," Zinc said.

Angels are always scheming, Zinc thought. However, he did have a point. The absence of my protective agents is obvious. Ugh, I didn't even give them a good excuse this time.

Zinc considered unburdening his collusion with Schitz to Constance. He trusted her. Yet, he hesitated. *I've already told my father and if there's one thing I know, secrets can only be kept in the smallest of circles.*

"I hope today goes well," he said to himself. "This agreement is providing a lot of stress and doesn't seem to be working out to my benefit as often as it helps the Demon. I wonder if I should just kill Schitz."

The Tehran apartment was unoccupied because its owner was at the front. Soon Coronavirus would be there as well. He had used the vacant abode for a rendezvous with his illicit lover. Coronavirus slid his robes back over his muscular frame. He had savored the moment of carnal indulgence, but his mind was already drifting back to less enjoyable matters, such as where he was headed.

"Must you leave already?" Vampirosis asked.

The pair had been part of the massive Second World War cohort and were some of the few survivors of their class.

"I have specific instructions where I am to be. I'm sure Anaphylaxis is already wondering where I am," Coronavirus said.

"Ah, come COVID, you're not needed there until morning," she said

"It is morning, and believe me, I wish I could stay," he said. He weighed his next snarky sentence for a moment. He considered keeping it to himself, then said, "I mean, it's not like you don't have someone else you can go spend some time with. If you're not satisfied."

Vampirosis laughed, a feminine giggle which annoyed him. Her enticing, naked frame slid across the bed and rose before him. She stroked his cheek.

"I am more than satisfied, my love. I hate when you talk about him," she said.

I hate that I have to, Coronavirus thought. Hypocritically, he overlooked the fact that like his lover, he too had a living spouse. Hatred for Haemophilus Influenzae, Vampirosis's husband, was omnipresent. COVID seldom thought of his wife, Borderline Personality Disorder, when he was with his paramour.

"I'm sorry," he said, feeling pathetic for apologizing.

"You will be," she said.

She had a playful glint in her eyes, but the mood had been killed for him. He loathed the clandestine nature of their arrangement and that he didn't have her to himself. He kissed her with mimed passion, more out of the desire to stake a claim than to express affection.

"Be careful my love, there's something going on," she said.

"There's always something going on," he replied. He draped a bandoleer of throwing knives over his robe, buckled his sword to his waist, then scooped up his heavy Celestial flail. He rested the chain over his shoulder.

Vampirosis smiled, "You look dashing."

Despite his mood, COVID broke into a small grin.

Vampirosis's guise shifted to one of gravity. "I'm serious. My father and other senior Demons think Schitz is not to be trusted. They are trying to investigate him."

"Isn't your father best friends with Schizophrenia?" Coronavirus asked.

"He is, but it doesn't mean Schitz isn't involved in some treachery," she said.

Coronavirus was not entirely certain he bought the whole "supreme commander is a traitor" idea.

"Because of your shoot down?" he said.

"That and other things. Look, you do what you want. I'm just saying be careful. You might be reporting to Anaphylaxis, but all of the orders came down from Schitz," Vampirosis said. Her voice had grown testy. COVID knew to back off.

"Alright, I'll be extra cautious," he said.

He made a portal and departed for the Iranian front lines. The hour was still early; the desert was mostly peaceful. The sun had yet to dawn on another day of carnage.

"And where have you been?" Anaphylaxis asked.

COVID rolled his eyes.

"Yes, indeed, where have you been?" Narcissistic Personality Disorder echoed.

"Just relaxing a bit. I haven't missed the battle have I?" he replied to his superior and his annoying brother. *NPD has always been friends with BPD; he should have married her. And he should keep his opinions about my other activities to himself,* COVID thought.

Neither seemed satisfied with the response. COVID didn't care. He stepped into a mortal and lit a cigarette. Anaphylaxis and BPD were both still staring at him in disbelief. He reclined against the wall of the trench and inhaled the smoke into his host's lungs.

"What? Look how many of us are here," he said and gestured toward the assembled squad of Demons. "Surely, with this many committed to the fight, you should have bigger concerns than me and what I was doing with my free time."

He pulled another drag from his cigarette, then stomped it out. *The problem is they were so quick to marry us off. If I had a choice, I would have preferred Vampirosis over BPD hands down, but nobody cared about what I wanted. They just wanted offspring for the war effort.* He lit another cigarette.

The morning arrived soon after his arrival at the front. The Fajr call to prayer took place at dawn. The sun crept over the barren desert expanse. Coronavirus had seen his fair share of fighting during the Second World War. Still, the sight of the mechanized Iraqi units rolling towards his position shook him to the core. He spotted Angels among the infantry, but his primary concern was the Soviet-built tanks that were pounding 125 mm shells. He fired back and shouted to Anaphylaxis. The zip and pop of incoming rounds plinked around the trench.

"Do we need to go into the Celestial?" His voice was buffeted by the vibrations of another tank shell exploding nearby.

The squad leader ducked debris from an incoming shell. "Stay in your host for now. We don't know how many Angels there are."

The flight of MiG-23 Floggers rocketed across the early morning sky. The Soviet built aircraft was one of the fastest in existence. Lord Plutonium spoke into his radio, "Yalla, yalla![28]" He eased back on the throttle. His Flogger drifted back behind the rest of the flight. He had led them into battle, but he wanted to be the last on the scene, so he could cover the flight's retreat.

The rest of the ground attack aircraft rolled in and dropped their payloads on the Iranians and Demons below. While he was lining up his approach, two contacts appeared on Plutonium's radar.

"F-14s, bug out!" he shouted into the radio.

---

[28] Hurry up, hurry up!

COVID fired his rifle again and tried to battle back the sensation of inevitable defeat. He was uncertain whether it came from his host or himself, but the doubt... the fear... the terror, were always present.

He dropped a possessed Iraqi with a shot to the chest. The Angel within seized on the ground about a hundred meters from his position. *There we go*, he thought. They couldn't move forward to dispatch the Angel, but it was still a positive to shoot one out of its host.

Suddenly, fire came from above – a flight of Iraqi Air Force MiG-23s. The Floggers were an exceptional ground attack aircraft. Their payloads incinerated the Iranian forward trench in a fiery explosion. His host fell and a departure seizure shook COVID, a nauseating paroxysm.

This is it; I am undone.

Plutonium scrubbed his approach and dropped his bombs without aiming. The others had already obliterated the enemy. The rest of the Angels steered their MiG-23s farther into Iraqi held territory. Their superior speed would outrun the F-14s. He noticed the cockpits of both enemy aircraft contained the dark aura of Demonic possession.

Oh, this is too good, he thought.

Plutonium pushed his throttle forward and pulled the MiG-23 into an arching turn. He looked through the canopy and saw one of the F-14s pursuing his squadron of fleeing MiGs; the other was engaging the advancing Iraqis. *He's trying to help his comrades on the ground, and expects I'm fleeing like the others.*

He threw his jet into a loop. The sudden gain in altitude from the maneuver would have left him incredibly vulnerable to the F-14s, however they had split their efforts and he had found a small seam between them. At the top of his loop, the target fell perfectly across his scope. The radar lock tone sounded. Plutonium fired a single R-23 Apex missile. He continued the loop, then fled for home.

He shouted when the F-14 erupted in a ball of flame. "That's what I'm talking about!"

The immobilizing fit was painful and never ending. From experience, Coronavirus expected an Angel to arrive and kill him while he was helpless. The overwhelming sensations receded from Coronavirus's mind; the departure seizure faded. He sensed an Angel bearing down on him and raised his sword to block the blow. He sliced the Angel across her leg. She fell, immobilized.

Instead of finishing her, COVID fled through the Celestial; he was still a little weakened from the seizure. Thoughts assaulted his mind.

How did they know to have such effective air support at the out-set of the engagement? Does this have anything to do with what Vampirosis mentioned?

Typically, either side tried to vector in ground attack aircraft after the presence of the enemy was confirmed. But Coronavirus and his squad had been struck within moments of contact with the enemy.

Were we so sloppy that their Familiars spotted us early?

He grabbed a rough, wooden plank from the floor of the trench and rested it across the gully. He carved the ancient symbols in the dirt and poured water from his canteen over them. He was relieved when the portal opened, but he could not shake his feelings regarding the ambush.

He looked up and saw a deployed parachute drifting toward the ground. The mortal dangling from the chute had an aura of Demonic possession.

"Sucks to be you," Coronavirus said.

He stepped through the portal.

While he walked through the Great Hall, the impact of the debacle hit home. They had lost Anaphylaxis, Narcissistic Personality Disorder, Dyspareunia, Central Hyperventilation Syndrome, and Gender Identity Disorder.

"Our whole squad got wiped out," he said. His feet wobbled and he sat on the cold marble floor. NPD *was annoying, but he was still my brother.*

He scooted out of the walkway and leaned against a pillar. He heard a familiar voice, the Supreme Commander Schizophrenia. He was on the other side of the pillar and could not see COVID.

"Is there something specific you want to ask?" Schitz said.

"Not really, I just want to know my six o'clock is covered," another voice replied.

COVID craned his neck. Schitz was speaking with Vampirosis's father, AIDS. So *she was telling the truth,* COVID thought.

"It was, and is despite your churlish nature, my friend," Schitz said.

I'm sorry," AIDS said. "I meant no disrespect. It just caught me off guard when I ran into her."

"Forget about it," Schitz said. "It was a rough day for all of us."

COVID heard one set of footsteps moving away while the other rounded the column. His pulse raced. It was too late to walk away. He looked up and met the gaze of Schizophrenia.

The ancient Demon seemed startled for a moment but quickly recovered.

"Oh, hello there, Coronavirus," Schitz said.

"Hello, Schizophrenia," Coronavirus said.

For a moment COVID wondered if that would be the extent of the exchange. Schitz reached down and extended his hand. He pulled COVID to his feet. The elder Demon adjusted COVID's robes. "See, this is what I've been saying to Titus, it's such an antiquated look."

"I'm sorry?" COVID said.

"The robes. Satan would never listen to me about anything, but I've been telling Titus that we need new uniforms. Come on, come with me," Schitz said.

COVID felt like he swallowed a boulder. He wanted nothing

more than to get away, but he followed the Supreme Commander, nevertheless.

They made their way to the library of Hell and then through a narrow corridor to a portion of the Great Hall COVID had never seen. Priests and Priestesses were coming and going, mingling, and pursuing mundane activities.

"I never realized there were so many clergy," COVID said.

"Well, how often do you pay attention to those administering the Return Ceremony?" Schitz asked.

"Ah, fair enough," COVID said. He felt a little more comfortable. Schitz was most likely not going to kill him in the company of Church officials.

"You also might not realize but there are also many supportive roles not trusted to the Wraiths, so yes, there are more Priests and Priestesses than you know," Schizophrenia said.

They entered a tailor's shop. The High Priest Titus and other clergy were overseeing several Wraiths who were working with lengths of fabric.

"Oh, my good friend," Schitz said. He shook Titus's hand.

"Good to see you, Schitz. Ah, Coronavirus welcome," Titus said.

COVID tried to shake his surreal feeling. *A little while ago I was fighting for my life, now I'm here looking at clothes,* he thought.

"Well, here are some different ideas," Titus said.

Schitz scrutinized the various outfits the Priests brought forth.

"I'm not trying to look like a Russian admiral," Schitz said to the first ostentatious number.

"Hmm, a little boring, no?" he said to the next.

This continued until Schitz settled on a gray and black trimmed tunic and trousers slightly reminiscent of a Schutzstaffel uniform in terms of color but more modern in its design.

"What do you think?" Schitz asked.

Everyone looked at Coronavirus.

"Ah, I'm not sure. I kind of like this one, casual," COVID said.

Some of the Priestesses and Wraiths giggled.

"Oh, um, those are just used for sizing and cutting material, they're not actually clothes," Titus said.

Coronavirus flushed.

"So what, you've imagined some sort of plainclothes attire for the field?" Schitz asked. He glared at the snickering individuals.

"Yeah, I mean I imagine some Demons will be resistant toward abandoning robes, others might like your modern military look," COVID said. "Some might be like me; they might like something plain and casual for the field. Maybe there could be another for more formal functions like weddings and funerals," COVID said.

"Perfect, do it," Schitz said. "Make my comrade here a contemporary field outfit, and start producing the tunic and trousers combo for those who would like to modernize," Schitz said.

"It will be done," Titus said.

Schizophrenia and Coronavirus departed the domain of the Priesthood. They made their way back through the library to the Great Hall.

"My life has a multiple aspects, many of which may go unobserved by the rank and file soldiers," Schitz said. "Witness the conversation you overheard earlier."

Coronavirus's mouth went dry. *Here it is*, he thought.

Schitz waved his hand as though he could hear COVID's concerned thoughts.

"No, no, don't worry. I know you didn't mean to be there. But I'm curious what you think," Schitz said.

"Well, if I'm being completely honest..." Coronavirus said.

"I would expect you would be. I'll be able to tell if you're not," Schitz said.

"I...well...Alright, so the thing is – ah...some senior Demons are concerned that you might be a bad actor," COVID said.

Schitz put his arm around COVID's shoulder. It was heavy – and cold.

"And what do *you* think?" the elder Demon asked.

"I don't know what to think," COVID said.

"Oh, come on, you're a bright guy," Schitz said. He punctuated his sentence by flicking COVID's Pentagram First Class.

"Today's ambush was suspicious, to say the least. I found myself wondering if something was afoot," Coronavirus said.

"A commander sends his troops out, knowing some may not return," Schitz said. He unhooked his arm from around COVID's shoulder and met his gaze.

"As opposed to ensuring they do not return," Coronavirus said.

Schitz's chuckle was unnerving.

"I'm involved in a very deep, very long game," Schitz said.

"And today's botch job was part of it?

Schitz nodded.

"Some Demons are concerned that you are directly involved in some of our soldiers meeting their demise," COVID said. "Or so I've heard."

There was an awkward pause in the conversation.

"I wonder if you might put Haemophilus Influenzae's name in that book," COVID said.

"And if something were to befall your girlfriend's husband, might you be inclined to forget about your concerns vis-à-vis today's action?" Schitz asked.

How does he know about us? Coronavirus thought.

"Indeed," he said.

"Consider your girlfriend liberated," Schitz said.

"Than—"

"Don't thank me," Schitz said. "Just know that you are in a very unique position. But remember I have survived foes more formidable than you."

Wynter Zinc looked at the report one last time. She balled it up and tossed it into the base of the cooking fire. *Korsakoff Syndrome and Haemophilus Influenzae*, she thought. Lord Zinc II, the Standard Bearer of her House had assigned her to the mission in Afghanistan.

The report he had provided detailed that two Demons would be arriving at the Afghan village within a squad of Soviet troops.

I wonder how the leadership acquires such detailed information, she thought. Wynter had recently graduated from the Angelic Academy and was anxious to complete her first mission. She was leading a squad of youngsters from the vassal Houses of the Zinc fiefdom. There were descendants of Gold, Silver and Iron in her squad.

Zinc had told her it was important to learn how to lead the House's subordinates. The weight of the responsibility felt heavy. She clutched her Kalashnikov and looked across the vacant, humble home. They had packed it with plastic explosives.

Wynter and Mikhail Silver, a lad of the unincorporated Silver House were the only Angels in possession of a host. The rest of the squad was outside the house in the Celestial Realm.

"What if they arrive in the Celestial? This trap will be useless," Mikhail asked.

"Just follow the plan, slave," Wynter said.

Her fellow seemed taken aback, but smirked and shrugged.

The squad of Soviet infantry walked through the village. The area outside of Jalalabad had been quiet and the troops seemed at ease. Wynter pushed open the wooden door of the house and raised her assault rifle.

The pops of the AK were deafening. She fired a burst in the direction of the Soviet soldiers and ducked back into the house.

"You know what to do," she shouted to her subordinate.

Wynter exited the rear of the house and entered a narrow alleyway. The Soviet troops were experienced and were approaching the source of the gunfire from several directions. Two Demonically possessed troops had just entered the house when Wynter's subordinate detonated the plastic.

The explosion destroyed the humble domicile and several surrounding buildings. Wynter hopped out of her host. The Afghan woman was thrown down the alleyway from the force of the blast. Within the smoldering crater, three Celestial beings wriggled and twitched from departure seizures.

Wynter drew her Celestial dagger. It shook in her hand as she approached the first Demon, a young male. Wynter stabbed him. The Demon's face contorted in unimaginable agony. She slashed again and again until he was still. Blood trickled from the Demon's mouth and nose.

Wynter made her way to the seizing Female Demon. She took a more measured approach. She put her hand over the Demon's mouth and steadied her, then stabbed her foe in the throat. The Demon twitched and stilled.

Wynter rose to her feet. She looked about the blackened, burning crater with glee. Her fellows joined her. They gazed at the butchered Demons and the seizing Angel. Mikhail emerged from the throes of his fit. He sat up cross-legged and rested his hands in his lap.

"That was rough," he said.

"You did your part," Wynter said blandly.

"Seems like it all worked out," the Silver youngster said.

"Of course it did; I was in charge," Wynter said. "Come on, let's head back."

Mikhail reached out his hand for assistance to his feet. Wynter brushed past and climbed out of the crater.

Coronavirus sat at a small desk in the basement of a Beirut apartment building. Around him lay piles of ammunition, mortar shells, rifles, pistols, and other assorted weaponry of the local Hezbollah fighters. The mortals that would use the equipment were otherwise occupied. COVID was using the downtime to map out the various connections between the spider web of the alliance that included the PLO, PKK, ASALA, Al-Tawhid, Jammoul, and other factions.

"Narcos, Communists, and Islamists sure do like their abbreviations," COVID said to himself.

"So does the USA, NATO, OAS, and UN," a voice said from the corner of the room.

COVID whirled to find a Wraith. She was thin and elderly in appearance. Coronavirus recognized her as Josephine, the most senior Wraith.

"Touché," he said. "What's up?"

"Schitz sent me to give his condolences," she said.

A wicked, evil grin spread across her face. It was followed by a look of pantomimed sorrow.

"Your poor sister, Korsakoff Syndrome was killed in combat in Afghanistan. She fell alongside Haemophilus Influenzae in a horrendous ambush," Josephine said.

"Tell him I appreciate his concern. I understand...I *understand* that he is very busy. It is most kind for him to take the time to inform me," he said.

"I'll let him know..." Josephine said, "That you understand."

The Wraith melted into the shadows of the basement.

COVID thought of his many siblings. They were not close: Marburg Hemorrhagic Fever, Alzheimer's, Huntington's Disease, NPD, and Korsakoff. Despite the lack of close familial bonds, they were all fond of each other, and all save Huntington's had survived the Second World War, no small feat.

Now two of us are gone in quick succession, he thought. *I know Schitz killed my sister along with Haemophilus Influenzae to make a point. There was a price to be paid for freeing up Vampirosis. There'll be a higher toll if I make waves.*

Coronavirus climbed the stairs. At the top doorway he stooped and traced the symbols for earth and air in the dust and grime on the floor. Before he could breathe onto the symbol he heard an enchanting, feminine voice coming from the residential floor above. The singer played the piano while singing her haunting tune, *Waiting Below the Surface,* wafted over the bomb-damaged apartment building and out over the ravaged district.

Still I'm waiting, never aging,
Still I'm waiting, what else to do,
Still I'm waiting, softly raging,
Still I'm waiting, here for you.

The sky above is dark and gray,
It whispers softly of decay.
The whistling wind seems to say:
The living have all turned away.

A chill ran through his frame. He listened for a moment longer then opened the portal.

Why did you leave?
To flee the pall?
And I, alone to grieve,
That we are liars, one and all.

Lay me down to sleep,
While outside the shadows creep,
There are secrets in the deep,
And they want my soul, to keep.

Wynter Zinc was presented with The First Order. The ceremony was not expansive. Only the House of Zinc and its subordinate Houses were in attendance. Nevertheless, Wynter was ecstatic and virtually glowed with exuberance.

"You did the hardest part," Melissa Silver said.

Her brother, Mikhail Silver, the detonator of the house bomb, shrugged. "I didn't kill any Demons. I just blew up my host and some Russians," he said.

"Still, it wouldn't have worked without you," she said.

"Eh, it was what it was. I'm glad I survived. Medals are for incorporated Houses. I'm perfectly fine to defer to Wynter Zinc, TFO," he said.

But you, still chose to leave?
To step from beneath the pall?
Leaving me alone to grieve,
That we are liars, one and all.

I am gone and can't be found,
Lost darkness all around,
Forever haunted by the sound,
Of rustling leaves upon the ground.

COVID milled about at the fringe of the cluster of mourners.

"I'm sorry about your sister," Titus said.

The Demon looked up from his cup of Brew to see the High Priest.

"She was a brave warrior," Titus said.

What am I supposed to say? COVID thought.

"Yes, she was. She'll be missed," COVID said.

Titus nodded and patted him on the arm. "We will mourn her loss and then recommit ourselves to the final victory. Your star is on the rise. It's not many Schitz takes under his wing," Titus said.

"I'm sorry?" COVID asked.

"The other day, at the shop. He doesn't take just anyone along with him. I assumed you, like AIDS, are one of our newest talents, someone he has taken to refining," Titus said.

Coronavirus swirled his cup and drained it. "Ah, of course, yes, it is quite the honor," he said.

"Your exploits will be an honor to your family and your sister's memory. To all of us really. Stay safe. We'll be counting on you," Titus said.

The Priest patted him on the arm again and departed.

"Hmmm, stay safe, it's not as easy as some would make it seem," COVID said under his breath.

He looked across the gathering and saw Schitz. He was immersed in friendly conversation with AIDS, Anorexia, and Autism. For a moment, his stare met the ancient Demon's gaze. Schitz nodded. COVID raised his cup and tilted his head in acknowledgment.

Still I'm waiting, never aging,
Still I'm waiting, what else to do,
Still I'm waiting, softly raging,
Still I'm waiting, here for you.
Below the surface, here for you.

CHAPTER 13

BITTERSWEET

Silver cursed under his breath and kicked the wall of the bunker. He immediately regretted it while hopping on one foot. The grumbling and swearing continued.

"What's going on over there?" Christa asked. She stood in the doorway of the large storage hallway.

"The cursed mortals," Silver replied.

Christa waited for him to continue. Silver rotated his ankle assessing the self-inflicted damage.

"They keep outpacing our efforts. I had adapted warheads to these Zvezda Kh-66 aerial bombs. Each bomb weighs six hundred and thirty-three pounds. I have just discovered this very munition was replaced by the Kh-23, which was made obsolete by the Grom-B. My arsenal of Kh-66s belongs in a museum. If we even snuck them into the Mortal Realm, they would raise suspicion, completely unnecessary suspicion, because the odds that they would be affixed to any attack aircraft are next to zero."

He drew back his fist to punch the wall, remembered his pained ankle and reconsidered.

"Some things still have to be up-to-date, no?" Christa asked.

"Yes, yes, the ammunition remains good," Silver said. "Thankfully, I have fabricated millions of rounds of ammunition and thus far they haven't invented laser guns or whatever."

Christa laughed, "Well, there's a plus."

Silver nodded and shrugged his shoulders.

"Perhaps you should focus on a small subset of weapons," Christa said.

"The only way this is going to work is if we can infiltrate our weapons into all aspects of a conflict," Silver said. "The Demons are cagey; they will figure out what is happening and develop a countermeasure. We have to wipe them out all in one go."

"Then I guess you just have to be prepared to face setbacks," Christa said. She kissed him on the forehead.

"I suppose so," he said.

"What are you going to do with these? The bunker's large, but we don't have infinite space," Christa said.

Silver chuckled. "I'll take out my components, then Lilly will have to find a way to take them to the Academy," he said. "I don't think she'll love the plan."

"You never stop terrorizing that poor Familiar," Christa said.

Silver's false teeth flashed in a toothy grin. "It's just how I am with my friends."

A heavy knock on the exterior door interrupted their conversation.

The pair made their way through the bunker to the entrance. Silver opened it just enough to peer out.

"Oh, Anna, what a pleasant surprise," Silver said.

"It's good to see you Uncle, Christa," Anna said.

Silver stepped through the gap in the door and embraced Anna. Then he turned her away from the opening.

"I'm not here for your secrets," Anna said.

Christa had followed Silver out and shut the door behind her.

"Well, in that case, how can we help you?" Silver asked.

"I'm in a predicament similar to what you went through," Anna said. She sighed and fidgeted with visible embarrassment. "Zinc wants me to marry his father."

A fit of laughter gripped Silver. He tried to stifle it, but his attempt only made him chuckle more. Christa elbowed him in the ribs.

"See, this is why I didn't even want to ask for help. Everything is a joke to you," Anna said.

"No, no, I'm sorry," Silver said. "I wasn't laughing at you. I was amused that Zinc asked you. Typically he commands, but I'm certain he was too terrified to do so on this occasion."

"Well, the pressure is increasing," Anna said.

"But doesn't he know you're—" Silver stopped.

"What?" Anna asked. She crossed her arms. "Doesn't he know I'm what?"

"...Not interested," Silver said.

"Zinc does not care about anyone other than himself," Anna said.

"Unfortunately, as a member of an unincorporated House, Zinc can instruct you to marry whomever he pleases," Christa said. "Your best bet is to exploit something he needs. Like you pointed out, he is selfish."

"Yes, he bought my loyalty and good behavior with our marriage," Silver said. He wrapped his arm around Christa's shoulder. "You just have to find something he values more than making his father happy. Which, if I recall his youth, is not a lot."

"Your help is astounding," Anna said.

"Well, hold on now," Silver said. "The stability of Angelic order is paramount to Zinc. If you had a rival suitor of high standing, he would probably back off. I doubt he values his father's interest over the peace he fought so hard to establish."

"Remarkably perceptive, Darling," Christa said. She playfully flicked his nose.

"Yes, thank you Uncle. That is actually... a good idea," Anna said.

"Why are you both acting like that's so rare for me? I found the Titan's sword! I'm bloody smart," Silver said.

All three laughed. Silver was happy to see Anna's mood brighten.

"Any ideas of who is senior enough for this plan to work?" Christa asked.

Anna scrunched up her face in thought for a moment, then said, "Ah, of course, Uranium II. I was instrumental in his installation. Surely, he'll do me a favor. Besides, he's fighting to remain relevant after his illness. Anything that takes Zinc down a peg will be helpful to him."

"Isn't he already married?" Silver asked.

"He is, but his line practices an old tradition where the Standard Bearer is permitted to take a new wife when his current bride is no longer able to bear children. The former wife retires to their ancestral monastery in the Heavenly Mountains," Christa said.

"Perfect," Anna said.

"Well, there you have it, sounds like a good plan," Silver said.

"I'm sure the charade will work, but have you ever considered actually settling down?" Christa asked. "It's not *all* horrible."

"Thanks wife, I'm right here," Silver said with mock offense.

"I know dear. You were meant to hear it," Christa said.

Anna sighed. "If I were lucky like you two, maybe I would, but thus far, that hasn't been the case," she said.

"Well, it might come along when you least suspect it," Silver said. "In the meantime, good luck securing Uranium II's cooperation. I don't foresee it being a challenge for someone of your menacing talents."

Anna bid them adieu. When she had disappeared beyond the nearest hill, Silver turned his attention back to his seemingly unending task. "Well, back to my slaving. Hopefully nothing else has gone out of operation," he said.

"Oh, come on Hephaestus, it's not all that bad," Christa said.

Coronavirus walked across Red Square past the colorful, pear-shaped domes of the Cathedral of Vasily the Blessed. The summer air was warm and pleasant. The mood of the common people was vibrant despite the current political situation.

He approached an elderly mortal with a dark aura of Demonic possession. The man was wearing a new suit that identified him as important. *Probably KGB, or a politician, or both,* Coronavirus thought.

"Ah, you were looking for me," Schitz said from within the host. He spoke without turning to look at Coronavirus.

"Correct as always," Coronavirus said.

"It's beautiful, no?" Schitz asked.

Coronavirus looked up at the iconic church. "I guess. I never really thought about it, but I suppose from a purely architectural aesthetic, it's alright," he said.

Schitz chuckled. "I get it, you're concerned I'm a traitor and now you find me admiring a church. They can be beautiful. Have you ever been to Notre-Dame de Paris?"

Coronavirus felt his skin crawl. "I can't say that I have," he said.

"Well, you certainly didn't come here to talk about sixteenth century architecture. So how can I help you?" Schitz asked.

Coronavirus felt a tremor in his body. He tried to find the right words, "Well, as you know, I well, I am involved with Vampirosis and, I really would like to marry her, but umm—"

"But you're married to Borderline Personality Disorder," Schitz said.

COVID was grateful for the interruption.

"So leave her," Schitz said. For the first time, he looked away from the church and met Coronavirus's gaze.

COVID felt a sudden chill as though winter had suddenly descended upon Moscow.

"You know, our laws don't permit..."

"Da, da, I jest, I jest," Schitz said. He waved his hand dismissively. "You would like your poor wife to join your girlfriend's late husband in the land of discarded Demons. So you come once more to the notorious source of Demonic demise."

"Something like that," COVID said.

"Well, you certainly have balls," Schitz said. "I might like you even more than I thought."

Coronavirus laughed nervously.

"Well, I've been learning about Russian tanks," Schitz said. "It seems the Soviets export woefully second rate variants. They also give...they also give..." He laughed uncontrollably and wiped tears from his eyes. "...they give customer nations training rounds and tell them they are as good as actual tank shells."

"Not a good time to be supplied with their equipment," Coronavirus said.

Schitz said, "Exactly, and Saddam looks like he's going to be in a fight with the Americans any day now. I might be inclined to investigate how woeful these export T-72s really are, but anybody I send to Iraq will be..."

"Exposed," COVID said, completing his sentence.

Schitz tapped his nose.

"I can't thank you enough," Coronavirus said.

"Don't thank me. You'll owe me later," Schitz said.

"Of course," Coronavirus said. *Great, I'll be in debt to the most vicious of Demons,* COVID thought. *Well, it will be worth it if I can simplify my romantic life.*

Coronavirus longed for something else to talk about other than his mariticidal conspiring.

"So what makes your disease so virulent with the mortals?" COVID asked.

"If I attacked their minds in a specific way, my disease would be rather mundane," Schitz said. "They might even develop some protections against it – even while I was still alive."

"Oh, I thought our diseases remained a mystery to the mortals while we were alive," COVID said.

"Yes, that is true, but if you fail to craft an effective disease, they might not develop a cure, but they may find a way to treat or minimize it. Conversely, if you develop an intricate disease, they might be helpless to it even decades or centuries after your death," Schitz said.

"Fascinating, so your disease is complex?" COVID asked.

"It is as intricate as the minds of the mortals and ever changing in the course it takes," Schitz said

"I'll have to apply that to my own," Coronavirus said.

"It's a must. AIDS has ensured that his virus is always changing," Schitz said.

"Your protégé," COVID said.

"Yes, he is a great warrior," Schitz said.

"Ever thought of taking on another one?" COVID asked.

"It's nice of you to offer, but I already have my hands full with your future father-in-law," Schitz said.

"Well, I appreciate the advice about disease cultivation," COVID said.

"Anytime, anytime," Schitz said.

COVID looked back up at the church. In the afternoon sunlight the building was spectacular, even if it was a house of the enemy.

"You know, I have to say, the building is quite beautiful," Coronavirus said.

He was met with silence. When he looked back over his shoulder, Schitz and his host were gone.

He gives me the creeps, COVID thought.

The corridors of the Great Hall wound before her like a great serpent. A Familiar had told Anna that Lord Uranium II was in residence. She was not sure what she would encounter when she propositioned the supreme commander of the Angels. She had heard much about him; mortal lore held him up as an archangel. He jointly held the highest office with only Zinc as a peer. He was a well-known firebrand, quick to anger and easy to rush to confrontation, but also a contemplative leader.

I wonder how he will take to my designs, Anna thought.

She knocked on the door.

"You may enter," a voice said from within.

Anna pushed open the door. The dwelling place was a surprise. Zinc was fond of oil painting depicting various moments of his life (some accurate, others fantastical), trophies from the battlefield, and all manner of fancied ornamentation. Conversely, Uranium's room was bare and spartan.

"How can I help you, Anna Gold of Zinc?" Uranium II asked.

He appeared older than any Angel she had seen. His hair was falling out, his skin was wrinkled and spotted. Uranium IIs condition was public knowledge, however seeing the effects up close stunned Anna.

"I have come to recall a favor," Anna said. *I wonder if I sound confident.*

Uranium II chuckled, then coughed. He punched himself in the chest, then chuckled some more. "I don't recall owing you a favor," he said.

"I was instrumental in your ascent to power, I—" Anna said.

Uranium II batted away words with a swat of his hand, "Girl, if I found myself beholding to every tool, I'd never get any work done. Anything you did for me, you did at the behest of Zinc. Therefore, I would owe him, not you."

Anna felt a twinge of frustration and the forming of a knot in her stomach. *Should I play my last card? There's no going back after that. Am I so repulsed by old man Zinc, that I would risk so much?*

"I thought you might say that, but tell me this. I have been told that the Asiatic Angels particularly venerate their ancestors. Is this true?" she asked.

Uranium II nodded curtly and said, "This is so. Why do you ask?"

"Well, you call me girl, but do not forget that I am older than you, Xiang Uranium II. Or should I say Xiang Cobalt or Xiang Mercury?" Anna said.

"I am familiar with my origins," Uranium II said.

"But do you revere your ancestors? Your adoptive father Cobalt got caught up in the succession crisis with you and your contemporaries, but what of ancient Lord Mercury? Does he hold your admiration and filial respect?" Anna asked.

"Of course, he does. Lord Mercury IV and all of the previous Mercury Lords are steeped in the history of the Asian Angels," Uranium II said. "The first three Mercury Lords reached retirement. They reside in the Heavenly Monastery, high in the mountains. In many ways they are our living Gods, somewhere between departed and living ancestors."

"So then, I wonder what the surviving Lords or you for that matter would think if you all were to discover his real killer," Anna said.

"What do you mean? Uranium II asked.

His face revealed his interest. His voice was intense. Anna braced herself and continued. She reached into her robes and retrieved a cloth-wrapped stiletto of a throwing knife.

"This is not the exact blade that killed him." Anna said. "I filed all of them down to the same width to hide their origin."

She unwound the bundle and handed the knife to Uranium II.

"Adapting weapons is frowned upon," Uranium II said.

"It is fitting for an assassin to behave like one," Anna said.

"And this assassination was ordered by Zinc?" Uranium II said.

Anna nodded.

"I knew he was duplicitous, but to have broken the chain of Mercuries, ah, umm, eh… I am speechless. Regardless of politics, all of his descendants would scream for blood. This is different than killing over a feud as I did with my brothers, this is something else altogether," Uranium II said.

"So, my favor?" Anna said. '

"What is it you ask of me?" Uranium II asked.

"I would like to be your fiancée," Anna said.

Uranium II coughed violently. His face was the picture of shock. "Excuse me?" he said.

"Only in name, to put off another suitor," Anna said.

"Oh, that makes more sense," Uranium II said. "Bowing to your request might cause some consternation in my House."

"What do you suggest?" Anna asked.

"What about my eldest, Hirohisa? He is ready to be the Uranium Standard Bearer, should I retire. He would be a better cover story with fewer headaches for me."

"That sounds good to me. What will you do with the information I have told you?" she asked.

Uranium II stroked his chin. "It is but a piece of a puzzle I am putting together. Centuries ago, there would have been an outcry for justice, but now such news would likely only arise to scandal, and I cannot know how the honorable ancestors at the monastery would respond. You need not worry while you remain his bodyguard. I will not act in haste. My illness has tempered my penchant for bold, rash decisions. I will use the information in the right way when the time comes," Uranium II said. "And I thank you for it. You've paid me quite the sum for escaping a marriage."

"It's worth it to me," Anna said.

"Yes, it is often that way. Value is oft relative to the party bargaining," Uranium II.

Anna nodded and saw herself out.

Zinc might fancy himself safe, but whatever Uranium II has in the works, must be massive, if something like this is just "a piece of a puzzle."

Anorexia walked along the banks of the Styx. She glanced up toward the entrance of the cave that housed her uncle, Bubonic Plague. *I wonder when he'll be permitted to return to the fold*, she thought.

Titus took note of her interest in the cave. He motioned as though to speak, but decided against it.

"So, do you think this Inquisition is ever going to happen?" Anorexia asked.

"It will," Titus said, "but Satan raised a good point. What if Schitz is working on something subtle, or what if the "evidence' you have is simply coincidence. It might do more harm than good."

The High Priest once more looked toward the entrance of the cave. "We all have our secrets. Do we deserve to have them forced into the light? Does Schitz deserve that? I thought you were fond of him?"

Is everybody always going to have my obsession with Schitz on the tip of their tongue? Why does he keep looking at the cave, does he know about Plague?

"Look, I get it, but this is a life and death matter," Anorexia said. "We're looking into instances where we lost important Demons. Vampirosis thought Schitz intentionally hit her plane with a missile. That's not some little secret. And yes, I feel quite deeply for Schitz. I've known him my whole life, but I have to put my personal feelings aside."

"You are an admirable Demon," Titus said. "Your dedication to our cause and your fellows is quite noble. We will have the day in court and we will have everything sorted – one way or another."

"I don't know what to hope for. I think I'd rather be wrong on all of this, but somehow, I don't think I am," Anorexia said.

"Try not to worry too much," Titus said. "We are all just small pieces in a massive machine. As long as we do our part, everything else will sort itself out."

Anna knocked on the door of Zinc's room. For a moment she heard the shuffling of clothes and whispers followed by the instruction to enter.

Constance and Zinc were seated on his bed. They met Anna's arrival with grins.

"Sorry, if I came at a bad time," Anna said.

"It's fine, I've been meaning to talk with you," Zinc said.

Constance motioned to leave, but Zinc shook his head. "If you're going to be my partner, you'll have to stop acting like you're only my bodyguard," he said to her.

Anna felt a mix of emotion. While she was happy Constance had finally gotten her man, Anna also wondered if Zinc was worth her friend's devotion and affection. *He is horrible in so many ways.*

"It would seem my poor father does not reside within your affections," Zinc said. His voice did not sound overly pained by the assessment.

"Ah, so you have heard from Uranium II?" Anna said.

"Uranium II?" Zinc said. He wore a puzzled guise.

"His son Hirohisa's proposal?" Anna said.

Zinc burst into a fit of laughter. "Oh, now this is rich. He's going to be so upset. All of a sudden you are quite popular Miss Gold. No, not Hiroshima. Apparently, you have received a marriage proposal from the Demon Schizophrenia. He did not know that you lived. Upon finding out you were still above ground, he unburdened his undying love for you and asked for your hand," he said.

Anna could not believe Zinc's words. Even as she heard them, it was as though she were suddenly within a dream. *Did I hear him right? Is this some ruse?* It was only after a few moments she realized that she was holding her breath. Anna exhaled, unsure of what to say.

"For once your poker face falls away," Zinc said. "I see you are happy with the news. And what of poor Hiromoto?"

"Hirohisa," Anna said.

"Hiro whatever. What is your answer" Zinc said.

"You would permit me to marry Schitz? How would it work?" she asked. Anna dared not hope for a positive answer.

"Well, he seemed to have a plan. He said something about eloping," Zinc said.

Zinc is something else. I knew he was familiar with the Demon, Spanish Influenza, but how is he tied to Schitz?

"Yes, of course, I accept," Anna said.

Constance jumped up from the bed and flung her arms around Anna. "At long last, we've both found our happiness. I'm overjoyed for you," Constance said.

Anna broke into a broad grin. She squeezed Constance with sisterly affection. Then turned her attention to Zinc. He was sat atop his bed with a mischievous grin.

"Thank you," Anna said.

"Say it. Say I am a good overlord," Zinc said. His voice was full of amusement.

"You really are," Anna said.

She recalled his teasing of Silver before he gave in and allowed him to marry Christa. Suddenly, a swell of guilt washed over Anna's happy feelings. *What have I done? Why did I deliver such damning information to Uranium II? If I had just waited, the suitor situation would have resolved itself.*

"But you look sad?" Zinc said.

"I'll miss you both very much," Anna said.

Zinc seemed taken aback. He rose to his feet and wrapped his arms around her and Constance.

"We'll miss you as well," Zinc said. "I know it hasn't always been easy, or pleasant working for me. But you have always been one of the two most reliable Angels in my life. I cannot ever thank you enough for all you have done for me. If this will make you happy, I more than owe it to you."

Anna felt the creases of her eyes burn. She fought in vain to stop a tear from running down her cheek. The three embraced with deep affection. Anna savored the moment and wished desperately to hold onto it.

Manning the Limbo Fortress was one of the least desirable details in the Heavenly army. The venture into Hell had ended in disaster. Yet, God seemed to be pleased to have acquired an enclave in Satan's domain. The fortress also offered a humanitarian service to mortals. Souls that jumped the banks of the Eunoe were permitted to remain within the countryside of Heaven if they chose to not return to the river of reincarnation. In Hell, souls that jumped the banks of the Styx were tortured by Wraiths before being dumped back into the river. The fortress of Limbo offered sanctuary to souls that reached its gates.

Eun-Sook Uranium contemplated the purpose of the fortress. Despite the good it accomplished for mortal souls and the insult it was to the Demons, she nevertheless hated spending time there. Across the Styx, the bodies of the Angels executed in the Limbo Accords were a permanent testament to her father's failed ambition. The bodies of the slain Angels, a payment demanded by the Titan who arbitrated the Divine Dictum, were a ubiquitous source of shame for her family.

The perpetual twilight of this dismal place is depressing as fuck, she thought. Her light steps carried Eun-Sook across the battlements. *Still, it's safer here than on the battlefield. Once father approves a bride for Hirohisa, I will be next in line, I wonder which House I will—* "Ow!" She clutched her head even while she kicked at the golf ball that had struck her. Eun-Sook turned in the direction from which the ball had come. Along the far bank of the Styx, she could see two figures in the distance.

"You fucking bastards! I'll fucking kill you," she screamed shaking her fist toward her far-off tormentors.

Downrange Titus and Salvatore were beside themselves with laughter.

The distance was too great to make out the words, but through a pair of binoculars, Titus could see a furious Angel shouting in their direction. She was clutching her head with one hand and shaking her fist with the other.

"Oh, you really pissed that one off," Titus said. He handed the binoculars to Salvatore.

The head of the Purists grinned broadly. "Still, I didn't knock her off the rampart. Have to try to put some more force behind the next one," Salvatore said.

"At over five hundred meters, just be happy you hit the target," Titus said.

"Fair enough," Salvatore said. Still looking through the binoculars he added, "There's something alluring about an angry female."

"Speaking of...how are things with Desdemona?" Titus asked.

A scandalous grin spread across Salvatore's face. "Very well. I appreciate your putting in a good word. I'm quite enjoying our illicit romance," he said.

"I'm glad to hear it," Titus said. "Oddly wholesome by your standards."

"Just because I recommended you might try fucking a corpse does not mean that I ever have," Salvatore said with a chuckle.

"That's a relief, and really, I'm happy for the both of you. Our lot can be a lonely one without companionship," Titus said.

"Excuse me your graces," Josephine the Wraith said.

Both Priests jumped. Salvatore grumbled about "sneakiness."

"Schizophrenia has asked for you, Titus," Josephine said.

"More shots for me," Salvatore said. He scooped a ball out of the bucket and set it upon his tee.

Titus nodded to Salvatore and followed the Wraith.

Anna looked across the bakery and said aloud to herself, "You have been faithful over a little."[29] The bakery was far from the most prestigious of assignments, yet she had improved it immensely in her time as its caretaker. She was proud of her incorporation of The

---

[29] Matthew 25:23 (RSVCE)

Confessoress's remedies into the production process. She was even more delighted in the program that allowed many of the drug abusing Familiars to reclaim their lives.

I'll miss it here, she thought. *This is what it must feel like to have a home.* She recalled the injured girl who used to sneak into the bakery after beatings from her siblings. *This place has been good to me. I am happy I could be good to it.*

"You called for me, ma'am," Patrice said.

"Ah, Patrice, it is so good to see you," Anna said. "I must entrust our operation to you for a while. Of course, on paper Beatrice will be the highest ranking as she is an Angel, but you and I know the operation will require your guidance if it is to continue to succeed."

She handed Patrice the Confessoress's journal. Anna had removed the confessions of Angels past and present and left only the recipes and concoctions. The heavily redacted volume looked ridiculous with chucks of pages removed.

"But what is happening to you?" Patrice asked. He had a look of worry etched across his face.

"Oh, I have to attend to something. It will take me away for quite some time," Anna said.

"But you'll be back, when it's done?" he asked.

"I can't say, and that is why you must continue our work in my absence," Anna said.

"This is so unfair, your place is here with us, not whatever Zinc has you doing," Patrice said.

"No, no, you misunderstand this is a good thing, a happy thing. It is only bittersweet because I will miss you and the others so much. But it is not a bad endeavor I go to."

"I am relieved by that, at least," Patrice said. "If I may?" He extended his arms.

Anna wrapped her arms around the Familiar she had come to know so well.

"What's with all the waterworks?" Beatrice asked.

"Oh, be quiet Beatrice," Anna said. She broke the embrace and wiped her eyes. She noticed Patrice was doing the same.

"We have to talk," Anna said.

"Fare thee well, my friend," Anna said to Patrice.

"All the best to you," he said.

Anna and Beatrice made their way to the back of the bakery. Once away from the others Anna said, "I'm leaving!"

"What do you mean?" Beatrice asked. Her eyes were wide with excitement.

"Schitz is alive. He brokered a deal with Zinc for me to marry him," Anna said. Speaking the words aloud suddenly made them feel very real.

"Oh, Anna, that's brilliant news!" Beatrice said. She threw her arms around Anna and kissed her on the cheek. "I'm so happy for you. Look at that, Zinc and your Demon being friends, that's probably how Zinc got his father back."

Beatrice wiped her face.

"Why is everybody crying?" Anna asked with a giggle. She thought of Zinc and Constance.

"Good news like this is so rare," Beatrice said through a sniffle.

"I suppose so. I didn't realize until I started saying my goodbyes just how hard leaving was going to be," Anna said.

"When do you leave?" Beatrice asked.

"Right now. Zinc gave me the symbols to meet up with Schitz. He said it's in Amazonia," Anna said.

"And you're going like that?" Beatrice said. Her was face full of amusement and feigned disappointment.

"Well, yes, I mean. How else would I go?" Anna asked.

Beatrice rolled her eyes. "It's your wedding. You can't go there in your everyday robes," she said.

"It's not a real wedding, Beatrice," Anna said. "He's a Demon. There won't be a ceremony or anything."

"That doesn't matter. It'll be as real as any other wedding. Come on," Beatrice said. She grabbed Anna by the hand.

They made their way through the Great Hall to the quarters of the Krypton House. Anna felt anxious and wondered why they were going to see Rachael's son. Beatrice knocked on the door. It was answered by an Angel of Arabic appearance.

"Ah, Maahjubin, so good to see you," Beatrice said.

"I'm sorry, how can I help you?" the young Angel said.

"I require a favor from you," Beatrice said. "Your wedding dress was absolutely splendid, and I need to borrow it. I promise it will go to good use, and I'll return whatever parts we don't employ."

"Are you ill?" the Angel asked. "My husband is Lord Krypton. My husband is the son of the Archangel Gabriel Hydrogen. My husband will wring your deluded neck when he…"

"That's right, your husband is Ahmed Krypton, right? And wouldn't you like to know what he does with his free time?" Beatrice asked. A broad smirk grew across Beatrice's face. She looked at Anna and said, "Scandalous."

"I'll get the dress," Maahjubin said.

"Thank you kindly," Beatrice said, collecting the dress.

"Where are you going? Tell me what you know about Ahmed," an irate Maahjubin said.

"As soon as I finish the rest of our errands I will return forthwith," Beatrice said.

She hurried Anna away from the door. The process repeated with Liza Promethium, Ichika Dubnium, and Talia Niobium.

"Alright Beatrice, you are ruining too many marriages," Anna said.

From under a pile of dresses Beatrice chuckled and said, "My reputation precedes me. They all assumed the worst. My gossip isn't restricted to intimate encounters. Maahjubin's husband is a gambling addict. Liza's man dresses in drag. I doubt Ichika will care much that her hubby maintains a secret menagerie of species extinct on earth, nor Talia that her spouse spends his leisure time possessing mortal race car drivers. All of their husbands are excessively boring. Yet, the women let their curiosity get the better of them, and now it cost them their wedding dresses."

"Oh, Beatrice you are the worst," Anna said.

"So I've been told," Beatrice said. "Yet, I did not lie. I will divulge the secret. But they will be more relieved to have been swindled than to have learned some damning truth."

"Let's hope for your sake," Anna said.

They made their way to the lodging space of Xiamara Silver. Anna had never met her distant cousin, a widow from Gold and Silver's rebellion.

"How can I help you," Xiamara asked after ushering them into her room.

"Anna here is getting married. Eloping actually, away from Heaven," Beatrice said. "We have some rough materials here. Oh, and we'll need some of the Gold family's jewelry."

"Beatrice!" Anna said. *Her big mouth just spilled everything.*

"Oh, X is a steel-trap, a vault," Beatrice said. "That's why she's the keeper of the heirlooms of both families."

"Even if I wasn't. You saved my life at the battle by the Red Sea," Xiamara said.

"Oh, I'm sorry I don't remember. It was a chaotic experience," Anna said.

Xiamara nodded and said, "It was, if only we had won. Eh, we'll get them next time."

Anna chuckled inwardly at the thought of a second Gold and Silver rebellion.

Xiamara Silver demonstrated herself to be an expert seamstress. In short order she transformed parts of the four separate gowns into one stunning piece. Anna marveled as she looked at herself in the mirror. Once more she felt tears growing in the corners of her eyes.

"Wait here," Xiamara said.

She returned with a large box. "The idiotic rules of Heaven forbid our people from wearing our House's adornments, but since you are once more leaving Heaven, it is only right that you have these," she said.

Anna chose a pair of gold earrings that fell to her shoulders, a pile of bracelets to cover her forearm from her wrists to her elbows, and several gold necklaces.

"Just beautiful," Beatrice said.

"Absolutely stunning. Fitting for the lady of a House," Xiamara said. She placed a veil in Anna's hair and made some final adjustments to her attire.

"I can't thank you enough," Anna said. She embraced Xiamara and then Beatrice. She held onto her closest friend, wishing that she did not have to bid her farewell.

Anna constructed a portal at the base of Xiamara's door.

"After I leave, you'll take care of the symbols?" Anna said.

"Stop worrying. We're the keepers of secrets," Beatrice said.

Anna stepped toward the portal. She stopped and looked over her shoulder. There was so much she wanted to say, but her words were caught in her throat. She forced a smile onto her face, then turned back and stepped into the unknown.

AIDS led a squad of Hezbollah along the border that separated Lebanon from the occupied Golan Heights. The troops were well armed with Kalashnikov rifles and RPG-7s. One of the squad members cut a hole through the border fence with a pair of bolt cutters. They filed through with efficiency and draped thick blankets over the rows of razor wire that lined the dusty, rocky ground.

AIDS's boots slipped as he made his way within the Lebanese squad leader. The Demon was impressed with his host and the other militants. The man he was occupying had an extensive knowledge of engineering, IEDS, communications, and artillery. He was a university educated mortal, nothing like the rag-tag depiction often portrayed within Western mortal media.

The raid had been choreographed for ruthless speed and finesse. The Israeli patrol consisted of three soldiers. AIDS knew the IDF troops felt confident in the daylight. When they went out to inspect the fence they did so in small numbers. If they encountered any problems, they knew they could call for backup from armor or gunships.

The three Israeli troops inspecting the fence did not have time to call for reinforcements. By the time they realized they were in trouble, they were surrounded. Their hands were bound and they were led back through the gap in the fence and into Lebanon.

Once they had returned to the Hezbollah safe house, AIDS possessed each of the captured IDF troops. He gleaned information about their readiness, morale, and areas of expertise, all vital to determining the likelihood of success should the Demons attack the Golan.

The strategic situation following the Second World War was complicated. The Angels technically held the United Nations and controlled a large swath of the globe. However, in practicality, controlling the Allies was more likely their high water mark in terms of influence in the Mortal Realm. The post-war world was fractured and volatile. Demons might fight on the side of a Communist regime one month and a Western power the next. The forces of the Devil made use of American forces in Vietnam, whereas in North America, the United States was mostly controlled by the foe.

Israel was an exception. When the Angels had acquired control of the Holy Land as part of their dominion over the British Empire, they had maintained control. This meant the Demons were constantly assessing the strengths and vulnerabilities of the Jewish State.

This was a pretty mundane mission. I wonder what Schitz is up to, AIDS thought.

Anna emerged from the portal to find Schitz standing beside another male. The second party did not have horns and appeared older than a Demon. *He brought a Priest; it is a real wedding,* she thought.

Anna pulled back her veil. She giggled slightly and threw her arms around Schitz.

She whispered in his ear, "I never thought a day like this would happen."

"I know," he said.

The Priest cleared his throat. "You'll have to forgive me," he said. "I've never done anything quite like this before. This is slightly unorthodox. I'll have to wing it."

His humor broke the tension.

"Take hands and face each other," Titus said.

Schitz took Anna's hands in his own. For a moment she felt like they were back in Egypt so many millennia before.

So much has happened since then, she thought. *Yet when I look in his eyes, all the same emotions are there.*

The Priest spoke. "We give thanks to… ah, well, let's see… we give thanks to the good fortune that brought you two here today. May you both love one another and remain faithful to each other for as long as you both shall live or eternally. As High Priest, I declare you married, at least as far as the Church of Hell is concerned." He looked at Anna. "You might have to take this up separately with your boss."

The Priest bid them farewell and the happy couple stood in silence.

"Let's take a walk," Schitz said. "I know a great place nearby for us to talk."

He led her through the vine-covered, stony ruins until they came upon a pool.

"It's beautiful," Anna said.

"It's yours," Schitz said. "No Demon will set foot in this forest. I can arrange that. You can fight the Atrophy by healing the various local tribes."

Anna grinned. "I will be Our Lady of the Amazon."

"An Amazon for the Amazon," Schitz said.

The water looked inviting. Anna opened her gown and allowed it to fall to the ground. She slipped into the water. Schitz followed her. She ran her hands over his body. His skin was smooth in the water.

He has more muscles than in his youth, and more scars, she thought. It was surreal to touch him again.

"How did any of this happen?" Anna asked.

"I will explain everything later," he said.

Schitz slid his hands down her back, sending waves of warmth through her frame.

"Good plan," she said.

Anna ran her fingers through the Demon's dark hair. She gasped when he caressed her breasts. She wrapped her legs around his waist.

"There have been others," he said.

The change in tone brought about by his apparent need to confess was annoying.

I have things to tell him too, but this is not the time for that, she thought.

Anna placed a firm index finger over his lips.

"The only thing I care about is if there will be others from now on. Will there?"

"Never," he said.

"Then take what is yours," she said.

She had barely finished her sentence when he entered her. Anna groaned and bit down on his neck. For a while all the rest of the world faded away.

The honeymoon in the Amazon was the happiest time Anna could recall. Schitz was an insatiable lover and a kind companion. It was pleasant to learn about his life and to tell him about hers. One day he took her to the ruin of Machu Picchu.

"So, this is where my absentee father met his end?"

They were making their way up the broken steps of what had been Gold's temple. The skeletal stones had long been picked clean of their glittering ornamentation. Schitz unstrapped the heavy item he had been carrying.

"Yes," he said. "This is where we fought." He unwrapped the sword he had taken from Gold. "From what I am told, this means something to Angels."

He handed her the sword by the handle.

"My father's sword," she said. "In my time, I could have never inherited it due to my questionable paternity, but it is amazing to hold it."

Anna thought of Gold. He had been the source of much hatred in her youth, yet in her early adulthood she had developed a deep bond for him. His death pained her. Though time had passed, she could still see his face, forever raging against the established order, always seeking his own elevation.

He was not evil, though he was portrayed that way. He was not selfish, though it was easy to mistake him as such. He was unique in a system that does not value individuality, she thought.

"Keep it," Schitz said, "my gift to you, Lady Gold."

"I've been thinking about that," she said. "I would like to take on your name. Anna Nervosa has a nice ring to it, or maybe Anna Gold-Nervosa. Yes, that's the one."

"Well," Schitz said, "since I am a Sir, you should keep your title as well."

"Nice to know I married so well," she said. "You must have put all that training in the desert to good use, Sir Schitz."

"Indeed," he said. "There is no doubt that I owe you my life."

"Well, then it only fits that you have pledged the rest of it to me," she said.

"Speaking of the rest of our lives," Schitz said, "I don't know what sense of normality we'll be able to enjoy."

"You mean since I will be hiding in the jungle, and you will remain in your world of double-dealing treachery?"

"Something like that."

"What you've given me is worth any inconvenience, and I do not mean this sword." She let the blade tumble to the ground. "I am free. I answer to no one. And you are mine. Just promise you will drop in from time to time."

"I do so pledge," he said.

"You said there had been others. I trust such will not be the case when you are away from here," she said.

A pained look crossed his face. "I say this not to question your loyalty, but to assure you that such is the same for me, while I am here," she said.

"Ah, so you too have...a past," Schitz said. "I mean, I had assumed it was a possibility. It has been a long while. I'm fine with that, it would be hypocritical not to be, I mean."

"You're rambling dear. I only mention it because I want you to know who I am, honestly. With you I have enjoyed the company of a male companion. I have also known the company of a female. It doesn't lessen what I feel for you, it's just a part of what makes me who I am and I wanted you to know," she said.

"You're rambling a little yourself," Schitz said. He grinned and added, "I'm grateful you feel free to tell me. I had a very close friend once. He was never able to openly express his love for his partner. It was a source of much pain for him. When he could be honest, it was a relief – and I hope you feel something similar."

A wave of relief washed over Anna. "It is my love. I am so happy to have a husband with whom I can honestly unveil all of me."

She kissed him. "Good," she said. She nibbled on his lower lip.

Schitz's only response was to step out of his robe.

A while later they made their way back down the mountainside. They had ascended to Machu Picchu after the closing time, so their visit within the Celestial had been devoid of tourists. When they reached the lower area they once again threaded their way through mortals.

A thought possessed Anna. For a moment she was back in the Great Hall of Heaven, pleading with Magnesium not to go to his ruinous final battle. She could hear herself.

"Let me go with you. Let me fight by your side," Anna said.

"Ususi," he said with a broad smile, "you must stay here. That is your path, this is mine."

"I don't know that language. I've never possessed a mortal from the New World. What does that mean?" Anna asked.

"If one day you ever make it to the Andes, possess one of the highlanders, the Inca, then you will know. Hopefully, there will still be some left by then," he said.

The memory faded. Anna spotted a local. She possessed the woman and was flooded with the mortal's memories and language.

Ususi means "daughter," she thought. It felt anticlimactic and jarring all at once. *I guess I always knew. Yet, he would never say. But he did in the end. He did tell me.*

"Are you alright?" Schitz asked.

"I've lost much on this mountain. I'm glad that I can now call it part of my home, though it is bittersweet," she replied.

Chapter 14
Angels and Archangels

AIDS's boots clunked on the marble in the Great Hall. He wore the new uniform Schitz had introduced to the army of Hell. It was fashionable and efficient, though not many had taken to wearing it. AIDS had decided to don the modern garb; he did not want to appear at odds with his sensei.

He approached a crowd of conspirators in a mixed array. The High Priest Titus was in his usual cassock. Anorexia was wearing the modern attire: a tunic and trousers. Autism and Vampirosis wore traditional robes. Vampirosis's new husband, COVID, was wearing some sort of monstrosity that resembled casual mortal garb.

This is the rabble with which we shall overthrow the most storied of Demons, AIDS thought.

"Well, today's the day," AIDS said when he reached the group.

"Hardly," COVID said.

I preferred the first husband, AIDS thought.

"And why is that?" AIDS asked.

"His holiness doesn't think it's a good idea anymore," COVID said.

Titus rolled his eyes. "I'm too old to be fazed by your disrespect, but in the presence of elder Demons perhaps you might allow them to brief your father-in-law rather than idly running your mouth."

I always liked this guy.

Anorexia snickered and picked up the conversation. "Titus has informed us that he is absolutely certain he has uncovered the reason behind Schitz's shadiness. He assures us it is both confidential and entirely above board."

AIDS groaned. He did not want to get into a contest with the High Priest, especially if COVID was the sole dissenter.

"And how do the rest of you feel?" AIDS asked

"It's pointless. The summons has already been sent, we have to go through with it now," Autism said.

"Hmm, but you have lost your zeal for uncovering the truth?" AIDS asked.

Anorexia shrugged. "It just seems like we might have been chasing shadows all along."

"And your thoughts, daughter?" AIDS said.

Vampirosis hated being singled out. "I've said from the start I was never completely certain about the shoot down one way or the other. Part of me wishes we had just gone on, business as usual," she said.

AIDS felt extremely frustrated. *I want my mentor to be free of guilt, I do. But I need to know the truth.*

"We will observe him during this farce and see how he reacts and what he says. If it is pointless then it's pointless; if it is of consequence so be it. The play's the thing, wherein we'll catch the conscience of the king, one way or another," AIDS said.

"Sounds good. You go check on him. The rest of us can wait in our rooms to see if he wants us to stand beside him in the dock," Anorexia said.

The group dispersed like the burst of an artillery shell over Fort McHenry. *Nobody really wants to be a part of this anymore, perhaps Schitz has already won.*

He rapped on Schitz's door.

"Come!"

AIDS entered the room. Schitz waved towards a chair.

"You look a little shook," AIDS said.

"I've been summoned," Schitz said. He sounded like a man announcing his intention to go for an afternoon walk.

"That must be a little nerve-wracking," AIDS said.

He seems calm. If he is guilty he has the cold blood of a reptile. Otherwise, I am harassing my best friend for no reason at all.

"No big deal," Schitz said. "If I am adjudged subversive, incompetent, or unworthy of the Lord's service, I will be executed in a matter of minutes."

He fastened the top button of his black and gray uniform jacket, checked the alignment of his medals, and slipped his Knight's Pentagram over his head.

"So glad we finally ditched the robes," he said. "I look so damn dashing in this."

If only the rest of Hell liked them as much. AIDS shifted his boots on the floor and wished for the comfort of sandals.

"You seem awfully calm for a man who could be dead soon," AIDS said.

"Do I have a choice?" Schitz asked. "I know I have not done anything wrong. So, I have nothing to fear; besides, no Demon lives this long without someone taking a run at him. I've traveled this road before."

"When do you have to go?" AIDS asked.

"Within a few minutes. Let's go find Anorexia and Autism. I would like my retinue to stand with me when I face my accuser."

Schitz walked directly ahead of Anorexia, who was tightly flanked by AIDS and Autism. They walked in grim silence through the eerily quiet hallways of Hell, past the Great Hall, and to the Judgment Chamber.

Each step felt heavy to AIDS. It was as though he were going to his own trial. *This poor fool took me under his wing. He counts Anorexia and Autism as his closest confidants. But all three of us have advocated for this Inquisition to take place. He was allowed to bring his closest supporters to stand beside him while he accounts for himself, and he chose us.*

The room was packed. It seemed as though all of Hell had turned out. The undertaker that doubled as the head of the Purists oversaw the proceedings. The Inquisition was much more of a Hitleresque rally than any type of trial. Schitz was charismatic, verbose, and seemed to enjoy the proceedings immensely.

Of course, he loves talking about himself. This format is hardly an interrogation. He's not going to slip up or reveal anything. If he is guilty of any subterfuge, this is more a victory lap than anything else.

AIDS took time during the Inquisition to assess the faces of those in the know. Titus visibly enjoyed Schitz's antics. Coronavirus was also amused and appeared at ease. Autism's face was of one mildly annoyed. He shifted on his feet and seemed impatient to leave. Vampirosis had a distracted guise.

Anorexia was the sole exception. She looked like a student in a lecture hall. She moved her lips, silently parroting everything Schitz was saying.

She's memorizing his accounts, AIDS thought. *She doesn't buy his innocence. Should I?*

The Inquisition ended with all in assembly showering Schitz with admiration. For someone accounting for his actions, Schitz did not even bother to stick around for the committee's official proclamation.

He's smooth. I wonder if my concerns were misplaced, or if I should dig deeper.

AIDS considered seeking out Anorexia, but in the hubbub at the conclusion of the meeting, she had vanished.

Uranium II looked across the tea house. It had been built in the 1980s, but the attention to detail transported him to yesteryear. While the decorations and furnishings had remained the same, the clientele was remarkably different. The locals were dressed in modern clothing, the courtly attire long abandoned to history. Additionally, across the large room there was a sprinkling of Black and Caucasian faces: tourists.

He watched from his seat in the Celestial as Anorexia infected half of the female patrons with her disease. She left the other half unmolested.

Some things never change, he thought.

Anorexia approached him. Uranium II rose to his feet and embraced her.

"Ah, Xiang, it is good to see you," Anorexia said.

"And you as well," he said. "Have you the results?"

Anorexia nodded. She reached into her oddly modern uniform top and retrieved a notepad.

"I've been trying to work out how they would know each other.

There is a massive hole in our theory; we're counting on their being in the same place at the same time, but of course they're going to be at hot places. Look at Kursk. You and I were both there, but we weren't in cahoots," Anorexia said.

"I've been thinking about that too. I was actually given the most serendipitous gift regarding the matter," Uranium II said. He shuffled his feet like an excited toddler. "One of Zinc's security detail recently came to me to parley. She offered up a damning secret, but not one pertaining to collusion."

"Which lends you to think she did not know of any collusion?" Anorexia asked.

"Exactly! She offered forward evidence of an ancient assassination, which although quite nasty in its nature, is hardly as diabolical as the allegations we are investigating," Uranium II said.

"His bodyguards go with him everywhere?" Anorexia asked.

"He makes a point of it," he said.

"So how can he collude with the foe?" Anorexia asked.

"Similar to the way porcupines make love," Uranium II said.

Anorexia chuckled, "With great care, or not at all," she said.

"Bingo. So it's not just about being in the same place at the same time, but about being *alone* in the same place at the same time. That takes attention to detail," Uranium II said. "So what's on your list?"

"A dogfight in Vietnam," Anorexia said.

"'67?" Uranium II asked, looking down at his notes from Zinc's inquisition.

"Yes, indeedy," Anorexia said.

"Zinc got shot down, survived the bailout," Uranium said.

"Schitz abandoned his aircraft as well," She said

"So together and alone," Uranium II said.

"Hmmm...Abandoned the aircraft," Anorexia said.

Suddenly Anorexia was far from the Beijing tea house. She was once more in the cramped, cold cockpit of a Bf-109, single-seater fighter. She had just shot down two Russian Yak-9s and had pulled along Schitz.

She rocked her plane's wings from side to side, celebrating her victory.

Schitz spoke to her over the radio. "Congratulations, ace," he said.

Anorexia rocked her wings side to side again and responded, "Horrido!" without any effort to conceal her feminine voice. "Two down on this side of the lines, infantry will confirm for sure."

Schitz gave a thumbs up. "This one's done for," he said. "I'm going to escort him down. I'm fine. Now, head back home."

Anorexia had throttled forward and pulled up next to Schitz's prey, a fatally injured Yak-9 with an Angelic possessed pilot. She had waved exuberantly to him before gesturing happily towards the ground. After the taunt, she rolled her plane over and dove for home.

Anorexia returned to the tea house.

"He followed him down," Anorexia said more to herself than Uranium II.

"I'm sorry?" Uranium II said.

"They met at the end of World War II!" Anorexia said.

"Zinc was shot down late in the war while flying with the Russians?" Anorexia asked.

"Yes, he and his bodyguard were shot down. They both survived. He bailed out, she crash landed," he said.

Anorexia smacked the table with vigor. A patron turned and looked at the vacant table that appeared to have rocked itself.

"I bagged his bodyguard. She must be Zen as fuck, to hide her aura, because I thought there was only one Angel up there. Schitz killed the Angel's engine and sent me back to base. He said he was going to 'escort him down,' which I took to mean he was going to make sure he crashed and died. Schitz never killed him. That's where they met. It's the only way," Anorexia said.

"It makes sense," Uranium II said.

They placed their notepads next to one another.

"Damn," Uranium II said. "Vietnam, Israel, the Congo, Cuba, Tunisia, Iran. This is too much to be coincidence."

"We have our answer," Anorexia said. She slumped in her seat.

"But who is betraying their side? And who is working the other?" Uranium II asked.

"Maybe both are traitors," Anorexia said. "Think about it, the world didn't even take a pause between the end of World War II and designs for World War III. Churchill wanted to rearm the Nazis and invade the Soviet Union in 1945. McArthur wanted to drop nukes on China like they were leaflets," Anorexia said.

Uranium II screwed up his face as though he had bit into something sour. The mention of nuclear weapons stung him.

"Ah, no offense," Anorexia said. "But think about it. The whole world has been engulfed in regional and global conflicts with countless nations armed with doomsday weapons. And I'm not just talking about nukes. They have chemical weapons, biological weapons, and powerful conventional weapons. Yet, no apocalypse has taken place. Similarly, among our ranks, neither side has developed any type of advantage, despite participating in countless conflicts.

"You think, they're in business together for...stability?" Uranium II asked.

"Or their own mutual benefit, probably one and the same," Anorexia said.

"Are we just seeing what we want to see, or is this really the case?" Uranium II asked.

"I feel like this is indisputable," Anorexia said.

Uranium II sat back and sighed. *I should have never pulled back the curtain*, he thought.

"What are you thinking?" Anorexia asked.

"Sometimes you don't want to see how the sausage is made," Uranium II said. "If this is the case, they may have well saved all of the mortals and by extension all of us Celestials as well. At the same time, it means all of the deceased Angels and Demons have given their lives for a charade. It's horrible, but what can we do now?"

"Oh, fuck," Anorexia said.

"What is it?" Uranium II asked.

"I just realized if that is the case, we've been safe. It's like they put us on some type of ark," Anorexia said.

"Oh, your side knows about that story?" Uranium II asked with a laugh.

"We're not cave dwellers, you know," Anorexia said. "If they're pulling the strings, we've not invoked their wrath."

"Hmm, not yet," Uranium II said.

I've been so snarky to Schitz since we never repeated our one-night stand. I wonder how he feels about me now, she thought.

"You look lost,'" Uranium II said.

"It's complicated," Anorexia said. "I went into just thinking Schitz is a traitor – wondering if he had a reason to be working for the enemy. But now, the idea he is working *with* the enemy, it seems believable. I'm wondering where I stand with him, and what will happen if I expose him."

"You've always felt very strongly about him," Uranium II said.

Anorexia felt herself blush. "I know. I've tried to put it to rest. He will never be mine, but I don't want my disappointment to turn to bitterness. It's not his fault, it's just the way things are sometimes," she said.

"And now we've made the biggest discovery ever for either of our sides, and what do we do?" Uranium II said.

"Nothing...for now," Anorexia said. "If I'm being honest, I wish I was on your side. I've always felt a closeness to Angels. Well, the Angels from your region at least. Hearing that Schitz might be helping you, I wonder if we could just tilt the scale so you win, but then I think of my brother and all those I care about."

"So we will wait, and we will tell no one," Uranium II said.

"We'll let it play out," Anorexia said.

Another Angel entered the tea house. He resembled Uranium II almost identically – before Uranium II was afflicted by his condition.

"Ah, this is overdue," Uranium II said. He rose to his feet.

The Angel approached and bowed, first to Anorexia, then lower to Uranium II.

"This is my son Hirohisa. He is the heir to my House. A nobler Angel there is not," Uranium II said. "Hirohisa, this is the legendary Anorexia."

Anorexia felt her pulse race and the nape of her neck perspire. *He is gorgeous,* she thought.

AIDS grumbled to himself as he unrolled the contents of the package of condoms. He used the smallest of pins to poke a nearly invisible hole in the middle of each prophylactic. Once all were damaged he returned them to the box and placed it back on the shelf in the airport pharmacy.

Hopefully it's someone's undoing, he thought.

He repeated the process for another box, then wandered out of the store within the Celestial. The Inquisition had been pointless. Schitz was unimpeded and nothing came to light. In the time since, he had been even more distant. *I wonder if he suspects that I suspect him.*

Boston's Logan Airport was crowded. The passage of mortals to and fro mirrored the Demon's swirling thoughts. AIDS snarled. The worst part had been the utter lack of action. Schitz seemed to be constantly away and content to fill AIDS's docket with mundane tasks. There was combat all over the world and yet Schitz seemed utterly disinterested.

All AIDS could focus on was the odd behavior of Wraiths traveling around the world via commercial aircraft. All Celestial creatures hated planes. Even the Demons that flew fighters, himself included, dreaded the notion of getting killed in a crash. His daughter, Vampirosis, was probably the sole exception.

She's a bit crazy. The Wraiths surely hate it, so why are they traveling this way all of a sudden? It seemed fishy. Additionally odd were the instances of Angels chasing after the Wraiths on the airliners.

It's all so cartoonish. There are countless conflicts around the world. But the Angels are chasing our Wraiths onto airliners like some cat chasing mouse bullshit. The Wraiths can make symbols for portals under any conditions, but the Angels require a stable platform. How would the Angels kill them? Why are the Angels interested in them? Why are the Wraiths even bothering with planes when they can make portals? This feels like time wasting at the end of a football match, when neither side is interested in playing the match anymore.

He was determined to get to the bottom of it. Luckily, he had met with Satan. The Dark Lord had bemoaned the lack of a global war involving the super powers. AIDS had quickly combined the two interests of looking into Wraiths with an event designed to trigger a global war.

AIDS had assembled four squads of the Al-Qaeda network. Within these, he had placed several Demons. These Demons were tasked with possessing the various male and female mortals and carrying out a massive terrorist attack on the United States.

AIDS was uncertain what the Wraiths were up to, but he knew they got their orders from Schitz.

Only after he had possessed his host and began boarding, the genuine fear of the hazards he would face crept into AIDS's mind. *It's alright*, he told himself. *It will be alright.*

Circades sat by the pool of his Italian villa. A servant brought him a chilled cocktail. The drink was a unique concoction of allspice dram, almonds, lime juice, and ginger. He savored a small sip while the servant waited for his approval.

"Yes, it is quite good, thank you," Circades said.

Another servant arrived and announced, "A Signore Louis Iraragorri is here to see you."

"At last, yes, please show him in," Circades said.

A few moments later the detestable Frenchman was brought before Circades. Louis was one of the Titan's top underbosses. He oversaw the production and distribution of heroin in a network that spanned from Afghanistan to North America, one of the more lucrative tendrils of Circades's syndicate. Nevertheless, Circades did not particularly care for the man.

Louis was in many ways an illusion. His name was adopted, his "designer" attire was comically imposturous, and his demeanor was of a man who wished to sound educated despite his lack of intellect.

"Oh, that looks good, I'll have two of those," Louis said to the waiter.

The servant looked toward Circades for approval. He nodded in a way that evidenced his frustration.

Louis sat upon a vacant lounge chair without waiting for an invitation.

"I'm glad you made it alright," Circades said.

"Yeah, it was tough, didn't really feel like flying, if you know what I mean," Louis said.

"I can't imagine why," Circades said with an eye roll.

"Yeah, I was in Somalia. Sorted out that problem there, but damn the Arabs really gave the old États-Unis a black eye, huh?" Louis said.

"That's one way of putting it," Circades said. "The attacks on New York and Washington will have far reaching consequences for our operation. Especially for you since the Americans will undoubtedly be invading Afghanistan any day now."

"You think?" Louis asked.

"One of us has to," Circades replied.

"Ha, funny one boss," Louis said. "But how do you want to play it?"

"The Taliban are good clients. They grow the poppies and are happy to be paid with weapons or with transportation of their people between Pakistan and Afghanistan, or farther afield. But even if they are annihilated, tribal leaders can step into the void."

"Do you think the Americans will interfere in the trade?" Louis asked.

Circades suppressed a grin. *As crude as he is, he is pragmatic and talented, of course that's why he's an underboss,* the Titan thought.

Circades fished his phone from the pocket of his suit. "That is an excellent question. One to which I would not presume to know the answer."

The Titan dialed a contact labeled CW.

"*Director* Craig Walters," the voice on the other side of the line said.

"Ah, congratulations Director, got a promotion did you?" Circades said.

"Hey, Larga Sombra!" Walters said butchering the Spanish with his Texan accent. "Yeah, after that shit show, you know the last boss had to go, and like they say in France, 'voila.'" He treated the French just as mercilessly as he had the Spanish.

The call was audible from a distance. Circades noticed Louis cringe at the mispronunciation, despite his own penchant for bludgeoning foreign languages.

"Louis would prefer that you not speak French," Circades said.

Raucous laughter blared through the speaker. "Hahaha, oh, Louis's there? Well, tell Monsieur Iraragorri that he still owes me for the Christmas safari," Walters said.

Louis gestured with his hand in irritation.

"He heard you," Circades said.

"So what's up, Shadow? What can I do for you?" Walters asked.

"What are your country's plans for Afghanistan?" Circades asked.

"Plans for what? Afghan-ni-what? Oh, that place that used to exist? Yeah, I think you'll find the plans are to wipe it off the map and then to wipe whatever was underneath it off the map as well," Walters said.

"But not my poppy fields," Circades said.

"Oh yeah, no, they'll be fine, how else are we going to bribe the locals we're not vaporizing into acting all democratized?" Walters asked. "I assume you'd be amenable to the Northern Alliance running your product at the same rates?"

"That's fine. Once they're in place, do you think we'd be able to transport directly to the U.S. via military aircraft?" Circades asked.

"Certainly, I'll send the details to Louis," Walters said.

"Wonderful. Congratulations again on the promotion," Circades said.

"Thank you kindly," Walters said.

Circades hung up the phone. "See, challenges and opportunities. He sounds all fire and brimstone, but that place is the graveyard of empires. Maintain our contacts with the Taliban as well. If we are going to give their rivals the fields, step up our arms sales to the Taliban. We can run weapons to them at a price deficit to help them out in their time of need. We can offer discount transport as well in case they need to relocate any high level operatives out of the warzone."

"Charity?" Louis asked.

"No, just keeping them on the hook. If they wind up back in power, we'll be in their good graces and stand to gain. We'll still be coming out ahead. Running directly to the U.S. on military flights will significantly lower costs," Circades said.

Louis drained his drink and rose to his feet. "I'm on it boss. I won't let you down."

Circades nodded.

Louis saw himself out.

Things are coming together, Circades thought. He closed his eyes and drank in the afternoon sun. In his mind's eye he could see his empire. Craig Walters was a powerful asset now at the apex of the Central Intelligence Agency. Gustav Schultz was a former General of the Staatssicherheitsdienst (Stasi), who ran a far reaching human trafficking operation. He worked closely with Makoto Tanaka, a powerful Yakuza Oyabun, who provided Circades influence in far eastern affairs.

I have the ability to rig elections and topple governments. I can disappear powerful people at my whim. The time will soon be at hand. I will have everything in order to bring about the end of times.

Uranium II banged on the bunker door. He was impressed by the stalwart design. *They constructed this whole place quietly in the middle of nowhere*, he thought. *Quite an achievement.*

There was a metallic clang on the other side of the door before it creaked open. Silver poked his head out of the space.

"Ah, hello there, Lord Uranium II," Silver said.

"Hello, Albert," Uranium II said. He pronounced the name with a French accent.

"What brings you here?" Silver asked.

Uranium II slithered through the doorway and closed it behind him.

"Interesting operation you have out here," he said.

"Eh, just a private hobby really, not much to do in my perpetual state of servitude," Silver said.

"Nothing to do with the sword?" Uranium II asked.

"What sword?" Silver asked.

Uranium II chuckled. "Indeed, well, I'm here for counsel. I'm told that in all of Heaven, you are perhaps the most knowledgeable in unorthodox arts."

Silver smiled and seemed amused. "I'm learned in some areas where other Angels have little interest, however, I am hardly a sage in any field," he said.

"Yet you and your brother unlocked the power of the Titan's amulet at the Red Sea," Uranium II said.

"That was a long time ago, friend. I'm not sure it will be of much use to you now," Silver said.

Uranium II coughed, a wheezing, grating sound. He spit. "I am desperate. I cannot heal mortals fast enough or kill Demons in requisite numbers to stave off this affliction. I need a cure, or I will quickly succumb to it," he said.

"And you think the powers of the Titan can alleviate you?" Silver asked.

"The punishment originated from him for violating the Divine Dictum. It only stands to reason that he would have the remedy," Uranium II said.

"Makes sense, but I do not have access to his ways or practices. Sadly, only the Titan himself could provide you with that knowledge," Silver said.

"Not unless I had something to offer him," Uranium II said.

"Well, yeah, I mean that's what makes the world go round; quid pro quo," Silver said.

"The problem is, what I have to offer him is not a benefit for myself or any of us," Uranium II said.

"Hmm, intriguing," Silver said.

"Yes, my House's Familiars are quite talented. The Ancient seeks to bring about what the Titans referred to as Ragnarok: the end of times. Armageddon." Uranium II said.

"The end of times? No, not at all. I have studied much of the Titan's religion," Silver said. "Their concept of Ragnarok is not like our Megiddo. The Titan's prophesied there would be a mighty battle that would culminate in the entire world being covered in water. Then, the world would reemerge from the depths and be repopulated by two mortal survivors."

"That makes a lot of sense actually," Uranium II said.

"Why is that?" Silver asked.

"Well, from what my Familiars have learned they believe the Ancient intends to halt the cycle of mortal reincarnation so he can be with his mortal love forever," Uranium II said.

Silver chuckled, "Of course, it fits their religion perfectly. The Titan fancies him and his mortal to take the role of Lífþrasir and Líf. So, he wants to end the world... great. Without the spiritual energy from the Eunoe we would perish, same for the Demons and the Styx."

"Yes, hence why giving him something that would help him in exchange for a cure, would be pointless," Uranium II said.

"Hmm, depends on how big your bollocks are," Silver said. He grinned.

"Go on," Uranium II said.

"Well, my brother always gave me some idiotic story about stalking the Titan to gain the knowledge of the amulet. From what I learned in my time in the library, I am certain he swindled him," Silver said.

"Swindled The Ancient?" Uranium II asked. His voice conveyed skepticism and awe.

"Yes, it turns out the Titans cannot lie or break agreements," Silver said. "So you would have to present him with a wager of some kind. You win, he gives you the cure. He wins, you give him the knowledge he seeks."

"I could challenge him to a duel," Uranium II said.

Silver shook his head. "His kind would be more than a match for one Angel, no matter your skill," he said.

"He likes chess. My Familiars have informed me he often dresses down and plays chess with strangers in New York City," Uranium II said.

"Ah, that's perfect," Silver said.

"Except I'm horrible at chess," Uranium II said.

"Really?" Silver said.

"Yes, why is that surprising?" Uranium II asked.

"Oh, nothing. I'm sure there was a culturally insensitive joke in there somewhere. Like, 'You must be the first Asian who isn't good at chess,' or something along those lines," Silver said.

"Ha...ha!"

"Well, you are in luck. The mortals would consider me a grand-master," Silver said. He put his arm around Uranium II and led him away from the bunker. "Come on, I haven't been to the Great Hall in a while. Let's find somewhere nice to teach you."

Anorexia pushed open her door, staggered into her room, and collapsed on her bed. She would not sleep as she had after her injury at Verdun, but she needed to be off her feet. Her entire body ached. The fighting in the Ba'athist stronghold of Ramadi had been fierce. Schitz had been leading the forces of Hell on an exhausting campaign in Iraq.

"I miss the days when Demons and Angels settled into one side of a conflict," she said with a groan. "All this constant switching of sides is exhausting."

"It's the modern way, Sis. It's never going to be like Waterloo or the Somme again," Autism said.

He had invited himself into the room and immediately helped himself to the liquor cabinet.

"This is the Brew, right?" he asked.

Anorexia nodded.

"I hated that other stuff Spanish Influenza gave you," he said.

"You never could hold your liquor," Anorexia said.

She gratefully accepted a cup. Autism flopped down into one of her reading chairs. He drained his own glass and refilled it.

"Schitz seems bent on fighting the Angels nonstop. Iraq has been even more brutal than Afghanistan," Autism said.

"It's almost like he's trying to compensate for something," Anorexia said.

I know Uranium said to keep things quiet but it's hard, she thought.

"Well, that's the thing. I never fully gave up on our questions after the Inquisition," Autism said.

Anorexia felt a chill run through her tired body.

"I've just came from the morgue. Salvatore allowed me to examine AIDS's body."

"AIDS is dead?" Anorexia bolted up in her bed.

"Aye, it just happened, a vicious fight outside of Mosul," Autism said.

Anorexia slumped back in her bed. She felt a knot grow in her chest.

"I liked AIDS," Anorexia said. "I mean he was kind of Schitz's annoying little buddy, but he was a good guy. Ugh, it doesn't get any easier even after all this time."

Autism did not show outward signs of mirroring her sentiment, but respectfully paused for a moment.

"I wonder how much of a friend he was to Schitz, because AIDS was killed by a Demonic weapon," Autism said.

"How could you possibly know that?" Anorexia asked.

"I was present for a mysterious incident at Teutoburg Forest when we lost Legionnaires' Disease and Chlamydial Lymphogranuloma," Autism said.

Anorexia felt further distress, recalling her long lost brothers. *We were never close in life, but it still hurts nevertheless*, she thought.

"The Wraiths were particularly interested in their deaths because their injuries were caused by Celestial weapons of unique dimensions. Apparently, Wraiths and Familiars use standard tools. So, my throwing knives are the same dimension as your throwing knives, which are the same as Schitz's throwing knives," Autism said

"I understand the concept," Anorexia said.

"Yes, well AIDS was definitely killed by a Demonic weapon. Salvatore is a bit of an autopsy expert and he concurred with my assessment. It's a bit of a hobby, examining the dead with Salvatore. He's been distracted as of late though," Autism said.

"You are forever odd," Anorexia said. "That's interesting but you know as well as anybody, weapons change hands in combat. He could have had his own weapon turned against him."

"Maybe, but so many coincidences? I think not," Autism said.

Ah, fuck it, I might as well tell him. She gestured for more Brew and was happy when he handed her the pitcher. She drank a deep draught straight from the bottle.

"Ahh, look Autism, here is the thing. I am certain that you are correct. Schitz probably had a hand in AIDS's death," she said. "Maybe he even killed him outright. But here's what I've determined since the Inquisition. Schitz appears involved in the deaths of many Demons at the same time, he appears to be responsible for a great many Angelic deaths."

"So, his treachery is balanced out because Angels are killed as well?" Autism was shouting.

Anorexia held up her hand for a moment of calm.

"I'm not saying it is right," Anorexia said. "We fought two global wars basically back to back. It's been almost a century since the end of the first one and still there is no third act. Perhaps Schitz is keeping us from tearing down the whole house, so to speak."

Autism fumed, swirled his cup, and said, "Does he fancy himself a higher order than Satan? He has elevated himself to the ranks of the Elementals? Schitz, the fifth element, the keeper of world order. Even if I don't believe the Church and the nonsense that Satan created the world. I'm not going to abide an old school chum treating me and the rest of us like toy soldiers."

"I agree, I agree, but I don't think he is betraying us to the Angels per se," Anorexia said. "And I don't think we can just stop what he's been doing. We don't want the mortals to annihilate each other. We need their souls passing through the Styx."

"So what, just keep waiting until it's our turn to die?" Autism asked.

Anorexia shrugged. "Do you think he would trade us?"

Autism sat in silence for a moment. He drank some more. He sighed. "No, I guess I don't think so. He might have spent more time with AIDS, but he is essentially a sibling to me. And I know you two, well...you know, but yes, I do not think he would ever do anything to harm us."

"So there you have it. We can't do damage outing him just to exert our own self-righteousness. He is our friend, still," she said.

"This might just be the Brew talking, but I have an idea," Autism said. He rose to his feet and fell to the floor.

"Are you drunk already?" Anorexia asked.

Autism picked himself up. "I'm trying to give these boots a try. I miss my sandals, it's not the same as when you're possessing a mortal," he said.

"You look sharp in the new uniform," Anorexia said. "So, what's your big idea?"

"I'm going to speak to Schitz," Autism said.

"Are you sure that's wise? You're really in no state to have a serious conversation," she said.

"No time like the present," Autism said. He stumbled to the door and exited, leaving it ajar.

"This is going to be bad," Anorexia said to herself.

Uranium II dropped his knight onto F2.

"Checkmate!"

"Here," The Ancient said after scribbling a series of unintelligible symbols in the margin of a newspaper and ripping the page free. "Put this on the wall with ash while the morning is still dark, then put your hands on either side of the sentence and keep them there until morning's first light has touched it. That will cure you of the Atrophy."

Uranium II's hand trembled as he took the paper.

"There's one more thing," The Ancient said. "The message you have there is different from mine. It…" He paused, thinking how to explain. "It pulls from a different source. If anyone other than you uses it, you will die. So, memorize it and then burn it."

"Sure thing," Uranium II said.

The Ancient pushed onto the back two legs of his folding chair. "What made you think I'd keep my end of the deal?"

Uranium II cleared his throat; it hurt, made worse with every swallow. "I've heard a lot of rumors about you, but three things I've heard consistently. One, you're dangerous. Two, you're obsessed with finding that lady human of yours. Three, you're an honest man with deals and accords."

The Ancient raised his eyebrows and cocked his head. "I wonder which one of those is most true."

"Well, I'll be seeing you," Uranium II said. He hoisted himself up with a lot of effort.

"Better hope not – for your sake."

Uranium II nodded. "You are noble and good, I can see why your kind were once the stewards of this realm," he said.

"Well, that's your job now, do the best you can with it," Circades said.

Uranium II departed Union Square. He made his way to the various hospitals of Manhattan, silently enhancing the effects of radiation in the treatment of various cancers. The day and night passed without remarkable events.

In the early morning hours he stood on the rooftop of a residential building in the Hell's Kitchen neighborhood. Uranium II waited until the last possible moment, just in case he was being watched. Then, as the morning light crept along the wall, he scrawled the message the Titan had provided him. He placed his hands on the cool bricks.

When the morning's light reached the letters, a warm sensation passed through his frame. The intensity of the heat increased. Fear flooded Uranium's mind. *What if he did deceive me? What if this is some type of harmful enchantment?* he thought.

When it felt like he could endure the burning sensation no

longer, it vanished. Uranium II looked down at his hands; they were no longer aged. He touched his face; the skin was smooth. He ran his hands through his hair; it was full and thick. *I'm me again.*

Uranium II fell to his knees and wept with joy and catharsis. He stood and constructed a portal in the roof's staircase. He stepped through the portal and rushed past the Return Ceremony, anxious to thank Silver.

"Ah, there you are Uranium II," Pyotr said.

All of Uranium II's joy evaporated when he beheld the head of the Priests of Purity, the secret, internal order. *They are quick!* he thought. *How do they already know that I dodged my sentence?*

"How can I help you?" Uranium II asked. He tried to imbue his voice with confidence and authority.

"God wishes an audience," Pyotr said.

"Now? I guess I'm free," Uranium II said.

"Is that an attempt at humor?" Pyotr asked.

"Something like that," Uranium II said.

Throughout the walk, Uranium II felt as though he were being led to the scaffold. *I've faced worse on the battlefield. Whatever is to be will be, but I will face it with dignity.*

Pyotr led him to a mysterious room Uranium II had never seen. It lay beyond the meeting hall where trials were held. The chamber was elaborate beyond anything Uranium II had ever seen. The floor was made of glass underneath which a tributary of the Eunoe flowed. Uranium II looked through the tiles and saw mortal souls passing through on their way to reincarnation. The walls of the room and its many pillars were also made of glass. The ceiling was open. The perpetual sunlight of Heaven shined through. The light struck the glass walls and columns and cast an array of color all about the room.

Uranium II squinted in the bright light. At the rear of the room there were three thrones. God was sat on the largest, middle throne. A male of Semitic appearance sat at God's right. A woman, also of Hebrew appearance, sat to God's left.

"Kneel when you first get to the carpet that runs up to the throne," Pyotr whispered. "When he tells you to rise, keep your eyes down, advance to the mark in the middle of the carpet, and kneel again.

Wait until he speaks, and then you may reply. When he dismisses you, walk backwards to the edge of the carpet and kneel again."

Uranium II completed the courtly procedure.

"Before you we have chosen to reveal ourselves: the Triune God, Father, Son, and Holy Spirit," God said.

Uranium II felt intimidated. *If this is punishment for reversing the curse, I'm in for it*, he thought.

God continued. "There has been a monumental shift in the balance of the three Realms. The Titan, the arbitrator of the Divine Dictum, appears to be taking actions that will lead him into conflict with all Celestials. His survival of the war between his kind and the Celestials, myself, my brother, and the rest of our kin was contingent on his non-involvement. Should this change, the petty squabble between myself and Satan would be moot."

All of this fighting for control of the Mortal Realm is merely a petty squabble to them? Angels have died in their multitudes in this quarrel. It dawned on him that the Angels were more of a tool than creatures respected by their creator. *We have no immortal soul; we have no purpose other than to fight and die. He seems to favor the Priests, but we might as well be Familiars, we are nothing to him. He is only concerned about the Mortals and the energy their souls provide. I have given so much, my kin have given so much, for what?*

"You look troubled," God said.

"I have recently cured myself of my affliction by hoodwinking the Titan," Uranium II said while continuing to look down at the carpet.

God chuckled. "As if we needed further reason to antagonism him. But I suppose if he permitted you to be healed, you have fulfilled your sentence," he said.

Uranium II felt relieved.

"Your son Uranium Hirohisa, he is your heir?" God asked.

"He is," Uranium II said.

"I have selected him to represent our contingent in a venture of cooperation with the forces of Satan, one which will conclude with the elimination of the Titan. Much like my son, he will go forth and be required to spend time in Hell though in a different way," God said.

Working with Hell, this sounds like Zinc. Was Zinc in on this the entire time?

"You look pensive. You are worried for your son?" God asked.

"I trust in Hirohisa's ability. He will be fine. I wonder what part Zinc is to play in this, he too is a Supreme Commander," Uranium II said.

"Ah, you both are the last of my Archangels. We have laid to rest Gold, Hydrogen, and Rachael. Zinc was not fully exonerated during the recent Inquisition. I have my concerns about him. But I trust he will come to the good. I do not want to lose him at this critical juncture. For now, I am entrusting you with ensuring that your son does well. I am also commanding you with a task of preeminent importance. If we are successful in eliminating the Titan, the Divine Dictum will be off the table. There will be no mechanism to enforce it. I hope this joint venture will be a bridge to my brother. However, if it is not, we must be ready for a war without boundaries or limitations. You must prepare our army for unrestricted warfare."

"I will do as you command," Uranium II said.

"Start with Silver. He has been working on something pertaining to the weaponry of the Titans. What, we have not been able to determine. I know he has assembled the sword of my father, Primogenitorous, but whatever he has been at as of late is a mystery. Tell him he will be reinstated and the Houses of Gold and Silver will be reconsecrated if he agrees to work with you," God said.

"I will do as you command," Uranium II said.

"Good. Go in peace, may your efforts be fruitful," God said.

Uranium II completed the exit routine and returned to the atrium of the Great Hall.

"Much has been revealed to you today," Pyotr said. "God even spoke the name of his father to you, a contradiction of our established religion, a contradiction of the Mortal's understanding of God, that he himself was born and that Satan is his brother and not a fallen creation of Heaven's Master. You would do well to keep this confidence until all of Heaven is ready for the complete truth."

Uranium II smiled. "He chose me because I can be entrusted with such revelations. I've bled and sacrificed for him across centuries.

Perhaps you would be wise to consider why he imparted this wisdom to me, rather than to caution me," he said.

Uranium II patted Pyotr on the shoulder and strode away. As he walked he entered into contemplation. *A unification of Heaven and Hell, could it be possible? Then Anorexia can be my kin. Of course, why can't they rule in tandem, the two brothers. Light and dark, creation and destruction, good and evil, two sides of the same coin. I have balanced power with Zinc all these years. Why can't they? Would it not be better for us all?*

CHAPTER 15

ELEMENTS AND ALLOYS

The waters of the Styx glowed with an incandescent blue hue as they wound their way across the plains of Hell. Serene, it returned the souls of mortals back to Earth. The banks of the river were a good place for contemplation.

"You are so predictable."

Schitz knew the voice before he turned.

"Oh am I, Autism?" he said.

He was shocked to see a cold, stern expression on his comrade's face.

"What's the matter, Autsy?"

"I knew I'd find you here," Autism said. "I just didn't know this would be so hard."

Confusion pricked at Schitz's neck; confusion... and fear.

"What's the matter?" he said again, this time with a more serious tone.

"Well, Schitz, terrible business about AIDS, wasn't it?" Autism asked.

"Yes. Although I didn't realize you two were so close."

"Yes," Autism said. "Did you know that the Wraith blacksmiths use standardized tools?"

"I guess," Schitz said. "Never gave it much thought."

"Remember how the Russians struggled when they tried to press into Prussia during the Great War?"

"Sure," Schitz said. "The Ruskies couldn't use their locomotives. The Prussian tracks were a different gauge."

"Right," Autism said. "The Wraiths have their tools and Heavenly blacksmiths have their own – different ones, like the Prussian train tracks."

The smile on Schitz's face faded. He knew where this was going.

Autism chewed the inside of his lip for a moment but never broke his gaze. "You see, based on the width of his injuries, it seems that AIDS was killed by a Demonic blade, not one from Heaven."

Schitz opened his mouth to speak, but Autism beat him to the punch. "Yes," he said. "I'm sure it was a captured weapon, or what have you. I'm sure there is some reasonable explanation."

Schitz was suddenly aware of his sword's weight.

I cannot defect. I cannot cross the river into Limbo. I cannot go into independent business with Zinc.

Autism noticed Schitz's hand touching the knob of his weapon.

"Are you willing to dispose of me to keep your secret even now?"

Schitz's eyes and voice were flat and hard. "What would you have me do?"

"There is no need to worry," Autism said. He smiled at his own ruse. "I am your friend for life. I simply came to tell you that if you have lost the path, there is nothing to stop you from regaining it. I have not said anything to anyone, nor will I ever."

It's a lie, Autism thought. *There is a growing list of those who expect his treachery, but there is no need to compound his humiliation.*

Relief washed over Schitz like the healing waters of the Styx.

"Thank you, Autsy," he said.

His friend saluted, then faded towards the twilight.

A nagging thought tugged at the back of Schitz's mind. "Wait!" he said.

Autism stopped and turned around.

"It was all a ploy," Schitz said.

"I'm sorry?"

"It started out from a moment of, I don't know, inspiration, weakness, call it what you will. But a long time ago, I realized I could use my relationship with the Angel to bend things in our favor. I want to survive. I want *all of us* to survive. I know I can use the trust I've earned with the Angel to be his undoing. Think about it. Killing Zinc will be a hammer's blow to Heaven. It might be the last thing we need to give ourselves the final victory," Schitz said.

Autism could hear the ravings of a madman in his friend's voice, but he could also hear honesty. "Perhaps, this is the masterstroke we needed all along. How will we do it?" he asked.

"I'm going to formulate a bulletproof plan and then we will kill him," Schitz said. "The Angels will be leaderless after the decapitation, and we will finish them."

"You're asking a lot considering what was just laid on the table. How do I know I'm not the next one to be traded in?" Autism asked.

"I know you well enough to know when you are lying. Your whole 'I haven't told anyone' shtick was not very convincing," Schitz said with a grin. "The truth is, you are not the only Demon who has found me out. I will assemble everyone who knows and we will kill the Angel."

Autism clasped Schitz by the hand then awkwardly transmuted the gesture into a full hug. Both chuckled.

"It's good to have you back" Autism said.

"It's good to be back," Schitz said.

Wynter Zinc made her way through the jungles of the Amazon within the Celestial Realm. She was the head of a squad composed of Angels from the vassal Houses and some lesser members of the Zinc House. The House of Zinc was massive. Although Zinc had sired a paltry number of sons, they all had produced many children before they met their demise. The same held true for his grandchildren and so on. Such had been the case for Zinc's brothers and cousins. Wynter was a descendant of one of Zinc's many siblings. She knew there was an impossible multitude between her and the Lordship of the House. However, the door had been opened to female Standard Bearers. Lady Rachael had been named head of the House of Hydrogen before her demise.

If I can show him my merit and worthiness, he might give me a House of my own, Wynter thought.

Her steps were fleet and full of purpose. Her heart rattled like a jackhammer. She had been warned who they were up against. Zinc's former bodyguard and assassinatrix. Anna was a fabled character in her own right. Wynter had grown up on stories that said, "If you misbehave, Zinc will send Anna to make you disappear." Now she hunted the hunter.

Zinc had instructed them to dye their hair dark and to dress in eastern style clothing – a ruse to give the appearance they were from the House of Uranium and his client Houses.

We'll kill her and I will be one rung farther up the ladder.

Anna sat up from her afternoon sunbathing. It was quiet in the clearing beside one of the Amazon's many tributaries. Still, her sixth sense screamed that she was in danger. *Yes,* she thought, *Celestial footsteps, many of them.*

She had taken to carrying her father's sword across her back. Unlike many other Angelic Lords, his namesake was sharp. It was far from ceremonial. Anna drew the blade. A throng of Angels entered the clearing from all sides.

It's always Angels. Demons almost never give me any trouble.

Anna readied herself. *I wish Schitz was here.* Not to protect her, but to fight alongside her for once.

The first Angel was a female with jet black hair. She swung her sword toward Anna. The blades rang out with a metallic clang. Anna tripped her attacker. The Angel stumbled past her.

Anna ducked the next swipe, spun, and decapitated the Angel. She barely had time to react as throwing stars sailed in her direction. Anna found herself beset on all sides. She disarmed one attacker, knocking his sword to the ground before running him through. She flung his impaled body into his comrades.

With the nearest Angels bowled over, Anna saw the opportunity to flee. She sprinted through the gap and ducked when more throwing knives whizzed past her. The Angels pursued her. Anna halted her flight at the tree line.

She drew a throwing knife in either hand and dropped two of her pursuers. Each blade caught its victim in the throat. Anna turned and vanished into the trees.

Wynter recovered from being pitched over to see the ambush going horribly awry. Anna was more menacing than she could have imagined. Zinc's bodyguard cut down members of the assassination squad with ease and then broke the encirclement.

Rather than pursue her directly, Wynter took a circuitous route through the jungle. *She'll want to open a portal by the ruins. I can beat her there*, Wynter thought.

Anna slowed her pace and stooped by an archway in the ruins Schitz had shown her on their wedding day. She traced the symbols for Earth and Water.

But where to? She thought.

She could not return to Heaven. Anywhere in the Mortal Realm would also be dangerous if Zinc had ordered her execution.

Limbo, she decided. She remembered the symbols from the incursion long ago.

Just as the portal opened, the shriek of a scarlet macaw breaking into flight alerted Anna. She jumped to the side and was met with a searing pain in her chest. She looked down and saw the handle of a throwing knife protruding from her chest. Had she not moved, the knife would have surely struck her through the heart.

Anna struggled to breathe. The blade had collapsed one of her lungs. With a final effort she stepped through the portal.

The banks of the Styx were bathed in perpetual twilight. Anna could not tell if it was the dim environment or her injury that limited her vision. She glanced up at the towering fortress of Limbo and slowly began to make her way away from it.

Each step was agony. Each forced breath was torture, and pulled more and more blood into her mouth and down her chin. *I'm dying,* she thought. *My life saving Manna is too far away. But I am here in Hell, perhaps there is a way for me to get a message to my beloved Schitz.*

Anna staggered to the edge of the Styx and fell to her knees. The twilight was growing dimmer. She could feel the end coming. *There is no message to leave. He knows I love him. At least we had our reunion.*

She looked down into the glowing blue waters and could just about make out her reflection. Though horrified at her blood stained mouth and robe, she smiled. *I am happy with myself and my life. I am at peace.*

"Hey, I know you," a voice called from the far bank of the river.

Anna's head felt like a cinderblock, but she managed to raise it. Across the water stood two Satanic Priests. Each was holding a golf club.

"From your wedding," the Priest said.

Titus! He can tell Schitz what happened to me.

"Drink the water," the Priest accompanying Titus shouted. He splashed into the flowing depths followed by Titus.

"Drink the water!" he repeated.

Anna reached down and cupped a small handful of the river. *The Eunoe drives Angels to madness, but at this point what do I have to lose.* She sipped.

A burning sensation coursed its way through Anna's body. It felt as though she had been tossed into a billowing pyre. She tried to scream, but no sound emerged from her gaping mouth.

"It's going to be very painful," the Priest said.

Anna fell onto her back. She was vaguely aware of the Priest kneeling beside her and unrolling something. He cut into her chest above and below the protruding handle of the throwing knife. Anna groaned. The Priest splashed her with the water from the Styx. It burned like acid. She shook and howled. He slid the blade out of her chest and guided her to the edge of the water.

"You have to drink a lot of it," he said. "Don't stop."

Anna gulped the burning liquid until she was choking on it. She gasped and realized she was still breathing. The wound to her chest was no longer suffocating her.

"Keep drinking," the Priest said.

Anna's vision grew blurry. She vomited a thick black liquid. It tasted like tar and bile. She was vaguely aware of one of the Priests patting her on the shoulder. Slowly the nausea subsided. Anna's vision returned and she rose to her feet. The world around her seemed brighter and more vibrant than before.

"You saved me," she said to the Priests.

The sound of footsteps approached. Anna felt her sword being pulled from its scabbard on her back. Anna turned and saw the Angel that had struck her with the throwing knife and a cluster of others walking toward them.

They must have followed me through the portal. Why did the Priest take my sword?

"What are you doing on our side of the river?" the lead Angel asked. She brandished her sword.

"We found one of your lot trying to cross over to ours," Titus said.

The Angel lowered her sword. She appeared interested.

"What did they look like?" she asked.

"Female. Dark hair. Olive complexion. Oh, and she had a knife sticking out of her chest," Titus said.

Does she not recognize me in the twilight? This is absurd. I'm standing right here.

"Where did she go?" the Angel asked.

"After we forced her back from our side she succumbed to her wound in the river. It carried her downstream," Titus said.

The Angel nodded and scrutinized the three of them.

"Where'd you get that sword?" the Angel asked. She gestured to the bag of clubs lying on the ground. The hilt of Anna's sword protruded from the bag.

"It's not a sword; it's a decorative club cover," the Priest who had saved her said.

The Angel squinted in the twilight, but seemed satisfied.

"Alright, well shove off," the Angel said. "You're not supposed to be over here. Get back to your side.

"Gladly," Titus said. He nodded in a friendly way to the Angel and led Anna and the other Priest back across the river. Anna cringed in anticipation as she stepped into the river. *She'll notice when I start burning,* but the water felt cool and normal. Anna peered down into its flowing depths and saw her reflection. She almost fell over from fright. She brought her hands to her head…

…and felt horns.

"Oh my God," she said.

"You're not going to be using that expression anymore," the Priest said.

When she lowered her hands and saw her long, pointy fingernails.

"I'm a… a Demon," she said.

"That you are. Oh, the name's Salvatore by the way. No need to thank me or anything," the Priest said.

They reached the far side of the river. Anna threw her arms around Salvatore. He stiffened, shocked by the gesture.

"I could never thank you enough. Why? How? I have so many questions," she said.

Both Priests laughed.

"Well, Titus here said he knew you, said he officiated your wedding. That seemed odd, but if he's a friend of yours, well, then you're at least an acquaintance of mine. I'm a skilled surgeon, but you were pretty much dead meat. Drinking the water was the only thing I could think of that would save you," Salvatore said.

"I'm Anna Gold-Nervosa, Schizophrenia's wife," Anna said.

Salvatore grinned broadly. He punched Titus in the shoulder. "Oh, you naughty dog. Performing inter-faith marriages, are you? How salacious of your Holiness," he said.

"I owed Schitz a favor," Titus said with a shrug.

"Is that why they were trying to kill you?" Salvatore asked.

"I have no idea. I was supposed to be safe from both sides," Anna said.

"Those agreements are tough to keep," Salvatore said. "Come on, let's bring you to the Great Hall. Everyone is going to be happy to meet you."

Anna Gold-Vermaca

Zinc walked through the Great Hall. He had been reading about Schizophrenia; the Demon and the disease. He was certain Schitz would respond violently to Anna's death. Zinc had just traded Schitz several Angels in a drone strike in Afghanistan.

He should not doubt that I am still on board. I will blame Anna's death on Uranium II. Thus, in one move I will have removed my peer at the summit of Heavenly power and deprived Schitz of Anna. This is perfect. He lost AIDS; now I will dispose of him. That will leave only Anorexia and Autism as the pillar Demons holding up Hell, Zinc thought.

He was so immersed in his scheming that he nearly knocked over Wynter Zinc, his distant relative.

"You were successful?" he asked.

She snapped to attention. "Yes, I was the one who threw the fatal knife," she said.

"Good. Where is the body?" he asked.

"We could not recover it," she said.

A crack sounded through the Great Hall when Zinc smacked her across the face with the back of his hand. She flushed tomato red and trembled in place.

"Are you going to cry?" he asked.

"No, Lord Zinc," she said.

"I told you to return with the body," he said.

"It floated downstream; we could not recover it," Wynter said.

"You couldn't find an Angelic corpse in the Amazon?" he asked.

"No, she opened a portal and fled to the area by Limbo Fortress," Wynter said. "She tried to cross the Styx but fell to her wounds. She was also attacked by a Demon and two Priests."

"Interesting she would flee there," he said. "And you are certain she is dead?"

"Positive, my Lord. Nobody could survive a knife through the chest like that. It's amazing it took her so long to bleed out," she said.

"She was strong," Zinc said. "You did well Wynter, but you must not forget, the definition of success comes from me, not you. If I ask for a body, I expect you to move Heaven and Earth to bring it to me. Do you understand?"

"Yes, Lord Zinc."

Zinc paused for a moment to scrutinize his young talent. She was a recent Academy graduate. Angels did not age, yet there was some imperceptible quality that spoke of her youth: a brightness in her eyes and innocence in her smile.

She is many good things, Zinc thought. *She is a good leader. She is smart academically and in the field. She is attractive, which will bend males and females alike to her will. She is ambitious. Rather like myself on all accounts.*

"Tell me Wynter, you know your ancestry all the way back through the House of Zinc?" he asked.

"I do," she said.

"Which of my brothers are you descended from?" he asked.

"Ervin Zinc," she said.

"Ah, my little brother. Did you know he once possessed the mortal, Alexander the Great?" Zinc asked.

"I have been told. He fought well. Died well," she said.

"So through him, you are related to my father Lord Zinc I," Zinc said.

"By a much, much longer path, but yes," she said. Her normal complexion had returned. She seemed more at ease again. *Good she retained her composure despite the public humiliation.*

"What do you seek for your career?" Zinc asked.

"I want to be a Standard Bearer," Wynter said.

Zinc chuckled. "You might have said the lady of a lofty House, but no, you want a House outright," he said.

"Lady Hydrogen had such," she said.

Zinc felt an aching pain of remorse run through his body. *I should not have given her up. I made the wrong choice.* Though he loved his father and cherished the times they had shared since his return, the loss of Rachael had driven Zinc to near madness. The thought of Schitz happy and free with his long-lost love while Rachael lay in a cold tomb had been too much to bear.

"Yes, she did. Do you fancy yourself like her? A destroyer of Demons?" he asked.

"Yes, Lord Zinc," she said.

Zinc nodded. "You are doing well. Don't get ahead of yourself. Next time do everything I ask. I have several dispensations stored up. I think there is no reason that I could not give you a House."

"You are most kind," she said.

She maintains the same decorum as when I slapped her. Dignified in both good and bad moments. Yes, she is an asset.

"I am. I am a kind Lord both to the Zinc House and those split from its lineage as well as the many unincorporated Houses I rule over," Zinc said. "There is a storm coming. I have the loyalty of Heaven, but this battle will test the solidarity I have built. Abraham, ah Lord Cadmium, has many sons, grandsons, and so on. So is the case for my son Gallium, and my grandsons Technetium, Rhenium, and Francium. But do you know the last time we could claim an Academy valedictorian?"

"You, Lord Zinc," she said.

"Yes, it would seem that my success has bred fine Houses, but also Houses led by those who have not been imbued with your hunger. There are many ahead of you in line for a House. How will you deal with that?" he asked.

"I will show them why I was chosen," she said. "I will embody a warrioress they have not seen since Rachael, The Destroyer," she said.

Zinc smiled, a bittersweet grin at the most recent mention of his late lover.

"Tell me, have you found an Angel willing to be the husband to a lady of a House in which he is not the Lord?" he asked.

"I've found an Angel to be the second lady of my House," Wynter said.

"Ah, how times have changed," Zinc said. "For a long while none of that would be permitted. Might I ask who?"

"Siobhan Argon," she said.

"Ah, Argon is one of the Houses of the Carbon line. Both of my late wives were from the House of Carbon," Zinc said. "Alright, continue doing what is required of you and you will have your House sooner rather than later."

The assemblage in the meeting room harkened back to the days of the Triumvirate. Schitz had called together a veritable host of Demons, Priests, and Priestesses – and a lone Wraith. Anorexia looked across the table at Autism, Coronavirus, Vampirosis, Pancreatic Cancer, Titus, Erin, Desdemona, Salvatore, and Josephine. Joining them was a mysterious female Demon Anorexia had never seen before.

It feels like Schitz's duplicity has diminished his allies. Still, my brother seeks counsel with him and Schitz is preparing here to speak to a "circle of trust." He's like a cat; he always lands on his feet, Anorexia thought.

Schitz spoke. "I have summoned you here today because we are about to embark upon a great and dangerous adventure. We are going to eliminate the last of the Archangels, Michael Zinc and Xiang Uranium."

Anorexia felt as though she had been struck by a bolt of lightning. *They want to kill Xiang? Of course. They always want to kill Angels, but they are targeting him. Killing Chu Hua was the biggest mistake of my life. I will not let them kill her son.*

Schitz continued. "I have been running a dangerous and at times costly side venture." Schitz paused for dramatic effect.

Is he pretending to hold back tears? He is shameless.

After collecting himself, Schitz said, "Many good Demons have paid the price for the strategy I have engineered. But their sacrifice has put us in a position where the Angel Zinc erroneously believes that I am working with him. Preposterous, I know. Nevertheless, he believes this to be true. We will exploit his naivete to eliminate him and the other Archangel. With their leadership decapitated, the Angels will be helpless when we launch one final campaign."

Anorexia's head echoed with thoughts. *He has fully exonerated himself. His duplicity is like a giant elephant. Autism touched a part of it, AIDS another, I yet another. Who knows how many other blind fools came into contact with it. But we could not see the whole beast. Now he tells us it was all part of a master plan. Everything he did was intended to set up the final victory. Was it? I feel like it wasn't but, my suspicions are not enough. I want to believe he would not have killed our comrades for personal gain. Why is it so hard to believe him? Why couldn't he have become mine after Kursk? We would have been so good together. Then I would know the truth. Then I could trust him. And who is this mysterious Demon? Where has she come from? I know everybody in Hell.*

"Anorexia...Anorexia..." Schitz said.

She looked up and realized Schitz had been talking to her. The weight of the collective attention was embarrassing beyond measure.

Schitz chuckled. "It's been a long while since you didn't speak in public. Back in our Academy Days. I was asking if you have begun your collaboration with Angels to eliminate the Titan?"

Anorexia had been asked by Satan to participate in a joint venture to assassinate Circades. The request had triggered much contemplation on her part. She feared that working with the Angels would reveal her close relationship with Xiang. She had just returned from possessing a dowager with a penchant for auditing psychology lectures at Oxford, a time when she contemplated whether or not to accept the assignment.

Now that I know his plan involves Uranium II, I must be in the mix.

"I have not agreed to the joint venture yet. Satan posed it to me as optional, since working with the Angels is such a detestable proposition," Anorexia said.

She noticed the unknown Demon screw up her face in response.

"However, I will agree to it," Anorexia said. "Satan informed me there is a meeting scheduled by the Limbo Fortress to discuss our first moves. The Wraiths and the Familiars have been tracking the Titan, is that correct Josephine?"

"Yes, we will be bringing our findings to the meeting," Josephine said.

She is always so condescending to me probably because she had Schitz first.

"Then yes, I will partake in the meeting with the Angels," Anorexia said.

"Good, it is important that you succeed," Schitz said. "We will time your elimination of the Titan to coincide with the assassination of the Archangels. Both the Angelic leadership and the referee will be off the pitch at the same time. We'll be free to run riot without rules or oversight while they are reeling from their loss of guidance."

There was a murmur of agreement.

Schitz gestured to the mysterious Demon sat at the table and said, "Let me take a moment to introduce you to Anna Gold-Nervosa. She is my wonderful wife."

Uranium II's jaw dropped. He stared at the massive, subterranean corridor the walls of which were lined with shelves and racks containing all manner of modern mortal munitions. There were mortar rounds, grenades, tank shells, aerial munitions, artillery shells, and crates upon crates of ammunition.

"This is remarkable," he said.

"Thank you," Silver said. He smiled at Christa. "We've worked very hard, both in finding the sword and in amassing this arsenal."

"Saint Eligius would be proud," Uranium II said.

"Yes, but you can also see why we have strived to keep it secret, even from Zinc," Silver said.

"Of course. Much of the impact will come from the surprise factor" Uranium II said. "Once the Demons know we can kill them in the Celestial even while possessing mortals, they will act with caution."

"Yes, we have to hit them with one decisive blow," Silver said.

"The Demons will come out if a superpower goes to war," Uranium II said.

"Indeed, but it needs to be on a limited battlefield," Silver said.

"This might seem like an impressive hoard of weaponry but a modern army in a conventional war will burn through it in no time." We can't spread out our armaments across a broad front."

Uranium stroked his chin. "You've thought this through. My initial thought is Taiwan. We could launch an assault from mainland China. The United States would get involved and the Demons would find the conflict irresistible."

"That's two superpowers involved. The potential for a nuclear war would be immense," Silver said.

"I thought you wanted a war involving the superpowers?" Uranium II asked.

"Yes, but just a conventional war. Look at Iraq. The Demons went all in. We need a superpower fighting against a small country, not an Armageddon style standoff. Zinc's always sought out the battle to end all battles. We will draw the Demons into thinking they have an opportunity for a tough, but regular fight. Then we will hit them with our little surprise," Silver said.

"Perhaps Russia," Uranium II said. "They took the Crimea without much of a fight, but should they try to gobble up the rest of the country…"

"It would be a big fight," Silver said. "Ukraine has been arming for years; it would be quite the contest. The opportunity would be irresistible."

"We need a system for securely moving the munitions to the Russian army, and discreetly marking them so we know where they are," Christa said. "And, we'll need time to fix the warheads to the missiles."

"I'm sorry, the missiles?" Uranium II asked.

"Silver's fashioned pieces of the warheads for NATO and Russian conventional rocket artillery and medium range missile systems. They also contain the Celestial killing element. But smuggling the entire rocket is absurd, so we will need to fit our components to the missiles the Russians will surely be using," Christa said.

"Hahaha." Uranium's laughter was harsh and humorless. "You two, you two are something else. This is my type of mission. I like it."

"Just no nukes this time," Silver said.

Uranium II shook his head. "I understand. We'll keep it conventional. What code do you want to use for marking the weapons?"

"Let's go with Zed," Silver said.

"The end of the alphabet. The end of the war," Uranium II said.

Silver tapped his nose. "And it's simpler to draw than an omega," he said.

"Good," Uranium II said. "I will select the most trustworthy Familiars and begin arming the mortals with our weapons. We can disguise the army's movements as a training exercise."

"Use Lilly's relatives," Silver said. "They're as reliable as she was when she was in the field."

Uranium II nodded. "Thank you Silver; this is immense," he said.

Silver's mouth drew into a thin grin. "Not too bad for a guy who's not even allowed to wear his medals, eh?"

The soldiers' boots struck the ground in unison, a relentless stomp above that rose upward to Heaven and sank down to Hell – the discordant sounds of a marching song. The notes of the Fallschirmjäger song, *Hört Ihr unseren Schritt?* floated over the parade:

> *Führ uns General, führ uns zur Hölle! Wir*
> *sind zur Stelle. Fallen wir einmal,*
> *siegen wird unser Fanal. Fallschirmkameraden,*
> *Ihr dürft nie Ihr dürft nie verzagen!*[30]

"Well if this is not ironic, I don't know what is," Zinc said. He was within one of the bystanders watching the Bastille Day international military parade.

---

[30] Lead us General, lead us to Hell! We are there. Let's fall, our end will be victorious. Parachute comrades, you must never despair!

"Not the first time the German army has marched through here, but Europeans always patch up their differences, eventually," Schitz said. "I like this parade, this song too, brings back memories."

"I'm surprised you wanted to meet," Zinc said. He looked about the crowd. Constance and his father were somewhere watching his back. *It's so much easier since they know about the conspiracy,* he thought.

"You know I could kill you now because of Anna and damn the consequence," Schitz said.

"I had nothing to do with it," Zinc said. "I can't control Uranium II. He's a hot head."

"If you can't control him, we have to get rid of him. It's as simple as that," Schitz said.

Zinc adjusted his host's cloth facemask. "I can think of someone who is out of control and worth trading him for," he said.

"Yeah, COVID came out of nowhere didn't he?" Schitz said. "But the mortals already have a vaccine."

"Yes," Zinc said, "but he keeps coming out with a new variant every few months. Eventually, the next one will be as deadly as the first."

"So Uranium II to make up for Anna and COVID as a bonus?" Schitz asked.

"Uranium II is a deal for Anna and COVID," Zinc said.

Schitz fumed for a moment then nodded. "Alright, you have a deal. I'll relay the location for the exchange through the network of schizophrenics." He disappeared into the crowd without further ado.

Wow, even after all this he is still onboard with our system. I'm going to catch him completely by surprise, Zinc thought. Now... do I remove Uranium II in the process? He may have outlived his usefulness. Yes, I think so.

Circades, The Ancient, emerged from the weapons room and returned to the study weighed down with holstered semi-automatic pistols under his suit jacket, grenades along his leather belt, an assault rifle slung over either shoulder and a metal ammunition container in his hand. A smile slowly spread across his face. The world was his for the taking, and for the first time ever, he had a guaranteed route to Pulwabi.

"I just have to get my people out of Afghanistan" he said to himself. "I can't afford for my operations to be compromised now. The worldly power I have built up must be sustained."

The United States' withdrawal from Afghanistan had complicated affairs. He had to protect his network to maintain his influence over the affairs of the nations. Then he could push the world toward doomsday. He had grabbed a veritable arsenal. *Can't be too cautious,* he thought.

When he reached his car he gave the heavier weaponry to his security. "Alright, let's get going boys," he said.

Anorexia and Hirohisa Uranium stood together looking over a map of The Ancient's known movements. The meeting took place under the towering walls of the Limbo Citadel on the Angelic side of the Styx. Their squads waited.

"So, for the time being, we will be working together," the young Angel said.

"At least until someone tells us to kill each other," Anorexia said.

"Don't be coy, you know you'd rather work with us than fight us," Hirohisa whispered.

Anorexia giggled. She had playacted as though it was their first meeting for the benefit of the others, but it was difficult to turn off her familiarity with Xiang's handsome son.

This is just what I need after the news of Schitz's wife, she thought. *Parading around his converted Angel – what audacity!*

She leaned against Hirohisa and continued to look at the map. It felt good.

"Nice to see we're all getting comfy with each other," Vampirosis said. "But what's the plan, we're on a timetable aren't we?"

Anorexia glared at her and adjusted her posture.

"Well, the good news is that most of the hard work has already been done by our Familiars and your Wraiths," Hirohisa said. "They've installed a tracker and a listening device in his phone. He's not a very good gangster. He talks on the phone all the time. I'm shocked he hasn't gotten arrested."

"He'll be in Kabul in a few hours, we can take him out then," Anorexia said. "There's an Islamic State cell active near the city center. We can cover the action under the guise of a terrorist attack."

"What is he doing in Afghanistan?" Pancreatic Cancer asked.

"Looks like he's overseeing the U.S. withdrawal. Remember a huge part of his operation is funded by heroin produced in Afghanistan," Hirohisa said.

"Alright, so we go in heavy and we take him out along with as many bystanders as possible," one of Hirohisa's Angels said.

"Let's look over the layout of the airport again," Anorexia said. "We can't afford to miss anything."

The crowd outside the Abbey Gate of the unfortunately named Hamid Karzai International Airport was nervous. There was a palpable air of uncertainty among all who wished to flee the collapsing country. It was as chaotic as the Americans' arrival two decades earlier.

Circades pushed his way through the crowd with his lackey Louis Iraragorri close behind.

"I've been doing the best I can, Boss," Louis said between exhausted gasps. "You said your double-dealing would keep us good even if the Taliban came back into power."

"Our operation is secure because of our people," Circades said. "The extremists will be more than happy to take our money, but where will we be in terms of distribution when they revenge murder all of our operatives?"

"I get it, I get it. I've been trying my best. Look, they're all here. Maybe you can convince this idiotic 'be all you can be' posterchild to let them in the base," Louis said. He pointed to the teenaged solider guarding the checkpoint.

The soldier, overhearing Louis, seemed even less inclined to let anybody through.

"Hi, let's be reasonable, all of my people have EU passports," Circades said to the soldier.

"Then by all means, go to the EU airport. But if you want to get on an American plane, you need to be on the list," the soldier said. "You must be cleared and until I get that confirmation, you must step back like I said to your man over there."

A claustrophobic sensation gripped at Circades's throat. He was not fearful for himself, but the twenty or so personnel that stood around him and Louis. All of the Afghans were highly skilled. They spoke numerous languages, carried many passports, and had connections all over the Middle East and Asia.

It's not just that they grow poppies and make junk, he thought. *They are all critical links in moving product, especially within American planes. I need to get them somewhere safe.*

"Fuck," Circades said. He had not planned on the country collapsing so fast. He considered reaching into his suit for his wad of cash, but assessed the soldier to be above bribery. Also, among the panicked mass, a veritable fortune of American money would likely start a riot.

"Alright, look. Here is *my* passport. Run that information up the line and you're going to get a call from a Mr. Walters," Circades said.

"When you do, he will not only confirm my security clearance but he will also rip your ass and have you busted in rank – perhaps run out of the Army. You will be inextricably fucked. You will not be able to get a job as a squeegee man on the street corner in some dump like downtown Atlanta."

The soldier accepted Circades's passport. Unfazed, he handed it to his superior.

"I wish there was some fucking reception here, so I could call Craig myself," Circades said.

Luis shook his head. "What can you do? That's Afghanistan for you."

An explosion ripped through the crowd. Bodies were torn apart as metal and fragments flew through the air. The ground outside the gate jumped and jostled with the intensity of an earthquake. Automatic rifle fire cut through the crowd.

The American troops at the gate began shooting indiscriminately into the sea of humanity. Circades drew a .45 ACP semi-automatic. Louis pushed him by his shoulder and shouted, "Stay down, Boss." Several gunshots struck him in the chest in quick succession.

Armor piercers, Circades thought. He knew Louis always wore a bulletproof vest. *They're here for me.*

Circades looked through the crowd and saw a mortal with a dark, Demonic aura. She was aiming a Kalashnikov in his direction. Circades fired his pistol. The round caught her in the eye and blew a hole the size of a fist out the back of her head. Thanks to Hyperion's ring, the bullet killed both the mortal and the Demon within.

More rounds sailed past him. Circades put his sight over a male with a light Angelic aura and fired. Another headshot. He aimed at another light Aura. A third hole in a third head. A grenade bounced along the ground in his direction. Circades threw himself to the ground.

The force of the blast was significantly smaller than the initial bombing, but jarring, nevertheless. Circades rose to a kneeling position and scanned the mayhem. The terrorists were shooting, the Americans were shooting, and in the midst of it, countless mortals were dying.

A round struck him in the shoulder and knocked him to the ground. He fell in a seated position, his left arm useless. Another bullet grazed his scalp sending blood running down his face. He screamed out as another struck him in the thigh. He dropped his pistol to the ground.

This is it. Damn it! I was too comfortable, to let them catch me off guard.

A wall of flames formed a circle around Circades. He shielded his eyes and squinted. Round after round of gunfire struck the infernal divider and exploded harmlessly.

Surely, some of those would have hit me.

Before Circades could figure out what had delivered him, he was pulled to his feet and propelled forward. A fiery portal opened in the gateway of the airport. He passed through it. His vision was filled with an orange hue, as though he were looking at the sun with closed eyes. When his sight returned, Circades was sat in the middle of his bed back at his villa. Svaha was straddling his lap.

"Where would you be without me?" she asked.

Circades's eyes were wide in stunned disbelief.

Svaha stuck her index finger into the hole in his shoulder. It burned for a moment. Then she pulled the round from his body and cauterized the entry wound. She placed her hand on his thigh and sealed the laceration. She ran the top of her hand over his crotch and up his chest. He winced as she stopped the bleeding of his scalp. Circades felt his heart racing and his own voice arguing in his head.

But what of Pulwabi...I've spent an eternity looking for her...I've been faithful...But she's spent lifetimes knowing other men... Can't I just once...

"You are mine, Circades," Svaha said.

She clenched his hair between her fingers and pulled him on top of her. She groaned as he kissed her neck. He pulled open her robes and kissed her chest. She released a guttural groan and dug her nails into his scalp. Circades felt her immense strength pushing him down until his face was between her raised legs. He lapped at her with the thirst of a man who had walked through the desert. Her taste inflamed his senses.

"Don't stop," she moaned.

A booming voice resounded through the bedchamber. "You whore!"

Circades looked up to see a flash of blue and gold moving toward him. Svaha extended her hand and sent a flame out across the bed. The fire held Varuna's trident in place. Elementals were swift and powerful. Circades knew Svaha had only bought him a fraction of a second. He reached to his holster and drew his one remaining pistol. He fired as soon as he brought the gun forward, there was no time to aim.

Varuna was knocked back to the floor. He fell in a seated position with his hands over his stomach. Blood oozed between his fingers. His complexion faded to a pale, sickly blue.

"You... found... the ring," he said. "I thought ... it was safe... in the deep, with... Hyperion."

He slumped to the floor. Circades slid off the bed and went over to him. Varuna was dead.

"Oh, I didn't think. This is bad, this is so bad," Circades said. He clutched his scalp and winced. "I got the ring to protect myself, but I killed an Elemental. What does this mean for the Universe?"

He looked back toward Svaha for an answer. She was sitting on the bed, her robe still open and wearing a lurid grin. "You've done it. We're free," she said.

"But that wasn't your husband?" Circades asked.

"No, my brother-in-law, but he was the strongest and always tried to control all of us," she said. "But now, we are free to do whatever and whomever we want."

She grabbed him by the hair.

"Now, worship your goddess," she said

Varuna

Water & Air

Schitz dipped his finger into the large bowl containing water and traced the symbols for water and air into the grooves of the departure columns in the Great Hall of Hell. He blew on the symbols. Nothing happened.

"That's odd. I haven't messed up a portal since my Academy days," Schitz said. He looked awkwardly at the faces of his squad.

"Try a different combination; we're on a tight schedule," Anna said.

He shrugged and dipped a finger in the pot of flammable oil. He traced the symbols for fire and air. He blew on the symbols. The portal opened.

"That's more like it," he said.

They stepped through on their way to Syria.

Fire & Air

Uranium II stood before the Departure Gate with a contingent of his House. He felt naked and cold.

"This is unexpected," he said to himself. "I've opened portals since I was a neophyte."

But the combination of water and air had failed. He knew Zinc was expecting him. *What should I do*, he thought.

He heard the loud murmuring of a crowd behind him. *They must be amused by my humiliation.*

His son rushed through the assembled trailed by Anorexia and another female Demon.

"Father," Hirohisa said, "the Eunoe is draining."

"What are they doing here?" Uranium II asked. He was baffled by his son's wanton disregard for protocol.

"We are a cooperative task force, are we not? And that's really beside the point. The Titan survived our ambush, and now the Eunoe is draining. It's the same thing for their River Styx. We've just come from there," Hirohisa said.

"But how did you get here?" Uranium II asked. "The portals don't seem to be working."

"Nothing with water is viable," Hirohisa said. "The other three elements still work."

"Thank you, I am meant to meet Zinc," Uranium II said.

"It can wait, we need your help. Before the Eunoe drains, Anorexia wants to drink of it," Hirohisa said.

"But it causes madness?" Uranium II asked.

"We believe only in Angels. The Angel Anna Gold drank from the Styx and was turned into a Demon," Anorexia said.

"And you think the Eunoe would have a similar effect on you? This is a big thing, Anorexia. Are you sure?" Uranium II asked.

"We've always said that we wished I had been born an Angel," Anorexia said. "Perhaps we have been afforded the opportunity to correct nature's miscalculation."

Uranium II looked down and saw Anorexia's hand gently resting against Hirohisa's. He smiled.

"Ah, I see," he said. "I'm so happy for you both, there is no reward without risk. Come let us to the Eunoe. Zinc can wait."

"Speaking of waiting," the other Demon said.

"Ah, forgive me, we were not properly introduced," Uranium II said.

"Vampirosis," she said, "and we have precious little time before we lose all of the energy afforded by the Rivers. If this is the Titan's punishment, then we have to meet with him. We have to beg him not to eliminate us; we are at his mercy. He killed Pancreatic Cancer and a handful of Angels. Do you have any Angels available to augment our number?"

"Take them," Uranium II said, gesturing to his retinue.

The Demon nodded. She patted Anorexia on the shoulder. "Good luck," Vampirosis said.

"Good luck to you too," Anorexia said.

Uranium II led the way to the Eunoe. "This is amazing, so you two are…"

The couple laughed. "Your son is an irresistible charmer," Anorexia said.

Uranium II gaped in terror when they reached the river. The water in the Eunoe was only ankle deep. Souls wandered about the stream and the banks in delight and confusion.

"We're in Heaven!" he heard one say.

"It's real!" another said.

"Oh, this is not good," Uranium II said.

Anorexia dropped to her knees and scooped the river water into her mouth. One gulp and then another and another. She fell onto her back and descended into a violent fit. While in the throes of the attack, her horns fell off; her teeth became flat. Her finger tips grew round and less pointy.

She lay still upon the grass, an object of interest to the two Angels and a cluster of mortal souls. She sat up and held her head. "Did it work?" she asked.

Hirohisa stooped and wrapped his arms around her. "My love," he said. "You are an Angel."

Uranium II dropped to his knees and pulled his long-time confidant and his son into a joyous embrace. "What a happy day. I only hope your colleagues are able to stave off this drought," he said.

The cloud of chlorine gas had drifted over the bombed out suburb of ar-Raqqah. The Syrian government helicopters had dropped countless barrel bombs at the break of dawn. The high explosives leveled walls and ripped off any remaining roofs in the already gutted neighborhood. Hours later, while the inhabitants attempted to attend to their injured and dead, the aircraft screamed past. Moments later, a thick cloud of deadly gas enveloped the area.

There were no mortal survivors in the immediate vicinity of the attack.

Just as I intended; no hosts in sight, Zinc thought. He stood in the Celestial beside his father.

"Where is Uranium II?" the elder Zinc asked.

"He should have been here by now," Zinc said. "If he doesn't show before Schitz arrives, we still take out the Demon. It is a must."

Zinc looked across the ruined neighborhood to the sniper's position. He could not make out where Constance's host was, but he knew she was there. Her mortal was outfitted with a gas mask and NBC protective gear. They had stolen some of Silver's Celestial 7.62 ammunition.

"Schitz will have no idea that we can kill him in the Celestial from range," Zinc said. "Even if he is on his guard, it won't matter. Constance is an expert sharpshooter. Today we will win a great victory."

"Your plan is well laid out. I only hope our forces were successful in taking out the Titan. He is wily," the elder Zinc said.

"Yes, I was hoping Uranium II would bring news," Zinc said. He looked about in frustration. "I have no idea what is holding him up. It is not like him to be late."

The elder Zinc chuckled, "What's that mortal saying? Late to your own funeral?"

Anna ran through the rubble of ar-Raqqah. Pebbles and rubble dislodged under her host's boots. It had taken her time to find a female SDF host and more time to find a silenced weapon. Anna's heart rattled like a machine gun. *I hope I'm not too late*, she thought.

As quick and quiet as possible, Anna made her way from building to building. Her host was a fit young woman from Aleppo, but under a gas mask and heavy clothing she was tiring in the afternoon swelter. Like driving a mule forward, Anna willed her host to continue.

She made her way across the top floor of a damaged apartment building. The dead – men, women, children, and elderly – littered the various abodes. The barrel bombs had ensured that all of the buildings were open to the air. The civilians stood no chance against the chlorine gas. Their wide eyes and froth-filled mouths spoke to the horrors of their final moments.

Anna almost stumbled over a mortal draped in a yellow plastic coat. She came to a gasping halt. It was Constance within a mortal sniper. Constance turned and met her gaze. Anna raised her silenced pistol and fired three shots into Constance's host. The silencer coughed and Constance fell into a departure seizure.

Anna grimaced. She hated that she had inflicted the suffering of the fit on Beatrice's daughter and her longtime friend. She forced the thoughts from her mind and scooped up Constance's weapon. A SVD sniper rifle.

But this is a mortal weapon? Anna thought.

She dropped the box magazine and looked at the top bullet.

This is not a normal 7.62mm, she thought. She had seen enough Soviet ammunition to know something was off. She popped the first cartridge and pressed it against her index finger.

She could feel the tip of the bullet not just in her host's finger but also in the Celestial. *What the fuck? You were not here to protect Zinc. You were here to kill Schitz.*

Anna looked down at Constance. She was still in the throes of the departure seizure, though it was fading. Anna returned the round to the magazine and slid it back into the rifle. Anna peered through the scope. Schitz was walking across the square toward Zinc and his father. She moved the scope across the ruins of the square. Autism and Coronavirus were in cover. The initial plan had called for Schitz, Anna, Autism, and COVID to surround the Angels on all sides in the Celestial. Zinc, Uranium, and any other Angels would have been trapped and destroyed. However, when Constance was not present, Anna had sensed a ruse.

This was your plot, she thought. She brought the sight over Zinc. Behind her Constance was emerging from her seizure.

"So, where is my wife's murderer?" Schitz asked. He held his hands out wide. "You were supposed to be here with him."

"Even if he was here, what were you going to do, talk him to death?" Zinc asked.

"Maybe I didn't come alone," Schitz said.

"Then you'd be giving away our collaboration," Zinc said. He looked awkwardly from side to side – a man trying to stall for time.

"We do still have our accord, don't we?" Zinc asked.

"You tell me. Do we?" Schitz asked.

Zinc looked past Schitz up into the ruins of a large apartment building.

There was a flash of light. Zinc felt a hammer blow to his body. He had been within enough wounded hosts to know he had been shot. Reflexively, he clutched at his chest. He fought to breathe, but no air was forthcoming. The impact of the ground felt dull and far away.

All of Schitz's battlefield experience melted for a moment. A *gunshot? In the Celestial?* He stood in disbelief and met the elder Zinc's gaze. Neither bothered to draw a weapon, both grappled one another with violence born of desperation. Schitz threw the Angel to the ground and attempted to pin him. The Angel reached up and choked Schitz. Schitz freed a hand and pulled a dagger from his waist. He drove it into the Angel's midsection three times in quick succession. He shrieked with each blow he landed. The elder Zinc went limp. His eyes filled with pain.

"I'm sorry, old friend," Schitz said.

"I told you... we would be enemies... if we were freed... from the dungeon," the elder Zinc said. He coughed violently with blood running out of his mouth.

"You died free," Schitz said.

The Angel nodded. "Free...and fighting," he said.

Schitz drove the dagger into the Angel's throat. He left the blade.

Zinc, incapacitated on the ground, watched the blurry image of his father dying by Schitz's hand. *I betrayed Rachael just so he could be free,* Zinc thought. *And now, he dies like this.*

Zinc swore he could see Rachael, and Carbon IV, and Cesium, and Uranium I, and Mercury IV, and Iron III, and Palladium, and Krypton II and Primrose and Bluebell and so many others, countless others. They stood over him behind Schitz.

"Any last words?" Schitz asked.

"So many, so many," he said. He coughed violently. "So many, for nothing. It was all... for nothing."

Autism and Coronavirus had crossed the square. Schitz held out his hand. Coronavirus handed him his virus-shaped mace. Schitz grunted when he crushed Zinc's head with the heavy iron ball.

"Ouch," Autism said. He laughed. COVID joined in. Autism jostled Schitz playfully. "To think we doubted you," he said.

Schitz chuckled. "I can't blame you. I might have doubted myself."

"Remind me not to get on your bad side," COVID said. "I mean, geez, he was already dying and you were all like 'Wah-pah, you go out on my terms.' Classic."

Schitz forced a smile. "Who said you're not already on my bad side?" Schitz asked.

Autism and COVID continued to laugh and grin. Schitz was quiet, wrapped in a blanket of contradicting emotions.

Constance stared at her erstwhile colleague and fellow assassin. "Anna? You're...you're a Demon?"

Anna nodded and continued to train the SVD on Constance.

"You, you killed him? How could you? Why? It was Zinc? Our Zinc?" Constance howled in disbelief.

"Did you know he was sending Angels to kill me after I left?" Anna asked.

There was an awkward and sudden stillness about Constance.

"I'll take that as a 'yes'," Anna said.

"He said it was necessary," Constance said. "So what are you going to do now? I can't hurt you from here in the Celestial."

"If I were in your position, I'd be thinking, 'Can I knock off her host's gas mask? Is the chlorine gas yet settled?' Am I right?" Anna asked.

Constance looked down. She knew her crouched, catlike stance was transparent.

"I told you once, I'm not going to be on the wrong end of the sword and Angels have caused me almost nothing but pain," Anna said. "So I don't mind killing them. I'm sorry only for Beatrice."

"Wait, An— "

Her head exploded before she could finish her sentence. A red, circular pattern of Celestial blood sprayed across the wall of the ruined apartment. Anna dropped the magazine out of the SVD and pocketed the exotic rounds. *I'll have to hand these over for analysis back in Hell... back home,* she thought.

The villa was picturesque, an elaborate display of Circades's vast fortune. When Vampirosis led her contingent through the grounds, she had expected to find the Titan enraged, seething, furiously planning. She never imagined he would be lounging beside a pool.

The joint squad encountered the Titan seated on a beach chair drinking a cocktail. He was in the company of a woman of South Asian appearance. She was clad in a small, black bikini, wore large sunglasses, and was also drinking a cocktail. Though she had come to speak with the Titan, Vampirosis was unable to pull her attention from his companion. The woman had amber patterns running through her skin and her hair seemed as though it was made of flames. The edges of her swimsuit burned and then regenerated.

The woman noticed Vampirosis's attention. She slid her sunglasses down. Her eyes were two abyssal, black pools.

"Never met an Elemental, have you?" the woman asked.

Uncertain how to proceed, Vampirosis looked from the Titan to the Elemental. "I am not sure how to address you," she said.

"Goddess Svaha," the woman said.

"Ancient Titan Circades, Goddess Elemental Svaha, we come to beg our most abject and sincere apology for...what happened earlier," Vampirosis said.

"Why are you here? Are you representatives of Satan and God?" Circades asked.

"Yes," one of the Uranium Angels in the squad said.

"We beg for you to restore the waters," Vampirosis said.

The Elemental broke into a thunderclap of laughter. "The waters will never flow again," she said.

"Then we'll die," Vampirosis said. "As Celestials, we rely on the cycle of mortal births and deaths. Without the rivers of reincarnation we will have no energy for opening portals or for inflicting our diseases or cures on humanity."

"Why did you try to kill me?" Circades asked.

"It was a mistake," Vampirosis said.

"But why?"

"We saw you as a threat to our existence," she said.

"Hmm, yet you come to beg for your existence now," he said.

"Not just for us, but for all of humanity, for all the universe of which we are a part," Vampirosis said.

The Elemental spoke next. "The water will not flow because the Ethereal of Water is no more," she said.

Svaha rose to her feet. She retrieved two notepads from the table next to her chair. She sauntered over to Vampirosis and her Angelic companions. Svaha handed each a notepad.

"You will recognize these as the incantation and meditations through which to resurrect the Eunoe and Styx as rivers of fire," Svaha said.

"Will the effect be the same?" Vampirosis asked.

"You might not enjoy drinking it or baking with it as much as you did with the previous rivers, but you will be able to utilize the molten flows for the same benefits," Svaha said.

"Will the mortals suffer more now?" the Angel asked.

"No, not really," Svaha said. "They'll have the same drowning sensation in the Styx and feeling of blandness in the Eunoe, but nothing new will happen. They won't feel like they're burning alive or anything. The fire will burn away the soul's memory much like the water washed it," Svaha said.

Hmm, I imagine she had some benefit from this change. She looks sexually aroused Vampirosis thought.

"Will you be able to overlook our indiscretion and return to the previous agreement?" Vampirosis asked.

"Time will tell," Circades said. "In the meantime, I'd get those rivers flowing again if I were you."

Uranium II, Silver, and Wynter Zinc stood beside the molten, fiery depths of the Eunoe. They were surrounded by a multitude of Standard Bearers and other Angels of varying levels of importance.

"Zinc left us no proof that you were to be given a House," Uranium II said. "There are a multitude of older Zincs. How could we know his designs without a will?"

There was a raucous murmur within the crowd.

"Besides," Silver said, "the law states that when a Standard Bearer falls, his House is rendered insolvent. His element no longer offers healing to the mortals, his kin are cast into subservience, and his dispensations are divvied out among the living Lords."

The grumbling intensified.

"Except during the duel with the Black Death or the case of the Hydrogen House," Wynter said.

"Very rare exceptions," Silver said.

"Zinc promised me a House. It is only fitting that I inherit the House of Zinc since he has passed," Wynter said.

The crowd bubbled as much as the fiery river.

Uranium II held up his hands, calling for order. "This is not the time for a succession crisis," he said. "There never is one, but now is an especially inopportune moment. God has trusted us to deal with the issue, so the law is whatever we agree upon. As the only Supreme Commander at the moment, the law is whatever I decide. But I would like an agreement if possible."

"She's lying," someone in the crowd shouted.

"Who said that?" Wynter asked. Her eyes blazed.

The crowd fell silent.

Wynter paced back and forth like a caged lion. She drew her Celestial sword and struck at the ground with it. "Say it again!" she said. "Call me a liar. Call me an entitled brat. A know-it-all. A youngster. Go ahead, say it to my face. Step up and say it again!"

Wynter pointed her sword at the crowd of Angels and looked toward Uranium II and Silver. "This lot is spineless and weak. Impotent. None of them deserves to lead."

Silver looked at Uranium II and shrugged. "She makes a good point," he said.

"Alright, this is what is going to happen for the Heavenly Army" Uranium II said. "Silver is to be reinstated. He will be dubbed Co-Supreme Commander and will have the former Houses of Silver and Gold under his dominion. Wynter will be knighted Lord Zinc III. She will maintain the rest of the Zinc Vassals and dispensations. I trust this is something everybody can live with."

There were muffled voices of agreement among the assembled Angels. Silver patted Wynter on the back and shouted to the crowd. "Aye, Lord Zinc II is dead. Long Live Lord Zinc III."

The assembled cheered with newly born vigor.

Lord Zinc II lay still upon a stone slab. It had taken Salvatore an eternity to reconstruct his head to any semblance of its prior likeness. The Demons had brought the Angel's body back to Hell. Schitz had intended for the proceeding to include both Zinc and Uranium II, however, he had only slain one. Still, he intended to hold the ceremony.

The Demons, Wraiths, and Priests of Hell filed past the fallen Angel lying in state. Schitz and Anna stood beside the body. An orchestra of Wraiths played the *Triumphal March* from Verdi's *Aida*. Around Schitz's neck rested a newly minted medal. It took the form of a pentagram with an upside down cross emblazoned in the middle of it.

"Congratulations," Titus said. He shook Schitz's hand. "I'm glad to see you are doing well Anna."

Anna smiled and nodded to Titus and Erin.

"You have won a great victory for our side and a huge amount of work for myself," Salvatore said.

"You did a wonderful job," Schitz said. He looked down at Zinc like a hunter gloating over a prize buck.

Salvatore and Desdemona gave Anna their well-wishes and moved on.

"At last," Josephine said. She smiled at Schitz and embraced Anna in a half-hearted fashion. "I hear you fired the shot that laid him low?"

"I did," Anna said.

"Fantastic," Josephine said. She continued past.

"Another medal. I'm never going to catch up," Autism said. He shook Schitz's hand with vigor and smiled at Anna.

"Well, it doesn't have to stop you from trying," Schitz said.

"You know it," Autism said. "We're all ready to finish them off now. One last battle to get some more decorations."

Schitz thought of Anorexia. Vampirosis had returned with word of her defection. The news had stung. *I will not let it dampen today,* he thought.

A hulking shadow was next in line. Schitz felt as though he would faint. Standing before him was Bubonic Plague. The leviathan rested his hand roughly on the Angel's corpse.

"This horrid creature killed my coven, murdered my children, and worst of all, dragged my reputation through the mud...I have longed...I have thirsted...I have agonized for the day when I would see him still and cold," Plague said.

Bubonic extended his hand. Schitz accepted it gingerly only to find himself pulled into a hearty embrace.

"Brother," Plague said.

Brother? Schitz thought.

"There is much for us to discuss, but I do not want my triumphant, though unexpected return to rob you of your moment," Plague said. "We will be in touch soon."

"Missus Schitz," Plague said with a nod to Anna.

"You never told me you had a brother," Anna whispered to Schitz.

"I... am at a loss myself," Schitz said.

Vampirosis was next.

"Ah, a Knight's Pentagram with swords," Schitz said, gesturing to her glittering neck.

"Well, saving Hell will do that for you, even if we missed the Titan," she said. Vampirosis looked past Schitz to the burning Styx. Schitz turned and viewed the fiery river.

"Well done indeed," Anna said.

When the last of the queue had passed, a cadre of pallbearers carried Zinc's body across a small stone bridge that spanned the Styx nearest the Limbo Fortress. The recent construction was a byproduct of the joint effort at killing the Titan. It bore a sign: El Puente de la Amistad, a placard placed by a humorous Wraith or Familiar.

Outside Limbo Fortress they left Zinc's body for his people to collect.

"That was an odd way to say goodbye to an enemy turned friend turned enemy." Anna said.

"I'm sorry if it was awkward, having known him and all. I felt I needed to rid myself of the stink of collusion once and for all," Schitz said.

"No reason to apologize, my love," she said. "I had a complicated history with him as well. It fits for Zinc that he'll have a funeral both in Hell and in Heaven."

Albert Silver stood alongside Christa at the front of a new formation. The Angels behind him were the descendants of his former House and his brother Gold's former House. An odd sense of anticipation ran through him. He felt his hands shake.

"It will be fine," Christa whispered.

"It's just so near at hand, I won't feel at ease until it is done," he said.

He was called to the high altar. Lords were usually knighted by their father, the one spending a dispensation to found their House. However, Silver's father, Iron II, had categorically refused to abandon his retirement at the Mercury Monastery to attend the ceremony. Wynter was an orphan who was inheriting from a deceased Standard Bearer. Thus, no fathers were present to preside over the patriarchal role in the ceremony.

The rite took on an almost comical level of complexity. First, Uranium II dubbed Wynter Lord Zinc III. The three Angels knelt to pray before the altar.

The High Priest, Carolus, said, "Ave Maria, gratia plena, Dominus tecum, Virgo serena."

Then he instructed Uranium II to rise. Carolus presented Uranium with the sword of the House of Zinc. Since Zinc did not carry it in combat, the sword had not been lost. The Priest rested the ceremonial weapon on Uranium's outstretched palms. Carolus instructed Wynter to rise. She placed her hands under the blade.

"Recite after me, young Lord," the Priest said. "I, Lord Zinc III, hereby accept The Zinszka, the sword of my House, the protector of my people, and the eviscerator of my enemies."

Wynter echoed the words of the High Priest. Next, the holy man removed a small, white dove from an iron cage resting atop the altar. He sliced the neck of the hapless creature with the razor-sharp edge of the blade and tossed the corpse into a basket beside the altar.

"I swear," he continued with Wynter repeating, "that this shall be the last innocent blood spilled by this sword or any sword of my House."

The blood of the slaughtered dove dripped from the blade onto the white marble of the Great Hall. "Kneel once more as a daughter of Zinc," the High Priest said. He turned to Uranium II. "Lord Uranium II, repeat after me. I dub thee Lord Zinc III."

Once Wynter had been invested, she had the right to free Silver, which she did. With Silver liberated, he was free to repeat the process. Uranium II re-knighted Silver as Lord Electrum I. He was presented with the Ur Lak, renamed The Elehtre.

Silver marveled how the Familiars had forged a white alloy of gold and silver in an elaborate pattern on the blade, handle, and cross-guard of the old sword.

I hope it still works on the forge, he thought.

With Silver knighted, Wynter gifted her subordinates of the Gold House to him. When she did, he incorporated them into his new House. Lastly, Uranium II dubbed Electrum I co-supreme commander of the Army of Heaven.

Carolus seemed unsatisfied as if everything had not been done in the right order. For a moment, all stood in silence while the Priest reviewed the order and actions of the day in his head. He mouthed under his breath. "And that rightly followed that, and then that, so we could do that... alright."

He stopped whispering to himself and addressed the assembled. "Go in Peace and serve the Lord."

There was a small celebration. The mood in Heaven was still dampened by Zinc's death and the transmutation of the Eunoe. Uranium II, Wynter, and Electrum gravitated to one another separate from the festivities.

"How is your family?" Uranium II asked.

"Relieved," Lord Electrum said. "Zinc wasn't a bad overlord by any means, but to be free again, that is like a breath of fresh air. I didn't appreciate it the first time I was made a Lord. I thought the ceremony was about me, about the ambitions I wanted to achieve, the heights I wished to conquer. Now I know a Lord is the lowest position within a House," Electrum said.

Uranium II nodded in agreement. "For he is a servant to all," he said.

"Yes," Electrum said.

Wynter looked on with fascination on her face. She drank from her cup of Elixir.

"You look nervous," Electrum said.

"I just...never thought of it that way," she said. "If I'm honest. Today *was* about me, about clawing my way up to the top. I am the first woman to survive in the job for any reasonable amount of time. I'm fine to fight and die, but the idea of serving everyone else is heavy. I heard what you said about Zinc. I want to be considered a good overlord to my remaining vassals," she said.

Uranium II laughed. "You sound like me. When I was young I loved only to fight. I thought I knew of politics, but I had an infantile grasp of it. I had this position thrust upon me by circumstance," he said.

"Yet you've thrived," Wynter said.

"Aye, I have, but a large part of that is luck. Luck, and relationships. I've been saved and I've grown powerful from those who I called friend and foe alike," he said.

"I have much to learn from both of you," Wynter said. "I am willing to, eager to."

Electrum smiled. "Wasn't it you just threatening to make the crowd eat its words,"

Wynter smiled. "That's the easy part. Doing the right thing might be harder."

"You'll learn," Uranium II said. "And come time, you will take my role as co-Supreme Commander along with Electrum here."

"I just got this job. Don't give me more responsibility," Wynter said.

"Always up, further and greater things," Uranium II said. "My time to retire comes soon. After this next campaign I will go to the Monastery of my elders. Between now and then I will impart my wisdom to you. My son has recently taken on a strong wife. He will inherit House Uranium, but you command the largest block.

It is important that a Zinc is a Supreme Commander. When the time comes, you and Hirohisa can sort out the next generation's leadership."

The three agreed that politicking for power would remain dead along with Zinc.

"We can solve our differences together," Electrum said. "Look how well today worked out. Besides, we have much bigger problems ahead than who has the unfortunate lot of leading us into the upcoming battle."

Chapter 16
Святий Дж

Anorexia tried to sit still. She was wearing Chu Hua's wedding kimono. In a world where photography had existed for nearly two centuries, sitting for a painting felt odd. She was reminded of sitting in the uncomfortable seats of the Hellish Academy. The Familiar had insisted they maintain serious faces, however, Hirohisa continually broke into a smile.

Oh, I love him, Anorexia thought. *He is so full of life and youthful exuberance. After a lifetime of missing out, I finally have something sweet, simple, and all my own.*

"Absolutely magnificent," Uranium II said.

He stood behind the Familiar and scrutinized the canvas.

"It is traditional in our Eastern Houses for a portrait to be painted in the days following a wedding or a funeral," Uranium II said.

Hirohisa rested his hand over Anorexia's. The Familiar sucked her teeth. The groom snapped his hand back to his side.

"Oh stop it, Chae-Yeong," Uranium II said. "You're only painting the background; you're already done with the couple."

The old Familiar released a grandmotherly laugh. "I fooled you three times before you caught on Xiang," she said. "Come, he's telling the truth."

Anorexia and Hirohisa rushed over to see the work.

"It's beautiful," Anorexia said. She felt her face glowing red.

"You painted me smiling?" Hirohisa asked.

"Well, you won't stop." Chae-Yeong said. "I think the ancestors will be forgiving."

"I hope so; I really can't help myself," he said. Hirohisa rubbed Anorexia's arm with affection.

"I'll deliver it to your room when I'm finished," Chae-Yeong said.

"Go, enjoy the time you have," Uranium II said. "All of Heaven is mustering for a grand campaign very soon."

Incorporation into Demonic society was a surreal experience for Anna. Nobody questioned her. She was immediately thrust into the position as wife to one of a legendary figure. She received little instruction as to the nuances of life in Hell.

URANIUM
ANOREXIA
HIROHITO

Here I sit at another Top Secret briefing, she thought. *So much for peace and tranquility in the Amazon.*

Anna was joined by Schitz, Vampirosis, COVID, Josephine, Titus, and a Wraith Anna did not know. Anna looked at Josephine.

She has the appearance of an elderly woman, but the spryness of her Wraith body conveys something of what she was like in her youth.

Anna knew the Wraith and Schitz had some sort of history. Part of Anna's acclimation to Hell had been coming to grips with Schitz's sordid past. Schitz had informed her in vague terms that it was almost customary for him to take a lover in each Academy class.

I must carry myself without petty jealousy. It seems that marrying Schitz is akin to being the Lady of an Angelic House. I am happy to have my husband and would gladly gouge out the eyes of anyone who looks at him too long, but that is not the way. We both have a lot of attention on us. It is best to be reserved and to appreciate being together. He has promised himself to me and I must trust him.

Schitz's friend Autism arrived at the meeting. "Sorry, I'm late, I got stuck… well, it doesn't matter, he said.

"Thanks Autsy," Schitz said. He passed out the bullets Anna had brought back to Hell.

"It's nothing new for us to bring back items from the Mortal Realm," Josephine said. "We bring back bullets for training in the Academy all the time."

"Yes, but the same process happens in reverse. If we take bullets modified for the Celestial Academy into the Mortal Realm, they lose any Celestial properties. These don't. They allowed Anna to shoot an Angel when he was in the Celestial Realm and she was in possession of a mortal," Schitz said.

There was a hushed silence.

"Yes, yes, I know," Schitz said. "It violates the Divine Dictum but so does the existence of such a weapon. It seems the Divine Dictum is rapidly deteriorating. Our conflict is spiraling out of control. The Elementals have torched our river and removed our ability to use water or air for portals. We can no longer worry about the rules. We need to knock out Heaven and then address the threats posed by the Titan and the Elementals."

"It is the product of the blacksmithing of the Titans," the unfamiliar Wraith said. He held the bullet between his fingers, then set it back on the table.

"There were Angels investigating the technology and weapons of the Titans when I was in Heaven," Anna said. *I miss Silver and Christa and the others*, she thought. A painful image of Constance slumped on the floor without the top half of her head flashed through Anna's mind.

"They must have been successful," the Wraith said.

"Oh, everybody, this is Vulcan, the head Wraith metalworker," Josephine said. "He oversees the manufacture of all of your Celestial weapons. His work keeps him out of public society and ignorant of things like introductions and etiquette."

Vulcan glowered toward Josephine and rolled his eyes.

Schitz chuckled. "Are you certain it is a Titan's weapon?" he asked.

"Yes," Vulcan said.

"I concur," Titus said. "The Church maintains that Satan created the Universe so everything I am about to say is heresy and things I have learned in my private time. Satan and God fought a grueling war against the Titans resulting in the deaths of all Celestials other than Satan and God. Before that, there was a pantheon of Celestials and a multitude of Titans. The war was so bloody because Titans possessed weapons that could kill Celestials even when they were not in possession of a mortal body. The weaponry could pass into the Celestial Realm with ease."

"That seems to fit with what we have here," Vampirosis said.

The rest nodded.

"Let's think from their point of view," Schitz said. "They assumed this advantage would result in their sniping me and anybody else with me. What's the next step? If they have these weapons at their disposal, they will want to use them in a large-scale battle."

"The Russians are massing on all sides of Ukraine," Josephine said. "It's going to be the largest land war in Europe in decades."

"Yes, they must be expecting us to come out for a fight," Schitz said.

"I mean, strategically, what if we bypassed the war – since they have Demon killer rounds and all?" Autism asked.

"We can't," Schitz said. He shook his head. "Let's say they roll over Ukraine in a week. It could be the Baltic or Poland or the Balkans next. Nobody wants a nuclear war, which means the Angels may try a worldly power grab. We can't take the risk that they might monopolize power on Earth. We know their leadership is fractured without Zinc. I suspect they are in the middle of a faction-fueled internal battle royale."

"We can't miss the opportunity to hit them when they're like this," COVID said.

"I agree," Schitz said. "Your pandemic has been instrumental in dividing and isolating many parts of the modern world. The mortals have been made ready for our permanent dominion over them. Now is the time to strike."

"But what of their arsenal?" Vampirosis asked. "We can't just fight our way through bullets that hit us both when we are in the Celestial or within hosts."

"Can it be reverse engineered?" Titus asked, posing the question to Vulcan.

"Come, let's try," the Wraith said.

The meeting moved to a hallway and then to a rundown portion of the Great Hall. Anna could tell from the looks of every face that like her, none had been to the abode of the Wraiths.

They arrived at a forge. Vulcan removed the bullet from the cartridge and examined the pieces.

"Hmm, as I expected. Only the projectile has been modified. The rest is of original Mortal design."

Vulcan used a pair of tongs to put the bullet into a furnace. After a few moments he removed a glowing pellet. The Wraith placed the molten bullet onto an anvil and began to hammer it. He burst forth with a thunderous voice that made many of the attendees jump.

"Yes, yes, yes!"

Anna watched as the orange metal expanded across the broad anvil.

"It is truly a special metal," Vulcan said. "Anything I have ever worked with is limited by the amount present. But look at what this bullet has yielded."

Anna peered at the forge and understood the Wraith's excitement. The small amount of metal had quadrupled when heated.

Vulcan dipped the metal in a vat of water. A violent gush of steam flowed over the audience. He held up the cooled metal. After a few moments he said, "Touch it. It's still Celestial and I would wager it will retain the properties of the bullet when returned to the Mortal Realm."

"So we can use these captured rounds to manufacture Titanic weapons of our own?" Titus asked.

"Yes," Vulcan said. "Like the cartridge, we can bring in mortal components and fit this metal to the projectile."

"But how long will that take?" Vampirosis asked. "The Angels are set to attack Ukraine in a matter of weeks. Who knows how long they've been preparing."

"Tell me this, Vulcan," Schitz said. "Would this metal work in things other than bullets?"

"It should work in any weapon that uses metal," the Wraith said. "I think it would even work in weapons with a warhead if the outside or parts of the explosive contained the Celestial killing components."

"It would be short-sighted to assume they only made bullets," Schitz said.

Coronavirus groaned. "We'll never catch up."

"We don't need to catch up; we just need to fight them on our terms," Autism said. "Look at the Iraqis. They consistently inflicted losses on the Americans with inferior technology by fighting them asymmetrically, or the Mujahideen, Viet Cong, or the Maccabees, take your pick."

"It's true," Schitz said. "We have to force the Angels into one area of combat and tilt the field in our favor."

"Where should we fight them?" COVID asked.

"If I may," Vulcan said. "Manufacturing rifle rounds like this cartridge will be time consuming and beyond tedious. Even with all of my Wraiths working around the clock, it would be a losing battle. A modern army burns through hundreds of thousands of rounds of ammunition. In a conventional war, we would need multiple factories to keep up. No, I would recommend a weapon system that offers more bang for the buck."

"Some type of MPAD," Schitz said. "Stingers, Verbas—"

"Javelins," Autism said. "The Russians are going to attack with tanks. The FGM-148 would be perfect."

There were nods of agreement.

"I could modify the HEAT warhead pretty easily. Five thousand even ten thousand of those are a lot easier to make than five million Kalashnikov rounds. And unlike a thousand bullets, the warheads will stop an army," Vulcan said.

"We'll need to force our enemies into a situation where they rely mostly on the tanks," Schitz said.

"Vampirosis cracked her knuckles. "Leave air defense to me. No one can touch me in the air, other than you," she said with a smirk.

"And we'll hit their infantry from distance. Lure them out, fall back, and take out the armor," COVID said.

"I think it can work," Autism said.

"Alright. Let's get to it," Schitz said. "Josephine, you and your Wraiths get a rotation going. Smuggle Javelins back here and then out into the field. Vulcan, nothing else is worked on by any of the smithing Wraiths until this is done. Titus, the fire of the Styx still heals us the way it did when it was water. Get working on a way to bring it right to the arrival portals. Vampirosis, go to the Ukrainian Air Force. Autism and COVID, divide our forces into fire teams. I'll head up one; each of you can lead one of the others."

Anna shook her head. "I was cut by the Titan's sword. Manna did not heal it. I fear water from the Styx will be equally ineffective," she said.

"How did you heal?" Vampirosis asked.

Anna held up her scarred palm. "With stitches just like the mortals."

"Salvatore is an excellent surgeon," Titus said. "I will liaise with him to get the rest of the Priesthood up to speed on how to heal injuries without Styx water. If we're not reliant on a healing source within Hell, we could provide aid directly in the field."

"Make it happen," Schitz said. "This is going to be a consequential and perilous battle. I've grown tired of talking about the 'final victory.' This time, let's just say we're going to fuck them up."

The nursery of Hell contained twelve Demons born of the three couples from the most recent adult generation. The youngsters shrieked and cried as they engaged in a violent game of Totem. Schitz chuckled as he recalled his own youth eons earlier.

"So many things change and so much remains the same," Bubonic Plague said.

"Thank you for coming. I didn't want to go into this battle without having spoken to you," Schitz said.

"It's good to see you," Plague said.

His large hand patted Schitz on the shoulder. The gesture was friendly in nature, but still buffeted the smaller Demon.

"You called me brother at the Jubilee," Schitz said. "Why do I get the sense you didn't mean it purely as a form of endearment?"

"Satan is your father and mine," Plague said. "That makes us brothers. There is much you don't know, but there is a family waiting for you – the Devil, our father, and his wife Lilith."

"His wife?" Schitz said.

"Aye, there is much you have to learn and unlearn," Plague said. "Like the mortals, our lore was crafted in a simplistic way to ease the minds of Demons marching toward their death. Satan made the Universe; we were fashioned in his image to fight the Angels. I mean there are sprinklings of truth, but the pantheon of characters in our history is as immense as any of the ancient mortals imagined."

"And he told you this forbidden history?" Schitz asked.

Plague continued, "Aye, he did. I've had time to contemplate and to learn – time to grow and meditate. Satan and Lilith have spoken with me about what came before – what they know, and what they don't know. It is an amazing tale. It stretches long past the ancestors of Fever and his wife Lupus."

"That is one of the banned names, stricken from our history," Schitz said, "but whispered to wayward children as a warning."

"Yes, they were not even the original Demons," Plague said.

His eyes were wide and wild. "There is so much more to us, it is astounding. If you win this battle there will be a chance for the final showdown and then, what I used to think was the final victory will be but the start of an incomprehensible future."

"And what of our past will echo into this bright future?" Schitz asked.

"You killed Vertigo," Plague said. "Satan ordered me to play a role in Rubella's demise. They are both gone. I tried to frame you at your sedition trial. You laid claim to my title of Antichrist. In small ways we were both in the wrong. I cannot see all of our people's past and all the future we could have scuttled by our feud. It does a disservice to all."

"You can just let go of all of it?" Schitz said.

"I see it like two children arguing," Plague said.

He gestured to the field where the Totem game was ongoing. A male youth clutched the totem while a female tried to wrench it from him. She pulled at the youngster's hair and sunk her teeth into his shoulder. He howled but refused to let go. His tormentor shook her mouth side to side like a rabid dog.

"The youth may quarrel. To them, it is a matter of the utmost importance. Yet, the father might so easily tell them, 'Stop it. Hug your brother.' The father knows more. He has already been a child and he knows what is significant and what is trivial. Our argument was sophomoric and I cannot continue it with you. All I can do is love you as a brother, an action that amplifies my greatness as the son of Satan. I hope you will do the same," Plague said.

Schitz felt his skin crawl. All of his experience, the fiber of his being, all that made him who he was, screamed to hate Bubonic. Yet, a larger part of him knew the old Demon was right. *How could I hate him forever? I don't even have that type of hatred for Angels*, he thought. *I have a sibling, a half-sibling, but nevertheless, a sibling. I cannot squander this reconciliation, this chance at family. I owe it to myself and to Anna to end the discord.*

"I accept," Schitz said. "Let there be unity in Hell."

Plague smiled broadly and embraced Schitz momentarily lifting him off the ground.

When he settled on his feet, Schitz asked, "So will you be fighting with us brother?"

"No, I long to be back in action," Plague said, "but Father has a specific prey in store for me. He starves me like a lion for the games. He will only unleash me on a singular foe when the time is right."

"The Nazarene?" Schitz asked.

"Aye, the Messiah," Plague said. "I am to combat him, as was foretold, as it should be. It is correct that the son of the Devil and son of God should settle their argument with one another, one on one."

"How do you know when he'll come out to fight?" Schitz asked.

Plague rested both of his hands on Schitz's shoulders. He looked deeply into his eyes and said, "That is where you come in, Baron of Tartarus. When you have laid waste to the armies of Heaven, God will have no choice but to send out his son. And when he does, I, the Crown Prince, will destroy him."

Electrum, formerly Silver, looked across the barren frontier outside of the village of Milove in Luhansk Oblast. With his night vision binoculars he could see the outlines of buildings and vehicles. He felt the nervous anticipation that always preceded combat. It had been the same when he and Gold possessed the army of Sargon; it was not different within a Russian Army host.

In his mind's eye he could see the strategy before him. He could see the forces he had arrayed around the region: Uranium II in Belarus, Wynter near Kharkiv, Wynter's many vassals in the Donbas. There were Angelic Lords such as Zinc's grandchildren, Francium, Rhenium, and Technetium and their Houses, stationed with the strategic forces. They were prepared to fire missiles all across Ukraine. Others such as Uranium II's clients, Thorium and Dubnium, were within the Russian Air Force. They would quickly gain air superiority in the skies above the steppe. Hydrogen's descendants, Actinium and Radium, were embedded among the

Special Forces. They would decapitate the mortal leadership and seize key positions.

"Everything is going to be fine," Christa said. She was within the body of an FSB operative.

"I still worry. Everything is riding on the element of surprise," Electrum said.

"And they will be surprised. Imagine how horrified they will be to be vulnerable in the Celestial," she said.

Electrum remained silent.

"What is it?" Christa asked.

"I'm sure it's nothing," he said, "but there was a moment when I was busy with Uranium II and you were tending to matters with the Familiars. Such a small window, but there was a time when the arsenal was unguarded."

"And?" she asked.

"You know I keep meticulous inventory. One box mag of 7.62x54mm ammunition was unaccounted for," he said.

"You put millions of rounds of ammunition, hundreds of thousands of artillery and tank shells, and thousands of missiles and rockets into the field, and you're worried because you can't account for one magazine of bullets? I think you might be going a little mad, love," Christa said.

"It's probably nothing. But when they recovered Constance, she had an empty SVD rifle with her," Electrum said.

"7.62x54mm," Christa said. "Do you think Zinc put two and two together and stole from the arsenal?"

"He wouldn't have thought of it as stealing," Electrum said. "He would see it as rightfully his. He would have taken it discreetly, knowing that I would have objected due to the risk of unveiling the operation early."

Christa looked at her watch. It read 0330. "You have about ten minutes to call this a training exercise. The troops could still all get the message and not cross the border," she said.

Electrum looked past her at a nearby T-72 main battle tank. It had been painted with a white Z indicating it carried modified shells.

"This is our one shot," he said. "We'll never be able to keep a track of all of these munitions. All of the Familiars that have ever existed or ever will exist could not recover all of our ordinance. If we scrub this, the mortal army will stand down and the weapons will be deployed to Africa, to Syria, to Yemen. They'll be sold by unscrupulous generals to ISIL and Hamas. If the Demons don't know about the modified weapons, they will and we could end up facing our own ammunition."

"That sounds grim," Christa said. "So you have a potential security issue versus a guaranteed one."

"Sitting second chair doesn't seem so bad right now," he said. He laughed and touched his silvery, false teeth. "Why did I ever put myself in a position where I was giving the orders?"

"Because nobody else would do as good a job as you love," she said. "No matter what happens, you and Uranium II are our best shot at victory. If Zinc bungled things up, it's not on you."

"It doesn't feel that way. It feels like it's on me. But we don't have time or the means to fall back. The only way is forward. Let's do this," he said.

Vampirosis sat in the cockpit of a MiG-29. She was incredibly frustrated with the lack of preparedness considering the circumstances. Despite medium range missiles falling all over the country, particularly Kyiv, only one aircraft was flightworthy, armed, and fueled.

I'm fine being without any other Demons, she thought. She remembered her father, AIDS. *He would value a challenge like today. I guess I'll never know what really happened to him. All the same, I wish he was here today. He'd love it.*

The air raid siren at the eastern Kyiv airfield blared through the dark, early morning sky. The muffled booms of explosions sounded across the city like echoing thunder.

Vampirosis's host, Stefania Ivanovych, had a wealth of experience though none of it in combat. *I hope her nerves hold up.* She pushed the throttle forward and the MiG rocketed down the runway and into the sky. She was still in her initial ascent when radar control was on the air asking for her call-sign: Привид (Ghost).

"Ghost. Three groups, wall 30. North group 0-7-0, rock 30, 25 thousand, hot, hostile. Middle group separation 10, 25 thousand, hot, hostile. South group, separation 10, 25 thousand, hot, hostile. Clear to engage," the radio said.

"Copy that ground," she replied.

The MiG-29 was armed with six R-77 air-to-air missiles. *Alright, two for each group. Better to hit each group some, than to leave any group fully intact.*

The hostiles were higher than her. Vampirosis kept her plane at a climbing speed and shot past her targets. The north group broke north and the south group broke south. Experience told Vampirosis that each group would turn in to cover the middle group.

Even before her warning alarms sounded Vampirosis had reached for the countermeasures and was maneuvering into a dive. By climbing she had put her jet into an inviting position. The middle group chased her and fired several missiles.

The enemies' air-to-air missiles screamed toward Vampirosis but impacted the flares she had launched from her BVP-30-26 dispensers. She pushed the MiG-29 down and climbed again from the bottom of the loop. She took an arching, northerly course in her climb. She looked through the glass canopy while rocketing back up to a higher altitude.

They're Su-27s. I can out-climb and out-maneuver them. She rolled the jet into position while the hostiles of the middle group were responding to her change in direction.

Vampirosis's arching climb put her above the north group. *Amazing!* Each of the three groups of four fighters each had maneuvered just as she had expected. She could see the middle and south groups in the distance.

She aimed at the nearest group and acquired radar lock. The Soviet wording came to Vampirosis's mind from her host. She pressed the trigger.

"Ghost, ushla odin," she said over the radio. One away.

Vampirosis shifted her targeting and locked on the next hostile.

"Ushla dva," she said. Two away.

As the missiles screamed off of their rails, she aimed toward the middle group.

"Ushla tri." Three away.

"Ushla čotiri." Four Away.

She adjusted her path and fired her last two at the furthest group.

"Ushla p'ât'." Five Away.

"Ushla šìst'." Six away.

In a matter of moments she had emptied out all of her air-to-air missiles. She pushed the MiG-29 to its utmost and fled.

"All hits! All hits!" ground control shouted through the radio.

"I'm all out. Returning to base," Vampirosis said.

The sun was creeping over the horizon when the MiG-29's tires squealed on contact with the tarmacadam. She taxied to the hanger and raised the canopy. The ground crew came running up to the plane cheering.

"This isn't some Hollywood movie. Reload the plane! There's plenty more up there. You think they only sent twelve aircraft?"

Vampirosis exhaled and removed her helmet. She ran her hands through her host's hair. The brunette locks fell out of their bun and cascaded down over her face. She pushed them out of the way.

Mechanical noises sounded as the crew began the process of rearming the fighter. The squadron commander climbed the portable ladder.

"You are hero, Stefania," the Colonel said.

"Use my call-sign, never my name," she said. "That way I can never be shot down. The legend of the Ghost will live forever."

"I don't know if anyone will believe this," he said. "An ace in a day. Twelve against one. It is fucking crazy," he said.

"Yeah, twelve against one," she said. "How are the other birds coming?"

The colonel shook his head. "Most of the good planes and parts are in the south or dispersed to avoid the bombing. Staying here was death wish," he said.

As though to prove his point, more explosions sounded across the city.

"Look, make yourself useful or something," Vampirosis said. "I could use a coffee before I go back up again."

"You are national treasure now, but don't push it," he said with a deep laugh. He climbed down the rungs.

Vampirosis watched the portly Colonel trudge off to the canteen. She looked down at her hands. Despite the power of possession, she could feel her host's hands trembling. *Or is it mine that are shaking?*

Chiyo Uranium sat in the turret of her Russian T-72 outside of the city of Chernihiv. Progress had been slow. Orders from both her mortal and Angelic superiors were often contradictory and confusing. Chiyo could tell that her mortal host was terrified.

A plume of smoke emerged from the woods in front of them – with another one right after it.

"Oh shit," Chiyo said.

The impact of the first warhead blew apart one of the treads without penetrating the armor. However, there was barely time to celebrate as the second tore through the interior of the tank. The crew was killed instantly. Chiyo was blinded in a fiery inferno that reeked of chemicals and burned her without mercy.

It didn't set off our shells, otherwise we would have jack-in-the-boxed, she thought. She tried to move but could not. Chiyo looked down and thought her host had lost her right arm at the elbow.

No, I've lost my right arm! How the fuck did that happen? I was in a host. Did they set off one of our special shells after all? No, of course not. I won't have survived? Do they have special shells too?

With horror she realized her legs were gone.

I need a tourniquet. I don't...I don't think I can reach the medi-kit.

She could feel blood running down her face. She raised her left hand to her head. *Oh good, I still have this one.* She touched her head; her hand came away gooey. Her skull was soft and squishy like a shattered egg shell.

I would have liked to have visited the sea one last time.

"Nice shooting!" Anna said. She and Schitz had used their modified Javelins to knock out a column of tanks outside of Chernihiv. It was a procedure they had worked out since the invasion. They double tapped the lead tank to create a traffic jam. Then they knocked out a tank farther back in the column. The tanks caught in the middle could be destroyed at their leisure. They had mined the countryside along the road in case one squeezed out.

The rest of the squad (Ebola, Marburg Hemorrhagic Fever, Esophageal Candidiasis, Anaplasmosis, Energy Drink Related Renal Failure, and Hand, Foot, And Mouth Disease) covered them from trenches dug into forested areas. From their entrenched positions they could mop up any survivors or supporting infantry.

"Yeah, no survivors," Schitz said.

They made their way back toward the trees, crouching low as they went. A high pitched whine cut through the air above them. The shriek was followed by a massive explosion. Dirt shot into the air like a geyser. A moment later another shell shook the ground, and then another.

Anna felt the clammy hand of fear clutching at her throat. A hot, liquid sensation ran down her leg – not just her host's. Hers as well. The shrapnel had clipped them both.

"They're Z rounds," Anna shouted. She hurled Schitz to the ground.

The shells continued to pound the area along the roadside. Metal fragments and dirt spit at them from everywhere. Shells blew trees apart, shattering branches and jettisoning splinters.

Anna looked up and saw Schitz bolting towards the tree line. She yelled at him.

"What are you doing?"

"We have to get back to the squad. They're gonna wipe them out!"

Anna caught up to him and hauled Schitz to the ground. They were both covered by a shower of dirt and debris.

"And what are you going to do – cover them with your artillery-proof umbrella?" she said.

Schitz stopped fighting.

"They're my responsibility," Schitz said.

"I know, but standing up in this is suicide," she said.

Anna wished for any type of cover. They lay halfway between the hulls of the burning enemy tanks and the tree line. The artillery barrage subsided and the pair hurried back to the trench.

There were small fires burning everywhere. Broken trees lay overturned and split in half. It was a miniature version of Verdun. In the trench they found many dead and injured mortals. Among them Energy Drink Related Renal Failure lay torn to pieces. His head was no longer attached to his body. His torso, like his mortal host's, was charred.

Marburg Hemorrhagic Fever was slumped in the Celestial holding her leg. Spurts of blood gushed between her fingertips. She looked toward them with a pale, panicked face.

"The Z shells cut right through my host," she said.

Schitz stepped into the Celestial and shouted. "Medic!"

Anna assessed the position. The rest of the squad seemed rattled but intact. The Priestess Erin led a junior along the trench. They began tending to Marburg Hemorrhagic Fever. The Priestesses looked shell-shocked but worked with dedication and poise.

Russian infantry advanced along the destroyed tanks. Anna could see light auras of Angelic possession among the troops and Angels in the Celestial alongside. She raised her host's rifle and fired in the direction of the enemy. The line of Ukrainian infantry followed suit. A hailstorm of outgoing and incoming lead sailed back and forth across the line.

Anna crouched for cover and reloaded her rifle with a fresh banana clip.

"We have to take the leg," Erin said. She drew a Celestial Liston knife.

"No, no, no. I'd rather die," Marburg Hemorrhagic Fever said.

The medics looked toward Schitz.

"We need you alive," he said. He looked at the Priestesses. "Do whatever is necessary."

Marburg howled when Erin cut above the shrapnel wound. Once she was done, she and her partner bandaged the wound.

"Fire from the Styx will heal the cuts we made," Erin said. "Come on, let's get her back to Hell."

The junior Priestess unfolded a stretcher and they carried off Marburg.

The Russian infantry pulled back.

"They're going to hit this area again," Schitz said. "Come on, fall back into the woods."

Wynter Zinc stood by the controls of the 9K720 Iskander short-range ballistic missile. *I wish the Air Force wasn't so scared of a fucking ghost,* she thought. Aerial munitions would be much more precise than her Iskander fired from 300 miles away.

Wynter wanted to be at the front, dangerous though it was. However, she had decided that her skills were best served commanding the missile battery.

The Demons outside Kharkiv were crafty and nimble. They would ambush mortal and possessed Russians and then relocate. The Demons used BTR-4 armored personnel carriers. Nicknamed "Bucephalus" after the horse of Alexander the Great, the APCs were a nuisance. They protected the Demons from the Z rounds of the infantry and allowed the foe to move in close to the Angels.

Wynter's radio came to life. She looked at her map. The coordinates corresponded to City Cemetery No17. There was a road intersection between the German Military Cemetery, Німецьке військове кладовище, and the local graveyard, Міське кладовище №17.

The terrified radio operator informed her the Ukrainian armor was overwhelming their position.

"Hold tight," Wynter said.

The Iskander was far from pinpoint, but with her experience she was certain the Z labeled missile would hit its target. With a deafening explosion, a cloud of exhaust and dust enveloped the launch site. The missile soared into the sky.

Autism fired his Kalashnikov in the direction of the Russian infantry. They were taking shelter behind war graves from the Second World War. *I wonder if any of my former hosts are buried here,* he thought.

He was crouched behind a Ukrainian Army APC. The armored personnel carriers were absorbing the small arms fire. *Their Z rounds are useless.* Earlier in the engagement, Von Willebrand had knocked out several T-72s and a newer T-90 with Javelin missiles. Von Willebrand tapped Autism's host on the shoulder while he was reloading his rifle.

"I can see at least three or four Angels still on the ridge. I can hit them," she said. She punctuated her sentence by tapping the launcher tube of her Javelin.

"It's a waste; we've already killed scores of them. They'll fall back any minute or we'll wipe them out. They have nothing to get through the BTR-4s," he said.

Autism had barely finished the sentence when the lead APC was obliterated in a fireball. Both Demons and their hosts were tossed to the ground. Lymphatic Filariasis and Swine Flu had been inside the personnel carrier and Hookworm had been taking cover behind it.

Von Willebrand stepped out of her host. Autism followed suit. She helped him to his feet.

"Another one of those fucking missiles," Autism said.

The pair rushed to the smoldering crater, prepared to defend their seizing comrades.

"Where are they?" Von Willebrand asked.

Typically, a Celestial creature remained in place even if the host was vaporized.

"The missile strike should have only sent them into a departure seizure," she said. Her voice was full of panic.

Autism crouched down and picked up a petite feminine hand. Everything around him seemed quiet. He could no longer hear the sound of gunfire, or the explosions of grenades. It was a Demon's hand, long fingernails, pale thin fingers. The nails were painted pink. The hand was severed at the wrist, but still bore a wedding ring. *This must be Swine Flu's hand. She was married to Lymphatic Filariasis. Any time I saw them they were together, even in the APC just now.*

"Is that a fucking *Celestial* hand?" Von Willebrand asked. "They have fucking Z missiles too?"

Autism snapped out of his stupor. "We have to fall back, there could be more incoming," he said.

Autism motioned to the surviving members of the squad to fall back. Within the Celestial the remaining Demons fled toward the nearby forest.

"Did you get all of them?" Wynter asked. She tapped her hand against her thigh as she waited for a response from the field radio.

"We lacked the unit coherency to follow the survivors after the strike," the forward observer said.

"Useless bastards," Wynter said to herself. She keyed the radio and replied. "That's fine, you took a beating. Regroup and await further instructions."

"Will do. Hey, don't sound so down Standard Bearer. You killed three Demons in one shot, back in my day that was unheard of," the forward observer said.

"That's right, with those two in Afghanistan and these three today, I'm an ace," she said.

"There you go," her observer said.

Wynter assessed the battery. It was preparing to fire another ballistic missile. *Might as well put it to use,* she thought. The current ordinance did not bear a Z, so she opted to fire the missile randomly into the city.

Katarina Kovalenko had spent most of her life in Kharkiv. She had died in Berlin, a suicide, and passed through the Eunoe on her way to reincarnation. Katarina was then born at the regional hospital on Nezalezhnosti Avenue.

During her formative years, the city was a part of the Soviet Union. Then the split came, which did not change Katarina's life much. She was a painter, a sculptor, and lover of the arts. When she spoke with a gallery in Köln, they had asked if she was Ukrainian or Russian. She had replied, "What's the difference?"

She looked out her window and thought, *What is going on? This is not Kosovo or Grozny. How can this be happening here?* Yet, deep within her Pulwabi was not surprised. She had seen violence, oppression, and genocide play out over the centuries. *It is not really that surprising,* she thought as she considered her many past lives.

Katarina's husband, Krystiyan, emerged from the bathroom. He held his mobile phone in his hand. It was vibrating.

"It's Kuzma again. He wants us to leave," Krystiyan said.

Katarina thought of her son Kuzma. He was studying abroad in America.

"Tell him we'll be fine," she said. "Besides, he should know, I'm not leaving my paintings."

Katarina walked across the living room and looked at a piece she had completed in her twenties. It was a scene based on Dante Alighieri's *Inferno*. Behind her she could hear Krystiyan. "Yes, yes, I know. I know. But it will be fine."

Katarina's attention was pulled away from the painting by a flash of bright light. She covered her face and felt an all-consuming heat envelop her body.

Svaha looked from her balcony at the stunning tower of the Burj Khalifa. The view from the luxurious penthouse was astounding when the sun struck the building. *Beautiful Dubai,* she thought. She looked over her shoulder and saw Circades sleeping in the over-sized bed. *This Titan has good taste.*

She looked over at the glass case that held his two pistols and the ring of Hyperion. Svaha had relieved Circades of the items after she had taken control of the Eunoe and the Styx. *He is easy to manipulate. He fears me enough not to fight me and hopes that through my good graces he might find his love.*

Svaha felt a sensation rip through her mind like a lightning bolt. *She's here.* She snapped her fingers and stepped through a portal in the balcony doorway.

She emerged with the molten flow of the Eunoe. She pushed her hands to the side and a wall of the lava formed on either side of her. She walked upon the dry river's bed. Svaha closed her eyes and hummed a tune she had heard long ago, *Song of the Volga Boatmen.*

Before her, the lava had formed into the barred structure of a burning cage. Within the molten jail cell awaited Pulwabi's soul. Svaha approached. She smiled broadly like a cat approaching a trapped canary.

"Ah, the elusive Pulwabi," Svaha said.

"What is going on? Who are you?" Pulwabi asked. She reached out and touched the bars. They did not burn her soul – neither had the fires of the river – but they did confine her. "Am I not permitted to pass on to reincarnation?"

Svaha laughed and looked around the riverbed. "How is it you end up in the Eunoe time after time?" she asked.

"I accept the world around me. My various incarnations benefit from that and I die at peace," Pulwabi said. "But why am I not permitted to pass? I have done nothing wrong."

Svaha snarled. "Oh, of course not. Sweet innocent Pulwabi.

Harmless Pulwabi. Always passing through life so gently. So mature. So Zen. You cannot pass because I have decided such. Do you know who I am?" she asked.

Pulwabi shook her head.

Svaha laughed, a thunderclap of a cackle. "I am the goddess of fire, Svaha. I am a Singularity Elemental, one from which all things came to pass."

"What interest could you possibly have with me?" Pulwabi asked.

"I am a jealous goddess. I cannot allow the devotion Circades shows to you to continue. I am the destroyer of all things and I will be the destruction of your union," she said.

"It's not possible. It will only die with us," she said.

"Hmm, I can arrange that as well," Svaha said. Her jaw unhinged like a serpent's. Her teeth grew into pointy fangs. Her liquid black eyes transformed into glowing red orbs. Then she quickly reverted back to her original form. "But not now," she said.

Pulwabi steadied herself on the frame of the cell. She had never imagined such terror as staring into the jaws of the timeless being.

"Your Titan has tasted of my carnal delights. As time passes, he will loosen the grip you have placed on his heart. And all the while, you will sit here, suffering, thinking about him ravishing me, you too will cool of your love. This is how I will consume your amor aeternus," she said.

Svaha turned and walked away from the cage. She resumed humming the tune and sung to herself, "Ey, ukhnyem! Ey, ukhnyem! Yeshcho razik, yeshcho da raz!" Behind her the river flowed back over Pulwabi's prison. Svaha snapped her finger and passed through the portal that emerged in the wall of fire.

Ey, ukhnyem! (Эй, ухнем)

Ey, ukhnyem! (Эй, ухнем!)

Yeshcho razik, yeshcho da raz! (Ещё разик, ещё да раз!)

Razovyom my byeryozu, (Разовьём мы берёзу,)

Razovyom my kudryavu! (Разовьём мы кудряву!)

Ai-da, da ai-da, (Ай-да, да ай-да,)

Ai-da, da ai-da, (Ай-да, да ай-да,)
Razovyom my kudryavu. (Разовьём мы кудряву.)[31]

Coronavirus walked through ruins of Mariupol. He was accompanied by his sister, Alzheimer's Disease.

"We're going to have to pullback soon before the city is cutoff. We can't afford to lose more well-trained hosts," she said.

"You don't think this is a good place to make a stand in the south?" he asked.

"No, they're going to wipe this place off the map. They need a land bridge between here and the Donbas," she said.

Coronavirus looked through the ruins of the column of Russian tanks and armored vehicles. They had massacred a haul of Angels and mortals with Switchblade drones and Javelins.

"I guess we can move this battalion to a more defendable position," he said.

Coronavirus looked up at a wall covered with graffiti. In the middle of the various marks there was a detailed piece of Mary Magdalene holding a rocket launcher. COVID chuckled. "Hey, look at that," he said.

"What, never seen good ol' Saint J?" Alzheimer's said.

"That's a good one," Coronavirus said.

---

[31] Yo, heave ho! Yo, heave ho! Once more, once again, still once more! Yo, heave ho! Yo, heave ho! Once more, once again, still once more! Now we fell the stout birch tree, Now we pull hard: one, two, three. Ay-da, da, ay-da!
Ay-da, da, ay-da! Now we pull hard: one, two, three.

Razovyom my kudryavu. (Разовьём мы кудряву.)
Ey, ukhnyem! (Эй, ухнем!)
Ey, ukhnyem! (Эй, ухнем!)
Yeshchɔ razik, yeshcho da raz! (Ещё разик, ещё да раз!)[32]

Lord Electrum felt his blood boil with frustration. The roadside in the Pryazovia countryside looked like a scene from the Second World War. There were shattered vehicles, shell craters, bits of crashed aircraft and bodies, so many bodies and body parts.

Electrum had been receiving reports that "surely Demons must have been killed in the blast" or "their remains must have burnt up." He did not trust the reports and so had assembled a specialty team. They had possessed soldiers of the Spetsnaz GRU. They had been tasked with killing the Ancient Demon Autism and the upstart maniac Coronavirus.

No longer trusting his Familiars, Electrum had called on an old friend.

"I keep trying to stay retired," Lilly said.

The aged Familiar was wearing more body armor than was reasonable.

Electrum laughed, "But you love me."

"Not enough to get blown to pieces," she said. "Ugh, I don't know how you got me here. And you, dear, how are you?"

"Holding up," Christa said, "hoping for some good news."

A pair of youngsters stood in front of them. One was a Gold descendant, the other was of the Silver lineage. For a moment, Electrum saw himself and Gold, fresh and hungry to prove a point.

"Alright, let's see it," he said.

The blonde youngster pulled back a tarp. Under it lay the bodies of three male Demons. Each had a hole the size of a U.S. half-dollar in his head.

"Did they surrender?" Electrum asked.

---

[32] Now we pull hard: one, two, three. Yo, heave ho! Yo, heave ho! Once more, once again, still once more!

"No, they all went down fighting. Why do you ask?" the Silver youngster said.

"Looks like they all got a visit from a medieval neurosurgeon," Electrum said.

"Oh, no, Wulfram's just a crack shot," the Silver youngster said.

"Wulfram is it? Well done, and you are?" Electrum asked.

"Mikhail Silver...ah...Mikhail Electrum," the youngster said.

"Well done to you both. And Lilly, do we have some good news for once?" Electrum said.

Lilly scrutinized the corpses. Despite having been long retired, her knowledge of Demons was superior to any of her fellow Familiars.

"Hmm...this is Cirrhosis, Great War vintage. This is Kawasaki Syndrome, post-World War II. This third one I'm not one hundred percent sure about, but judging from the age and the likeliness, I'm going to go with HAB Illness. I think he's Kawasaki's son. Not bad by any means, but not Autism or COVID," she said.

The youngsters both swore.

Electrum held up his hand to quiet them. "You have performed well. I will call on you again soon."

My po byeryezhku idyom, (Мы по бережку идём,)
Pyesnyu solnyshku poyom. (Песню солнышку поём.)
Ai-da, da ai-da, (Ай-да, да ай-да,)
Ai-da, da ai-da, (Ай-да, да ай-да,)
Pyesnyu solnyshku poyom. (Песню солнышку поём.)[33]

Circades scrolled through his phone. He rubbed his temples. *Things could be going so well,* he thought. *Craig Walters is about to run for president in the United States. Gustav had reached the pinnacle of underworld power. Makoto Tanaka controls the governments of Japan and the Republic of Korea. All the pieces to create a nuclear war.*

He read a message from a ranking official within the Taliban thanking him for a recent gift. Circades had sent the Islamic Emirate

---

[33] As we walk along the shore, To the sun, we sing our song. Ay-da, da, ay-da! Ay-da, da, ay-da! To the sun, we sing our song.

of Afghanistan engineers and instructors to repair and teach them how to use discarded American military equipment. *The drug trade has stabilized despite the power change in Afghanistan. My funds are untouchable both in the Middle East and South America. The nuclear war can happen. The nuclear winter that follows will be the Ragnarok I seek, and then the cycle of reincarnation will grind to a halt with the death of humanity. The Celestials will die without humanity's energy.*

Circades had long ago learned the symbols requisite to travel to Hell and Heaven. *I'll find her wherever her soul ends up and take her back to earth where we can be together forever. The pieces are in place, or are about to fall into place. Yet, after all of this effort a part of me wonders...*

Circades looked up from his phone. His yacht was an extravagant affair. Beyond his chair he saw Svaha. She was sat in the hot tub. Her presence within the water sent cascades of steam up from the surface of the water.

"Put down your phone and come join me, Circades," she said.

She's taken the ring, and essentially turned me into a prisoner. But, a prisoner with benefits. I stayed true to my quest for so long. For so long, Pulwabi got to live mortal lives, have other loves. Did she not get the idea of living together after Ragnarok from a Demon, a Demon who loved her and wanted to spend eternity with her? Would it be so bad if I remained with the Elemental?

"Of course, goddess," he said and rose to his feet.

> *Ey, Ey, tyani kanat silney! (Эй, эй, тяни канат сильней!)*
> *Pyesnyu solnyshku poyot. (Песню солнышку поём.)*
> *Ey, ukhnyem! (Эй, ухнем!)*
> *Ey, ukhnyem! (Эй, ухнем!)*
> *Yeshcho razik, yeshcho da raz! (Ещё разик, ещё да раз!)*[34]

Anorexia unstrapped her flight helmet and scratched her host's scalp. She was exhausted. She climbed from the cockpit of the

---

[34] Hey, hey, let's heave a-long the way to the sun, we sing our song. Yo, heave ho! Yo, heave ho! Once more, once again, still once more!

Mi-35 gunship. Hirohisa pattered her on the shoulder from within the Mi-35's gunner.

The pair had been dodging shoulder fire rockets while trying to knock out the Demons around Kyiv Oblast.

"This is a lot more difficult than I thought it would be," Hirohisa said.

Anorexia watched as the ground crew rushed to rearm the gunship's S-8 rockets. The rockets were onloaded from a crate marked with a Z.

"We'll get them," Anorexia said.

Ekh, ty, Volga, mat'-reka, (Эх ты, Волга, мать-река,)
Shiroka i gluboka,(Широка и глубока,)
Ai-da, da ai-da, (Ай-да, да ай-да,)
Ai-da, da ai-da, (Ай-да, да ай-да,)
Volga, Volga, mat'-reka (Волга, Волга, мать-река)[35]

"Push them out of the way," Uranium II shouted to his driver.

The T-72 operator, possessed by Chao Uranium, one of his nephews, rammed the tank into the burning, turretless shell that had been knocked out in front of them. It smoldered with the charred remains of Russians and Angels.

"As soon as we push this out of the way, they're going to knock us out too," Chao said.

"Just do it!" Uranium II ordered.

The T-72 jostled as it impacted the wreck in front of it.

"Come on, come on," Uranium II said to himself.

He fired without an exact target as soon as the wreck was cleared. An enormous explosion rocked the tank a moment later. The T-72's shell had impacted an incoming Javelin missile.

---

[35] Oh, you, Volga, mother river, mighty stream so deep and wide. Ay-da, da, ay-da! Ay-da, da, ay-da! Volga, Volga, mother river.

"What the fuck...your host should play the lotto," Chao said.

The autoloader clanged as another Z shell slid into the breath.

Be faster than them, be faster than them, Uranium II thought as he sighted on the Demons position.

The gun was ready. He fired. The shell exploded among the Javelin crew.

"Got you!" he shouted. "Got you bastards!"

No sooner had he spoken than the tank was engulfed in a fireball. The heat and the suffocating vacuum overwhelmed Uranium II's host and threw the Angel into a departure seizure.

Oh, thank God, it was a conventional weapon, he thought.

When the fit subsided he and his fellows emerged from the burnt shell of their tank. The battlefield had grown eerily quiet. Both sides of mortals and the Demons were gone. He looked up into the sky and saw a solitary MiG-29 zip by.

Ey, ukhnyem! (Эй, ухнем!)

Ey, ukhnyem! (Эй, ухнем!)

Yeshcho razik, yeshcho da raz! (Ещё разик, ещё да раз!)[36]

---

[36] Yo, heave ho! Yo, heave ho! Once more, once again, still once more! Yo, heave ho! Yo, heave ho!

Vampirosis made another pass over the battlefield. She had rendered close-air-support for an embattled ground unit containing Schitz and Anna. She keyed her radio again.

"Ground, come in," she said.

There was no response.

"Schitz, Anna, come in. I took out the last tank, you should be clear," she said.

She was once more met with silence.

"Oh, for fuck's sake, please be alright guys," she said.

A warning alarm sounded in her cockpit.

"Ugh, low on fuel," she said to herself. "Well, I did all I could guys, I hope you are alright down there."

She pulled back on the throttle and plotted a course for her home base.

Ey, ukhnyet! (Эй, ухнем!)
Ey, ukhnyet! (Эй, ухнем!)

Our Lady

The machinery of war continued to hum: the clank of metal, the whine of engines, the reverberations of explosions. The symphony of destruction echoed up to Heaven and down to Hell. It rumbled in the Ethereal. Interlaced among it were the notes of the old song *Unser Liebe Fraue*.

Unser Liebe Fraue
Von kalten Bronnen,
Bescher' uns armen Landsknecht'
Eine warme Sonnen!
Lasst uns nicht erfrieren,
Wohl in des Wirtes Haus,
Ziehen wir mit vollem Säckel,
Und leerem wieder ,naus.

Die Trommel, die Trommel,
Larman, larman larman,
Hei ridi-ridiran,
Ridiran, frisch voran!
Landsknecht voran!
Der Trommler schlägt Parade,
Die seid'nen Fahnen weh'n,
Jetzt heißt's auf Glück und Gnade
Ins Feld spazieren gehen.
Das Korn reift auf den Feldern,
Es schnappt der Hecht im Strom,
Heiß weht der Wind von Geldern,
Herauf den Berg op Zoom.

Die Trommel, die Trommel,
Larman, larman larman
Hei ridirideran,
Ridiran, frisch voran!
Landsknecht voran![37]

---

[37] Our Dear Lady of Kaltenbrunn bestow to us poor landsknechts, a warm sun! Don't let us die of cold, into the landlord's pub we go with pockets full of money, but they are empty when we go out. The drum, the drum, the alarm, the alarm, the alarm, Hi ridi-ridiran, Ridiran, heartily ahead! Landsknecht ahead! The drummer drums parade, the silken banners wave, now it's up to good luck and grace, when we march for battle. The grains ripen in the fields, The pike hunts in the stream, hot blows the wind from Geldern, up to the Berg op Zoom. The drum, the drum, the alarm, the alarm, the alarm, Hi ridi-ridiran, Ridiran, heartily ahead Landsknecht ahead!

Below the Surface

Still I'm waiting, never aging,
Still I'm waiting, what else to do,
Still I'm waiting, softly raging,
Still I'm waiting, here for you.

The sky above is dark and gray,
It whispers softly of decay.
The whistling wind seems to say:
The living have all turned away.

Why did you leave?
To flee the pall?
And I, alone to grieve,
That we are liars, one and all.

Lay me down to sleep,
While outside the shadows creep,
There are secrets in the deep,
And they want my soul, to keep.

But you, still chose to leave?
To step from beneath the pall?
Leaving me alone to grieve,
That we are liars, one and all.

I am gone and can't be found,
Lost in darkness all around,

Forever haunted by the sound,
Of rustling leaves upon the ground.

Still I'm waiting, never aging,
Still I'm waiting, what else to do,
Still I'm waiting, softly raging,
Still I'm waiting, here for you.
Below the surface, here for you

About the Author

J.L. Feuerstack holds a BA from Washington & Lee University and a MA from Queens College, both in the study of Psychology. He has worked in various investigative and supervisory capacities for the City of New York. He is a diehard supporter of Liverpool Football Club and the German National Football Team.

About the Illustrator

Alana Tedmon is an award-winning fantasy illustrator working in publishing for the past half-decade. She developed her body of work under the tutelage of world-renowned artists Sterling Hundley and Edward Kinsella through the Visual Arts Passage. She enjoys painting subjects that capture the dark, the whimsical, and points in-between. She's also an ardent lover of rats.

ACKNOWLEDGMENTS

The author would like to thank:

My wife Eileen Feuerstack for her unwavering support and encouragement as well as her companionship in traveling to many of the locales featured in the story.

Editor, Arthur Fogartie, for his unparalleled skill and patience. His insight and wit were paramount in ensuring that this story was told.

Illustrator, Alana Tedmon, for her talent and dedication. Her creativity was vital for the creation of the characters of *The Saga of Fallen Leaves*.

9 781961 624511